DARKNESS BEHIND THE MOUNTAIN

BOOKS 1 & 2

THE LONGER PATH

&

THE LEGEND OF BROKEN FINGERS

by

Amir A. Sada

ISBN 978-965-93212-2-3 (paperback)

Cover Design by Creative Covers, Ken Dawson

Typesetting by Book Polishers

I thought I knew what love is.

Now that you two came into my life,

I can absolutely say that I know what love is.

I dedicate this novel to you, my precious daughters Tooti & Baby.

I can't wait until you're old enough to read it.

Love, Dad

Contents

Darkness Behind the Mountain

Book 1
The Longer Path

PROLOGUE
THE MISSION

"He's going to send you on some quest," said Matar.

"Get down from there," said Kamanar.

Matar stooped and looked down. The castle wall he stood on stretched downwards, disappearing into the gray fog far below. Barefoot, he continued to walk on the stone ledge.

"Maybe this time you'll find what you're not looking for."

"What do you mean?" asked Kamanar as he strolled beside his friend but remained on the floor of the long balcony.

Matar skipped over a small gap in the ledge and stopped.

"Careful. Why don't you walk here, on steady ground, like a normal human being?" asked Kamanar.

"Left death, right life. Left is wrong and right is right. Simple. Or maybe not?" asked Matar, pointing his left hand down to the fog and his right to where Kamanar stood.

"What are you saying?"

"Left real, right fake." Matar faced his friend, staring him in the eye.

"I …" Kamanar looked away.

"The fog is thickening. Still, it's a nice evening, don't you think?" asked Matar. He stood above Kamanar in his tattered clothes, his eyes glimmering in his young face. He raised his gaze to the gray sky, leaned back, and dropped off the ledge.

Kamanar leaped, slammed his body against the stones, and grabbed Matar by his coat. Matar hung on the side of the wall, his arms and legs limp.

"Hold on to me," said Kamanar, one hand clutching his friend, the other gripping the ledge. "Come on."

"Let me go."

"Never. Give me your hand!"

"You did it before."

Kamanar's eyes widened for a moment. "Don't go without me, please."

"When you learn how to unmask evil, when you find your soul, then you can come."

Matar shook himself. Kamanar squeezed the coat with all his strength. But his friend slipped from his grasp.

"No!" cried Kamanar, his eyes locked on his friend's.

Matar plunged down, disappearing into a sea of mist.

"No," said Kamanar, sobbing.

The fortified castle stood surrounded by the evening fog. Kamanar remained leaning over the stone ledge that framed one of its square towers, his arm outstretched. The pale stones underneath him were still warm from the heat of the afternoon sun.

"Come," bellowed a voice.

Kamanar stood up and looked ahead, ignoring the call. Gazing beyond yielded nothing. The mist had engulfed the world. The halo of a single torch flickering above him on one of the castle's balconies caught his eye. The small flame cast swirling lights and shadows in the fog.

"Kamar. Come."

At the top of the stairs leading to the tower's upper level stood a short, narrow-shouldered man. The darkness concealed his facial features.

"Kamar. Come," said the man again, beckoning.

Kamanar drew in a long breath and took a moment to

straighten his clothes before climbing the stairs. The man's face became distinguishable: his close-set eyes shone with a spark of madness. His lower lip was split open, and behind it sat a row of large, yellow, decaying teeth. The odd man smiled while he nodded.

"Lead the way, Bosh," said Kamanar.

By the time Kamanar had reached the top, Bosh's playful look had all but vanished. He stepped back as Kamanar rose in front of him, mountain-like. His tall figure dwarfed that of the peculiar man.

"Come," he said timidly. He vanished into a dark passage in the side of the tower.

Kamanar followed with his long strides as Bosh scurried ahead, half running, half jumping through the dark, narrow corridor.

Torches were scarce in this part of the castle. They made their way in complete darkness. *This is it,* thought Kamanar, groping along the stone walls.

The short man led the way while talking to himself. Whenever Kamanar got close, the skittish man would let out a scream, rush forward, and say, "Come," in a nervous tone.

After walking for some time, they reached a corridor flooded by light coming through an open side door. Bosh stood in the doorway.

"Here." He pointed inside and entered.

Kamanar squeezed through the opening and found himself in a small, windowless hall lit by four torches hanging in its corners. A cushioned yet simple and undecorated throne stood on a stone dais. On it sat King Creeden, who was stroking his white beard. Not daring to disturb his liege's ponderings, Kamanar remained silent.

Bosh giggled and hurried out of the hall, still mumbling.

The king continued to stroke his beard without saying a word, still not looking at the tall man in front of him.

Behind the modest throne a remarkable mural spanned

the entire back wall. It depicted, with great skill, an epic battle; the accuracy of its details was almost overwhelming. Knights wearing shining armor filled the right side of the mural, some on horseback, others charging on foot, wielding swords and spears. On the left side, diabolical hooded figures attacked with dreadful, blackened weapons. Their skin was dark, their mouths fanged, and their ears large and pointy. Their half of the mural was painted in dark and reddish shades, while the knights' half was embellished with blues and bright colors. The demon-like creatures' faces were twisted with frantic, taunting expressions, whereas the knights had a noble, strong-willed look to them.

The clash between the two forces was brutal, notably in the center of the great painting. Both sides impaled and slashed each other mercilessly. Kamanar tilted his head to get a better look at the bottom of the mural. Many bodies from both sides were piled beneath the fighting figures' feet, drenched in pools of blood and mud, some missing limbs or heads, others horribly mutilated.

As Kamanar's eyes shifted back to the small throne, he noted that the king was staring at a sword that leaned against the wall, as if it had been forgotten there. It was massive, larger than any he had ever seen. The black hilt had no crossguard, and odd-looking engravings covered the blade, which glistened in shades of blue. The weapon seemed simple yet somehow imposing.

"Well," said the king, as if he were talking more to himself, his eyes drifting toward the tall man.

Kamanar bowed.

"I did not suspend you of your duty in vain," said the king in his thick, commanding voice.

A chill ran down Kamanar's spine as he realized the wait was over.

"Kamanar, your finest hour is upon you. You are about to embark on the mission of your life. You and a select few." He spread his hands as he shook his head. "It amazes me how, every time, the peasants truly believe we are the victors. Just by announcing that we are such … Those mindless fools. But change is coming. I am about to set in motion a stratagem that will alter everything. At last, after endless defeats and so much loss, I will finally tip the scales."

King Creeden rose from his throne, clenching his right hand into a fist as he paced forward, his eyes staring deeply into Kamanar's. "From among all my predecessors, the entire Dummah dynasty, I, Creeden Dummah, will be victorious. I will make Mellethya whole! Those Dalusians will be struck so hard that they will run like rabid dogs back to wherever they spawned from. Good will banish evil, with you and my loyal subjects as the instruments of justice."

He placed both hands on Kamanar's shoulders. "Loyalty is rare." After releasing his grip on Kamanar, he turned around and walked back to his throne.

"You know, Kamanar, there are few people whom I can turn my back to like this," he said as he sat down again. "It is better to have subjects like Bosh, the creature who led you here, close to me than many others. He's a foolish half-wit but infinitely loyal. He'd jump off the highest tower of the castle if I asked him to."

Kamanar listened to the king, somewhat bewildered. He knew him as one who spoke to the point.

"And without further ado," the king said, as if reading the warrior's mind, "the essence of my request is very simple. I want you to assassinate a prominent general in the enemy's army: a key figure whose demise will diminish the Dalusians' power significantly, thus shifting the balance in our favor. Once you and your men reach a certain point at the bank of the elevated river—stealthily, of course—beyond it you will discover an unfortified structure, a tower of sorts, where this minister of evil is dwelling. It will not be difficult to identify him. Let your archer take aim and shoot an arrow right through his heart. You should have no further encounters with the enemy, ensuring a safe return … hopefully."

"In that case, we will need our best archer. Even two of them," said Kamanar.

"You will have only one. Your party must be very small, lest you compromise the secrecy of this mission." The king leaned back in his seat. "You are aware, Kamanar, that the difficult part will not be the assassination …" The king began stroking his beard again as the worried look returned to his face. "It will be the journey itself, its treacherous paths. In hundreds of years, few have made it back, and those who did … returned without their sanity. It will not be an easy quest. This task requires an experienced commander, an exceptional warrior: the best. And that is you, Kamanar."

"I will do anything and everything to fulfill my king's wishes. I owe so much to Your Majesty that I will move mountains. I will push each one of my men beyond the limit of human ability. This mission will be accomplished."

The king sighed and gave Kamanar a faint smile. "That is what I wanted to hear. Though you do not need to be taught about the value of trust and loyalty." He rose to his feet and turned to face the mural near a certain section depicting two evil-looking human figures. "Without those, we are like grains of sand scattering in the wind: powerless. I want you to be vigilant. If you have any suspicion of treason among your men, you must act swiftly. We can't risk having any traitors on this quest. You and I both suspect there might be a few of those hiding among us. Meet me here after dinner and we will discuss the details, including the identity of your men."

The warrior bowed and turned toward the exit.

"Humanity's sake and everything that is good are depending on you," said the king. "And I must have vengeance, for my son's sake. Maybe that will lessen the torment of my soul."

"I understand."

"One last thing …"

"His Majesty can ask me for the world, and I will not hesitate to deliver it."

"This last thing, it is for your sake. I know you are haunted by demons of the past."

Kamanar was taken aback. He turned and fixed his gaze on his master.

"If you succeed in this task, as a reward, I can erase it. Your past, that is."

"Impossible! Excuse my insolence, Your Majesty, but that can't—"

"It can be done. There is an instrument that can perform such a feat. Now go."

Kamanar nodded and exited.

Bosh led the tall warrior out through the maze of dark corridors to a walkway that connected the castle's towers. The man muttered something then disappeared as quickly as he had appeared.

The fog had thickened. Only a few eerie halos of remote torches were visible in the murk. The castle was enveloped but for the well-lit tower at the end of the walkway on which Kamanar stood.

Engrossed in thought, the warrior paced. The goal was clear, although the exact route he would follow had yet to be revealed. Yet this didn't bother Kamanar as much as the unusual sword he'd seen. He wondered why the king had made no mention of it and whether it had something to do with the mission at hand. And, most importantly, the offered reward. *Could it be true? To erase my past!*

His musings were interrupted when a silhouette emerged from the darkness and escaped toward the balcony that surrounded the tower. Kamanar dashed, stretching his arm out to grab a corner of the swirling cloak. He yanked the cloth, forcing the suspicious figure to spin in his direction. He stared in amazement as the hood fell back to reveal a familiar face.

"Naiya." He let go of the woman and took a step back. "Why are you sneaking around? Are you spying on me?"

Naiya's pale face shone in the darkness. She straightened her cloak. "It's nothing that concerns you," she said.

"Fine," he said, turning to leave.

"Wait."

Kamanar stopped for a moment then continued to walk away.

"It does concern you."

Naiya chased him and grabbed him by the arm, forcing him to face her. "Listen, just for a moment. For the sake of what was between us."

"Whatever was between us is now over, and not through any fault of mine."

"Just listen … please." She let go of his arm but stayed close to him. Her brown eyes swept across Kamanar's face, and she took a step back.

"Speak," said Kamanar.

"I know … I know about your mission. You are about to leave on some task … to do something. I'm not sure what it is. I do know it's important, but—"

"How do you know these things? Your father didn't tell you, I'm certain of that."

"Lately he's been mumbling in his sleep. I hear things from my chamber … names, places."

Kamanar stepped closer to her. "The way you behave … I often forget you are the princess. I hope you haven't told anyone about this."

"No, of course not."

"Keep it that way. You mentioned names and places?"

"They're not important … Please! Do not go on this mission. Make an excuse or something!"

"You must be out of your mind."

"Maybe it's time for you to stop running away."

"I'm not running from anything."

"You know that my father is not a well man—"

"There you go again. Your talk verges on the treasonous." He lowered his voice. "You two aren't as close as father and daughter ought to be. One day you'll find yourself in the gallows."

"I don't care."

Kamanar threw his hands up in the air.

"Please, I beg of you, don't be like my brother."

"That arrogant fool! Please don't tell me that he's going on this mission!"

Naiya stood silent. Kamanar groaned and turned to leave.

"Just hear me out, please." She wrapped both of her arms around one of his.

"No," he said, wrenching his arm free and walking away, the princess's sobs echoing in his ears.

CHAPTER 1
SOMEONE ELSE'S FORTUNE

A carving of a skewered lamb on a double door caught Naji's eye. The door swung open and a large, middle-aged woman wearing a dirty apron walked out. She poured a bucket of water onto the street, splashing a bit on the boy. The aroma of roasted lamb coming out of the tavern wafted over him, and he chewed with his mouth empty.

As he approached the entrance, an old woman's voice distracted him.

Beside the tavern stood a small, tattered tent. A heavyset, bearded man knelt in front of it. His clothes were dark and neat. He was nodding his head to the stuttering voice coming from within the tent. Strange bluish smoke drifted from the entrance. *A fortune-teller,* Naji thought, and he began climbing the three steps to the tavern. Stopping for a moment, he noticed the man walking away.

She'll take my coin for nothing. He tightened his fist around his coin and climbed another step, only to stop again. Muttering, he staggered back toward the fortune-teller.

The boy stood in front of the tent holding the coin in his hand.

"Zig, you owe me one big, fat piece of lamb," he said to himself and knelt.

He saw the figure of an old woman inside. She was covered from head to toe in a shabby cloak and had worn-out gloves on her hands. Sitting in her tattered tent, she looked like a pile of rags.

"How can I help you, young man?" a weary, screechy voice asked from beneath the veil. She pulled something out from under her cloak and threw it into the fire. The sweet scent of incense filled the air. Naji breathed in as much as he could.

He tried to find her eyes behind the dark veil.

"I'm looking for my friend. He was kidnapped by bandits."

The veil rose a bit as she studied the young man. "I am a fortune-teller and, thus, only tell fortunes. Would you like to know yours?" She threw another handful of incense into the fire, and the smell intensified.

Naji shook his head while scratching his crotch. "Can you tell my friend's fortune? Maybe it will tell me something."

"I can try, but I need a strand of hair from his head."

"But my friend's gone. He was kidnapped."

"If I try to foresee his fortune without a sample, I might foresee someone else's fortune, some other friend of yours."

"That's not a problem. He is my only friend."

"Is he?"

"I have no other friend in the whole world. So?"

The old woman remained silent for a moment. "Perhaps. Kidnapped, you say … Tell me about that. Tell me everything, starting with his name."

"Zig. His name is Zig. Back in Masta-Dahl, I think four days ago. Zig and I had a pretty good act: 'Naji and Zig, the Dragon Slayers'. Heard of us? Naji and Zig?" he asked, again trying to catch a glimpse of her hidden eyes. She shook her head.

"Anyway, it goes like this: I keep the crowd entertained with my fancy storytelling. Zig blows out candle flames with arrows, without hitting the candles—"

"Interesting."

"Interesting? Not fantastic? Incredible?"

"Do you want applause, or do you want to find your friend?"

"To find my friend … In the crowd were five strange fellows, all odd and evil-looking. One was dressed in fur, and another had a long staff strapped on his back. The very tall one, who was scary-looking, I think he was their leader. I saw that he was *very interested* in Zig's performance. At the end of the act, we picked up the food that people tossed to us and ran like crazy, because we knew those five were up to something. We slipped into an alley, but those bandits found us. They closed in on us from both ends. We were trapped. The tall one started asking Zig about the bow and stuff. When I saw him getting too close, I cursed him." The boy paused and felt the bulge above his left ear.

"Then?"

"I don't know. One of them hit me. I felt my head bounce … When I woke up, they were gone, and so was Zig."

The fortune-teller leaned back with a sigh. "They must have taken him for his skill. But for what purpose?"

"I—"

"Describe to me this Zig."

"Describe Zig? Hmmm, he's slightly shorter than me and has a thick mop of hair."

"Curly?"

"Yes, curly hair, brown eyes … They are pretty big, come to think of it. He sometimes has this surprised look even when he's not really surprised. What else? He dresses like me, more or less, but the good shoe is on his right foot." He pointed to his left foot. "Just like this one."

"You share the same pair of shoes … All right, let's try it."

Naji grinned and moved closer to the woman. "What now?"

"First, you pay."

Naji gave her his copper coin.

"Kneel. Give me your hand." He placed his dirty palm between her hands. She spat into it, and Naji was intrigued.

She sprinkled a handful of red powder across the boy's palm and tilted it sideways, studying how the spit picked up the dust. With a pair of tongs, she took a burning coal and held it over the reddening saliva.

Naji felt the heat of the ember radiating towards his fingers, but he didn't pull his hand away.

The hag's face became stern. She returned the coal back to the fire and wiped Naji's hand with a rag while she mumbled, "I am done."

"Well?" asked Naji, his arm still extended.

Still mumbling, the woman pushed his hand away and smoothed out her garments.

"I gave you money. Tell me what you saw!" His voice rose when he noticed she was evading his gaze.

"It is best not to know, for your own good."

Naji wiped his hand on his pants as he stood up. "I'll tear down this ugly tent if you don't tell me right now!"

"Do you really want to know?" she asked in her screechy voice. "I foresaw many fortunes and fates. But I haven't seen one as disturbing as this in a long time. Come closer."

Her words startled Naji, but he approached.

"I saw your friend standing on a battlefield teeming with clashing soldiers, on a great mountain, far away. Rain and wind lashed at him. His wet hair stuck to his face. A wicked knife, its blade shaped like a snake, was buried deep in his chest. He collapsed and died." She threw the copper coin back at Naji.

"It's a lie! I don't believe you."

Shaking her head, the old woman let out a sigh.

"You're a fake!" he said. He left, grumbling.

Disturbing thoughts haunted him as he walked under the scorching sun and left the town, heading north toward the forest. As he marched, he looked at the old coin in his palm. He and Zig had been planning for so long to split a decent meal with it. *We'll have to decide: a whole stuffed chicken or slice of lamb. That's a hard one.* Zig's words echoed in Naji's head.

He was hoping to find the bandits somewhere around Narrow Woods, a well-known hunting ground, but a place that was unfamiliar to him. The path before him twisted around the trunks of felled trees before disappearing into a great pine forest.

"That fake hag. What does she know?"

Naji walked on a carpet of needles under the shade of the big trees. The trees grew denser the deeper he went.

The top of a fir, much higher than the surrounding trees, stood out.

"That's a good lookout," he said to himself.

He climbed past the height of the surrounding treetops. Everything below looked so small. The winding path looked like a ribbon, appearing and disappearing among the pines.

He straddled a thick branch, his feet dangling down either side as he leaned his back against the trunk. To the north, he spotted a group of men on one a hillside. Straining his eyes, he counted a dozen mules being driven by the group.

"Too many, not them."

Naji stayed in his nest within the shade of the branches for some time. His tired, aching body grew limp, his eyelids closed, and he fell into a slumber.

As the sun began to set in the west, Naji stirred in his sleep, trying to get into a more comfortable position. The air whistled in his ears and his stomach dropped. His eyes opened wide and saw the earth coming at him fast. He screamed as he flailed his limbs.

He managed to grab a branch, and all traces of weariness vanished as he clung on for dear life.

"Damn it!" Still shaking, he pulled himself up to settle on the branch.

The world grew dimmer in the reddening light.

Naji heard voices coming from somewhere below. Between the branches, he spotted a couple of men walking alongside their mules.

"One, two, three!" He counted the mules as they flashed by among the trees. "Cross-eyed Godfried said they had three mules," he said, recalling the words of the old man, one of many he'd questioned along the way.

Sliding from branch to branch, he climbed down and sprinted after the group.

Naji recognized the long staff wrapped in cloth on one man's back. He felt both glad and apprehensive as he advanced parallel to the path, hiding behind bushes, making as little noise as possible. When he heard them talking, he got as close as he could and peered through the bushes.

"Zig," he blurted when he recognized his friend's curly head.

Not bound or chained, Zig walked alongside his captors.

Naji waved his hands, but Zig didn't notice him. He waved with a stick.

A hand grabbed the back of his shirt, pushing him out of the vegetation. He fell on his stomach in the middle of the path, right in front of his friend.

"Naji!" Zig called.

Naji jumped to his feet and spun around to face the man who had tossed him. It was the one with the staff. He was wearing a peculiar hat. He came closer to the boy.

"I'll hit you! Wanna fight?" asked Naji, lifting a stone.

The man with the strange hat smiled as he strode toward him. "Really?" he asked, stopping close to the boy and folding his arms across his chest.

Naji pulled Zig towards him; they were surrounded. On one side stood the tall, scary man wearing a sword on his belt, accompanied by an olive-skinned, bald man clad in furs. On the other side, in front of the mules, stood an older man with a round belly. Behind them stood the fifth, who had a longbow hung on his shoulder.

"This way!" yelled Naji, tugging Zig down the path. They passed the chubby man, running as fast as they could back toward the town.

CHAPTER 2
TWO USELESS FOOLS

Naji glanced back as they ran. The bandits didn't give chase. As Zig overtook him, Naji slowed, his head still turned. He saw the men walking away and he stopped, still panting.

"Wait." Naji took a moment to examine his friend's body. "Are you all right?"

"Yes," said Zig.

"I was really worried. I thought I'd never see you again."

"And I was worried. When the nasty one—the one with the hat and the staff—knocked you out, and you just lay there…"

"Why didn't you run away or something?" asked Naji.

"I—"

"Come on, tell me on the way. I want to reach Kameltur before it gets dark." Naji prodded him along.

"Kama Altur."

"Whatever. Let's go," said Naji as they marched side by side. "Why didn't you escape?"

"They weren't awful. When you fell, Marbel, the old chubby fellow, and Sarik, the good-looking one, tried to help you. They said you'd be fine."

"Not awful, huh …" said Naji, touching the bulge above his ear. "Go on."

"They said they wanted me to help them hunt some rare

bird, that it would take a couple days. I didn't want to go. I was worried about you. Their leader, Kamanar—"

"Kamanar? What kind of name is Kamanar? Go on."

"He said if I helped them hunt this bird, I'd get an equal share of the gold. His condition was that I join them right away. I don't know why I said yes. I suppose I thought this was the chance you always talk about. I thought we'd hunt the bird, take the gold, and come back. Of course, I regretted it the moment we left you behind and have not stopped regretting it."

"And then comes your best friend Naji to save you."

"I was surprised when I saw you, really. I couldn't believe it. How did you find us?"

"Witchcraft, dear Zig. My magic powers are growing stronger." Naji smiled, raising his fists to his face. "And don't be naive. They're not good people. There are no good people anywhere, understand? There is no rare bird, no nothing. It's all nonsense. You think they'd pay you in gold, really?" he asked, kicking a pinecone.

"No, it's all true."

"I told you—stop being so naive."

"Here." Zig pulled a gold coin from his pocket.

Naji fell silent. His eyes shone as he stared at the coin in his friend's palm.

"Kamanar gave me this without me even asking."

Naji took the coin. "Judging by the weight, it's real." He passed the coin from one hand to the other and grinned at his friend. Zig smiled, too.

"Come on. Let's go back to the bandits," said Naji.

The smile disappeared from Zig's face. "But you just said they weren't good people, that I was being naive."

Naji threw the coin back to Zig. "Come on." He turned around and walked back up the path.

"Wait. Take it. I don't want it."

Naji pushed away Zig's hand. "Forget this one miserable coin. We can have many more. This is our big chance."

"No…"

"Don't you trust Naji?"

Zig rolled his eyes. "I do, I do."

"Off we go," Naji said and dashed back up the path, followed by a reluctant Zig.

The sun began to set, and the forest darkened. The deeper they went into the forest, the more the pine trees huddled together. The nervous boys, peering around, quickened their pace without uttering a word.

"Light," said Zig, pointing ahead.

The two ran toward a light that flickered through the bushes and between the trunks.

"It's them. Something smells good," said Naji.

They got off the path and moved between the bushes. A twig snapped under Zig's foot. They froze.

"You can stop sneaking around," said a voice.

The boys stepped into the light of a small campfire. Three of the bandits stood before them.

"You have decided to come back," said the tall man.

Zig nodded. "That's Kamanar," he whispered to his friend.

"You must be Naji. Zig spoke much about you," said Kamanar. "We told you he'd be fine. Come, join us for dinner." He pointed to a bubbling pot tucked into a pile of stones on the fire.

The boys exchanged looks. Smiling, Naji approached the fire and sat down close to the pot. Zig sat next to him.

"We've decided to accept your offer. We want to join," said Naji. His gaze shifted to the bald, dark-skinned man in furs who was stirring the embers with a branch.

"I asked Zig to join. I wanted to hire his skill, not yours … If you have any."

"You need to understand, Mr. Tall Man, that without me, Zig couldn't even hit that tree over there. He gets nervous, and if I'm not there, expect a miss. Then, no bird. This stuff smells good."

Scratching his unshaven chin, Kamanar tapped on the

scabbard of the sword on his hip. "Is that so? Marbel, serve some soup to our guests."

Naji waited for the bowl of hot soup to land in his hands and immediately took a sip. "Delicious," he said, slurping the hot liquid until the dish was dry. "More, please."

"Very well." Kamanar knelt in front of the boys. "You may both join."

"Really? I mean, sure," said Naji in between gulps.

Kamanar stared at the two lads, the reflection of the fire burning in his eyes. "Zig has already met our party. Allow me to introduce the others. This likable fellow, who is so young at heart, is Marbel." He pointed at the older, heavyset man, who displayed a smile amid plump cheeks, patting his belly at the same time.

"Pleased to meet you," said Marbel.

"This bald fellow wearing all the furs despite the heat is our tracker. His name is Motehro."

When he heard his name, the tracker stood to attention.

"At ease—I don't need anything." Kamanar waved his hands in dismissal.

The tracker scratched his head and went back to stoking the fire.

"Motehro does not speak our language, but we manage. And my name is Kamanar. I'm the commander of this party, which is missing two at the moment. They should be back any minute. We are headed toward the Dwarves' Passage. I must warn you that we are going on a difficult and dangerous journey, which may take much longer than a few days … You have until tomorrow evening to decide whether or not you wish to come along."

"We've decided. We're coming," said Naji.

The tall man's blue eyes were fixed on Zig's curls. The boy raised his head, looked at Kamanar's gaunt face, and nodded.

With a rustle in the brush, a young man appeared in front of them carrying a bundle of twigs, a longbow slung across his shoulder. His light brown hair was highlighted with streaks of gold.

"This is Sarik, our archer," said Kamanar. Sarik came closer and placed his bundle next to Motehro, who was still tampering with the campfire.

"I bet Zig can shoot better than him," said Naji.

Sarik smiled. His face was bright and gentle, the color of his eyes peculiar and impossible to determine in the dim light of the fire.

"I'm sure he can," said Kamanar.

The last member of the group soon followed Sarik. His long, wrapped staff was still on his back. He, too, had a bundle of twigs.

"What are those two useless fools doing here?" he asked.

The boys were startled by his audacity.

"They're joining us," Kamanar said without even looking at the man. "You don't have to be acquainted with this one."

The man mumbled something, walked up to the fire, and dropped his twigs on Sarik's bundle. He rearranged his strange hat, which covered every hair on his head, and threw a piercing look at the boys. The two avoided his eyes and pretended to study the fire.

"We are ready for dinner," Kamanar said.

The chubby old man nodded. "Right away," he said as he rummaged through the provisions lying in a pile near the mules.

That evening, Kamanar's party, joined by the two hungry boys, had a feast of dry bread and smoked meat.

At the commander's order, after putting out the fire all seven settled in for the night.

CHAPTER 3
PUSH ON

"Wake up."

Zig sat up. It was early morning. The sight of his friend lying on his back, drooling, brought a smile to his face.

"You, too, get up." Kamanar kicked Naji.

The boy sat up and looked around as if confused. Kamanar stared at the boy, then at Zig.

"This is normal," said Zig, smiling.

Kamanar smirked and went to help Marbel and Sarik with loading the mules.

Naji stretched. He patted his dusty clothes and walked straight up to Kamanar. "I want to talk to you about something."

"Talk," Kamanar said as he fastened the leather saddle straps on the mule.

"About our fee …"

The tall man threw the boy a stern look.

"I understand, thank you," said Naji, turning away.

Marbel dealt each member of the expanded team an apple and a wheat biscuit. When everything was packed and loaded, they moved on, taking a path carpeted with pine needles and cones. Kamanar and the tracker, Motehro, led, and behind them came the two boys, followed by Marbel and the frowning man. Sarik was last, leading the mules.

As the pale-yellow light of the morning sun wove its way through the thick branches, the dew evaporated. The birds filled the forest with a variety of melodies: some nice, some annoying.

"What's with that one?" asked Naji.

"Which one? Sarik?" Zig pointed at the archer.

"Don't point. No. The one with the goofy hat and the staff."

"They just call him *Soldier*. I don't know why. He's always in a bad mood."

"What's that on his back?"

"I'm not sure. I think it's a sword. One thing's for sure, though: he doesn't leave it for a moment, not even when he sleeps."

"Don't fall behind," Kamanar said and picked up the pace.

Walking at a quick but steady rate all day, they followed the trail that crossed the forest.

As the sun began to set, Kamanar took a sudden turn, leaving the path and heading westward. They made their way among the trees and bushes until they reached the edge of the forest.

As it grew darker, a great, gently sloping valley unfolded before them. At the edge of the valley stood an imposing mountain range, its many darkening peaks running from north to south.

"Rest for a bit," said Kamanar.

"And I was just thinking about a snack," said Naji.

"Show any more of this attitude, and you'll have to find your own way back. We eat when I say so, understand?"

"We don't have to snack. I was just thinking. Is it a crime to think?"

The tall man beckoned for them to gather around. "From the moment we cross the Dwarves' Passage and until we reach Fir Forest, there will be no stopping—not for rest, not for peeing. I don't care if any of you sprain an ankle or break a leg. We must cover the entire distance in one go. We stop only after we reach the tree line."

"You said we were heading for the Dwarves' Passage. You

didn't say anything about crossing it into the cursed woods of Turundia. People never come back from there," said Naji.

"Those woods are crawling with giant, bug-like creatures, and monsters, even Dalusians!" Zig said.

"The evil Dalusians!" said Naji. "With their fangs and horns, and they shape-shift, turning into a helpless man or a little girl, and then, when you're fooled …" He pretended to slit his own throat with his index finger.

"I'm aware of the risks, but this is our route. Beyond the passage, there is no changing your minds, no way back. We will continue until our goal is accomplished. Now is your last chance to decide. What's it going to be?" Kamanar eyed them.

The two friends exchanged glances.

"Send them home," someone said with a mocking tone.

They all turned to look at the one called Soldier. He was leaning against a tree staring at Zig and Naji.

Kamanar turned to the boys. "I would prefer it if Zig … well … if both of you join. But I must inform you that we are not dealing with a rare bird here, but with something much more significant. Don't ask for details. I will not reveal anything, not before we cross the passage. So?"

"We're coming," Naji was quick to answer.

"But. But …" said Zig.

"We're going with you all the way," said Naji. He patted Zig on the shoulder. "I'll explain later."

"What does Zig say?" asked Kamanar.

Zig sighed and nodded.

Kamanar smiled. "Dwarves' Passage is guarded by a company of Mellethyan soldiers," said Kamanar as he gazed at the mountain range. "The passage has been closed for years, but tonight, and only tonight, it will open." Kamanar led the six, along with the mules, straight for the mountain range.

"Cheer up," said Naji. "We are lucky."

"I don't know. If we go there, to that forest, I'm telling you…"

Naji pulled his friend closer to him and smiled.

"Whatever you say, Naji, whatever you say."

As they reached the foothills, a great, dam-like wooden wall appeared before them. It had been built into the mountain. The wall was high, and there were a few rooms at the top of it. Faint lights flickered in the windows, and whispers could be heard from dark corners. The few soldiers manning the structure appeared more like shadows in the dim light, their armor rattling and squeaking.

The party walked up to a large gate in the center of the wall that was bolted shut with a sturdy beam. A soldier stood by and leaned against the wooden bolt.

The group halted behind Kamanar. Everyone but the boys began to unload the beasts, each man gearing up with a backpack and a sword.

Sarik pulled the mules away, handing their reins to one of the soldiers. Much to the boys' chagrin, instead of swords, Zig got a small bag packed with supplies and Naji a waterskin with a leather strap to carry across his back.

"Soon we will be out in the open, exposed, with no trees for cover. Remember, no stopping," said Kamanar. "We will proceed in the following manner: the tracker and I will go first, then Sarik and the boys, and Soldier and Marbel closing the rear. Check your packs, make sure they're fastened tight."

Kamanar signaled to the guard standing by the gate. He slid back the wooden bolt.

They heard the guard's faint, "Good luck," as he slammed the gate behind them.

They pushed forward through a dark tunnel for a few minutes, soon finding themselves out in the open on the other side.

Kamanar raced ahead with the others close behind. They welcomed the cool breeze stroking their faces. Stars glittered in the sky, illuminating their surroundings. In front of them, the starry night sky blended with a wide field on the horizon. It was a vast, open area, with small bushes scattered about. The ground was firm, which made running easier.

The boys began panting. The rest were still keeping pace, including Marbel. Zig and Naji slowed down.

"Come on—run!" came a whisper from behind. Soldier caught up and kicked Naji's butt hard. "Run. We've barely covered half the distance. You and you, run, I say!"

Naji turned to face Soldier, only to see him coming in for a second kick. Naji sprinted, followed by Zig, his hand clutching his side as he tried to keep up.

"I can't go on … I have to stop," said Zig, struggling for air, feeling his body about to go numb.

"Push on. I can see the trees," said Kamanar.

As the commander reached the tree line he slowed to a walk, as did the rest, and disappeared into the shadows of Fir Forest.

"I saw you two taking rolls from the mules. That's what happens when you run on a full stomach," said Kamanar without looking at the panting boys. The two glanced at each other before they turned their gazes to the ground.

All were eager for respite, awaiting a sign from Kamanar. But he kept on going deeper and deeper into the forest. The world became darker with each step, until the dense fir branches finally blocked out the starlight.

"Here," said the commander at last.

The boys dropped to the ground, sprawling at the bulging roots of the nearest tree. Old Marbel sat down beside them. All three panted and dripped with sweat.

"Sarik, stay at watch to the rear," said Kamanar, who knelt, peering into the dark.

"Caleem, come beside me," said Marbel in a low voice to the man they called Soldier.

"That was hard," said Zig once he caught his breath.

"Silence," whispered Kamanar. "From now on, we don't talk unless we must—" he approached the boys "—and if we do, we whisper. Understood? Naji, pass the waterskin around." Naji did as he was ordered after taking a few sips for himself.

Following a frugal meal, they went to sleep. The camp was

guarded in shifts of two. Naji and Caleem were first, keeping a silent distance between them. Next were Sarik and Zig, followed by Marbel and Motehro. A little before sunrise, Kamanar, who had kept watch on his own, woke them all up.

CHAPTER 4
IT'S PROBABLY NOTHING

"We'll try to be on the move either at dawn or around sunset, when visibility is lower. We'll need to avoid moving at night. Dalusians can see well in the dark. We can't," said Kamanar.

The boys shuddered at the mention of Dalusians.

As dawn was breaking, Kamanar noticed Sarik scanning the trees, his bow in his hand.

"What is it?"

"I thought I saw something on my watch last night. Two big figures among the trees, there," said Sarik.

"And only now you're telling me this? Why didn't you wake me up?" Kamanar looked him in the eye.

"I wasn't sure. It's probably nothing. I may have imagined it."

The tall man grabbed Sarik by the shirt. "Imagined? Your imagination could cost us dearly."

Soldier jumped in and pushed Kamanar away from the archer. "Don't touch him!"

"Caleem, know your place," said Kamanar, his tall frame looming over him. Caleem clenched his fists in response.

The others watched in silence as the two men sized one

another up. It seemed that a fight was inevitable, but after they exchanged a few menacing looks, Kamanar threw his head back. "Finish breakfast and prepare to leave," he ordered the others.

"What just happened?" whispered Naji.

"I don't know, but this isn't the first time," said Marbel.

After breakfast, they covered their tracks and moved on through the cover of the trees. It was a long walk with no breaks until sunset.

"Twilight … perfect timing," said Kamanar as they approached the northwestern edge of Fir Forest.

Beyond the last tree was a barren clearing that extended all the way to Turundia, the great oak forest.

"We must reach the other side swiftly. Straight for the oaks, one by one," said Caleem.

"That's not necessary," said Kamanar. "We will run as a group. It's a short distance. If we cross one by one, we will stay exposed for a longer time. Come on, let's go."

"I disagree—"

"It's not your decision." Kamanar dashed, leading the way, and the rest raced close behind him.

Halfway across the clearing, Motehro overtook Kamanar and came to a sudden stop. Dropping to his knee, he raised his hand, signaling for everyone to halt. Kamanar knelt beside him. The two exchanged a few whispers.

Kamanar looked back to the others as he drew his sword. "Lie down."

Before any of them could do anything, sharp whistles tore through the quiet evening. They stood, paralyzed, trying to figure out what was happening. "Run back. It's an ambush!" Kamanar yelled as volleys of arrows flew in their direction.

He dashed back, only for a small arrow to pierce the back of his neck. He gritted his teeth while pushing Motehro back, who was wobbling left and right. The latter fell to the ground, dropping his sword, his eyes wide open. Two short arrows protruded from his abdomen.

Kamanar ducked, grabbed the tracker by the arm, and dragged him back toward the trees amid a rain of arrows.

Sword in hand, Caleem dropped his backpack, ran past Kamanar, and headed straight for the shooters.

"What are you doing? Come back!" said Kamanar.

Caleem screamed as he charged.

As Kamanar continued his retreat, he noticed Marbel diving into the bushes ahead.

Zig whimpered, rolling his body into a ball and covering his head with his hands.

"Get up and run! Before I kick you all the way back," shouted Kamanar.

Zig dove into a small bush as a barrage of arrows flew over his head. He saw the waterskin on the ground and, next to it, his friend lying on his back.

"Naji, get up!" he yelled, coming to his aid. Zig noticed a small arrow sticking out of Naji's chest; blood stained his shirt.

Naji moaned as he held the arrow. "Help me."

Zig began to weep as he looked into his suffering friend's glassy eyes. Still whimpering, he helped his buddy up.

The arrows stopped. The clash of swords reached them along with the noise of Caleem shouting and cursing as he battled the unseen assailants.

The two friends limped past Marbel to the trees.

"Well done, boys, you made it. Keep going a bit farther … behind the bushes.

They reached Kamanar, who was sitting on the ground. Motehro lay on his back next to him, both arrows still in his abdomen.

"How could this be?" asked Kamanar as he held his neck and the arrow sticking out of it.

The two boys sobbed.

Marbel peeked over the bushes. A figure emerged from the shadows, heading straight at them. "It's Caleem," said the older man. Zig noticed at least a dozen arrows jutting out of his body.

Caleem was about to collapse, his blood-stained sword almost slipping from his hand.

Marbel took a deep breath and leaped out of his hideout, his eyes fixed on his friend while he ran. He slammed into Caleem and wrapped his arm around his shoulders.

"The sword, the sword … The other one!" Caleem mumbled, pointing at the staff-like thing that had fallen from his back.

Marbel picked it up and slung it on his back.

Caleem collapsed, and Marbel carried him with great effort. As they reached the fir trees, a fainting Caleem released his grip on his sword.

Still some distance from the safety of the bushes, Marbel glanced behind him. Zig followed the direction of his gaze and saw several dark figures approaching fast. The attackers stopped suddenly, only paces away. They wore dark cloaks, and their faces were concealed by oversized hoods. In their gloved hands, they held unusual swords with long hilts and short blades.

"Dalusians!"

One of the Dalusians turned around and ran to the oaks, and the rest followed and vanished.

Marbel put Caleem down and knelt beside him. He began to pull the short arrows out of his body. When he was done, he slung the young man's body over his shoulder. As he continued to where his friends lay, three giants emerged from the greenery. Each was as tall as two men and wider than four.

They looked heavy, their faces round and their bodies bloated. They wore gray pants and shirts, and short orange hair covered their bodies, even most of their faces. Under their small, widely spaced eyes sat wide, flat noses, almost as broad as their plump lips. Two of the giants held huge hammers in their hands. One of the orange giants extended his hand towards Caleem.

"You scared away the Dalusians … Thank you," Marbel said in a trembling voice. No reply came. "The enemy of my enemy is my friend … I hope."

With his three-fingered hand, one giant pulled the unconscious man from Marbel's arms, lifted him onto his massive shoulder, and motioned for the other giants to follow him. The three giants approached the other members of the defeated team.

Zig was the only one still on his feet; all the rest were now unconscious. The boy panicked at the sight of the giants and began to drag Naji away.

"Friends," said Marbel, smiling. "I think they want to help."

To Zig's speechless wonderment, the giants carried the rest of the party on their shoulders.

"Did you see Sarik anywhere?" asked the chubby man. Zig shook his head, his eyes still fixed on the giants.

"Sarik! Sarik!" Marbel called. There was no answer.

The giants continued into the forest.

"Marbel, come on. Looks like we're leaving," said Zig.

Marbel stumbled around in the darkness until he reached the boy.

"Where do you think they're taking us?" asked Zig.

"I don't know. Far from here, I hope," said Marbel, peering behind him. "No Dalusians following, thank God."

Zig marched after the creatures, his head drooping. Naji's limbs bounced up and down with each of the giant's steps.

"I told you we should go home, but you didn't listen," he said to his friend. "Damn you!" Zig yelled, turning to Kamanar. "It's all your fault."

Marbel placed a hand on the boy's shoulder and pulled him closer.

"Come on, boy. Relax. That won't do anybody any good."

Indifferent to Zig's shouting, the giants walked on. A branch released by one of them sprang back and slapped Naji's buttocks. The boy moaned.

"He's still alive," said Zig.

"They've passed out, that's all."

An hour later, they entered a clearing. Several tall poles, some topped with torches, encircled the perimeter. Three giant-size log cabins, one bigger than the other two, were visible in the flickering light. In the center of the clearing, a brighter torch hung on a short pole. On either side of it were two large pits.

There were many more orange giants around, some bearing hammers. All looked at the new guests.

The giants carrying the wounded walked toward the center. Marbel and Zig followed.

"Notice the little horns sticking out of their foreheads?" asked Zig, pointing to one of the giants.

"Don't point," said Marbel. "It's not polite."

A giant approached Zig and pulled the bag off his back.

"Thank you." Zig bowed.

The big creature reached for Marbel's sword, which he willingly surrendered. Then he grabbed Caleem's long sword from Marbel's back.

"I would prefer it if you didn't take that one," said Marbel. The giant took it anyway.

"It looks deep," said Zig, as he and Marbel peered into one of the pits. In a flash, a giant shoved them into it with a sweep of his hammer.

They plummeted into the depths of the dark hole. Zig threw his arms out, trying to grab on to something. He squealed with his eyes shut as he braced himself for the crash. The impact was sudden. Dizzy, stunned, and groaning, the two sat up in the soft, muddy ground. Something landed next to them with a splash.

Pulling themselves together, the two crawled to the pit's wall. They heard three more splashing thumps. A torch a giant held above brightened the pit just enough for them to see their friends lying in the mud.

They rushed to Naji and Kamanar, who had landed face down. They wiped their faces clean and tugged the men to the side of the pit to lie next to Caleem and the tracker.

All the two could hear were the giants' booming voices, grunting among themselves as they looked down at their prisoners.

CHAPTER 5
SOUNDS LIKE A GOOD IDEA

"Let us out. Please!" yelled Zig hoarsely.

"Let it go, boy. We've been fooled. These are no friends. I should have known better," said Marbel.

"What do they want? Do you think they're going to eat us?"

"No … they're not carnivores. I think they are called Guzuds. Did you notice their hooves?"

"If you knew what they were, why did you trust them?"

"I wasn't sure. I know nothing of their nature. I once heard that they're some kind of tribe, inhabitants of the far-northern plains. We really had no option: it was either them or the Dalusians," said Marbel as he examined a wounded Caleem, whose hat remained firmly on his head. Marbel pulled out the last short arrow from Caleem's body. The tail of it had broken off, and instead of a metal tip, it had a sharp, wooden point. Marbel brought the arrow close to his nose and sniffed it.

"It's some kind of sedative."

"Sedative?"

"These arrows weren't meant to be fatal. They only penetrate deep enough to deliver the drug."

Marbel pulled all the arrows out of each of his companions'

bodies. "I wonder what happened to Sarik," Marbel said while tending to the wounded.

"Well, what do you think?"

"They'll be fine. Time will fix them, like it does all problems."

They sat down on the muddy floor, leaning against the pit's rock wall, their gazes alternating between their unconscious friends and the pit's mouth high above.

"Maybe we should do something, Marbel," said Zig after a long silence.

"Do what? Eventually, Kamanar will wake up. He'll know what to do."

Zig looked at his friend Naji lying beside him, his chest rising and falling slowly. "Coins, coins, coins. There's nothing more important than coins. Well, look where your love for coins got us!"

"Coins can solve many problems, yes. But they also make even more of them. My late grandfather used to say that the three truly important things in life are the woman, the belly, and the woman's belly. Not coins."

Zig nodded, pondering Marbel's words.

"You know, I have a son, maybe a year or two older than you," said the old man.

"What's his name?"

Marbel's expression became grave. Then he sighed and his eyes became gentle again. "It doesn't matter. Lie down, and try to get some rest," he said as he slid down and lay on the wet soil.

The silence at the bottom of the pit lasted for a few hours. The droplets of water trickling down the rocky walls formed a small puddle at the bottom. Marbel sat up. "This Dalusian drug is annoyingly potent. No one is waking up," he said, wetting Caleem's lips with water from the puddle. "How come you're so adept with a bow, Zig? Or is it a trick?"

"No, no tricks. I just aim and shoot. I wish I didn't even know how to hold a bow."

"Talent, boy. It's called talent."

Clouds covered the night sky, and darkness filled the pit as the light from the torch above weakened. Gentle rain began to fall.

The inside of the pit was almost pitch-black. Zig felt cool drops landing on his head as he hugged his knees. A muffled thud came from the stone wall behind him. He listened, hearing it for a second time, then a third. "Did you hear that? There's something behind the wall."

Marbel listened for a moment. "I'm sorry, son. My hearing isn't what it used to be. If I'm not mistaken, the second pit is on the other side of this wall."

"Maybe it's Sarik."

"Could be. Let's try to find a loose rock or something. Maybe we can dig a way to the other side."

After a thorough groping of the wall, to their disappointment they found that most of it was solid rock.

"It's useless. I can't see my own hands in this darkness. We'll continue in the morning … If there is a tomorrow for us," Marbel said as he settled down. "What I'd give now for a big, fat chunk of pork!"

The boy dug through a triangular patch of soft dirt he found between two rocks.

Marbel rested his head on the wall and dozed off.

The boy, intent on his task, scraped and pulled, removing the soft mud until he'd dug a narrow tunnel in the space between the rocks. To the sound of Marbel's snoring, Zig worked until he was able to squeeze his entire body into the tunnel.

"Marbel," he called, his voice muffled by the tunnel. "Marbel!"

The chubby old man woke up and jumped to his feet. He looked for Zig next to him. "Yes, boy, I can hear you," he said while searching.

"Come, help."

Marbel stuck his head into the opening of the tunnel. "Where are you, boy?"

"I think I made it to the other side … Yes, Marbel, I did it!" he said after he broke through with his hands into the other pit, encountering nothing but empty space.

He squeezed his head through the hole and peered, but it was too dark to see anything. "Sarik," he whispered. "Sarik!" But there was no answer. Zig stretched downward and groped the wall, searching for the bottom. This pit seemed to be deeper. As he inched his way farther down, he slipped and slid to the ground.

He got up, wiped the mud off his face, and spat out some dirt.

"Sarik," he whispered, unable to see anything.

"What's happening?" Marbel's voice floated through the tight tunnel.

"I don't think Sarik's here. Or maybe he is, but he's unconscious." He began to explore the muddy pit.

"*Garum bara'a!*" roared a voice, making the whole pit tremble.

Zig's heart almost stopped. He shrunk, not daring to move.

"*Garum bara'a* … Come here, boy. Don't be afraid."

Zig could only make out a pair of catlike glowing green eyes, very big and far apart. The boy let out a choked scream. Attempting to escape back into the tunnel, he jumped up and down, fumbling to find the opening.

"What's happening there?" asked Marbel. Marbel's voice helped him find the opening. Zig lifted himself up and tried to crawl as fast as he could back to his friend. Something grabbed his legs and pulled him back out to the wrong side of the tunnel.

"Marbel!" he yelled as something lifted him up in the air. A huge hand clenched his body and another blocked his mouth. The pair of feline eyes appeared before him once again. He tried to scream but failed to make a sound. He felt as if he were wedged between rocks.

"Calm down, little boy," said the deep voice.

Zig was so close to the creature's mouth he could feel its hot, foul breath. His arms and legs trapped, the boy tried to struggle, but to no avail.

"I will let you go. Calm down."

Zig was panicking. After a long moment, he felt the hand loosen its grip and put him down on the floor. He stood, motionless. Marbel's voice had echoed through the opening the whole time, yet Zig had only just noticed it.

The voice addressed Marbel. "Be quiet, please."

"What did you do to the boy?"

"I'm here," said Zig.

"I'm a friend, don't worry," said the voice.

Zig sensed he was speaking to a gigantic figure. "The last friends I made threw me into this pit," he said.

"That's what they did to me. We're all in the same predicament here," said the deep voice.

The sky cleared, and starlight began to shine into the pit. A gigantic figure, much larger and more daunting than any of the fat Guzuds, stood in front of him. The creature had a large, bright mane that extended from his head all the way to his back. Its giant torso was dark and muscular.

"Can I go back to my friend?" asked Zig.

"Of course. Here, let me help you," said the creature, coming closer to Zig, who was still awed by its sheer size. The creature lifted him up and inserted him headfirst into the tunnel. The boy crawled back and emerged at Marbel's feet.

"What was that?" asked the old man.

"A huge, scary creature with a white mane and glowing eyes. He's huge! Bigger than all those Guzuds put together," whispered Zig, struggling to wind down. "What do you think it is?"

"I don't know …"

"Hello, human," whispered the creature through the tunnel.

"His breath stinks," Marbel whispered. "Identify yourself."

"I'm a captive like you. Maybe we can help each other and get out of these rotten pits."

"How, exactly?"

"Send the boy to me."

"What will you do with him?"

"You'll have to trust me."

"I don't know." Marbel turned to Zig. "Do what you think is right, boy."

"He didn't hurt me before. We have nothing to lose," Zig

said and crawled back into the tunnel.

Once his head appeared on the other side, huge hands grabbed him again and pulled him out. Only when the creature had placed him on the muddy floor did Zig's fear subside.

"I understand … my size."

"You could crush me like a bug," said Zig, noticing a very long, hooked nose curving down from between the monster's eyes.

"I can, little boy. But why would I? Don't worry … I've tried to climb out, but the rocks can't bear my weight. I won't try again, for the whole pit will collapse."

Zig scratched his head, looking at the rocks scattered around.

The creature stooped down. "There is a way, though I doubt you will like this."

The boy stared at the giant's face: apart from the strange, beak-like nose, it looked a lot like a cat's, only hairless. The features that most caught the boy's attention were the long, sharp fangs protruding up from its lower lip.

"I'll scoop you in my hand … and hurl you out."

"Sounds like a good idea."

"The challenge is, what will you do then? I suppose you should look for a rope or a log and lower it into my pit."

"What about my friends?"

"You have other friends?"

"We are seven: four unconscious, me, and Marbel. The seventh is lost." Zig paused. "We have no chance."

"You'll have to trust me, boy. Once I'm out, I will take care of these ugly, fat creatures. Then I'll help your friends."

"But those Guzuds—there are too many of them."

"Leave them to me. What do you say, boy?"

"Don't have much of a choice …"

"Come on, boy. The sun will rise soon, and it'll be harder for you to elude their gaze. Then we'll have to wait for tomorrow night, and who knows what will happen before then. We must act now."

"Fine. What do I do?"

CHAPTER 6
GARUM BARA'A

The creature opened its huge palm. "Sit here."

Zig sat down on the hard fingers, wary of the long, sharp claws. The humongous beast stood up and exhaled. Zig tried not to breathe as the stench hit him again. He looked down into the darkness, and although he couldn't see the bottom from where he sat, he knew he was high up.

When he was catapulted out of the pit and into the night sky, he shrank with fear as the air whistled in his ears. He regretted this idea, but it was already too late. His eyes shut tight, he failed to contain a long scream as he continued to fly upwards.

The monster had thrown him too high. Sensing that his rise was slowing down, the boy stopped screaming. Opening his eyes for a moment, he saw the two pits far below him. As he began his descent, he screamed again. Something scraped his limbs before a hard blow hurt his back. He'd landed at the top of a tall fir tree outside the camp's perimeter.

The boy spread his arms, trying to grab onto anything, but only managed to break some twigs as he continued to fall, bouncing from one branch to the next and eventually crashing on the ground.

The Guzuds began grunting loudly, breaking the silence of the night.

"*Guzud bala! Guzud bala!*"

Lights were lit in the three wooden buildings, and dozens of Guzuds poured out, bearing large hammers and torches, all yelling in their unfamiliar language.

One of the guards ran out leading a group of about a dozen other Guzuds. Others hurried to check the pits. The rest of them searched around the camp. Then the majority went deeper into the forest, leaving only a few in the camp.

The grunting creatures closed in on Zig's hideout. Though weary and bruised, he raced back toward the torches surrounding the camp. The clumsy giants caused a racket as they stomped in all directions, making it easier for him to evade them. He took a better look at the camp and noticed only a small number of giants clomping around, torches in hand. Once they were at the far end of the camp, he entered. Stooping down, he sprinted to the nearest wooden building and hid in its shadow.

Apart from the shadows near the buildings, there was nowhere to hide from the camp's open, well-lit central area.

Zig stayed glued to the wall as two Guzuds came toward him, holding their ubiquitous hammers. They approached quickly, and he couldn't tell whether they could see him. Either way, it was too late to escape.

The two giants increased their speed. Zig crouched down, burying his face in the wet earth by the wall. Their steps got closer and louder. As he waited for the crushing blow of a hammer, his whole body began to shake. He wanted to scream, but the two Guzuds walked right past him and opened a nearby door. They entered while snapping at each other and left the door open.

Zig lifted his head up. Light came through the doorway. He was still caching his breath when the two Guzuds returned, even more upset. Zig ducked as they slammed the door behind them. When the sound of their hooves had subsided, Zig noticed that the door was ajar. Protected by the wall's shadow, he peeked inside and saw a large and empty room, so he entered swiftly.

Zig closed the door behind him, leaving just a small crack.

In front of him were three huge doors. He crossed the hallway and reached for the high handle of the middle door. Though he was terrified, he opened it and peeked inside. There was no one in there, just three colossal beds standing against the walls.

He went for the door on the left and opened it. It was a storeroom full of hammers, pitchforks, and other tools. His eyes opened wide when he spotted a long, thick rope rolled into a coil.

He grabbed the rope and rushed to the main door. He peered outside, but the light of the torches inside made it hard to see far into the darkness.

He hurried out, staying in the shadows as he had before. The Guzuds were returning from the woods. As he paused to exhale, he glimpsed a log's edge sticking out of the corner of the adjacent building. Ignoring the approaching Guzuds and with trembling hands, he fastened one end of the rope around the log then grabbed the rest of the coil and dashed toward the pits.

"Which one?" he yelped, trying to identify the correct pit.

The Guzuds grunted, "*Guzud Gara! Guzud Gara!*" as they charged, shaking the muddy ground with their hooves.

The sight of the lunging mass of giants petrified him, but still he continued sprinting toward the nearest pit. He peeked but couldn't tell if this was the creature's pit. The angry giants were nearly upon him. He threw the rope down the pit and fled, not sure whether it was the right one. Racing toward the far torches, he tried to escape into the forest, but two Guzuds blocked his way, one holding a hammer, the other a torch. They charged while more closed in from behind.

Zig was on the verge of tears. He ran back to the buildings, but yet more hammer-wielding Guzuds emerged from behind them. He was besieged on all sides. He stopped, terrified, glancing all around, wondering which one would strike him first.

The pale sky was becoming brighter in the hour before sunrise. He heard the sound of a tightening rope. The Guzuds halted and became silent. The rope creaked as if it were about to tear.

One Guzud shrieked in horror as his peers looked on, and so did the frightened boy. The Guzud's tiny eyes were wide open. He screamed in panic, displaying his brick-like teeth, and pointed to one of the pits. A silvery-white mane emerged, followed by the dark, muscular back of the mighty creature climbing up the rope.

The Guzuds stared at the creature in disbelief. The boy lying at the mercy of their hammers was all but forgotten.

The monstrous creature stood up, raised his arms, gazed up to the sky, and let out a deafening roar that shook the entire forest. Flocks of birds fled in every direction, and the orange-haired giants trembled. The feline-faced creature shook its head, its mane swaying from side to side as it bellowed its prolonged, horrifying roar. When the creature finally ceased, the camp was left in absolute silence.

The monster walked up to the nearest Guzud, who was a dwarf in comparison. He knocked the hammer out of his hands, grabbed him by his orange head and, with no effort, lifted him and threw him into one of the pits. The cry of the falling Guzud woke the rest of them out of their stupor. The Guzuds charged, their screams filling the air.

Two Guzuds swung for the creature, but he grabbed their hammers before they could hit him. They tried in vain to pull their weapons free. The monster kicked one, sending him crashing into the building. The heavy giant fell facedown, motionless. The other Guzud attempted to wrench his hammer free from the creature's hand. The beast seemed to be smiling as drool dripped down his narrow chin. The terrified Guzud turned to run but was struck on the head with his own hammer. Other Guzuds continued to come, grunting. The monster was now armed with two hammers, and it swung them as if they were sticks, crushing the orange-haired giants one after the other.

Zig took advantage of the confusion and hid behind one of the buildings, observing the massacre from its corner.

When a pair of Guzuds attempted to flee the camp, the creature threw the hammers at them, neutralizing them both.

He lunged straight for the others. The orange giants went into a panic when they realized their ruthless foe wouldn't allow any of them to escape unscathed.

The monster swung his long arms left and right, slashing the Guzuds, tearing their limbs off with his claws. He approached the large building and pulled one of its logs out, causing its walls to collapse. He then brandished the log as he roared menacingly.

A Guzud jumped into a pit, and the others followed suit.

"*Krashnagz wad Guzud Ha'a Ha'a*," said the beast, smirking, as he dropped the unused log and walked up to the pit to peer down at the terrified Guzuds. "*Garum bara'a*," he said then searched around. "Where are you, boy?"

The grave voice called, yet Zig remained hidden behind the building.

"Boy, please answer me."

Zig worked up the courage to walk toward the pits. He pretended to be looking for any hiding Guzuds. He approached the brutal beast with trepidation.

"There you are, little boy," he said with a smile, displaying his long fangs in the morning sun. The creature raised his head and straightened his mane, then grabbed a dead Guzud, turned him on his stomach, opened his gigantic jaws, and took a bite of the Guzud's behind.

Zig recoiled in disgust.

"Forgive me. I haven't eaten for a long time," he said and threw the boy an apologetic look, wiping the blood off his chin in embarrassment. "I will help your friends, just let me finish this tasty meal."

CHAPTER 7
A TREE?

Opening his eyes, all Kamanar could see was a blurred mass of green. He blinked a few times until his vision cleared. Feeling quite dizzy, he tried to get up. His head hurt terribly, and his body was heavy and feeble. When he finally managed to sit up, he took a look at his surroundings.

He was in a large, strange room, almost a perfect cube, yet its corners were rounded. The entire room was covered in thin, carpet-like greenery, some kind of moss growing on the surface of the brownish walls. Tiny holes in the walls let through a reddish-yellow light.

Kamanar felt his aching head. Naji, Caleem, and Motehro all lay unconscious next to him. All their wounds were coated with purple ointment. "What is this place?" he whispered. The thought that he was in some Dalusian dungeon crossed his mind, but the pleasant perfume of flowers, blended with a nice but musty smell, made him reject that notion.

With some effort he rose to his feet, noting a large opening that led to a round, curving tunnel. Its walls were covered with the same moss as the room.

"Rough start. What now?" came a familiar voice.

A tall young man leaned on the green wall and stared right at Kamanar. He was barefoot and wore torn, dirty clothes.

Kamanar sighed and turned his face away. "I don't know. I'm evaluating …"

"Evaluating, hmmm," said the young man, smirking.

"Matar, just let me rearrange my head for a moment, please."

"All right … That's it, the moment has ended. At this rate, you'll never get your *reward*," said Matar, his big, dark eyes in his pale face fixed on the warrior.

"My reward?"

"Deleting or extracting your past, whatever that means. I know how much you want it. To undo what has been done. Wouldn't that be convenient?"

Matar smiled then faded into thin air.

Kamanar took a deep breath and went toward the exit. He was disoriented, and he felt an urge to explore the tunnel. A crate had been placed near the entryway. He opened it to find fruit and vegetables inside. He grabbed an apple and bit into it. Kamanar devoured the apple, then a carrot, and a sweet pepper. Somewhat satisfied, he closed the crate and entered the green tunnel.

The tunnel descended in a gentle slope. Kamanar staggered ahead until he exited onto a round balcony inside a gigantic, tower-like structure. Its walls, made of ancient wood, stretched high up. Above there was no ceiling; a multitude of luminous orange spheres hung in the void. Their light dazzled the confused commander.

To his right, he noticed a wide staircase spiraling up and around the imposing structure that reached all the way to the bright spheres. At the various levels were many balconies with openings leading to more tunnels, just like the one he had emerged from. To his left, the staircase descended far down the great tower.

Kamanar froze. At the bottom of the stairs sat a huge creature with a silver mane covering its head and running the length of its back. The warrior rushed back into the room and grabbed the heavy crate before returning to the balcony. He peered down, and the beast was still sitting at the bottom of the staircase, preoccupied with something. The warrior carried the large box on his shoulder as he descended the wooden stairs. The closer he got to the creature, the larger it became. From high above, it had looked to be about the size of a large man, but it slowly dawned on him that it was a being of a different scale altogether.

Kamanar stood a few steps away from its enormous back. He raised the crate over his head. His arms began to tremble under its weight. He took a final step and let out a scream as he smashed the crate against the creature's head. The crate shattered, fruit and vegetables flying in all directions.

Without turning to face its aggressor, the creature swung its claws backward, grabbed Kamanar's shirt, and hurled him up in the air. The warrior flew across the tower and crashed into the far wall, and his body slid down to the floor in a heap.

Roaring menacingly, the monster jumped to its feet. Kamanar moaned and struggled to get back up, then stood facing the mighty creature, whose angry green eyes were fixed on him.

Marbel and Zig appeared, seemingly flabbergasted.

"What's going on?" shouted Zig.

"Kamanar!" Marbel called.

"Marbel! Strike him with the sword!" Kamanar yelled, his hair covering his face.

"Calm down, Kamanar. This creature saved us back at Fir Forest," said the older man. "He defeated the Guzuds. Trust me, Commander, he's a friend." Marbel approached.

"Guzuds?" mumbled Kamanar. He examined the beast with suspicion.

Marbel patted Kamanar on the shoulder. Then, with a wave of his hand, he gestured to the creature. Much to Kamanar's surprise, it nodded and exited the tower in giant strides, disappearing into one of the tunnels.

Marbel helped his dazed commander sit on the stairs then sat down beside him.

"How are you feeling?" asked Marbel.

"What the hell is going on here? Where are we? What was that thing?"

"He is a friend," said Zig.

"Listen, it's a long story," Marbel began. "We'll tell you everything in good time, but for now I'm asking you to trust me. You're hurt and exhausted. You've been unconscious for three days."

"Three days!"

"Come, I'll help you up. Let's go upstairs and check on the rest," said Marbel.

The three of them returned to where their friends lay. An exhausted Kamanar dropped to the ground near the entrance and sat against the wooden wall.

"Where's Sarik?" asked Kamanar.

"No idea. We haven't seen him since the ambush. The Guzuds didn't take him, that's for sure. I hope the Dalusians haven't got the poor bastard," said Marbel.

"What are these Guzuds?"

"Big, fat, orange—" began Zig.

"Wait until the others wake up, and then we'll tell everything," said Marbel.

Marbel sprinkled cool water on the faces of the unconscious men. Motehro and Naji opened their eyes. "About time," said Marbel.

Naji and the tracker sat up, both dizzy and weak. They looked around the room. Motehro mumbled something to Naji, and the latter answered unintelligibly.

Zig was delighted to see his friend was well. No sooner had he sat down by his side than he was assaulted by a barrage of questions.

Marbel emptied the entire contents of the urn onto Caleem's face. He shook him and called him by name, but the man remained pale and motionless.

"Don't worry, Marbel. He'll wake up soon, like all the rest," said Zig.

"I sure hope so. Bring some fruit for the lads."

Yawning, the men stretched their limbs.

The chubby man didn't wait any longer to relate what had happened, starting from the Dalusian ambush, then the Guzud camp, and finally ending with meeting with Gudjewkan, the carnivorous giant. He described how they were on his shoulder for a whole day, journeying through the enchanted forest of Turundia, ultimately arriving at this enormous tree.

"It's called the Allmother in the common language," said Marbel to his gaping listeners, who had just finished eating.

"A tree?" asked Kamanar.

"A very big one," said Zig.

CHAPTER 8
GIVE US A TOUR

"We've wasted enough time. We'll continue immediately when Caleem wakes," Kamanar said while looking at Naji and the tracker still stretching and yawning.

"I thought we'd be going home, after all that's happened," said Zig.

"You were told, before we crossed Dwarves' Passage, that once we went through there would be no turning back," said Kamanar.

Zig lowered his eyes and stepped back.

Kamanar held him by his shoulder. "I have not thanked you yet. For your courage."

Zig smiled.

"I'm all in, to the very end, as bitter or as sweet as it may be," said Naji.

"Marbel, give us a tour of the place," said Kamanar.

Marbel nodded, heading for the exit. "Follow me!"

The older man took one last look at Caleem, who was lying in the corner, and left the room, followed by his peers.

They went into the colossal tree trunk and headed up the staircase. "These tunnels are actually the branches of the tree," Zig said as they passed them.

"And what's that orange light?" asked Kamanar.

"In a moment, you'll see," said Marbel without looking back.

They reached the top of the staircase, which led to a large, circular doorway. Marbel went through and they all followed him onto a great patio. High above their heads floated myriad bright-orange, luminous spheres of many sizes. They all gasped at the sight. "These are the fruits of this great tree," said Marbel. "The darkness behind the fruits is not the night sky. It is created by layer upon layer of leaves, creating a big, mushroom-like dome, preventing the sunlight from entering."

The five friends wandered about, fascinated.

Huge branches stretched up from the edges of the patio, their ends disappearing beyond the bright spheres and into the mock night sky.

"Incredible," said Kamanar. "Is it day or night outside?"

"Noon," said Marbel.

Kamanar said nothing for a moment, then tore his eyes away from the orange wonder to focus on the men. "This place is fascinating, and our host may be generous. However, we're running out of time."

"Before anything, you promised to tell us where we are going, and what we are doing there," said Naji. He sat down in front of Kamanar, and so did Zig.

"Very well. We are on a mission of the highest importance, entrusted to me by King Creeden Dummah himself."

The boys looked at one another then continued listening attentively.

"I was the commander of the Royal Guard. Marbel, Sarik, and Caleem are soldiers specifically selected for this mission, which is to assassinate a high-ranking commander in the Dalusian army. To do that, we must get inside Dalusian territory in occupied Anathoria. And we have to complete our task before the war begins."

The word *war* sent a shudder down the unsuspecting boys' spines.

"Unfortunately, it is inevitable. The evil Dalusians, the scourge of the earth, are mongering for it. Don't be alarmed. Mellethya shall be victorious yet again, as it always is. Perhaps, this time, we will defeat them once and for all. And Anathoria will be ours once again. Have no fear. The war's affairs are none of your business," he said, turning to the two boys. "As far as you two are concerned, the mission is the only thing you should be worried about. If we succeed—and we will—it will tip the scales. This will lead to a glorious triumph for all Mellethyans."

"I want to go home," Zig whispered to Naji.

"Shut up! Stop whining," said Naji.

Zig frowned, got up, walked briskly away, and then ran down the stairs.

"He sometimes acts like a coward. Don't worry—I'll fix it," said Naji.

"Not at all. He's a brave kid. But he hasn't realized it yet," said Kamanar. "Still, I can't force him, even if he's the best archer in the world. Perhaps I made a mistake by bringing the two of you," he said and headed for the stairs.

"No. With my help, he can kill this Dalusian with one arrow, I tell you," Naji called after him.

Kamanar did not reply but continued down the stairs.

"He's the best archer in the world!" Naji yelled.

Marbel caught up with his commander as he descended.

"Come," invited the older man, overtaking Kamanar. "After we eat, I want to show you something."

***

After he finished his meal, Naji went down to the bottom of the tree. He ran through a large tunnel, which was actually one of the tree's giant roots, and soon was outside the Allmother entirely. He looked back at its enormous trunk, rising high and disappearing among the thick branches and spheres. The canopy was filled with those glowing spheres, hanging among the leaves, filling the atmosphere with their warm, orange light. The ground he trod on was moist, cool, and devoid of undergrowth. A pleasant smell of greenery filled the air. A muffled cry sounded from behind a large root. Naji walked over to its other side and found his friend slouched, his head between his knees, leaning on the root.

"I'm sorry I shouted at you," he said to Zig. "But this is it. We have to stay with them until the end. You heard what he said—they're on a secret mission for King Creeden Dummah himself. That means a big reward will be waiting for us at the end."

"All you care about is money. You saw what happened at the beginning of this damn quest. We're lucky to be alive. You didn't see the Guzuds or the Dalusians. There's no chance this stupid mission will end well. I want to go back to the city."

"What do you have there? You're a beggar, and you'll always stay that way if you go back. We have a chance to be a part of something big. If the choice is between risking my life or going back to Sontira to starve in the alleys, in the rain … I've just had it with you!" Naji stopped, fuming, then walked back inside the tree.

"I can't go on with this craziness," Zig called after him.

CHAPTER 9
I LIED!

"What did you want to show me?" asked Kamanar as he got up.

Marbel finished chewing the last piece of meat, patted his belly with satisfaction, and pushed himself off the floor.

"Follow me!" he said, heading upstairs. He soon entered a tunnel, followed by Kamanar. At the end of the tunnel was a room filled with a variety of items: engraved walking sticks, leather bags, chairs, wooden cabinets, plates, knives, dusty clothes hanging from racks, and many other objects Kamanar could not even recognize. Everything was old and worn.

"This used to be Gudjewkan's father's room," said Marbel.

"Either his father was smaller, or he was a man," said Kamanar as he examined the room.

Marbel cleared a path through the dusty piles toward a corner of the room where there was a bare wooden door. He gestured for Kamanar to follow him.

They entered a room brimming with books of various shapes and sizes neatly ordered on shelves that lined every inch of the space.

By the door stood a timeworn table and a chair, and on the table lay an open book. Its pages were made from broad green leaves. The writing was in white characters. "Gudjewkan's father was a sorcerer who served King Daneer Dummah. He either fled or was banished into these woods, which he made his home. The giant creature is his adopted son," said Marbel.

"King Daneer died nine hundred years ago. How is that even possible?"

"Listen, it's all written in these books. The sorcerer himself wrote all the books in this library. There are books about the mapping of the stars, medicine, herbs, animals, food, witchcraft, and any other subject you can think of. And there's also his diary." He pointed to the book on the table.

"Tell me, does the big creature know you're rummaging through his property?"

"Yes, he knows. He asked me to read this book to him. In fact, he stressed that I do. But I didn't divulge to him what he wanted to know … I lied!" Marbel said, closing the book.

"Why?"

Marbel sat down on the dusty chair. "According to his diary, a bunch of carnivorous giants, like Gudjewkan, lived in caves in the northern area of the Tan-Mirus range. Occasionally they would venture out to hunt. They hunted everything: deer, elk, boars … men."

"Go on."

"One day, some men—it doesn't say who they were—poisoned the beasts' water supply. The Wakashees, that's what the sorcerer calls them, began perishing. He assumed that they had all been wiped out until he stumbled upon one of their caves. He found all the giants dead except for one. A youngling who was barely alive. He brought him here with the help of ants."

"Ants?"

"Ants. That's what the book says. The sorcerer treated the moribund giant for a long time. When Gudjewkan recovered, he had no knowledge of what had happened to him or his kin. He didn't even know his own name. The sorcerer took care of him, taught and educated him as if he were his own son. He called him Gudjewkan, which means 'My Big Son' in the old tongue.

Gudjewkan learned many things yet, despite tremendous efforts, reading remained beyond his grasp."

"I think you should have told him the truth."

"Listen, humans killed off his entire kind. The sorcerer didn't want Gudjewkan to feel resentful toward humans. Or worse, to crave revenge. That's probably why he kept it a secret. Gudjewkan somehow figured out that the book has something to do with him. I think his weird helpers can't read either."

"Weird helpers?"

"He can't fit in this room, you know, because of his size, so they fetch stuff for him. I caught a glimpse of one, very odd looking."

Kamanar approached the table, picked up the diary, and began to leaf through it. "This whole story is extraordinary, but we don't have the luxury of wasting time on reading. Tell me, is there anything else in this book that I need to know?"

"There are some obscure details about improving the forest. I'm not sure what the sorcerer meant by that. Maybe it's not important."

Kamanar headed for the door with Marbel, who took several bags with him in tow.

"I tucked some food into these. And I've found a couple of swords—one has a rusty blade—and a shield, but that's all I could find."

"You did well, my friend," said the commander as he relieved Marbel of some of the load. Marbel nodded with satisfaction.

"Let's check on Caleem on our way down," said Kamanar.

The two stopped by Caleem's room, hoping to find the wounded man in better shape. To their dismay, he was lying in the same position, pale and motionless.

They knelt beside him, and Marbel splashed some water on his face, yet Caleem remained as still as a corpse.

"What's this purple balm?" Kamanar asked.

"It's a healing ointment made of the Miprona plant. It says so in the sorcerer's guide to plants."

"He's not getting any better. We can't wait much longer," said Kamanar. "Come on—get me out of this tree. It feels like I'm trapped in a dream. I need to see some sunshine."

They went down the staircase and exited the great trunk, leaving the provisions near its entrance. They found their friends strolling around outside the tree.

Marbel approached the wall that encircled the Allmother. It was made of dense, rounded leaves, so large that even the smallest one could cover Kamanar's whole body. Gently, they cleared an opening.

Both men walked through. Kamanar found himself in the open air, under the shade of old oak trees. As massive as their trunks were, they were still dwarfed by Gudjewkan's tree, which, from the outside, looked like a giant green dome.

Rays of sunlight peeking through the canopy dispersed light to the twisted, claw-like roots. The moist ground was bare of any twigs or leaves. Kamanar stopped to take in the pleasant scent of the forest. He spread his hands upwards, toward the sunlight, savoring the moment.

Marbel surveyed the forest. "There are creatures here, the nature of which we might not understand. I saw some drawings in one of the books—"

Marbel's words were interrupted by Naji and the tracker running toward them in a panic.

"He's coming! He's coming!" shouted Naji.

Motehro also cried out, looking behind them nervously.

As the terrified pair approached Kamanar, he gestured for them to stop, but the two dove into the bushes. The men heard loud rustling noises and the breaking of branches. The canopy shook and deep thuds made the earth tremble. A shadowy figure, as tall as the trees, emerged and approached them.

"Don't be afraid," said Kamanar to his frightened companions.

The mighty giant stood in front of the four.

"Greetings, Gudjewkan."

"Greetings," Gudjewkan answered.

"I am sorry for what I did. I was not aware of your nature … And I want to thank you. You have been most generous."

"You should be thanking your young friend." The giant's deep voice filled the air.

"How did you end up in that pit? If you don't mind me asking," said Kamanar, sitting down. He motioned for the others to do the same.

The giant sat before them. "The fat ones set a trap for me, but it was my fault as well. I shouldn't have left my father's domain," he said and scratched the cracked soles of his enormous feet.

A horrendous stench came from the beast's feet, and Kamanar was the only one who didn't turn his head away.

"The fat ones, what were they doing in Fir Forest? I know they are foreigners."

"They arrived here in father's domain recently, from the north. They tried to settle in the forest, destroying the trees and building camps, like the one you saw, but I chased them out. They eventually moved to the small forest, which is outside my father's domain."

"Your father's domain is Turundia, the great oak forest?" asked Kamanar.

"Yes. On his deathbed, my father commanded me to watch over the forest and prevent strangers from coming here."

"The small forest … You mean Fir Forest?"

"Yes," said the giant as he smoothed out his mane. "What were you doing there? It's been years since I've seen humans in these lands."

His companions turned to Kamanar, waiting for his answer.

"Indeed, a fair question," said Kamanar uneasily. "We're farmers from the west. We would be grateful if you helped us to return home, or at least to reach the Mobinar."

For a moment, they fell silent, all eyes on the giant.

"Liar!" yelled Gudjewkan, and the men shrunk back. "Are all humans deceiving? My father was right. You are an unworthy race."

Kamanar raised his hands in protest, struggling to find the right words to appease Gudjewkan.

"West of here lies the realm of your enemy. That is not your home," the creature said. He rose to his feet and walked away.

"Forgive me," said Kamanar. The giant stopped. "Forgive me. We are on an assignment of great importance. Its success is critical to our people. But it is of a confidential nature. We need to leave this forest and head west."

"The forthcoming war," said Gudjewkan, still with his back to them.

Impressed by the giant's knowledge, the men whispered among themselves.

"How do you know this?" Kamanar asked.

"I have subjects watching over the forest. Before every one of your wars, there is a sequence of events. Both your nation and your enemies begin to stir, moving forces along the borders of my father's domain. A small contingent of the cloaked ones crossed the forest a few days ago. At about the same time, your party emerged from the east. This is not a coincidence."

"The Dalusians that ambushed us! What can you tell me about them?"

"They are no longer here. I try to keep them out, but they are of an elusive nature."

"Damn Dalusians. Those vile creatures," Marbel blurted.

The giant turned to face them, picked his huge, hooked nose, and said, "Kill each other as much as you want—I couldn't care less—as long as you do it far from here." The giant was quiet for a moment then said, "My subjects have informed me that the Guzuds are building another camp in the northern part of my forest. This time, I will chase them away for good."

"Can you help us make our way west?" said Kamanar.

"I will ask one of my subjects to guide you to the foot of the great mountain." With that he turned and vanished between the trees.

"It's getting dark. Get back to the tree and start packing. We leave tomorrow, with or without Caleem," said Kamanar.

The moment they were all out of sight, Kamanar turned and ran into the forest after the silver-maned giant.

CHAPTER 10
FRIEND OR FOE?

The weak light grew even dimmer as evening set in, and Kamanar found himself running along a wide path. The massive green canopy blocked the sky completely. Following the immense footprints, he ran as fast as he could on the smooth, soft ground. He could feel his body recovering from the lazy heaviness with each stride. The creature's muscular back soon appeared before him.

"Where—?" He stopped when he noticed they were surrounded by several dark silhouettes. Getting a better look, he realized they were wolves.

The giant began to croak in a peculiar way. The wolves sat down like obedient dogs. There were about a dozen of them. The giant, still ignoring the man, became silent. One of the wolves let out a gentle, broken howl. When he finished, another picked up the howl. Gudjewkan croaked and howled along. Kamanar relaxed, folding his hands on his chest while he waited for them to finish their unusual conversation.

The wolves turned and ran, disappearing into the night.

"My subjects told me that there is another one of you close by. Your missing friend, I suppose."

"Sarik. I must get to him."

"I will take you. I don't want strangers wandering through

the forest. Hurry up! I have been informed that more Guzuds have arrived at the camp to the north. I will head there tonight."

"Tomorrow we, too, will be on our way. There's a chance that our wounded one and the two boys will stay at the Allmother temporarily. Is that possible?"

"Yes."

"Gudjewkan, about Marbel …"

"I know he lied."

"He did. Because there is an awful secret in that book."

"I don't think I'm ready …"

"Isn't that why you brought us here?"

"What if the never-ending search is better than knowing? What if self-delusion is a gift?"

"Maybe it is," said Kamanar, lowering his gaze, reflecting on his own deeds.

"Well then." Gudjewkan exhaled and turned to him.

"Once, there were many of your kind living in the mountains. They hurt some humans, and they, in turn, poisoned your people, all of them. You are the last of your kind."

"So, it is true. I'm the last." He let out a roar before slamming a tree and storming away into the dark forest.

Kamanar ran after him.

The giant stopped then uttered a strange sound, as if he were calling for someone.

"You said that you were heading west," said the giant.

"Yes."

"You will have to go over the thicket."

"Over the thicket? Will we be exposed?"

"Yes, it's a path that goes over the bush to the edge of the forest."

"We can't risk being seen by spying eyes from the mountain. Can't we simply head west?"

"Then you'll have to go through the thicket, home to the ants."

A humming noise came from between the tree trunks as five

oval-shaped creatures appeared in front of them. Dumbfounded, Kamanar tried to figure out what they were. The white, fluffy furballs, about as high as a man's waist, emitted a white glow.

They had thin, stick-like arms and legs; their feet and hands were flat and round like small flatbreads and were also white but furless. Their glassy, black eyes were set close together, almost touching. Their eyeballs were very large and bulged out of their sockets.

Kamanar stared at the beings but couldn't figure them out.

"These are the five keepers of the forest. They are the fabulls: Zimo, Taxo, Terlu, Pesko, and Justo. They guard the ways in and out of the thicket. Justo will go with you. She will guide and protect you," said the giant, pointing at one of them.

"How is that little thing going to protect us? It doesn't matter, as long as she can show us the way out of the forest. We'll manage from there."

Four of the creatures disappeared as quickly as they came. The last one stayed where it was.

"Come on—your friend is not far," said the giant, sniffing the cool night air with his long, beak-like nose as he continued walking.

Justo followed him with short, quick steps. Kamanar was last, still examining the white creature.

They walked down a winding trail. Darkness shrouded everything except for the nearest trunks, which were illuminated by the glow of the small fabull.

Soon, the giant stopped to sniff the air again.

"He is close. Go to him. I don't want to startle him." Gudjewkan pointed in the right direction.

Kamanar continued forward, feeling his way through the darkness.

After a short distance, a young deer crossed his path. It had a strange aura around it. Though the night was very dark, the deer was visible. It did not run but stood staring at him.

"Friend or foe?" a voice came from somewhere.

It took Kamanar a moment to recognize it. "For a moment, I thought you were another confusing being. What do you mean 'friend or foe'?" asked Kamanar, looking back at the deer.

"Sarik," the deer answered.

"Friend or foe, I don't know Matar," Kamanar said and continued on his way.

The bright deer lowered its head, sniffed the ground, flicked its ears, and caught up to Kamanar in a couple of playful jumps.

"My guess is Sarik is a friend, but you never know," said Matar.

"I think I will sit with you for a bit." Kamanar stopped.

"Some other time. That beast is waiting for you back there, and Sarik is pretty close ahead—I can smell him." The deer sniffed the air, then leaped into the darkness, vanishing.

It became quiet again except for the rustling of leaves.

"Oh, Matar." Kamanar closed his eyes and took a deep breath, then continued walking.

"Sarik, Sarik," he called repeatedly.

"Kamanar, is that you?"

"Yes. Come to me."

Sarik materialized before him; he was still carrying his bag and had his sword at his side. Only his longbow was missing.

"Where is everyone? Are they well?"

"Follow me. We'll talk later." Kamanar turned around and retraced his steps. "Bear in mind, we're about to meet a rather big fellow. He's a friend, so don't do anything foolish," said the commander before they reached the beast. "This is Sarik, a soldier of mine."

"I am Gudjewkan, and this is Justo."

"Nice. Nice …" stammered Sarik.

Gudjewkan headed back to the Allmother, followed by Justo and the two men, who said nothing to each other the entire way. They arrived at the Allmother at midnight.

"The rest are upstairs, inside the tree. Go to them," Kamanar ordered Sarik.

"Very well. I shall head north at once," said Gudjewkan.

"Right. Thank you for everything—and good hunting," Kamanar said, smiling.

"*Garum bara'a*," the giant said and turned to leave. "One more thing—" he looked back over his silver-maned shoulder "—the rats. The rodents that betrayed my father: he banished them from the forest. Now they infest the caves at the foot of the great mountain. They dwell by the Wall Cliffs. They take their victims deep into their lair where they burn them alive before they eat them … Beware, Kamanar."

"By the Wall Cliffs," murmured Kamanar as the giant left.

The tall man climbed all the way up to the top of the trunk, lay down on the wooden surface, folded his hands under his head, and reflected on things.

Trying not to be fooled by the never-ceasing orange light of the spheres, he guessed it was almost sunrise. He went down to his sleeping subjects.

"Time to go," he said as he kicked them, one after the other. They all woke up except for Caleem.

Marbel sprinkled some water on the man's mouth and forehead.

"Kamanar, why not stay one more night? I believe he's getting better," said the chubby man.

"We leave now."

"Someone should stay and take care of him."

"The boys will stay. With all due respect, I don't believe the 'dragon slayers' are ready for what lies ahead."

"I'm not staying. I won't stay here because of that coward," Naji yelled, pointing at Zig, who said nothing. "I have a talent, too!" Naji said and broke off a small branch from the wall. He threw it in front of Kamanar. "Look." His eyes were fixed on the small stick.

Naji stared at the branch. It began to levitate. Everyone gasped except for the commander. After a moment it fell back to the floor.

"Nice trick, but it will do us no good. If you want it that much, you can come. But know this: my patience for your behavior is reaching its limits. Understood?"

Naji smiled and looked at Zig. The boy returned a downcast look and left the room.

Chapter 11
A Good Friend is Better Than Family

As they exited the Allmother they saw Justo waiting by one of the long roots. "Gudjewkan assigned this little fellow, Justo, to be our guide," said Kamanar.

Each carrying a backpack, they gathered around the little white creature. Kamanar picked up the swords and the shield, which was hexagonal in shape. "You will take this good sword, and I will carry Caleem's," said Kamanar to Marbel. He took the long sword, still in its cloth sheath, and hung it on his back, under his bag. The commander gave the shield to Naji and the rusty sword to Motehro. Sarik still had his own sword.

Kamanar noticed Zig standing at the entrance to the Allmother. The commander walked up to the boy, making sure the others were out of earshot. "I have a request. Caleem, if he doesn't wake up … I ask you to bury him in an appropriate manner."

The boy met Kamanar's blue eyes. The tall man's expression was as serious as ever.

Zig nodded.

Kamanar glanced at the group standing around Justo. "Better say your goodbyes properly. Who knows what might happen tomorrow?" he said to the boy. Zig shrugged.

"A good friend is better than family," said Kamanar.

"What do you know about friends?"

Kamanar looked up and sighed. "Take care of yourself, boy.

"Come on—off we go!" Kamanar ordered the group, none of whose members could help but stare at the furry white creature with the big black eyes.

"I tried to get him to talk, but it looks like this thing doesn't even have a mouth," said Marbel.

"It's a fabull, and she's a girl."

"A girl?"

Waving his hands, the older man looked at Justo's head and tried to prompt the creature to move. Justo glanced at Marbel's bouncing belly, then began to walk on her short, stick-like legs.

"I hope Gudjewkan knows what he's doing," Kamanar said to himself as he led his men behind the little fabull.

Naji was last. He darted a final glance back at the Allmother. He could see the silhouette of his friend. For a moment, it seemed that Zig wanted to wave goodbye, but he didn't. Sprinting forward, Naji soon caught up with the others.

They plowed their way through the Allmother's external wall of leaves and marched out into the forest, leaving the orange lights behind.

It was early in the morning, and the giant oaks' tight canopy blocked out the sky. Bright Justo, who seemed weightless, moved in short, hasty steps. Slowly, the light of day grew stronger, and visibility improved. The forest floor was soft, devoid of twigs and leaves. Justo made steady progress, never looking back at those who followed.

"How does she eat if she doesn't have a mouth?" asked Marbel.

"No mouth, no nose, no ears, nothing ... Nothing but those big black eyes," said Naji.

"Can she hear us?" asked Marbel. "Justo!"

The fabull stopped in its tracks and spun around at once. They all stopped, too, staring at the thing.

"Go on," prompted Kamanar. The creature turned and continued. "Well, she can hear."

"White dongha, nice dongha …" said the curious tracker while gesturing wildly.

The party followed the fabull for the entire day.

The forest grew darker, and night came. Still, they marched on, following the fabull's light. They heard the trickle of water and soon found themselves marching alongside a stream that led to a clearing.

"Justo, stop," said Kamanar.

The glowing creature stopped.

"Naji, fill the waterskins. Marbel, get us something to eat," said Kamanar.

They all sat down and dined on dried meat and some berries that Sarik and Marbel had gathered. Marbel tried to offer berries to the white creature, but there was no response.

She sat down on a thick root, lighting up her surroundings with her pleasant glow.

"Don't become complacent," said Kamanar while they dined. "Our encounter with the Dalusians was no coincidence. It was a planned ambush, without a doubt."

"But how could that be? You and Caleem never revealed—even to us—any exact route," said Marbel.

"A Khandalus. I can't think of anything else," said Kamanar, clenching his hand into a fist.

"No, impossible!" Marbel said then glanced at the party members. "Maybe one of the guards at Dwarves' Passage?"

"No. All they knew was that we were going down south, which was wrong. Whoever gave our position knew exactly where we were and when," said Kamanar, chewing on a mouthful of berries.

"What's a Khandalus?" asked Naji.

Kamanar and Marbel exchanged looks.

"A Khandalus is worse than a Dalusian," said Marbel. "It's a man who sold his soul to the devil and became a servant of the Dalusians."

"But why?"

"Greed, I guess. The Dalusians tempt people with vain promises … Or maybe charm them using forbidden ways," he said then looked at Kamanar. "The Dalusians could have killed us, but they didn't."

"Yes, the sedative," Kamanar said while shifting his eyes to Sarik, who sat apart, staying out of the conversation. "They wanted us alive. Information is more valuable than a few dead men … Right, Sarik?"

There was a sudden silence—only trickling water and rustling leaves could be heard—as they all wondered what Kamanar meant. Kamanar rose, grabbed Sarik by the shirt, and yanked him up to his feet.

"What do you want?" asked Sarik quietly.

Kamanar jostled the young man violently. "I want the truth! I know what you are: a spy—don't deny it. Where are your Dalusian friends? Are they close?"

Marbel and the rest got up, unsure how to react.

Sarik's face turned pale. He put up no resistance. "Why are you saying these things? I don't understand …"

The lofty Kamanar looked more menacing than ever as he held Sarik, who was tiny in comparison.

"Where did you disappear to the moment the Dalusians fired the first volley? Where were you when we were all lying there, wounded? You dirty Khandalus bastard!" yelled Kamanar, grabbing the hilt of Sarik's sword, pulling it with one hand, and pushing him with the other. Sarik lost his footing and fell to the ground.

"Calm down, please!" said Marbel.

Kamanar stood above Sarik. The archer attempted to sit up, but Kamanar pinned him to the ground with his foot. The stunned Sarik didn't even resist. Kamanar pressed the edge of the blade against his neck. "What did you tell your masters? What do they know?"

"No! No, Kamanar. I got lost when I was evading the arrows. Please, wait!"

Marbel approached his commander, his arms stretched forward in a calming gesture.

"Stay where you are, Marbel," said Kamanar, his eyes fixed on the man at his feet.

Marbel complied.

Sarik pushed Kamanar's leg away from his chest. "What's wrong with you? I'm a proud Mellethyan. I'm loyal to King Creeden, no less than you are!"

The tip of the sword trembled, and Kamanar's demeanor softened and became one of distress. He dropped the sword to the ground and turned his back on Sarik, covering his face with his hands.

Silence reigned.

"All of you, go to sleep. I will wake you before dawn, which isn't long from now," said Kamanar calmly, as if nothing had happened.

The tall man sat down behind a tree and leaned back against the trunk.

"Well, goodnight, everyone," Marbel said in a joyful manner. But there was no reply from anyone. He helped Sarik back to his feet. "Don't worry, he's probably just upset about some other stuff. Tomorrow will be a finer day."

Sarik offered no response as he stared at the tree behind which Kamanar was sitting. He walked away and sat by the stream. Naji and the tracker lay down not far from him without uttering a word.

Marbel approached his commander. "May I give my opinion?"

"No."

Marbel took a deep breath. "I know him. He's among the best and most loyal soldiers I have ever met. He's really a fine lad."

Kamanar sat, staring into the darkness, saying nothing.

"Who do you want to be on watch first?" asked Marbel.

"Go to sleep. I will stand watch alone tonight," said Kamanar.

Marbel joined his comrades. They had made their camp for the night near the stream, which was lit by Justo's gentle, pale aura.

It took them a while to fall asleep that short night, unsettled by the incident, a feeling of gloom still hanging in the air. The tired men eventually surrendered, except for Kamanar, who stood watch, and Sarik, who did not stop tossing and turning all night long.

CHAPTER 12
HE TAMPERED WITH NATURE

Just before dawn, the commander rose to his feet. He stretched his limbs in the crisp breeze and headed for the creek.

Justo was still sitting on the same root. Kamanar glared at Sarik, who lay with his eyes open. "Get up and wake the rest."

Sarik jumped up and went about waking everyone.

All got up in haste, except for Naji, as usual. "Naji!" barked Kamanar. The tired boy rose, still half-asleep, stretching like everyone else.

"It's chilly this morning. Autumn is here—" Marbel began but stopped when he noticed Motehro, alert.

The tracker pointed at a movement beyond the trees. Kamanar and the others recognized a figure, much like Justo, in the distance.

"Another one," said Marbel, looking at Justo.

"That's how Justo looks from afar? Not very stealthy, is it?" asked Kamanar, pointing at the fabull's twin in the distance.

When they turned around, they saw Justo standing perpendicular on a tree trunk. She walked up to the top with ease, as though she were on flat ground.

The fabull disappeared into the branches.

"Now what?" asked Marbel.

"We wait," said Kamanar. "Only she knows the way. If she doesn't come down soon, we'll have to do without her. In the meantime, wash your faces in the stream and get ready."

The water was cold and refreshing. They packed their bags and sat down by the stream, waiting for the fabull. The world around grew brighter, which meant that the sun was already up somewhere above the green canopy. That morning, there was less conversation than usual due to the late-night episode with Sarik.

Justo reappeared about an hour later, walking down the trunk the same way she had gone up. She landed on the ground and stood before them, her fur and aura much brighter than before. Her eyes were white, but they then turned to gray before eventually returning to their original gleaming black. Kamanar's men looked at each other, not even bothering to ask for an explanation. Justo passed between them and began to walk ahead. Even in the light of day, she glowed with a white aura.

Kamanar, a bit more relaxed, followed the creature into the forest, his team behind him. Justo continued at a steady pace. With her short, quick steps, she led them deeper into the vast oak forest. Afternoon arrived and the air got a bit colder. They ascended a gentle slope, taking one of the forest's numerous paths. Motehro, who walked behind Kamanar, stopped and raised his hand, signaling for everyone to stop. Gazing ahead, he listened, turning to Kamanar and pointing.

"Duck!" whispered Kamanar. They all dropped to the ground. Kamanar raced to the nearest tree with the rest of the team stacking up behind him, except for Justo, who stood in place, motionless.

"Come here!" whispered Kamanar.

The fabull looked at him but didn't budge.

"Come here, you overgrown bug. You'll expose us."

Kamanar jumped from his hideout and ran to Justo to pick her up. Justo was very light and pleasant to the touch. Her tiny, stick-like limbs flailed while Kamanar ran. Back under cover, he placed the fabull behind one of the tree's thick roots. Along with the rest, he gazed ahead. The crunching of leaves become louder.

"Be ready," said Kamanar, resting his hand on the cloth-wrapped hilt of the long sword. His companions grabbed their weapons, ready to pounce.

A round, brown mass rolled down the path. As it drew closer, the shape of the thing became clear. It was a ball of dirt and sticks, and it was huge.

"Looks like a rock. Maybe not," whispered Naji.

The huge mud ball rolled closer. Gathering momentum, it rolled past them and slammed into a nearby tree.

"It stinks," whispered Naji, plugging his nose with his fingers.

Something else appeared up the path.

"What in heaven's name is that?" said Marbel.

"A beetle," said Naji. "A dung beetle."

It was a gigantic beetle, larger than any animal. It was black and shiny, and although its head and facial features were visible, it was impossible to understand them. It had six long hairy legs, the front pair thicker and covered with spikes. Slowly, it came down the path and crawled right by them. It was the size of a loaded wagon. When it reached the mud ball, it began to push it using its hind legs, touching the ground with its front pair only. Slowly, the ball began to roll as the beetle continued to thrust it along the path.

Kamanar emerged from cover, followed by the others.

"Bizarre!" said Marbel, still looking down the path.

"Zig and I used to play with beetles like that. We'd race them," said the boy. "Can they grow so big?"

"They can't," said Kamanar. "That mad sorcerer surely had something to do with this."

"What sorcerer?" asked Naji.

"Gudjewkan's adoptive father was apparently a sorcerer with great abilities. He was a man like us. He died long ago. He tampered with nature. Distorting it somehow …"

"Unbelievable! I wonder what else he did."

"I hope we don't find out. But I have a feeling we will!" said Kamanar.

Justo continued walking up the path.

"Let's go," said Kamanar, picking up the pace to catch up with the little guide.

"This is why the forest floor has almost no leaves on it," said Naji.

All the talk about the sorcerer had excited the boy, who kept asking Marbel about Gudjewkan's father for the rest of the day.

Soon it was early evening, and Justo's aura glowed brighter as darkness set in. Evening turned into night. Justo marched and marched, followed by the tired men, who were eager for the stop command.

It was close to midnight, and Kamanar had not yet given the order. "We will walk a little more today. This forest is vast," he said hoarsely. "We have to make up for lost time."

They all frowned, whispering their complaints to each other.

This part of the forest started to look different from what they had passed through. The trees were even closer together, their roots sprawling longer across the ground, meshed in the roots of other trees and even crawling up other trunks.

"This place is spooky," said Naji as he stumbled on a snake-like root.

"We're closer to the thicket," said Kamanar. Fatigue was manifesting in his heavy body after two sleepless nights.

Bushes began to appear around the oaks, and some tree branches reached all the way down, clinging to them. On the ground were layers of leaves, crisscrossed by the long, rope-like roots. Little Justo found her way quickly, walking down narrow paths between the bushes. The men now had to walk single file, struggling through dense greenery. It got even worse, and they felt as though they were digging through a never-ending wall of vegetation. Kamanar struggled just to keep Justo in sight, even losing her occasionally.

"It's so dark. Where is this crazy creature taking us?" asked

Marbel. He straggled behind Naji, trying to evade the relentless springing branches that the boy pushed away. The answer to his question was a series of unintelligible grunts from the men in front of him, who were all weary and covered in scrapes, just like he was. The old man sighed in frustration.

Finally, they found themselves entering a wide tunnel. The tunnel's entrance was perfectly circular as though it had been cut into the tight vegetation. Its walls were made of leaves and those long, crisscrossed branches.

"Who trimmed this thing? At least now we can walk like human beings," said Marbel as he looked down the tunnel, which extended deep into the thicket.

Justo's bright light had a limited range; beyond, it was pitch-black.

"Let's get some rest," said Kamanar.

The weary men took off their bags and threw themselves on both sides of the tunnel. Marbel spread a piece of cloth on the ground and served a few slices of meat and some berries.

Everyone sat around the cloth, enjoying the meal. Soon, there was only one piece of meat left. Many hands tried to snatch it, but it was Naji's catch, and he shoved the whole thing into his already-full mouth. It took him some time to chew his prize. Pleased with himself, he patted his thin belly, then lay down on his side and fell asleep with his bag under his head, using the hexagonal shield as a makeshift cover. One by one, they were all dozing off.

"I'll stand watch first," said Kamanar.

Marbel nodded, lay down next to Naji, and fell asleep at once.

Kamanar glanced at Justo, who had settled down a bit farther into the tunnel and was glowing, not moving a limb. The commander fought against his heavy eyelids until his watch was finally over. He stepped over Naji—the boy was drooling on his bag—to reach Marbel, smiling at the sight of the two, who slept like the dead.

"Marbel, wake up."

Marbel sat up, still sleepy and mumbling.

"You and Sarik will take this watch, Naji and Motehro the next," said the commander.

Marbel nodded. Kamanar pulled him aside to whisper in his ear. "I want you to keep an eye on him, especially when I'm asleep."

The old man opened his eyes wide, then nodded, too tired to protest.

The exhausted Kamanar stepped over Naji once again to lay down on his side and settle in for sleep. He placed the long sword beside him and soon was immersed in a deep slumber, the likes of which he had not known since the beginning of the journey.

CHAPTER 13
PALILU NAJI!

Kamanar awoke with a start to the sound of screaming. He found himself in the dark tunnel with Motehro staring at him, rambling on dramatically. The dark-skinned man seemed terrified. Kamanar groped on the ground for Caleem's long sword, but he didn't find it. He jumped to his feet and noticed that Marbel was also wide awake.

"*Garba wani, garba wani palilu* Naji … *Palilu* Naji!" the tracker said hysterically, pointing farther into the tunnel.

Kamanar looked around, noting that Sarik was standing with his sword drawn. "Where's Naji?" Kamanar asked.

Screams of terror came from deep inside the tunnel. It was the boy, now shouting Kamanar's name. Kamanar sprinted into the darkness, followed by the tracker, who brandished the rusty sword.

Marbel grabbed one of the bags, pulling out two brown fruits. "Wait!" he yelled as he peeled off the skin, revealing a pair of luminous spheres that lit up the tunnel with orange light. He propped Justo up on his shoulders and ran deeper into the dark tunnel after his comrades. Meanwhile, Sarik, sword in hand, slung on the rest of the bags: three on his back, two on his arms. Following the white-orange lights, he ran into the curving tunnel.

Kamanar raced in total darkness, guided by Naji's incessant

shrieks. The screams became weaker each time he stumbled on the branches protruding from the tunnel floor.

The commander stopped. The tracker slammed into his back, and Kamanar steadied him.

"Shhh … quiet," he said.

Motehro stopped his grumbling.

Naji's voice was now coming from their left. "Turn left at the intersection!" Kamanar shouted. He pressed on, tripping and stumbling on the jutting, twisted branches. The tracker followed, groaning, stumbling on the same branches, colliding with Kamanar every few steps.

Marbel ran, Justo and the orange balls lighting his way. Sarik, carrying all the bags, caught up and overtook Marbel.

"Here, take one," panted the chubby man as he tied a sphere to a bag on Sarik's back while they ran.

The young man dashed forward, passing through many splitting tunnels. The orange light hanging over his shoulder lit the tunnel, revealing long, intertwined branches, their shadows twisting like snakes to the rhythm of the bouncing light.

"Kamanar said right," Sarik yelled back to Marbel. "I mean right after the left!"

"Now up the slope," shouted Kamanar. He felt he was getting closer by the sound of the boy's cries. He also heard strange crackling noises.

He fell into a hole.

Reaching out with his arms, he managed to grab onto a branch, and then his body swung and he slammed into a wall of branches. He was hanging in total darkness. Before he could warn Motehro, the tracker plummeted past him, shrieking. He tumbled down the pit, his fall culminating in a snap of metal from his rusty sword.

By the sounds, Kamanar assumed that the bottom was not far below. An orange light appeared above him, allowing him to discern Sarik's vague figure.

"Kamanar," the young man called to his hanging commander.

"Get down here," said Kamanar, trying to understand the manner of the light source on Sarik's bag.

Sarik climbed down into the hole. The wobbling light sent the shadows crawling eerily across the walls. By its glow, Kamanar descended to the bottom of the pit. He landed on both feet, followed by Sarik. Muttering, the tracker lay on his back. After glancing at the broken sword, Kamanar helped him up. "You're fine," he said, throwing one of the bags at Motehro. The dark-skinned man complained one last time and flung the bag over his shoulders. Kamanar took the sword and a bag from Sarik's hand and charged ahead.

The boy's shouts were becoming faint again. Ahead, the twisted, rope-like branches stretched, spanning the length of the tunnel. It was impossible to tell what lay beyond: earth or rocks or just more layers of twisted branches. The slope of the tunnel, now painted orange by Sarik's luminous ball, became less steep. Kamanar stopped to listen; he couldn't hear Naji anymore.

The tall man ran as fast as he could, fearing for the boy. Out of the corner of his eye, he saw strange black shapes moving in the darkness. As he got closer, their form became clearer. They scurried in all directions on their many legs.

The men were astonished by the gigantic black ants, bigger than the largest of pigs. They snapped their huge, jagged jaws as they moved among the tangled branches. Kamanar and his two soldiers were almost out of breath, yet they caught up to the fleeing insects. Letting out a loud scream, the commander kicked the closest one. It went flying over its army of friends and landed on its back. Brandishing Sarik's sword, the warrior slashed through the ants, cutting them to pieces. Slimy green goo gushed out of their torn bodies as their legs still twitched convulsively.

Kamanar spotted Naji's limp body being dragged away in the grip of the jaws of five or six insects. A cluster of ants turned and blocked Kamanar's way then charged at him. The warrior leaped onto their backs, stomping his feet with all his strength. Their shells cracked open under his boots and splattered his legs with green slime. Overcoming a wave of nausea, he focused on the black jaws pulling the boy by his limbs. He jumped over a row of ants and ran on.

Sarik and Motehro were confronted by a wall of snapping jaws. The tracker tried to jump over the insects as Kamanar had, but a pair of jaws clamped around his leg in midair. Motehro let out a scream and crashed to the ground. He shoved his rusty, broken blade into the ant's head. Green slime splashed, yet the creature did not let go. The tracker shrieked as he stabbed his aggressor again and again until, finally, it loosened its grip.

Sarik kicked the heads of the ants blocking his path. To his surprise, the giant insects backed down. He ran up to one of them, and it turned its head away before he could even swing his foot. Sarik glanced at the orange sphere dangling from his shoulder. He yanked the ball, held it up, and walked straight to the ants.

"Go back. Back!" he shouted.

The ants shrank away and went for the fallen tracker instead. Sarik leaned over Motehro, swinging the sphere at the insects. Covering their tiny eyes with their front legs, they retreated farther back into the tunnel, crackling loudly.

Sarik helped Motehro up. He rolled up the man's slime-stained pants and found long, blue marks on his flesh.

"It's not so bad. Come on."

Sarik ran, holding the sphere in his hand. The tracker followed, limping, trying to keep up.

Thanks to the dim orange light, Kamanar was able to tear the leg off one of the insects holding Naji. The torn limb still hopped on its own. The tall warrior stabbed the ant's backside with his sword, yet the creature didn't let go of the boy.

Kamanar pulled the sword out of the ant's body and jammed it into another one. He turned to the first ant, pulled it with all his strength, and hurled the giant bug up in the air, its five legs flailing as it tightened its grip on Naji's leg. The boy screamed. Kamanar pulled even harder, stopping the ants tugging the boy to the other side. Naji screamed hoarsely. The ant's body tore from its head, and when Kamanar fell back the ant's headless body landed in his lap. Kamanar threw it aside, stood up, and charged again. The insect's head was still clamped to the boy's leg. The commander kicked the head until it broke free and went rolling down the tunnel. The warrior, wielding his sword again, beheaded the ant clamping the boy's waist and shoved it away.

He swung his sword again, determined to hack at the other four ants still dragging the exhausted boy. But before he could make another move, the ants dropped their victim. Covering their eyes with their legs, they fled as Sarik emerged swinging the orange sphere.

Naji, bruised and trembling, lay in a heap on the ground. Sarik ran farther down the tunnel, chasing the ants away. Kamanar stooped over the boy while he caught his breath. "Are you all right?"

Naji only whimpered. The tall man gave the area a sweeping glance then knelt beside the boy to inspect the marks all over his body; some had turned dark purple. Naji sat up, trying to contain his moans.

"Are you all right?" Kamanar asked again.

"Yes, yes, I'm fine," the boy said faintly. He stood up and almost collapsed on Kamanar, who helped him to his feet. "I'm fine, don't worry," the boy said and stood on wobbling legs.

Motehro appeared, limping and breathing heavily.

"*Galim gala*, Naji," he said. He smiled, patting the boy on the shoulder. Naji squealed in pain, pushing the bald man away.

Sarik returned with the orange light. He also had the hexagonal shield in his hand.

"They're gone," he said.

CHAPTER 14
ANY SIGN OF MARBEL?

Kamanar noted that the tunnel they were in split into several smaller ones. Because they were all identical, he had no way of knowing which way to go.

He scratched his stubble as he scanned each one. "Well … let's wait for Marbel and the fabull."

The boy sat down and suppressed a moan as he rubbed the gashes and bruises on his body. The tracker sat down next to him and started comparing his wounds to the boy's, shaking his head and mumbling all the while.

Kamanar took the shield from Sarik. "Where did you find this?"

"There," he said and pointed. "It was lying on the branches."

"Hand me the light." Kamanar tossed the shield next to the boy and walked ahead into the tunnel. He advanced carefully, searching for the long sword, but returned empty handed. He hung the luminous sphere on the tunnel's wall, and the gloomy tunnel was flooded with a pleasant orange hue. "This will keep those bugs away." Kamanar looked at his weary men and the boy, his hand covering his face, sprawled on some branches next to Motehro, who was scratching his bald head. Sarik had dropped the bags and was standing guard. Water trickled from above and slid down the branches.

"It's raining outside," said Kamanar, but he received no response. "I know everything looks a little grim right now. Caleem was left behind, wounded, and Marbel could be lost. But remember, it's an honor to have been chosen for this mission, to serve the king and Mellethya."

Naji didn't budge, the tracker showed no interest, and Sarik half listened. Kamanar gave up his motivational speech and lay down along the tunnel wall.

The tall man opened his palm under one of the dangling branches and caught a few drops of water. "I love the rain."

"Who loves rain? It's cold and wet," said Naji.

"You're right. Cold and wet. Ever since I was a little boy, I've loved the rain. During the winter, the first thing I'd do each morning was look at the horizon to see if any clouds were approaching. The sight of raindrops on puddles inspires me. I don't know why. I just love the rain, even when it's pouring down on me."

Naji shivered. "You're crazy!"

"What is the meaning of the name 'Naji'?" asked Sarik after a short silence.

"Survivor," said Naji.

"Survivor of what?"

Naji looked at the young man and shrugged.

"Maybe there's some truth to that," said Kamanar. "You survived the Dalusians, the Guzuds, and the ants. Let's just hope those don't come back."

"What kind of a weird name is 'Kamanar'?" Naji asked.

"Just a name. After my grandfather."

"And Sarik?"

Sarik shrugged. "I don't know if it even has any meaning."

"I wonder if Motehro's name has any meaning," said Kamanar, looking at the bald man, who raised his eyes to him as soon as he heard his name. "I suppose we'll never know,"

Kamanar said, smiling. Returning the smile, the tracker scratched the three tiny tattoos at the crown of his bald head.

It became quiet again. The four settled in, and each retreated into his own thoughts. Without intending to, Kamanar dozed off. Eventually, they all slept for a few hours, except for Sarik, who watched over his friends.

Kamanar, woken by Sarik rummaging through the bags, sat up quickly. "How long were we asleep?"

"Not too long," said Sarik, who was still searching through the bags.

Kamanar got up and stretched his limbs. He discerned that the orange ball's light had dimmed, yet the tunnel's visibility was better. The darkness had somewhat dissipated.

The commander blew air on the sphere, trying to revive the light, but it still faded by the second until it went out.

"Any sign of Marbel?" asked Kamanar.

Sarik shook his head and sighed.

"What are you looking for?"

The archer groaned, tossing the bag aside. "Flint," he said. "Fat Marbel's only concern is his stomach. There's plenty of food in the bags, but nothing to light a torch with."

"He did bring those orange balls. Maybe there are more in the bags."

"There's none of those."

"The sun must be high in the sky. That's why it's brighter. We must take advantage of this … with or without Marbel. Wake everyone up, quickly!" Kamanar ordered.

Sarik nudged and slapped the two. When Naji and the tracker got up, the commander noticed that the boy's wounds and the tracker's shin had been daubed with the Miprona ointment.

"Did you do that?"

Sarik nodded.

"Did you get any sleep?" Kamanar asked.

"No, but I'm not so tired, really."

"This purple stuff works," Naji said while feeling his bruises.

"Now, tell me what happened. Starting with the sword," said Kamanar. His tone was stern.

Naji avoided the tall man's gaze, murmuring something.

"Speak!" said Kamanar.

"I was standing and … I was alert. Me and Motehro … And we stood watch for a long time, and …"

"Go on!"

"And then I took Caleem's big sword. I was fooling around with it, and with the shield, and … I sort of wandered into the tunnel. Then an ant bit my leg, and another knocked me down." The boy pointed to his leg. "I tried to hit it with the sword, but it was too heavy, and one ant grabbed it with its big jaws. Another bit me on my hip, here and here …" He pointed to all the sore areas.

"And the sword?"

"The ant took it, dragged it away … I held on to my shield almost till the end, but I lost that, too."

The commander swung his palm and slapped Naji hard on the cheek. The boy raised his hands to protect himself from further punishment.

Kamanar threw one of the bags over his shoulder. "We're moving! Pick up your bags."

Although the blow on his cheek was still tingling, Naji was relieved that the confrontation with Kamanar was over. He opened his bag, found a blue shirt, and threw it over his old, torn rags. In high spirits, he picked up the bag and his shield, not allowing the occasional twinges of pain to hinder him.

"Where did you get that?" asked Kamanar.

"I took it from the Allmother. And these," said the boy, showing him his new pair of shoes.

"You stole them."

"As if Gudjewkan could fit into these. Wouldn't it be a shame to just leave them there?"

Kamanar marched on, Sarik's sword strapped to his hip, and the rest followed close behind.

CHAPTER 15
DAMN IT

They went deeper into the tunnel. Kamanar had no idea in which direction they were going, yet he was determined to make the most of the faint light of day.

"Kamanar," called Naji. "What about the big sword? Aren't we going to get it?"

"Marbel is more important, don't you think? If we happen to find it on the way, great. If not, so be it."

Kamanar strived to maintain a consistent course, which was not an easy task with so many identical, twisting tunnels.

"This isn't going to work," said Kamanar after hours of wandering. "It's impossible to navigate here. We'll generally move uphill. That's the only direction guaranteed to take us out of this bush."

Kamanar choose the options with an upward slope, regardless of their degree of incline. Yet this strategy bore no fruit, either. Most of the tunnels sloped downhill. Despair began to set in, even with the commander, with some unintelligible curse escaping his lips at each intersection. "Well … Anyone have a better idea?" he asked eventually.

"Why don't we call to Marbel? Shout?" asked Naji.

They all looked at the tall man. Kamanar stood with his arms akimbo, his thumb fumbling with the hilt of his sword. "I doubt there are any Dalusians around," he said as if to himself. He groped the wall of branches. "Sound can travel through. Marbel!" Kamanar's voice ripped through the silent tunnels, startling everyone. "Let's hope those ants don't have any ears," he said. "On the count of three, we all call together. One, two, three …"

"Marbel!" they all shouted in unison, their voices echoing through the maze.

"Again."

"Marbel!"

Their yells grew louder. Even if the old man couldn't hear them, the shouting gave them a joyful release, putting broad smiles on their faces.

"Quiet now. Be quiet," said Kamanar. They all listened to the dreary silence in the tunnel, aware of every little trickling sound, even that of the light wind breezing by.

"I hear something," said Sarik. Then he shouted, "Marbel! We're here!"

"*Jangu, jangu*," the tracker said, grinning. "Marbel! Marbel!"

Finally, a muffled sound reached their ears.

"It's Marbel!" Kamanar said. They repeated their calls to the old man in a noisy, cheerful choir. With each pause, they could hear Marbel's voice getting closer until, eventually, they were able to make out some of his words.

"Where … Kamanar … Tunnel … Damn it …"

A rustle came from somewhere in the tunnel. They looked ahead. They all knew that those shuffling noises were not Marbel's footsteps.

"Damn insects!" said Kamanar.

The rustle now came from both ends of the tunnel.

Kamanar motioned his men to follow him, intending to flee to a nearby intersection, but there was rustling there, too. Retreating, he drew his sword. "We're surrounded!"

Marbel's voice was still somewhere in the distance, barely audible over the rustling and crackling.

Kamanar stood his ground, brandishing his sword. Naji was

poised beside him, his shield up. Sarik and Motehro, armed with his rusty, broken sword, stood back-to-back with Kamanar and Naji, facing the ants approaching from the opposite direction.

All at once, an entire army of the giant insects invaded the tunnel, filing in from both ends in a synchronized attack.

The noise of a pair of jaws slamming against Naji's shield sounded like the blow of a hammer. His legs shaking, Naji managed to repel the first ant. Kamanar started hacking at the charging ants with his sword, cutting them to pieces as they came, green slime splattering all over. Behind him, Sarik kept the insects at bay with his kicks. Motehro managed to hit a few ants with the stub that was left of his sword. but the insects kept on coming, climbing over their fallen siblings to bite the men.

These were bigger than the ants they had encountered earlier: their jaws larger, their teeth sharper. The dead insects were piling at Kamanar's feet, but this didn't deter others from pressing on. Glancing behind, he realized that the situation there was the same.

Swinging his sword in all directions, Kamanar hacked at the insects. The boy's wails signaled a turn for the worse. Motehro's shrieks joined Naji's. Kamanar found himself drowning in a tidal wave of ants; all he could see around him were hairy legs and snapping jaws. The pile of ants rose high, burying the tall Kamanar. Sarik tumbled in the swell while trying to fight the ants off with his fists. His shouts drowned by the commotion, the tracker disappeared under a mountain of insects.

Naji shot one last terrified glance at Kamanar. Dropping his shield, he reached out to the commander with a trembling hand, but he was sucked into the black mass.

Dozens of ants closed their powerful jaws around every part of Kamanar's body.

His sword was yanked out of his hand. All he could see were insect body parts trampling over him. The thought of the mission failing disturbed him more than anything. He was overwhelmed and felt dizzy.

He was losing consciousness.

Chapter 16
We're Not Going Anywhere Without This Thing

A pandemonium of flashing lights and loud crackling noises brought Kamanar back to reality. Ants crawled all over him, but he pushed them off and lifted his head.

The ants were biting themselves and one another as they scurried in all directions and jammed into piles of their dead siblings, which were meshed with the battered bodies of unconscious men. They were retreating as fast as they could, all the while covering their eyes with their legs.

A sudden flash of bright, white light blinded Kamanar, forcing him to shut his eyes. When he opened them, a small, white, furry creature with big gray eyes materialized before him. The creature tilted its head, watching Kamanar and the ants. Its eyes turned from gray to snow white and emitted another dazzling flash. Kamanar covered his eyes with his hand.

"Why did you stop calling?" he heard Marbel say. "Looks like we made it right on time."

Marbel's vague silhouette leaned over one of the men. Trying to get up, the commander stumbled and fell back down. Bruises covered his entire body. Marbel helped him up, and the tall man leaned against the wall.

"Made it on time? I would disagree a little," he said, forcing a smile.

"Why wait for fat, old Marbel? We can manage on our own. A few ants don't scare us. Who needs Marbel?" asked the old man. "Did you see what this little thing can do?"

Touching his aching bite marks, Kamanar chuckled while Marbel began helping the others.

"This is becoming a habit," Marbel said while daubing Naji's wounds with Miprona ointment. The boy lay inert, and only his eyeballs shifted from side to side. "You get hurt, and then Marbel comes to tend to your wounds. There, now rest for a bit."

"No!" said Kamanar. "We need to get out of here." Marbel approached him with the ointment. "Treat the others. I'm fine." He pushed the chubby man gently back. The latter turned to Sarik and Motehro.

"Make it quick, Marbel," Kamanar said as he knelt by the boy. "It's more bruises than wounds."

The boy answered with a meek smile as the commander helped him to his feet.

"Damn big ugly ants!" Naji said and kicked a dead one.

Marbel helped Motehro up then gathered the bags and weapons that had been scattered during the battle.

"What about the sword? I mean Caleem's?" asked the older man.

Kamanar shrugged. "We'll do without it."

"But Caleem alwa—"

"I said we'll do without it!"

They all stood up and were ready to leave. Justo turned and walked back through the tunnel, the rest of the bunch limping after her.

"From now on, we're not going anywhere without this thing," said Kamanar, pointing to the fabull.

A few hours later, the tunnels became dark again. Justo's pleasant aura lit their way, although it appeared to be a bit dimmer.

"It was amazing how Justo scared them away. Pshh ... Pshhh!" said Naji, raising his fists to his face, imitating Justo's big eyes.

"Did you know that those ants used to serve the sorcerer?" asked Marbel.

"What?"

"I read it in a book at the big library."

"If I ever make it back to the Allmother, I'm going to read all the books there."

"Most boys don't favor books so much."

"I want to be a sorcerer."

"A sorcerer ..."

"One day, I will be a great sorcerer, like Gudjewkan's father."

Everyone laughed at the boy.

"I will."

After several long hours of walking uphill, the tunnels became brighter. The small creature's light was now fainter than ever.

Heart-shaped, bright-green leaves began to appear on the bare branches.

"We're at the top of the labyrinth. We'll be out soon," said Kamanar.

A few rays penetrated the meshed branches, and the men slowed down just to take in the light.

Justo stopped under an opening in the ceiling. Rays of sunlight sneaked in, making the white creature glow. She strolled up the tunnel wall on her round, flat feet toward the crack and exited through it. Kamanar stood under the opening and looked up at the blue sky. The others huddled next to him under the warm light. Motehro's tanned bald head shone.

"If the fabull continues over the top, we'll have to go on without her. We can't risk being out in the open," said Kamanar.

All four of his subjects frowned.

"All right, a little sunlight in a concealed position won't hurt anyone."

Nodding, they smiled.

Kamanar put down his bag, jumped up, grabbed the ends of some branches, and hoisted himself up through the hole. The others followed.

"Help me up!" Marbel called. He jumped up a few times, trying to grab the branches.

"Drop the bag," said Kamanar, lowering a long, rope-like branch into the tunnel.

"God forbid. There's food in it."

He grabbed the branch, and the entire team lifted him out into the open.

Once outside, Marbel looked around, squinting and blinking repeatedly. As his eyes grew accustomed to the light, it was clear he was enthralled by the wonderful sight of green, rolling hills extending in all directions. They were now above the thicket and could walk on the dense carpet of leaves, almost as if they were on solid ground. Kamanar raised his eyes to the cloudless blue sky, spreading his arms to soak in as much light as he could.

They all stood in silent awe. Her white eyes turning gray, Justo seemed better. She stood as still as a statue. Her fur swayed slowly, and she began emitting a soft humming sound.

"What a strange creature," said Marbel.

"I think she's feeding … on sunlight, as she did before in the forest," said Kamanar.

"The creation of a mad sorcerer …"

Marbel and the rest lay down on the carpet of leaves to enjoy the sun's warm caress.

Kamanar surveyed the area. "Stay here. I will take a look around while this fellow is feeding."

He walked around the small, leafy hill they stood on. Many more leafy hills of different shapes and sizes appeared in front of him. Above the hills, a great mountain range stretched from north to south, its numerous peaks jutting like sharp blades into the sky. Some were rocky and bare, others capped with snow. Kamanar recoiled and took cover behind the branches and leaves, never removing his gaze from the mountains. Crouching, he fixed his eyes on the ridge. It was as uninviting as it was mighty.

"The infamous Mobinar."

CHAPTER 17
WHERE'S THE SWORD?

A high-pitched whistle caught Kamanar's attention. An eagle, soaring in the sky, descended and landed close to Kamanar.

The warrior recognized the golden eagle by the shade of its distinctive feathers. "Hello, Matar," said Kamanar.

"Kamanar," the bird uttered back then transformed into a young man.

Looking toward the mountains, Matar said, "Doesn't look so infamous to me. There are probably lakes and rivers around it that we can fish in."

Matar dusted off his ragged clothes and sat near Kamanar to face the far range.

Smiling, Kamanar asked, "Remember when we used to escape working the field to go fishing? Not returning home till the next day? My father would be furious."

"Remember that time we went fishing and we saw those girls washing in the river?" Matar asked with a chuckle.

"Then their dad, or uncle, caught us sneaking. He came out of nowhere, waving his ax."

"When we were running and I looked back, I couldn't believe that this old man could keep up like he did. I was actually worried."

Kamanar laughed. "It took him some time to give up."

The two friends gazed at the mountain range and went silent for a while.

"I wish you were here with me," said Kamanar.

"I wish it, too. I wish I could join your mission as one of your soldiers."

Kamanar smirked. "You probably would have been the commander, and I would be your soldier."

Kamanar's demeanor became serious.

"What?" asked Matar.

"I'd better go."

"Have you reflected on what I said?"

"I have to finish my task. We still have a long way—"

"Your true task is to close the gap between your head and your heart. Right now, it's greater than the distance to your Dalusian target. How do you unmask evil? How do you tell right from wrong? You can never join me if you persist in choosing ignorance and denial."

"I …"

Matar's figure faded into nothing.

"Matar!" called Kamanar, but no answer came. The warrior rose to his feet, took a deep breath, shook himself, and returned to the others.

Appearing from behind the hills, Kamanar said, "We have covered a good distance. I saw the Mobinar range. It's not far." He looked back. He closed his eyes for a moment, and when he opened them he put on his usual serious expression, making sure his encounter with Matar remained unsuspected by the others.

He approached the four friends, who had gathered around a piece of gray cloth. On it were strewn pieces of dried meat, crushed mushrooms, and a few figs.

"Very good. So, we've made progress," said Marbel between mouthfuls. "Come, Kamanar, eat something."

They all sat and stuffed food into their mouths. The last piece of meat was contested again, going to Motehro this time.

The tracker celebrated by vigorously feasting on the meat right in front of Naji. The boy shrugged, putting on an expression of faked indifference.

"I wonder what those tattoos are on the top of his head," said Sarik. Everyone looked at the three strange, small, word-like drawings on the tracker's head as he wiped his hands on his fur jacket.

"Too bad he speaks only the language of nonsense," said Marbel.

Because all his companions were staring, Motehro stopped chewing, his mouth still full. "*Blandi gucho seban*," he said and took the last bite out of his mouth, offering to share it.

"No, no, no!" they all cried in disgust, gesturing for him to stop.

"All right," said Kamanar after they'd had a good laugh. "Let's make the most out of this respite … till Justo finishes whatever she's doing," he said, glancing at the creature, whose aura was being restored to its original brightness.

And so they did, rubbing their bruises while they dozed off.

The sun began its descent to the west, and the sky became cloudy and dim. They all bundled up against the cold breeze.

Hearing footsteps from behind one of the green leafy hills, Kamanar opened his eyes and sat up. He placed one hand on the hilt of his sword while the other tapped the old man on the chest. Marbel woke up and, realizing that something was wrong by Kamanar's grave look, strained to sit up.

Drawing the sword from its scabbard, Kamanar noticed Sarik, kneeling and alert, his eyes locked on the space between two green hills ahead. The rustling of dried leaves grew closer. It was the unmistakable sound of someone—or something—approaching, but not ants. Kamanar woke the tracker and Naji with hard pokes. As the unknown guests drew closer, an incomprehensible conversation reached their ears. Sarik sat back down at ease.

"I think it's Zig," said the archer.

Caleem appeared from behind the hill, followed by Zig.

They all were stunned for a moment.

"Caleem!" called Marbel, jumping up and running to his friend. The chubby man embraced his friend, lifting him up in the air. Caleem still wore his strange hat firmly on his head.

"You fought through … I knew you would," said the older man, examining what was left of the wounds on his friend's arms.

"I'm fine, Marbel. Everything's fine," said Caleem.

Marbel embraced Zig the same way.

Naji stood up and rubbed his eyes in disbelief. Zig walked up to him and placed a hand on his shoulder.

In return, Naji hugged his friend tightly. "How the hell did you get here?"

"Uh … we walked," said Zig.

"I thought I'd never see you again."

"I wanted to head home, but I felt it would be wrong to go without you. Caleem wasn't too thrilled with the idea of me joining, but I did it anyway … That thing is still with you?"

"Justo is much more than she looks."

"How did you find us?" Marbel asked.

"That book you left me," said Caleem, producing a little book from inside his shirt and then tucking it back in.

As if searching for something, Caleem's gaze went past the old man to focus on Kamanar. "Where's the sword?" Caleem asked. Receiving no answer, he went up to Kamanar. "Where is the sword?" he asked again, his temper rising.

Kamanar looked him straight in the eye. "Lost."

"Fool! You call yourself a commander?" Caleem spat on the ground.

"Don't be insolent. I'm warning you!"

"That sword is very important."

"It's just a sword as far as I'm concerned. Your father said nothing to me about it. He left it in your hands, which makes it your problem, not mine … Prince!"

Caleem did not argue. He approached Marbel and took him aside for a whispered conversation while their peers watched in silence. Caleem patted the older man on the shoulder when the exchange was over, and Marbel's expression became stiff. Caleem walked up to the crack through which they had climbed earlier.

"I'm going to find the sword. Beware!" he said. "Beware of he whose motives are purely personal—especially you, Sarik."

He jumped down and disappeared into the crevice.

The men stood in silence. The only sound to be heard was that of the leaves trembling in the wind.

"What was that book?" Kamanar asked.

"It's a kind of navigation book, from the big library. I thought it would help him find his way home if he woke up," said Marbel.

"That book could have been useful to us, don't you think?"

"Honestly, I didn't think it was reliable … Look, Kamanar, I don't know what exactly is going on between you two, or you three … but you should know that this is all quite disturbing."

"Marbel, don't worry about it. Don't take that royal boy seriously. I am the commander of this mission, and anyone who doubts my integrity is betraying the king himself as far as I'm concerned. Even if he is the prince, it pains him to take orders from me. That's all."

Marbel cast his eyes down and turned away.

The rays of sunlight were beginning to fade, and the air became colder. Justo, whose eyes had returned to black, stirred back to life. The fabull walked to the opening and jumped in.

"We're moving—come on," said Kamanar.

They lowered themselves into the crevice one by one, last of all Marbel with the bag on his back.

Justo took the lead again. Marbel took the rear, together with the two whispering boys, as they made their way through the thicket once more.

"Kamanar called him … a prince!" said Zig.

"He doesn't look like any prince to me," said Naji.

"What is this place?" asked Zig, feeling the tunnel's walls with his fingers.

"Come on, I'll tell you all about it."

Chapter 18
I Hear Rumbling

From the way the boys chatted and giggled, Kamanar felt the tension among his party had dissipated a bit. Things were getting back to normal.

Justo increased her pace. Kamanar made sure everyone was keeping up.

A pair of jaws appeared from behind a bend then retreated. Kamanar noted that this happened several times. Zig, who was seeing the insects for the first time, was the most jittery.

"Stay close to each other. Especially you, Naji," said Kamanar.

Although sweating from the exertion, Marbel was keeping up.

The tunnel grew narrower, forcing them to walk single file. It sloped down, making it easier to maintain pace. Of all the tunnels they had passed through, this was the longest. The deeper they went, the darker and bleaker it became. The group's mood changed accordingly.

As they marched, Naji quickened his pace to catch up with Kamanar.

"What do you want?" asked Kamanar.

"Kamanar, listen. Zig is back, and …"

"Speak."

Naji looked back. Zig was still immersed in conversation.

"Listen, I went to a fortune-teller. She saw Zig's future! She said she saw him on a battlefield full of soldiers. A knife shaped like a snake was stabbed in his chest, and then … he died."

Kamanar scoffed.

"Look, at first, I thought it was a hoax, especially after he stayed at the Allmother. But now that he's back … and what you said about the war stuff …"

"A man's fate is determined by his actions … and luck. I don't believe in predictions. Don't worry about it. Fortune-tellers are frauds who prey on desperate people."

The boy nodded, somewhat reassured, and returned to his friend's side.

The way became steeper, yet Justo maintained a steady rhythm. The tunnel was now composed of muddy earth and roots as they descended.

"Justo is shining brighter," said Zig, still very much intrigued by the little white guide.

"No. The tunnel is darker," said Kamanar.

The tunnel began to branch more often, and ants still lurked behind some of the openings.

"I'm a bit worried," said Marbel.

Pointing at the glowing fabull, Kamanar said, "Worried or not, we have no choice but to follow this thing."

"Why don't we go over this bush instead of under it? Zig says there's a path that goes over the top," said Naji.

Kamanar stopped. "Are you questioning my course of action?" He glared at the boy. The latter threw his hands up in the air and retreated.

Turning to Zig, Kamanar said, "Let's hope that you and your friend Caleem didn't expose us to the enemy. The Mobinar range is filled with malicious eyes."

"He is not my friend," said Zig.

Kamanar turned and quickened his steps, narrowing the distance between him and Justo, who moved in smooth, tiny steps as if she were gliding. The sloping path began to level out again. The drip of water echoed through the dreary tunnel;

its flat, muddy floor was becoming flooded. Justo floated on without hesitation, paddling forward into the water that filled the bottom of the tunnel.

"What now?" asked Naji when the sight brought them all to a halt.

Kamanar stepped into the shallow water and began wading forward. After hesitating for a bit, the rest followed. They soon became accustomed to the water, which was not as cold as they expected. It wasn't unpleasant at all, as opposed to the annoying, constant cold dripping from the ceiling, which often found its way down the back of their necks.

The wading and splashing in the darkness of the never-ending tunnels began to take its toll on the group, yet none of them asked for food or rest. The water in the tunnel got deeper, reaching up over their knees. This didn't trouble Justo, who paddled on. As wading became difficult, the men behind slowed their pace. A considerable gap had opened between the creature and them.

"Who wants a rest?" asked Kamanar.

Nobody answered.

"Fine. We will stop for a bit anyway. Sarik, pass some food around. Hang your bags and sit down, everyone."

In the underground stream, they rested their tired muscles as Justo trod water, waiting. Sarik produced a piece of cloth containing some dried meat.

"Only two pieces each," said Kamanar.

At the end of the meal, they rested for a while, somehow dozing off in the water while leaning against the muddy walls.

A gentle touch on the cheek woke Kamanar up.

He opened his eyes only to be startled by the proximity of Justo's enormous black eyes. She was standing on his belly, dripping wet, caressing his cheek. The sound of the falling drops, stronger and faster than before, was accompanied by the sound of a flowing stream. Kamanar placed Justo back in the water and got to his feet.

The tunnel had become colder and darker. More water leaked

through the ceiling, pouring down in a steady flow. "Get up, get up!" said Kamanar, shaking the men awake. "The water is rising." He rushed to retrieve their bags.

Justo paddled forward once more. In their wet clothes, the men followed.

"Something's wrong with Justo," said Zig. All eyes turned to the fabull.

"Her light is fading again," said Kamanar. "We need to get out of this place."

As Justo's aura grew fainter, the darkness became deeper. Water gushed from the ceiling and walls, and the current became stronger.

"The water is still rising," said Marbel.

"Thank you for the information. We didn't know that!" said Kamanar. "Come on—keep moving."

The commander looked up, searching for any way out. The tunnel was now wider and the ceiling much higher. The few leaking holes he found were infrequent and narrow. Picking up the pace, he got closer to the white creature, who paddled even faster.

Soon, the water rose above Kamanar's waist. Naji and Zig, immersed up to their chests, began to paddle with their hands. Progress became cumbersome for everyone.

"Well, I don't mind me a short swim … I think," said Marbel, failing to amuse his peers.

"There's got to be something …" Kamanar muttered to himself as he scanned the ceiling once again. In the dark, he noticed a dripping shaft. He stood right underneath it. "This opening seems to go up. If the tunnel is flooded, we can float through. This might be a valid option. We're not continuing. It's too risky."

"What if it's blocked?" Marbel asked. But no answer came.

A sense of helplessness filled them as the water rose and they floated under the opening.

Justo, whose glow was almost gone, swam back toward

them. She hummed as she motioned them to follow with her round palm.

"I hear something," Sarik whispered. They all listened. "I hear rumbling!"

Soon, all heard the sound.

CHAPTER 19
A WAY OUT OF THIS NEVER-ENDING, ANNOYING, DAMN FORSAKEN BUSH

Kamanar was about to say something, but he was overwhelmed by a powerful gust of air coming towards them through the shaft. A deafening noise shook the whole tunnel. Everyone looked up and shuddered in anticipation.

"What the hell is happening?" cried Marbel.

With a loud blast, an enormous tidal wave of brownish-white foam thundered down from the tunnel above.

All Kamanar could do was cover his face as the full weight of the water hit him and washed him down the dark tunnel. His companions' hapless bodies crashed against the muddy walls and one another. The tide of foam and water splashed in all directions, taking everything in its path, flushing the muddy walls and making the water murkier.

Kamanar struggled to keep his head above the water. Each time he managed to emerge for a breath, he saw one of his men being thrashed by the current. The raging wave pushed them at an extraordinary speed, sending them tumbling. Kamanar was submerged for a few minutes. His lungs felt like they were going to burst. Enormous pressure built in his chest; his muscles twitched, and his head spun.

Kamanar closed his eyes, and his body went limp. A second before losing consciousness, he felt himself being flung out of the water and thrown into a dark abyss.

Opening his eyes, he saw only black nothingness. He gasped for air, taking breath after breath. Still in free fall, he regained full awareness. His friends screamed above him.

Waiting for the impending crash, he tried to hold his head up and legs down. The air whistling past his ears intensified the terrifying sensation of the fall. He closed his eyes and clenched his teeth.

He plunged into water and sank deeper and deeper until he spread his limbs and swam up to the surface. Taking a deep breath, his head still spinning, he heard his falling peers scream and then splash around him. It was too dark to see anything, and for a moment only pouring water could be heard.

"Zig? Naji? Marbel? Motehro?" Kamanar called.

"Kamanar!" Zig cried, gulping for air. "Naji, are you all right?"

"No. Yes," Naji said and coughed.

"Marbel! Motehro!" Kamanar called again.

"Motehro is next to me. He passed out. We need to get him out of the water," Sarik shouted.

"Look for Marbel," said Kamanar.

They all called for the chubby man as they thrashed their arms about to find him in the dark water.

"I'm taking Motehro to the green spot over there," came Sarik's voice, accompanied by the sounds of splashing.

Kamanar looked, noting a wall emitting a green aura.

"Here's Marbel, here!" Zig shouted.

Kamanar swam toward the boy's voice. Searching with his hands in the darkness, he felt that it was indeed the fat man, floating on his belly. The commander flipped him over and tugged him toward the green wall.

"It's shallow here," said Sarik from close to the wall.

Something soft and wet touched Kamanar's shoulder. He was startled at first, but then he recognized the fabull. Kamanar laid the limp little creature on Marbel's belly. The furry wet lump no longer gave out any light.

Everyone swam toward the green wall, glad to finally be able to stand on firm, almost dry land. In the green aura, they could see each other. Zig laid Justo on the ground, and Kamanar went about trying to revive the fat man. Sarik tended to Motehro, who coughed up water and foam and then began to ramble. Everyone left the tracker and stood around Marbel. Although Kamanar tried to breathe air into his lungs, the fat man did not respond. Sarik knelt by his side and placed his hands on his chest. He pressed his hands up and down. Water spurted out of Marbel's mouth and nose. Sarik turned the fat man on his side, and Marbel coughed, threw up water, and coughed some more.

Finally, he sat up and looked around, dazed. "Am I so handsome … Why are you all staring at me like that?" he asked hoarsely. Everyone laughed. "Where are we?" the fat man asked. There was no answer.

The group gathered around the small, furry, motionless figure. Her black eyes reflected the green light, but they bore a dark and lifeless glint. Kamanar caressed the mud-soaked body, at a loss as to what to do. He shook the creature, but this elicited no reaction. He stood up. "Zig, take Justo."

"Is she dead?" Zig asked, but no answer came.

The tall man looked at his soaking comrades, noting that everyone, including himself, had lost their bags, except for Sarik. Kamanar drew his sword, the only weapon they had left. Tightening his grip on the hilt, he began striking at the green wall of vegetation.

"There's light behind this wall," he said, hacking through the thick branches.

Sarik joined him, pulling and tearing branches away. Naji, Marbel, and the tracker got up to join the effort.

"I hope it's a way out of this never-ending, annoying, damn forsaken bush," said Marbel as they worked.

Sarik and Kamanar attacked the wall from one side while Marbel, Naji, and the tracker tore at it with their bare hands a few paces away. Only Zig remained kneeling by Justo.

Kamanar hacked at the branches. "Sarik, faster, they're catching up."

The fat man pulled at a thick branch with all his might. It snapped, sending him tumbling on his back. "You're using a sword, and we have nothing," he said, getting back to his feet as he rushed to help Naji and the tracker. The three had already penetrated deep into the wall.

"There's three of you and only two of us," said Kamanar.

Naji signaled Zig to come to their aid. The boy sneaked into the small tunnel they had dug.

The commander heard laughter coming from the other tunnel, followed by chants of victory: "Hey! Ho! Hey!"

"We won. We made it first," said Marbel.

Kamanar and Sarik crossed over through the new passageway to the other side of the vegetation.

Zig stood with a mischievous look on his face. Kamanar smiled. From behind Zig came a blinding light reflected by an array of white stones.

"Zig, bring Justo here," said Kamanar, his eyes still adjusting.

They found themselves standing on a muddy surface. Sharp-edged rocks bulged from the ground, and an assortment of stones were scattered about. Surrounding the space were gray rock walls towering high above them. Hanging from the bright opening at the top, a narrow, wooden ladder reached all the way down to where they stood.

"This is a pit," said Marbel. "Not the work of Guzuds."

"No. This is a waterhole, a kind of well," Kamanar said. "The question is, who's using it?"

He approached the long ladder, noting that some of the rungs were bones.

Motehro knelt at the bottom of the ladder. He pointed at strange footmarks in the mud while emitting a sound: "Tss … Tsss …" Sticking out his upper teeth above his lower lip, he waved his arms up and down.

"Can anyone understand what he's trying to say?" asked Kamanar.

Moving over to inspect the tracks, Marbel said, "He's imitating a bird, a sick one."

"I think he's imitating a rat," said Naji.

Kamanar froze for a moment, his eyes wide open, but said nothing.

"What about Justo?" asked Zig.

"Let's take her up," Kamanar said.

They climbed up, Marbel and Kamanar coming last.

Grabbing the ladder, Marbel looked up. "It's really high … Motehro looks so small."

"Come on," said Kamanar.

Marbel forced a chuckle as he placed his foot on the first rung. "It's just that … I'm a little big, and this thing doesn't seem to—"

"It's sturdy enough," Kamanar interrupted. "Start climbing—go on. Just skip the bone rungs."

The older man exhaled and, trembling, began to climb. "I hate heights!"

"Look at me, look how tiny I am," said Kamanar. "You'll explode like a watermelon if you fall." He chuckled. Marbel shut his eyes and dashed up.

One by one, they emerged from the pit onto a wide, sunlit, rocky area. Kamanar was the last out, following the fat man, who threw himself across the bare rocks far from the hole.

Only a few clouds stained the clear midday sky.

"Hooray!" said the old man, still trying to get his breath back.

CHAPTER 20
I'LL BE THERE BY YOUR SIDE

They were on the shoulder of a steep mountain, surrounded by clusters of rocks with pine trees scattered around. The slope descended to the east where it bordered the formidable thicket.

The peculiar formation, which they had only seen mostly from the inside, extended in various directions. Viewed from this vantage point, it looked like a small, very green mountain range.

"Thank God we made it out of that pile of leaves," said Marbel while taking in the wonderful sunlight.

Zig placed Justo's limp body on a rock right in front of the tall man.

"Let's hope the sun will do her good," said Kamanar.

Zig sat down on a patch of soft ground between the rocks beside little Justo.

Fatigue had caught up with all of them. They all curled up in different postures and sunk into a long and pleasant slumber on the sun-bathed rocks.

Kamanar's sleep was restless, a series of nightmares disrupting his peace. In one of them, a furry little creature stood in front of him, waved goodbye, and disappeared. Then came nightmares about enormous ants, Dalusians, and even Guzuds, which he still had never seen. A dream of Naiya chased away all the horrors plaguing his mind. The great dining hall was decorated with red wall hangings, and there she was, wearing an ornate white gown and sitting opposite him at the long royal table. All the guests disappeared one by one until only she was left. She was holding a golden goblet in her hand when her moist eyes met his.

"Kamanar … when will you wake up? You know my father's will is tyrannous. What is yours? Do you have any? Or are you merely an extension of his arm?"

"My king is my master."

"What is this quest of yours worth if you don't know how to love? What is anything worth?"

"What?"

"You care so much for everyone around you, yet you always make sure to keep a distance. And make sure that you don't love. Can you love?"

"Of course I can," said Kamanar, lowering his gaze to the empty plate.

"Then there must be someone. Who is she, or he? Tell me."

"I …"

"Maybe if you learn to love, really love, maybe then you can free yourself from this magical hold that my father has on you."

"I can't … not now. I must finish my task. This is my only aim."

"Yes … your precious reward. Do you believe that eliminating your past will lift you from your gloom?"

"I have to believe. Otherwise, death is my only salvation."

"Your past is of sorrow. Don't let it consume the whole of you. Maybe it's time to face it."

"No!" he shouted.

"I trust you. When the time comes, I know you will make the right choices. You are a good and courageous—"

"I'm a coward and an evil man!"

Kamanar sprung from his slumber, panting.

Returning to reality, he sat up straight and looked around. Scattered clouds sailed across the sky; the sun was already behind the mountains.

He rose to his feet. A cool breeze caressed his face, blowing away the last vestiges of sleep and agitation.

"Another bad dream? We're all having those lately. Mine was full of those big, hairy insects. I must give thanks to my growling belly—it woke me up," said Marbel as he sat with the rest of the gang around the only remaining bag. "Did you? Dream of those nasty bugs?" he asked.

"Worse … a woman," said Kamanar. Marbel chuckled.

Sarik stood alone, leaning on a rock, gazing at the thicket, his light-brown hair blowing in the wind. The young man shot the commander a long glance then turned away.

Kamanar walked straight up to him. "Is there anything you want to say?"

"Yes," said Sarik after a short pause. "You don't trust me, and that is degrading. You have no idea how much … I believe in my king. My loyalty to him is absolute. What do I have to do to prove it?"

The tall man looked into Sarik's bright eyes then turned and walked away.

"We're starving. Let's eat something," Marbel said, changing the subject as he opened the bag.

"Where's Justo?"

Marbel shrugged. The others looked around.

"I remember something," said Kamanar. "She woke up while we slept. I think she went back home." He smiled and sat with the others.

"I can imagine she did. It's just like that fabull to leave without saying goodbye," said Marbel.

"I'm going to miss her," said Zig.

Marbel produced the cloth containing the food. "The meat is soggy. Shame. Now we will have to eat the whole thing, or it will spoil," he said, smirking.

"No, we don't. It's better to stay light. We have a steep incline ahead," said Kamanar.

Still, the men devoured the meat until there was none left. Kamanar and Sarik had only half a portion.

"That's it—now we're out of provisions," said the older man.

"We'll manage. Get ready to move," said Kamanar.

Sarik flung the bag over his shoulder. The others were slow to get up.

Kamanar led them up the steep, rocky slope.

An odd sensation of freedom swept over them. They were all enjoying the hike, climbing among the rocks and scattered trees.

"Stay low," said Kamanar as they reached the top of the hill.

In front of them, the mountain range extended north and south as far as the eye could see.

"What huge mountains," said Naji.

"The Mobinar," said the commander. "Its tops are infested with Dalusians, some of whom are looking this way right now."

Naji and Zig crawled back with exaggerated caution. They were still able to see some of the snow-capped mountaintops, but others were hidden by the clouds.

"I'm not sure I'm ready to kill someone," Zig whispered to his friend.

"What? Why not?"

"I don't know …"

Kamanar overheard the boys. "First, we need to enter their territory, beyond this ridge." He pointed to the sharp slopes. "There's a path there, the Spy Trail, which should lead us to this Dalusian general, also known as the commander of the Ivest. Then …" Kamanar stared at Zig, who looked disconcerted. "And then, one arrow will be shot with great precision, right through his heart. Right, Zig?"

Zig's face turned grim; he did not respond.

"Right, Zig?" asked Naji, tapping him on his shoulder. Zig offered nothing.

Kamanar got closer to the boy. "This shot will save many.

Fear is normal, is in every being, and we cannot survive without it. But we must learn to master it, not the other way around. I'll be there by your side when you do it."

Zig nodded, a faint smile touching the corners of his lips.

"Good," the commander said and crawled back down the slope with the rest behind him.

"But we have no bow, no arrows," said Naji.

"We'll make them," said Kamanar. "Come on, we'll move on the side of the hill—it'll provide cover. Once we get to the foot of the mountain, the ridge will protect us from prying eyes. Any questions? Good, off we go."

They began a short descent, circumnavigating the hill. They found themselves entering a ravine going up between two hills. The trees around grew denser, their branches meshing. "The mighty oaks of Turundia make these pines look tiny," observed Marbel between gasps.

No one answered on account of the increasing effort.

The men disappeared under the cover of the trees in the ravine that led to the ridge. They continued uphill, and, despite the steep incline, they made fast progress through the forest. Bushes flanked the base of the trees, but they were small and far apart, and passing them was no trouble.

Distance grew between the commander and the others, who were sweating and panting. Kamanar waited for them. "You're lucky the trees give us cover. Otherwise, we'd have had to run."

"We're keeping up—no problem," said Marbel, breathing heavily and leaning on Motehro.

"Are you now? Very well, we'll pick up the pace."

The old man's face became pale, and the boys didn't look too thrilled, either. The food, still heavy in their bellies, was causing them much discomfort.

Kamanar kept up a rapid rhythm, occasionally glancing at the evening sky. He heard coughing behind him.

"I don't have to remind you about Dalusian nocturnal eyesight. We have to take advantage of the twilight time."

It was Naji who coughed. As he approached the others, he coughed again, then began to vomit. Marbel and Zig rushed to his assistance.

"I warned you not to eat like pigs. One day, this will cost us dearly," said Kamanar.

CHAPTER 21
THE STORY

They were all out of breath, except for Sarik, who helped his straggling friends, pushing them ahead. Kamanar slowed, but the rest still lagged behind. The sky began to grow darker. At this slower pace, the panting stopped.

Naji made sure the commander was out of earshot before asking Marbel, in a whisper, "What's the story between Kamanar, Caleem, and Sarik? Hear anything new?"

"Nothing yet. Maybe it's the notion of taking orders," said Marbel, "or maybe because Kamanar was captain of the Royal Guard, and Caleem isn't too fond of that institution. I don't know."

"Not too fond? Why?"

"They're a corrupt crowd with close ties to the king and his court. They receive land, titles, and gifts. They have the finest horses and the best swords. They wear fancy clothes," said Marbel.

"What's corrupt about that?" asked Zig.

"It's at the people's expense. Worse than that: in battle, we, the infantry, march first. The guards, along with the cavalry, wait behind on their horses, doing nothing, just monitoring the battle. If we're about to win, they join, but if we're about to lose, they flee. They are arrogant, selfish hypocrites, and they treat us with disdain."

"Kamanar isn't like that," said Zig.

"No. He's certainly different. Well, he's a famous warrior, but I didn't really know him before this journey. I heard he was known for being brutal. I figured he was just like the rest, but now I can say with certainty that he is not. I did notice him talking to himself a couple of times, but I guess we all do that once in a while."

"So what does Caleem have to do with that?" asked Naji.

"Caleem is an infantryman. Like me," said the chubby man.

"I thought he was the king's son, a prince," said Zig.

"So he's not a prince?" asked Naji.

"He is. He wears that strange hat as a disguise. He's one of King Creeden Dummah's two sons. Prince Caleem didn't want to be a part of the Royal Guard, the place to be for all noblemen. So he joined the infantry against his father's wishes. He came to us when he was very young. That's when I met him, shortly after the war. What a kid he was …"

"Wait, wait. You two were in the war?" asked Naji.

"I was. Not Caleem. He was too young back then." Marbel tripped. "Damn stone! It's getting dark."

"Quiet back there," whispered Kamanar, who began to argue with Motehro. Each man pointed in a different direction.

"Caleem's older brother fought in the war," said the old man in a whisper after the distance between them and the commander had widened again.

"Tell us about it, Marbel, please, about the war," said Naji.

Kamanar, far ahead, was immersed in finding their way and the occasional disagreement with Motehro. Eventually he stopped and waited for the others to catch up. "The three of you wait here. Sarik, Motehro, and I will search for an easier path," he said and jumped over a bush, the archer and tracker behind him.

"Well, let's rest a bit. Great timing," said Marbel. "It was about thirteen years ago," he began as the boys sat down next to him. "It wasn't the first confrontation between us Mellethyans and the Dalusians. Some say it was the thirtieth war, others say the hundredth. Anyhow, it was after the last winter rains. I'll never forget it. We marched for a week from the ancient wall, northwest to Anathoria."

"Anathoria … Heaven on Earth. That Anathoria?" asked Naji.

"Yes. Long-lost Anathoria. Once a part of Mellethya, now infested by Dalusians. Anyway, we marched and marched, all hopes and fears, until we reached the Polikolion Valley. The ground was muddy—I remember it like it was yesterday." Staring at the top of a young tree standing against a starry sky, the chubby man fell silent. Not even the delicate slice of a crescent moon appearing above the branches distracted him from his memories.

"That's where the Dalusians struck us. At the Polikolion, as in all previous wars. Always at the damn Polikolion. I was in the back rows of the infantry. The cavalry and the Royal Guard were aligned behind us. We heard whizzing high in the air, and a blanket of arrows cut across the sky. It came from the tops of the trees. The screaming of the injured began, and arrows rained nonstop. You two had a small taste of that, so you know what it's like … Anyway, they aimed at the weak points of our armor, so no one was safe. Within minutes, everyone in the front lines was on the ground, either dead or in agony.

"Our forces panicked, breaking up in total disarray. Our company commander regrouped and rallied us to the tree line. To his yells we advanced straight to the source of the arrows. The enemy was hidden from sight. Our battle cries expressed more fear than courage. Behind, the company commander and his likes struck down anyone who dared to turn back. So it was death from both sides.

"As I lunged forward, my fellow soldiers around me fell, one by one. When the first of us reached the bushes under the trees, arrows still flew over our heads, striking the others behind. I could hear the sounds of the bowstrings as they were drawn and released nonstop.

"Out of nowhere, a group of Dalusians appeared in their camouflage. Some had strung bows, others swords. My friends and I desperately tried to defend ourselves, waiting for their malicious arrows to tear us to pieces. But their archers shot over our heads, busy aiming at the cavalry. Riders fell off their horses, some collapsed together with their mounts. Chaos reigned … Chaos."

The chubby man fell silent once more, his breathing heavy with anxiety. Their eyes glued to him, the boys were enthralled.

"Despite the barrage, a group of armored cavalry charged. A great number of sword-brandishing Dalusians lunged at them and at my company. Before the forces clashed, I ducked and pressed myself against this tiny bush, barely avoiding our galloping cavalry. The riders ran over the Dalusians, trampling and killing them with their swords, forcing them to scatter and retreat. A hand grabbed me and pulled me up to my feet. It was one of the Royal Guards. 'Fight beside me!' he ordered.

"I watched him bravely strike down the Dalusians, swinging his sword in every direction. He shouted at our frightened archers to shoot at the treetops. I felt my courage surging, and I joined the fight. Dalusians are also master swordsmen, but his ability went beyond belief. He struck them down one after the other while dodging the arrows and swords coming at him.

"Cavalry reinforcements soon arrived. The surviving Dalusians fled before our eyes, and those hiding in the treetops simply vanished. With a warm smile, the heroic warrior approached me and patted me on the shoulder. At that moment, I would have followed him to the end of the earth. There was a charm about him, his voice was cordial but commanding … It was Prince Ansseur, Caleem's older brother." Marbel finished with a smile.

"Caleem's older brother!" whispered the boys.

"Tell some more, tell some more," said Naji.

Chapter 22
At the Time

Crickets chirping and the tiny white glowing flowers gave the three friends a sense of serenity.

"When the awful sounds died down, a gruesome sight was revealed. Dozens of bodies lay scattered across the valley, many brought down by arrows. Riderless horses galloped in circles. Flags depicting the deer head, our royal emblem, were scattered on the battlefield like rags. Soldiers were fleeing far to the south. Ansseur declared, 'It is over.'

"He ordered me to flee, which I did … Though we won that skirmish, the war waged on and was lost in less than a day. It was a humiliating defeat. It was an indescribable feeling to run with my life still mine … I was already a long way from the battlefield. When I glanced back, I could see Polikolion Valley swarming with cloaked figures.

"Not far from me grazed a riderless horse. Seizing its reins, I jumped on the saddle, clinging to it as if it was my savior. Before riding away, I shot one last glance behind me. Far away, surrounded by the Dalusian horde, I saw the flash of a sword. A last fighter with a great commotion around him. I watched intently until the glint faded. Slowly, it dawned on me that it was the same brave man I had known for a brief moment. It was Ansseur. I went on my way. Riding back to the walled city,

I passed many fleeing soldiers. They looked as dejected as I did. How could we stand before the king? His glorious army, defeated and humiliated. And worst, the loss of his firstborn." Marbel paused.

The three pairs of eyes rose to the night sky; the stars twinkled through the spaces among the trees.

"Lower your voices or shut up!" Kamanar said, emerging from the brush only to disappear immediately on the other side.

"Are we lost?" Marbel asked.

"No. I know exactly where we are," Kamanar whispered. Motehro followed him, grumbling; Sarik was close behind, shaking his head.

"We're lost," Sarik said before he disappeared into the vegetation.

"What did the king say?" Naji asked in a whisper once their commander was gone.

"Nothing," whispered Marbel as he found a new position on the hard ground. "The grief was too great for him and his family. As it was for all families who lost a son, a brother, or a father. Royalty, nobles, and us peasants—the entire kingdom sank into sorrow. The queen, Ansseur and Caleem's mother, refused to leave her chambers. She was in deep anguish, unable to cope with her loss. So was her daughter, Naiya."

"Did Kamanar fight in the war?" asked Zig.

"Yes, he did. Kamanar was still a new recruit in the Royal Guard. I don't know much about what he did—I only heard that he fought well, but in the end, it was the same sad outcome. What I do know is that after the war, he became very close to Princess Naiya. She found solace in Kamanar's arms. They were even engaged to be married, and they were together for a few years. But eventually, they separated.

"Now, going back to the main story. King Creeden was troubled by his wife's depression. Three months after the war, a surprise awakened the kingdom from its stupor …"

Naji and Zig begged Marbel to continue, unable to

comprehend the reason for the irritating break in his riveting narration.

"Just removing this nasty twig," said Marbel, pulling a broken twig from under his behind. "Several horsemen rode into the castle grounds. These were men who were thought to be dead. Turns out they had been taken captives by the Dalusians, but then, miraculously, they were set free. They were led back by Ansseur, who was alive and unscathed … It was a miracle.

"Yet the royal household's joy and relief were short-lived. The men were interrogated thoroughly by King Creeden, who had been restless since their arrival. He ordered them to be locked in the dungeon. It turns out they had undergone some kind of evil manipulation or some kind of dark spell had been cast on them. Acting like madmen, they talked endlessly about the Dalusians. Ansseur himself wreaked havoc wherever he went, having loud, repeated confrontations with his father, until he, too, had to be locked up."

"What …? Did they become Khandaluses?" asked Zig.

Marbel nodded, sighing.

"The king tried to restore their sanity. But the spell cast by the Dalusians was so strong, they gradually lost their minds completely, ultimately dying one by one. The damn Dalusians had infected them with demonic spells, planting madness and divisiveness among them. Ansseur was the last to die. The kingdom plunged into grief once again, this time even worse than before. It would have been better had they died in battle …

"A week later, the queen died—of a broken heart, they say. She was especially loved by the simple folk, as she was the daughter of peasants. She had treated her subjects with fairness from the day she married the king. All mourned her death. King Creeden confined himself to the castle, becoming a different man from that day.

"At this time, Naiya was still engaged to Kamanar. Caleem, just a boy, grew more and more distant from the royal family and their courtiers, who not only continued to spread negative rumors about Ansseur, even after his death, but also openly defamed others with their gossip. The young lad came to us, to the infantry. We were surprised but, of course, accepted him gladly. Despite his young age, he proved to be a gifted fighter and in time became an extraordinary warrior. We became good friends, regardless of the age difference. We remained close even after he left."

Once more, they heard rustling in the bushes. Motehro's mumbling got closer.

"We're moving—on your feet!" Kamanar ordered and led the way.

"Back to the world. Off we go," said the chubby man as he rose.

Marbel, Naji, and Zig were last. Storytelling time was over, but they still reflected in silence as they followed their commander into the dark.

They marched, stumbling around until midnight, when Kamanar stopped under a big pine tree. "We'll rest here until the break of dawn," said the commander, producing a ball of string. "Marbel, take this. Make two bows and a trap. Maybe we'll have a catch by breakfast. Sarik, give him a hand."

The two went between the bushes and began to work on the task.

"I still don't understand the problem between Caleem, Kamanar, and Sarik. Nothing Marbel said had anything to do with it," whispered Naji.

"It is not right, the way Kamanar treats Sarik," said Zig.

"Right."

Kamanar approached the boys. "How many times do I have to tell you to be quiet? We're being careless, all of us," he went on in a hushed tone. "The ridge, it's teeming with Dalusians. Any unnecessary word could give us away."

Kamanar's warning made them uneasy, and they became alert once again.

"Sarik and Marbel will stand watch first while they finish their job, then the rest and I will guard together, just to be on the safe side," said Kamanar, giving the boys a sharp glare.

Sarik and Marbel chopped a few branches then crafted two bows and three traps, which they set around the trees.

When it was Kamanar's turn to watch, he took Marbel aside and whispered in his ear, "Are you keeping an eye on that fellow, like I asked you?"

"Listen, Kamanar, the lad is a jolly good fellow …"

"Just do it, and that's it! Don't wake the others. I'll take this watch on my own."

Marbel sighed and lay down by the sleeping boys.

Sarik saw everything from the corner of his eye. He walked away and found a patch of earth for himself. He bundled up and fell asleep with his back to the rest.

Chapter 23
We Are Not Lost

Just before dawn, Kamanar woke the team with a few kicks. The commander examined the bows and drew their strings. Naji took one and drew it. "Arrows, too, Zig. Come take a look."

Reluctantly, Zig took the bow.

"Cheer up, boy. This will make a hero of you," said Kamanar.

To everyone's disappointment, Sarik soon returned with empty traps.

Kamanar, laying down a sizable amount of the strange, red fruits he had gathered on two big leaves, said, "Here. That should be enough for now."

"Not bad. With a piece of ham this would have been perfect," said the chubby man.

"Come on—we need to move now," Kamanar ordered after they had finished.

The world grew brighter. Kamanar set a fast pace, and under the cover of the trees they pushed west. The rows of trees growing along the ridgeline provided some cover, allowing them to advance during the morning and afternoon hours.

The commander stopped and scanned the area from north to south, and they backtracked up the same path. Then they went up a tight ravine and backtracked again. All the while, Kamanar stretched his neck, looking around and puffing.

"Is everything all right?" Marbel asked.

"That damn Spy Trail."

"It's getting dark, and it's a big mountain. It'll be easier to find in the morning."

"Looks like rain," said Kamanar.

"The boys said you like rain—there you go."

"That's—Where's Sarik?" Kamanar stopped and looked around.

"I'm here." Sarik emerged from the bushes carrying a bird impaled with an arrow. Giving the commander a resentful look, he dropped the bird at Kamanar's feet and took the bow off his shoulder.

"Roast bird tonight," said Marbel.

"No fires from now on. The light and the smoke will give us away," said Kamanar.

A light drizzle began to fall.

"How will we eat it?" asked Naji.

"Raw," said the commander. "Listen, I'm leaving for a while." Taken aback, they all looked at him. "The way to our destination is hidden, and it might take hours, maybe days to find it … If we all go, it will increase our chances of being exposed."

"So we're lost," said Naji.

"We strayed a little off course—we are not lost. There is no time to waste. I'm leaving. All of you, stay close together until I get back. Don't even think about lighting a fire." He gestured for the old man to come closer. "I leave you in charge. Make sure they stay quiet and that someone is always standing watch."

Marbel nodded. Kamanar gave the old man a hard look and squeezed his shoulder. Lowering his voice, he said, "If I am not back within a couple of days, you must take command."

Marbel's eyes widened. "What …? All right," he said with a nod.

"Don't forget to keep an eye on you-know-who."

He turned to the others. "Goodbye," he said and disappeared into the darkness, leaving them standing in the rain.

Marbel noted that all eyes were fixed on him. "It's going to be fine. We can hunt and gather berries, and we can catch up on some sleep. Come … Let's start with this bird." He picked up the bird and began plucking its feathers.

Late in the evening, after an endless argument between Marbel and Motehro, who was unable to grasp why a fire could not be lit, they dined on raw bird meat.

Despite its taste and rubbery texture, no flesh was left unconsumed.

After supper, very few words were spoken on that wet autumn night.

CHAPTER 24

HOW CONVENIENT IT IS TO BE ON MY OWN

Caleem spotted the long sword, its blade buried halfway in a rock near a stream. It was surrounded by a strange, bluish aura. Mesmerized, he was drawn to it. As he placed his hand on the dark hilt, a disturbing shadow crept behind him. The prince turned, his heart beating harder, every breath cumbersome. It was a tall, dark figure with sharp features. He recoiled in horror. The pair of menacing, metallic eyes met his, and its long, dark-bluish arm stretched over Caleem's shoulder and drew the sword out of the rock. It struck the prince.

Drenched in sweat, Caleem woke up with a start, gasping for air. This nightmare had haunted him ever since his father had entrusted the sword to him.

He looked around. Everything was still in the tunnel's gloom. He re-covered himself with leaves and rested his head on the twisting branches of the tunnel's floor.

Caleem heard rustling and closed his eyes. Within a moment,

he was surrounded by a multitude of giant ants. He flashed his eyes open, getting a glimpse of the jaws of the ants crawling all over him. One of the huge jaws snapped shut on his leg, and the pain was sharp yet bearable. Another pair of jaws closed on his other leg. He was dragged by two ants as two more bit his arm and hip. With his eyes shut, Caleem grinned. *It's working! Stupid bugs!*

They hauled him deep inside the thicket maze. Caleem felt pressure building in his arm, yet he remained motionless, resisting the urge to shake himself free. He was dragged into a huge garbage dump, and its foul smell made Caleem screw up his face. Along with mounds of twigs and branches, there were old wooden crates, rusty bits of armor, shields, and shattered weapons.

A helmet rolled between the insects' legs and bumped against Caleem's head. The gaping, cracked skull inside it came face to face with the prince.

In a sudden panic, Caleem punched the ant biting his arm. The insect, along with its three friends, dropped the warrior. They crackled as they retreated.

Caleem was surrounded by huge piles of junk and debris. The human and animal bones lying among piles of torn garments made him shudder. Keeping calm but wary of the baffled ants, he began to search while shaking his numbed arm. He didn't notice the ants approaching him.

He found the cloth sheath of his sword and flung it over his shoulder. "It has to be here," he said while rummaging through the trash.

Spotting the tip of a black hilt, he grinned and took a giant leap, reaching for it. He snatched it out of the pile and rolled over the black mass of ants, then landed nimbly on his feet.

"Now, I dare you!" said the smiling warrior wielding the sword above his head.

Dozens of ants lunged. Ready for the onslaught, he swung his sword in all directions, its heavy blade slicing through the insects' bodies as if cutting through eggshells. Within minutes, he was covered in green slime from head to toe, standing amid piles of oozing heads and quivering limbs.

More ants poured into the hall through the entryway, which was the only way out.

Spitting and wiping his eyes clear as he sought to escape, he noticed a mesh of twigs covering the floor between the piles of trash. He slashed an opening in one swing then slipped through and down into another tunnel. He ran, having no idea which way he was heading. After taking dozens of turns, he halted and spun around a few times. Finally, he smiled. "Up," he said. He climbed to the top of the tunnel wall. By jamming his sword into the ceiling, he made an opening wide enough to hoist himself through. He repeated this in each subsequent tunnel until he broke through the thicket's roof.

Outside, the black sky was sprinkled with a few twinkling stars between the clouds. The crescent moon shone above the mountain.

"The moon sets to the west," Caleem said. Recognizing the Mobinar range, he was now certain of his direction. Placing the sword back in its sheath, he began his journey westward between the hills of the thicket. He ran for several hours until he stopped near a pile of rocks. "Earth and stones … I'm out of that bush."

He began to wobble on the uphill slope. He had to rest, so he threw himself between some bushes and fell asleep with one blink of his eyes.

Waking up to the sound of rustling, he saw the world bathed in faint morning light. He climbed out of the bushes to investigate. *Probably an animal*, he thought. Feeling the hilt of his sword, he smiled with satisfaction.

"How great it is to be on my own."

Hearing rustling again, Caleem crouched down and crept to peek behind the bush. Three dark figures huddled together tampering with something on the ground. From their lower backs hung long, hairless tails. Their heads, almost hidden by humps, had big, pointy ears.

These things are not Dalusians.

They were unfolding a net on the ground, and one of them spun around and stared straight at Caleem. It rose up and walked in his direction.

The prince froze at the gruesome sight. A huge pair of glimmering black eyes bulged out of a gray and elongated face, ending in a long, black snout. The creature's arms grew forward from its shoulders.

Rats. Giant rats, walking on two legs!

The rat began twitching its nose and sniffing. As it got closer, Caleem did not dare to move a muscle. The other two, who were busy with the net, squeaked. It squeaked back and returned to its friends to help them cover the net with twigs and leaves. The prince sighed.

As they finished, about a dozen rodents came out of the bushes. A brief, squeaky conversation ensued, after which all hurried away and disappeared behind the trees. Caleem waited, listening to the fading rustle of the bushes. He came out of hiding to examine the trap. It was simple yet effective.

"You're not catching me."

He walked away, picking his steps, and then pulled the small navigation book out of his pocket.

"The Spy Trail," he said out loud. Nothing happened. "Spy Trail," he said again, but still the pages didn't move. The prince put the book back in his pocket with a sigh. Hoping for the best, he marched on. "I hope you're still safe," he said, thinking of Sarik. "I should've taken you with me."

The prince scanned the ground, looking for any tracks left by his friends. The hidden path, made by wild animals, was easy to walk on. By nightfall, he had covered a distance that would put a horseman to shame. The sky, visible over the canopy, turned red as the treetops swayed in the light wind. Down where he marched, there was no breeze, yet the falling leaves and the browning vegetation reminded him that autumn was here.

The prolonged hunger had sharpened his senses and made

him feel light and alert: a feeling he enjoyed. Darkness enveloped the Mobinar, and his worries weighed heavier on him than fatigue. Every now and then, he would stop to listen, knowing that his ears were now his eyes. Despite the thickening fog, he pressed on. The more he advanced, the more he realized that finding his friends or stumbling on the Spy Trail in this vast range was a daunting task.

Caleem went on like a blind man. He stumbled against a rock wall, then he climbed, clinging to rock after rock, grasping as the sharp rock ledges cut and bruised his arms. Adding to his woes was the long sword, which kept getting stuck between cracks and protruding roots. Breathing heavily, he tried to find a level position where he could get some much-needed rest. Looking down, he knew there was a deep precipice, though he couldn't see it hiding beyond the fog. He was concerned that if the cliff became any steeper, it would be impossible for him to continue.

CHAPTER 25
IT SHOULD BE ME

Caleem found a niche, crawled in, and lay on his back. It was relatively comfortable and, more importantly, he was out of sight of potential enemies. The prince put his hands under his head and began to reflect on the evening when his father gave him the sword.

He remembered every detail and, more than anything else, his disappointment.

***

King Creeden sat on his festive throne at the end of the long dining table.

Before the king, and facing each other, sat Princess Naiya and his loyal officer, Dolegg. Next to them sat Caleem facing Kamanar. The rest of the long table, although filled with various platters of food, was empty of chairs. Around them dined, while standing, many clusters of noblemen and women. Nervous, blue-uniformed servants scampered about the great hall, carrying trays and pitchers.

Caleem glared at Kamanar while he chewed his food. The latter ate with a great appetite, indifferent to the prince's gaze. The prince slammed his fist on the table, and the food jumped off the plates. Everyone stopped eating except for the tall man in front of him, who was still enjoying his food. King Creeden shifted his eyes between the two.

The prince threw a piece of chicken at Kamanar.

"Stop it," said the king.

"What's wrong with you?" asked Naiya.

Caleem went back to staring at Kamanar, who, in return, smiled at the prince and sipped his wine with a loud slurping sound. Caleem flipped the whole table with a scream, startling everyone in the great hall.

"Caleem!" shouted the king.

"It should be me!" the prince shouted.

"Don't raise your voice to the king," said Kamanar.

The prince yelled, "Shut your mouth!" and lunged at the tall man. The two fell to the ground and started brawling, with everyone's eyes upon them. They thrashed each other on the floor, and Caleem punched Kamanar twice in the face. The latter looked to the king and, after receiving a nod, punched back, then thrust the prince off him. He jumped to his feet and lunged at the charging prince.

"Father, stop this!" said the princess.

"Let them play a little," said the king.

She clearly wanted to intervene, but short, plump Dolegg held her by the arm.

No one dared to intervene while the two warriors continued pounding and throwing each other around the hall.

"Stop," said the king.

The two paused for a moment, but then Caleem continued punching. Kamanar remained motionless, receiving the hits like a rag doll.

"Stop this, fool," said the king.

A bunch of Royal Guards ran in, overpowered the prince, and pulled him away.

"See, Father … I bested him," said Caleem while pushing against the guards. They let him be after he calmed down a bit.

King Creeden patted Kamanar on the shoulder as he walked

past. The tall warrior stood straight, keeping a tranquil demeanor as he wiped his bleeding nose.

"It should be me!" said the prince again.

"Thank you for proving my point," said the king to his son.

"What point?"

"Fix the table," the king ordered as he went back to his throne, ignoring the prince.

Smirking, Dolegg approached the prince. "The point is that you're an immature child."

"Get out of my sight before I stick my boot in your mouth!" said Caleem.

The officer's ugly face was Caleem's last memory before he fell asleep.

***

He awoke with a heavy head and struggled to open his eyes, only to be reminded of his aching body. The sun was up. As he examined the small cuts on his hands, he scanned his surroundings. Squinting, he noticed a dark, winged creature flying nearby. The strange bird disappeared behind the thin veil of fog.

Caleem was at the top of a rocky ridgeline, and, to his disappointment, he was now certain that this was not the Mobinar he had climbed. It was a smaller ridge, one of many stretching down from the formidable range. There was no way he could climb up the mighty mountain face in front of him, which stretched into the clouds. He pulled out the navigation book.

"The Spy Trail," he said to the little book on the palm of his hand. The book remained inanimate.

"Marbel, Sarik," he said, louder this time. Nothing happened. The warrior cursed and threw the book away.

After scanning all the folds and flanks along the endless mountain range, he kicked a dead bush. Picking up the book again, he shouted, "The Spy Trail!"

"I don't know where it is. I don't know! Stop repeating that," a voice said out of nowhere.

Caleem looked around, the tips of his fingers on the hilt of the sword. "Who's there?"

No answer came. The warrior looked around the rocks and bushes. "I'm not losing my mind, right …? So who said that, damn it? This can't be." He pored over the book once more. "Talk to me." He hurled the book at the rocks and drew his sword. "Talk now, or I will chop you into a thousand pieces."

"No, no, no. Please don't," a voice sobbed from the book.

The prince froze. "Who … what are you?"

"I'm a book," it answered in a man's voice. "The navigation book."

Caleem chuckled then became serious again.

"Could you please take me back to the library?" asked the book.

"What library?"

"The library. My library."

"If you mean in that giant tree, then you can forget about it."

"Why? What do you mean?"

Caleem stooped down and picked up the little book. "Look around. We're far away."

"I'm sorry. I have no eyes, although I've always wanted a couple, or more … There is always a shorter path, I can lead you."

"You hear and you talk," said the warrior, examining the book. Inside, it contained only directions written in small characters without any mention of specific names or places. The hard cover looked like that of any other book. On closer inspection, he noticed the shape of a mouth and a tiny pair of ears. He watched in astonishment as the lips drawn on the cover began to move.

"Please, foreigner, return me home."

"If you help, I'll take you back. You are the Map Book, right? Tell me where the Spy Trail is."

"I told you. I don't know that trail."

"The trailhead is somewhere at the foot of the Mobinar. You do know the Mobinar?"

"Of course. I am familiar with every rock and tree from the Tan-Mirus to the mighty Mobinar range and more."

"Can you locate people?"

"No."

"Could you at least tell me where I am?"

"No. I can only show you the way to a place when you say its precise name. There is nothing else I can do."

"You're not worth much to me right now, are you?" He shoved the book back into his shirt pocket. It mumbled something in return. One look at the ridge leading up to the Mobinar brought him back to reality. Facing west, he descended into a gorge that was covered with trees and vegetation. He came upon a bush that looked like it had been trampled on recently. He stooped down and noticed long paw prints on the ground, each bearing the marks of four claws.

"Are we in a cave?" The book's voice was soft and muffled. "I miss my master. We used to hike all around Turundia."

Caleem pressed the book tighter against his body. "Quiet! We are in a dangerous place."

"Dangerous?"

"There are giant rats lurking around. You don't want them to sink their dirty teeth into you, do you?"

"Those ungrateful rodents," whispered the book.

"Do you know them?"

"Yes. They betrayed the master. They only wanted to exploit. They killed many animals of the forest, but that didn't last long. The master was a kind, forgiving man, but he also knew when not to be. He banished them from the forest to the caves under the mountain. The wise master sent them a terrible nuisance to keep them busy … So, when are we going home?"

"We're not going home. Now shut up. For days you haven't said a word, and now you can't stop talking."

"From the moment they pulled me out of the library, I knew these were not my master's hands. I was afraid …"

"I don't care. Shut up!"

Chapter 26

I'm Dying to Try This Thing Anyway ... On Real Flesh!

"I hope you're looking after him, Marbel," said the prince to himself as his concern for Sarik grew.

The fog had somewhat dissipated, but vegetation on either side of the path concealed the tree trunks. He heard the murmur of water, and soon a crystal-clear creek was visible. The closer he got, the more frequent the footprints became.

Rats. Hordes of them.

Examining them up close, he noticed that the prints were fresh. He was unable to discern any human footprints among them.

He dipped his head in the cool water along with his hat then jumped in. Alert, he waded across the creek. At the opposite shore, he noticed a huge, round imprint left by some enormous, cloven-hoofed beast. It was covered in many rodent footprints. Caleem marched along the corresponding path. The bushes on either side began to close in on him; the denser they got, the more broken and trampled the bushes were.

Evening began to set on the mountain range. The sky turned darker while tiny drops of rain sprinkled the surrounding leaves.

A shriek made Caleem stop right in his tracks. Beyond the steady drizzle, he heard a commotion close by. *Maybe the rest were captured by those rodents.* Caleem resolved to run as fast as he could. He dashed toward the racket. Disturbing sounds of screaming and squeaking got closer with each step.

As Caleem stepped over a stone, he lost his footing and slipped. He fell, landing flat on his belly. In the twilight, through the bushes, he saw a multitude of raging rats. Some held bone-tipped spears, others dagger-like bones. They were ecstatic about whatever was trapped in their net and now hanging from the branches above.

Caleem drew his sword and unwrapped it, his eyes fixed on the net, which hung like a huge sack. He was about to lunge at the creatures but then he noticed the prey: they were not men, but giants. The two giants wore dark metal armor over their entire bodies. They hung upside down, squeezed together, their big hammers pressed against them. They thrashed their limbs, trying to break free.

Caleem observed from cover. The rats stabbed and beat them, not intending to kill but only to abuse. The rodents squeaked and squealed nonstop. One of them was taller and chubbier, with gooey saliva and mucus dripping from its mouth and nose, its left ear punctured with holes. It pointed in various directions as if doling out orders.

Two more rats appeared on the scene riding two bull-sized, eight-legged rats pulling a big wooden cart. To the prince they seemed like a cross between a spider and a gigantic rat. The creatures stopped near the net. The big rat screamed, and some of the rodents pushed the cart, aligning it under the net.

Through the net, a rat pulled the helmet off one of the giants, exposing a wide, orange face with small eyes, and big, flat nose. Recalling Zig's descriptions, Caleem could tell they were Guzuds.

A couple of rats climbed up a tree and chewed on the ropes

holding the net. It fell and crashed onto the big cart's platform. The rodents bound the Guzuds to the cart. Each time one of the giants moved, a rodent dealt him a blow to the head or stabbed him in a crack between his armor plates. The exhausted Guzuds eventually stopped offering any resistance and lay groaning side by side.

The riders of the eight-legged spider-rats spurred them on. The beasts pulled the oversized vehicle but barely moved it. The big, fat rat squealed, and some of the rodents got behind the cart and pushed.

The giants' whimpering echoed in the warrior's ears as the wagon started to move. The cart's wheels got stuck on the rocks. The fat rat screeched in rage, looking as if it were about to explode. It climbed onto the cart and stood on the helmet-less Guzud's chest then squeaked and stamped on the giant's face. This brutal act galvanized the rats into action. They pushed harder, freeing the cart from the obstacle, and the bizarre procession continued under the trees. The leading rat continued abusing the hapless Guzuds, who howled in pain, and this drove the horde of rodents into a mad frenzy.

Caleem stepped out of the brush, unwrapping the cloth around his sword. "Filthy freaks. I'm dying to try this thing anyway … on real flesh!"

He looked at the mysterious engravings etched along the silver-blue blade. Then the prince took a deep breath, gripped the hilt with both hands, and charged.

A rat that lagged behind heard his footsteps. It turned around and shrieked.

Its peers, recognizing the threat, readied their spears and knives. Squeaking, the rodents hurled themselves at the warrior. The leading rat saw what was happening and urged the riders to go faster.

Caleem charged straight ahead, undeterred by their screams and repugnant looks. An instant before colliding with them, he swung the sword. The blade struck the side of the closest rat.

To Caleem's amazement, the blade exited its body only to hit another rodent. The blade then cut the second one in half and, of its own volition, it then slashed a third one as if it were cutting through nothing. The blade continued on.

For a split second, all the victims' body parts remained hovering in place until they collapsed into horrific lumps. With a single swing, Caleem had six rats lying at his feet in a long, hideous mess. Although the sword had only grazed its belly, a seventh rat lay on the ground, its face twisted with pain. The sight did not deter an attacking rat, who lunged at Caleem's face with a sharp bone. Caleem dodged, and the bone scraped the tip of his ear. He grabbed the back of the rat's long, furry neck and pulled it toward his blade, slicing it in half.

The other rodents scampered in a panic around the cart as it careened down the path, trampling everything that stood in its way. The large, fat rat, still jumping on the Guzud while screaming out orders, glanced at the fierce warrior, whose long blade had turned red.

Caleem looked at the blade with awe; blood was gliding down to his hands and then dripping from the edge of its hilt. The squeaking brought him back to reality.

He was surrounded.

The rats were closing in on him. With a quick swing, Caleem dismembered the four closest to him. Out of the corner of his eye, he glimpsed one coming from behind. The warrior thrust his left elbow backward, surprising the attacker, who held a knife in both hands high above its head. The powerful blow crushed the creature's chest, sending it reeling to the ground. The rats facing Caleem recoiled.

The bouncing cart rolled under the trees.

The warrior dashed forward, passing the hesitating rats in favor of the vehicle. Caleem jumped up and stood on one Guzuds's armor. The cart jolted. The fat rat fled to one of the corners.

Caleem glanced at the dozens of rodents running around

the cart, their bulging, black eyes fixed on him. Some began to climb onto the cart from the rear and front.

A sharp pain shot through Caleem's foot. He tried to pull it back, but it was trapped between a rat's grubby teeth. The creature gnawed on his boot while pulling and slashing at it. The prince lost his balance and fell back onto the platform beside the Guzuds. His leg was still trapped in the rat's bite, causing him excruciating pain. Rats were coming in from all directions. The jerking motion made it impossible for him to get back on his feet. He tried to stand yet fell once again, but this time he lost his grip on the hilt and the sword lurched to the edge of the cart, almost falling.

Caleem leaned back. Without even seeing it, he kicked the head of the rat biting his foot until its skull cracked. The rodent went limp and fell under the cart's wheels. Another pair of rodents lunged at him. Caleem kicked one off, but the other landed right on top of him, going for his face. Revolted by the rat's saliva dripping on him, Caleem finally managed to wrestle himself free and tumble toward the sword. He rolled over the Guzud's armor and snatched his weapon's hilt with his fingertips. He swung the sword as he rose, hacking at the rats lunging at him, while glancing at the fat rat fleeing to the other end of the vehicle. The prince sprung in its direction, ignoring the waves of pain from his wounded foot. He decapitated the few rats trying to block his way with two neat strokes of the steel.

The rat leader turned to jump off.

Caleem drove the sword deep into its back and pulled it toward him by its moist fur. As the creature slid on the blade, it uttered a few choking cries, thrashing its tail, until it fell limp. Like a madman, Caleem cursed and punched the dead rodent.

The remaining rats fled in all directions.

Caleem didn't stop his attack until he was certain not a single rat was left in sight. Soon, the only noise he heard was that of the rolling wheels. Caleem withdrew the sword and kicked the fat rat's corpse off the cart. He cut the spider-rats free, and the odd creatures ran away, still tied to each other, and disappeared down the path.

The cart stopped. There was no other sound apart from Caleem's breathing and heartbeat. He remained alert, relaxing ever so slowly.

Only then did he notice it was still drizzling.

Chapter 27
Me, You, Friends

Night drew nearer. A shiver went through Caleem's body. Incredulous, the warrior stared at the blood-red blade. Still, he couldn't fathom how this weapon would *bring about the doom of the Dalusians*, as his father had said. He figured there was more to this mysterious blade.

A sound of clanking iron came from the cart. The giants were trying without much success to wiggle their way out of their bindings. Caleem got on board again and cut through the net. Stepping off, he winced at the throbbing pain in his foot. The battered giants threw the pieces of torn net into the mud as they climbed down. The one wearing the helmet untied his hammer from the cart, and the other stood silently in front of the prince.

Sword in hand, Caleem remained alert. The Guzud flung the hammer onto his shoulder and stood next to his friend, facing the little warrior. "Indeed, big you are … I am friend. Me, you, friends," Caleem said.

The giants stared back.

Caleem planted the long sword into the ground. "Me, you, help. And you, me, help." He pointed at them and then at himself. Pressing his palms together, he said, "Friends. We'll be friends."

The Guzuds looked at each other, exchanged a few grunts, then nodded.

"Good," said Caleem.

They nodded again, and Caleem laughed, taking a couple of steps forward. He extended his hand in a welcoming gesture. One Guzud scratched his orange head, and then he, too, extended his gigantic, three-fingered hand. Caleem smiled yet stayed near the sword. The Guzud came closer. The warrior, intimidated by the creature's size, stood his ground, his hand still outstretched. The giant lowered his hand toward Caleem's. The Guzud dropped his hand to the ground then yanked it away. The motion was so fast that Caleem had no chance to react. He had been standing on a piece of net buried in the mud, which the giant pulled from under his feet. He flew up in the air, tumbled, and finally landed flat on his back.

The Guzud lifted the hammer high over his head and smashed down. Caleem rolled but felt the hammer crush the ground right next to him and splash mud everywhere. His sword was a few steps away, and he sprung for it. A giant hoof slammed into his back and sent him flying past the sword. He rolled and hit a tree. Dizzy, he jumped back to his feet, covered in mud. The giants ran straight at him, one ready to strike with the hammer again.

"Ungrateful beasts," he said and vanished behind the tree.

The Guzuds ran around the tree from either side, but all they did was bump into one another. They looked around, trying to figure out where the little warrior had disappeared to. After exchanging looks, they saw Caleem in the clearing, strolling toward his sword. The Guzuds charged.

Caleem stood with his back to them, his hands on the hilt. He glimpsed back to see one of them already taking aim with the hammer but held his ground.

The Guzud lifted his hammer, ready to slam it down. Caleem pulled up the sword and, quick as lightning, stepped to the side. The hammer hit the muddy ground and sank in. The Guzud didn't even notice the warrior had dodged. Splattered in mud, Caleem jumped up to stand on top of the hammer and raised his sword above the giant's head.

He met the giant's gaze for a moment. The Guzud began to lift his hammer. Caleem struck right between the shoulder and the neck of the giant's armor. The sword sliced the metal. Caleem was amazed, unable to comprehend the ease with which he had accomplished such a feat. Once the blade had reached the center of the Guzud's chest, Caleem pulled it out. The hammer fell back into the mud, and the Guzud groaned, blood gushing out of his armor. Caleem jumped off the hammer's head and stepped away as the giant fell dead on his face.

The remaining opponent stood eyeing the bloody blade. The Guzud recoiled, bellowing as his heavy hooves carried him toward the cart. Finding the second hammer, he picked it up, throwing away the bits of net and rope still stuck to it, and returned to face the prince.

Caleem lunged, screaming like a madman, but stopped midway, startling the Guzud, who then stumbled backward. Caleem chuckled. "Afraid of small Caleem? Rightly so. You are going to die now, ungrateful cow." He lowered the sword as he jumped left and right in a playful manner.

As the prince got closer, the Guzud flung the hammer at him. The warrior dodged, letting the huge hammer fly past. His arms extended, the Guzud charged. Caleem aimed the tip of the sword at the center of the giant's chest. As the Guzud closed the distance, Caleem sprang against him. The sword pierced through the breastplate, gliding in, and its tip shot out the victim's back. This didn't stop the giant's momentum. Caleem found himself suspended in the air, holding on to the hilt. The giant tried to grab the swinging soldier, but he began to falter. The blade slid out of the collapsing giant's torso, and Caleem fell to the ground. Roaring in agony, the Guzud fell to his knees. Caleem rolled and bounced back to his feet, poised for another round. But the Guzud's groans had ceased, and he fell facedown on the ground.

After the intense fight with the rats and then the Guzuds, it took Caleem a few minutes to wind down, and he let out the last of his tension with a long sigh.

"What was all that racket?" asked the book, startling the prince. "Is it raining? It's wet in here."

"It's my sweat," said Caleem.

"Eww! Get me out of here," said the book in his pocket.

Slinging the sword over his shoulder, he came closer to one of the dead Guzuds. Upon closer inspection, Caleem was intrigued by the black armor's plates, which covered the body from head to toe. "This craft is familiar," he said as he felt the cold metal plates.

"What craft?" asked the book.

"This armor."

"What armor?"

Caleem didn't answer. He tapped the book as he gazed at the sky, hoping the stars would show him the way. But they were all hidden behind a curtain of clouds.

Slouched and limping, the warrior still carried on, making his way between the rocks and bushes, trying to leave as few tracks as possible. His injured foot made it hard for him to walk. The ascent uphill turned into a strenuous climb. His energy waned until he couldn't push his exhausted body any longer, and he slipped off a rock. His limbs refused to move, and he couldn't get his eyelids to open.

The book mumbled some words in a protest, but Caleem plunged into a slumber.

Rambling for hours, he tossed and turned on his bed of bushes.

Caleem opened his eyes. It took him a few moments to recognize the incessant, rambling voice. Sitting up, he noticed he was gripping the hilt of the sword, which was drawn from its sheath. He leaned back, still dazed, trying to relax.

"… behind a rock. We walked along the shore, the master said—"

"Shut up," said Caleem. The book stopped talking.

The morning fog was dissipating, revealing the snowy ridgeline of the mighty range rising up into the clouds. He stood and wiggled and stomped his foot a few times; the stinging pain was almost gone.

"Can I ask you something?" said the book.

Caleem didn't answer.

"When do you think we'll be back at the Allmother? If you just say the word 'Allmother', I will get you there, through a shortcut with stunning views …"

CHAPTER 28
I HAVE TO CONTINUE MY TASK

Another look at the great mountain range killed the prince's hopes. But then he spotted the strange, winged creature he'd seen a day before circling the sky just north of him, as if searching for something. Caleem climbed up the nearest tree to get a better look, and the big creature began to descend. As he watched it swooping down in circles, a crazy idea popped into his mind. He jumped off the tree and raced in the creature's direction.

"What's happening? Why is everything shaking?" asked the book.

"There's a giant bird over there," said the warrior as he sped downhill.

"It could be dangerous. Run, foreigner, run!"

"First, we get closer. Then we mount it …" Caleem said in between gasps.

"No! Run away! That's a bad idea."

"After we catch it—excuse me, after *I* catch it, since you're useless—I will make it fly over this damn mountain."

The book continued to complain until it eventually gave up.

The warrior ran, trying not to lose sight of the creature as it glided in and out of the fog.

"I have to continue my task at any cost," he said, "maybe even at the expense of Sarik's life."

"What task? Who is Sarik?"

After reaching a hilltop, he gazed at the sky but was unable to find the flying creature. Hastening his pace, he faltered down into the dense vegetation; his only concern was locating the bird.

"This morning, you said something about taking a sword to some river … Are we going there?"

Caleem's steps slowed down. "I was probably sleep babbling … I have no idea what you're talking about."

"Maybe it's better just to let the bird roam the sky."

"When I'm done, I guarantee you that with my own hands I will return you to the library. Or … throw you into a pit of fire. It's going to be one or the other."

"Maybe it's better if I keep quiet."

The elusive bird was nowhere in sight. Weary and frustrated, the prince slowed down. As he plowed through a large bush, he glimpsed a shadow flashing by on the canopy. The huge bird circled above him and then descended into the fog nearby.

The warrior dashed forward.

"What's happening?" asked the book.

"Shut up. We're close to it. Don't utter a word!" Caleem ran up the hill to where the vegetation was scarcer. He inched forward, scanning the bushes before him. Voices came from behind the trees, and the prince stopped to listen. "Could it be …?"

He continued in silence and got close enough to distinguish a cacophony of agitated shouting. As he emerged from behind one of the bushes, he discerned a strange, dark figure moving about a hundred paces away. It seemed alert and interested in the noisy commotion. Caleem moved faster, his footsteps drowned out by the shouting.

Elated, he recognized Marbel's voice.

The mysterious figure was a two-legged creature, its dark-brown body striped with a lighter brown. The huge hump on its back was its folded wings. Just like Caleem, the giant, winged, demon-like figure had also taken cover behind a tree and was peering in the direction of the noise.

Why is it spying on them?

He moved towards the winged being and felt for his sword. *It can tell me nothing if it's dead.* He released the hilt.

Close now, the prince was ready to pounce on the creature with his bare hands. He took a deep breath.

"Why is it so quiet? What's happening?" the book asked from inside his pocket.

The creature turned. Caleem froze, gazing into a pair of yellow eyes framed by a lustrous, brown head. The creature opened its toothless mouth to reveal a long, pointed tongue and hissed.

Caleem lunged at its head, only then realizing that it was topped by four twisted horns. The demon caught Caleem in midair then slammed him to the ground. The creature gave him one last glance and jumped into the air, spreading its enormous, bat-like wings to soar through the branches. It disappeared into the fog before Caleem could even move.

He stood and gazed up, but the demon was gone. Caleem kicked a bush in frustration, pulling out the book. "I hope you burn!" he said, slamming it to the ground. "If it weren't for your big mouth, I would have caught it."

He left the impertinent nuisance and didn't look back.

CHAPTER 29
WHAT SCHEME?

By the tone, it sounded more to the prince like a heated argument than anything else.

"So much noise in this dangerous, abominable place …" said the warrior as he raced forward.

He skipped over the bushes and came into full view of the group. The boys and the tracker were standing to one side, and Kamanar, his sword drawn, was looming over Sarik, who was on the ground. A distressed Marbel, with his palms pressed together, looked like he was pleading for Kamanar to stop.

"Caleem!" said Marbel.

Without a second's hesitation, the prince charged at Kamanar. The latter swung his sword at Sarik, who lay at his feet. A moment before the sword touched its victim, Caleem crashed into Kamanar, knocking the sword from his hand. The two fell to ground, Caleem on top, his hands griping Kamanar's neck.

The rest stood around the fighting duo, unsure of what to do.

"You've brought this on yourself," said Caleem as he squeezed with all his might.

Kamanar tried to escape, thrashing with his fists, but with no success.

Caleem looked straight into Kamanar's eyes, watching as they rolled back. "Die!"

Marbel tapped the prince on the back. "Caleem, what are you doing?"

He received no answer. The prince pressed on, choking Kamanar.

"Please …" said Marbel.

Naji threw himself at Caleem and grasped the man's head together with the hilt of the sword on his back, its edge scraping the ground. "Let him go!" the boy shouted and bit Caleem's ear. The prince refused to let go. Kamanar was no longer offering any resistance, and his body went limp.

Letting out a muffled cry, Naji bit harder and drew his head back, tearing off a piece of Caleem's ear. Caleem released his hold and pushed the boy away. Groaning in pain, he covered the bleeding ear with his hands.

With great effort, Kamanar managed to roll from under Caleem. Coughing and gasping, he pushed down on his arms to get up. Caleem picked up Kamanar's sword and attacked again.

"Caleem, stop! Get a hold of yourself," said Marbel, positioning himself in between the two.

"Get a hold of myself? This man has no honor. He took on this quest only as a personal vendetta. You've disgraced yourself, your family, your rank, and everyone else here!" After shoving Marbel aside, he pounced on Kamanar again.

Kamanar clutched the prince's hands to divert the sword's tip then rammed Caleem in the face with his forehead. The prince fell on his back, the sword still in his hand.

"I've had it with you," shouted Kamanar raspily. Looming over Caleem, he stepped on the arm holding the sword. When Caleem tried to rise, Kamanar kicked him in the face, sending him rolling. His nose and mouth bleeding, Caleem forced himself back up. Kamanar picked up his fallen weapon while Caleem drew the long sword from its sheath.

"This is unbelievable," said Marbel.

He again stepped in between the two men, gesturing for them to stop. "Stop, right now. Just stop!"

The two halted.

"What do you think you're doing, Marbel? Get out of my way!" said Caleem while he wiped the blood from his nose. The chubby man stood his ground.

"Marbel, step aside," said Kamanar. "This needs to be settled, once and for all." He glared at Sarik. As he tightened his grip on the weapon, his steely eyes returned to Caleem.

Marbel turned to Kamanar. "What is *this*? What needs to be settled? I won't allow you to bring disaster on us all. Look at yourselves." He shifted his eyes from one man to the other. "In a lifetime of serving the king, I've never witnessed such behavior. A duel between two senior officers … Instead of leading and setting the example."

"That's where you're wrong, Marbel," said Kamanar. "Even if he is the prince, there is only one leader, one commander here, appointed by the king himself, and that's me."

"You are not worthy. I don't care if God himself appointed you," said Caleem.

"You think you are so important, high above humanity. You can't follow orders from the likes of me. You disgust me, Prince!" Kamanar took a step toward Caleem.

"Kamanar, stop!" Marbel was ready to push him back.

"I must say, I'm impressed with your deceptive ways. Despite your scheme, you managed to keep up a friendly facade. Beware of this hypocrite, men," said the prince.

"What scheme? What are you talking about?" Marbel asked. "What's going on between you three? It has been a burden on all of us from the beginning of this journey. In the end, it will bring about our doom."

"Ask your commander why he really wants Sarik dead."

All eyes turned to Kamanar.

"Sarik is a traitor, a Khandalus. It's because of his doing that we walked into the Dalusians' ambush," said Kamanar.

Sarik stood by, taking in each word but offered nothing.

Kamanar went on. "I suspected him from the very beginning.

And just now, my suspicions were confirmed. When I told you I was going away to seek the trail, I was in fact hiding behind those bushes. I was keeping an eye on this devious Khandalus.

"When it was his time to stand watch, you, Marbel, trusted him, though I had warned you not to. He walked to a clearing farther down, unaware that I was following him. He whistled a strange, repetitive call. A raven appeared out of nowhere and landed on his shoulder. He petted the bird and gave it something, then it flew away. You gave away our location, again! Didn't you? You dirty Khandalus!"

"A raven?" Caleem laughed. "This is so amusing … You're quite a storyteller. Has anyone seen this raven?" The prince turned to the others, but no answer came. "Ah, yes—they were asleep, or maybe busy dancing."

"You're calling me a liar?" asked Kamanar.

The prince tossed his sword from hand to hand in a playful manner. "Why don't you tell them about the girl? About your true motive? They deserve to know."

The commander seemed taken aback. For the first time, the men saw their leader falter as he failed to conceal his troubled expression.

Caleem fixed the tip of his sword in the ground and leaned on the hilt. Marbel lowered his arms, backing up a step to stand beside Caleem, and stared at Kamanar.

"There is no girl," said Kamanar.

"I will spare us all this pointless argument. Your commander desires my sister, Naiya."

"What are you blabbering about? What was between us ended a long time ago."

"Everyone knows that you still want her. Now, what exactly does that have to do with the matter at hand? Naiya, my sister, used to suffer from long bouts of depression, keeping to her room for days on end. Though Naiya and I were close, in recent years I haven't exactly been the best soulmate for her. Everything changed the day she met Sarik. In his gentle way, this man pulled her out of the gloom, returning a smile to her face. Obviously, they have kept this a secret, even from me. Who would allow a princess to marry a common soldier? Certainly not my father."

"If you're hinting that I'm jealous of this traitor, you are truly insane."

"Do you deny that you still have feelings for my sister?"

"It's a natural thing. I still care for her, but not in that way."

"What about Sarik? Did you know about him and Naiya?"

"I knew."

"There you are. This man, with the consent of my father, plotted for Sarik to go on this mission so that he could make sure Sarik didn't come back. Then my sister would have no choice but to go back to him."

"What? That's nonsense."

"So please explain, if you'd be so kind, why on earth, out of all the Mellethyan army, did you choose Sarik?"

"Supposedly, he is the best archer. Your father chose him for this mission, not me. You should ask him this question. If I wanted him dead, he would have been dead long ago. I don't need an excuse."

"Yes, you could have easily killed him, but what would you have told poor Naiya afterward? You needed a convincing story—you thought it through. As soon as Sarik went to pee behind a bush, you'd blame him for planning a second ambush—how very convenient. You'd pin this whole fabrication of treason on him by proving it with an implausible story about a raven! Which none other than you saw. You'd kill the man, blacken his name, and end up a hero. By the way, that's why you needed Zig … as a substitute archer! When you get back, you make amends with Naiya and, with my father's blessings, take her hand in marriage. My sister may be naive in many ways, but she is far from stupid."

"How would she—?" Marbel blurted out then covered his mouth with his hand.

"Do you know how I know she isn't naive, Marbel?"

"No," said Marbel, his hand still covering his mouth.

"Because she asked me to watch over Sarik. She wanted me to protect him from you, Kamanar. Not from Guzuds, not from Dalusians, from *you*."

"What?" asked Kamanar.

Motehro interrupted. Mumbling gibberish, he pointed at something behind the brush as he scanned the area.

A rustle came from the bushes near Marbel. "Something's moving behind there," said the chubby man.

"She deemed it necessary to warn me. She suspected it might be part of a scheme when she heard Sarik was recruited to this mission," said Caleem as he, too, became alert.

Kamanar shook his head. "How did you come up with this fantasy? Long after our relationship ended, I was always a friend to your sister, someone she could rely on like a big brother. I was there when she needed me, unlike you."

"We had an older brother who could never be replaced. Not even by the likes of you!"

The rustling now came from every direction, along with the creaking sounds of tightening ropes.

"With all this bickering, every single creature on this mountain has heard us," said the prince.

"What are these things?" asked Marbel, trying to recognize the figures moving in the bushes.

"A tail! I saw a tail!" Zig shouted, pointing.

"Rats," said Caleem. "Hordes of them."

CHAPTER 30
RATS

"Rats?" asked Marbel.

"Very big ones, and not very friendly," Caleem said and raised his sword. "Form a point of defense. Stand back to back!"

Arming himself with an arrow from the quiver, Marbel manned the position behind Caleem. Also grabbing an arrow, Motehro joined in and shifted the arrow from hand to hand. Sarik stooped to pick up his bow, but a furry paw shot out from the bushes and snatched his weapon from under his nose. Startled, he moved back to his friends. The boys remained in place, glancing around nervously.

A huge rodent dashed across the clearing holding a net. The net's edge snagged on some invisible branches inside the vegetation, forcing the grubby creature to a halt beside the party. The men scrutinized the almost human-sized rodent standing upright on its hind legs and covered in repugnant gray fur. The rat seemed to be just as anxious, squeaking while it tugged frantically on the net. Another appeared and they tugged together until the net came loose with the sound of a snapping branch. The rodents went about their tasks, latching the nets to the surrounding trees, creating a tall, circular, weblike trap around the men.

"Kamanar!" Marbel yelled, but the latter didn't budge.

By the intensity of the squeaking and the movements behind

the bushes, they inferred that there were many more rodents around. Rats armed with sharp bones and spears scaled over the nets in droves and spilled into the enclosure.

With no visible escape route, the men stood still, terrified by the revolting sight of the giant, drooling rodents. Their big, bulging, black eyes relished their prey. Kamanar had yet to say a word.

"Don't worry. They're not as terrible as they look," said Caleem. "Sarik, you and Motehro watch our backs. Marbel, stand there by the bush. I'll take the front."

The boys huddled close to Kamanar for protection. Naji gave Zig an arrow from his quiver. Zig's shot was weak, landing at one rat's feet.

Noticing the fallen arrow, Caleem shook his head at the boy. He then shot a scornful glance at Kamanar.

"Drop your weapons!" Kamanar ordered, breaking his silence, and laid his sword on the ground.

"Your commander has lost his nerve," said Caleem.

"Kamanar, what are you doing?" asked Marbel, his eyes alternating between his commander and the rats.

"You heard me. Put that arrow down. You, too, Motehro."

The tracker set the arrow down. Marbel was reluctant but obeyed as well. Zig dropped his bow to the ground next to Kamanar's sword.

Caleem shouted, "Pick it up, Marbel. You, too, Motehro—pick up that arrow! It's clear that our commander has lost it. Ignore him. We can win this."

Marbel picked his arrow back up with a menacing motion, ready to stab the first creature who dared come close. The tracker became tense again, muttering his gibberish while he recovered the arrow.

Caleem let out a battle cry, charging ahead with the long sword. He stumbled and fell. Looking behind, he was astonished to discover it was Kamanar's foot he'd tripped on. "You bastard!" he screamed, but before he could get up, a group of rats lunged at him. One of them bit the hand that held the sword while another one snatched the weapon away.

"Kamanar, why? Haven't we had enough for one day?" asked Marbel.

"Marbel, you must trust me, as you have until now."

"Don't listen to him!" screamed Caleem, still struggling with the rats, which had multiplied tenfold. "We can take them on."

Before Marbel could do anything, a rat sneaked up from behind and hit him on the head with a large bone. Clutching the back of his head, Marbel fell to his knees. The rodents jumped on him and pinned him down while tying his hands.

The tracker stood next to Kamanar. Dropping his arrow, he raised his arms in surrender.

"Kamanar, what do we do?" asked Naji, remaining close to Zig. Both were terrified.

"Don't worry. Let them tie you up," said Kamanar in a calm tone.

Reluctantly and with eyes shut, the boys and the tracker extended their hands. The rats were quick to bind all their captives, forcing them to the ground.

Sarik jumped on the net and climbed. Several rats sitting at the top of the net emitting horrible squeaking noises began swatting at him and gnashing their teeth. The archer stabbed left and right with his arrow and managed to slip from the rodents, hurling himself to the other side of the encircling net.

"Run!" screamed Caleem.

Sarik looked at his friends and stood his ground, ignoring the hysterical rodents around him. A rat lunged at the young soldier, but Sarik jammed his arrow in its head and pushed it away. He climbed the net and jumped back in the enclosure.

"Why?" asked Caleem, who was buried under a furry mass of rodents.

"I will not make that mistake again," said Sarik. He was pushed to the ground, his hands and legs bound in a moment.

Marbel's head ached as he regained his senses. Caleem

struggled to break free from his bonds. The prince cursed, Kamanar being the main target of his obscenities.

"I'm sorry," Marbel said to Caleem, who now lay on his belly beside him. He was still cursing and spitting, not bothering to respond.

The men were heaved onto three small wooden carts. Caleem and Marbel were loaded side by side on the first cart, and Sarik and the boys were dumped on the second one, arranged in a messy pile, one on top of the other. Kamanar and Motehro were loaded on last. The huge, eight-legged spider-rats towed the vehicles.

The grotesque convoy rolled into the trees while hordes of rats paraded behind, some taking excited peeks at the captives as they squealed in delight.

"Damn you! And damn my father for appointing you commander," said Caleem, still fighting to break free but surrounded by rats who beat him with their blunt bones.

Kamanar said nothing and neither did the others. All they could do was lie still.

The first stars began to appear in the night sky. Reddish leaves glided down onto their faces as they pondered their fate.

CHAPTER 31
FAULTY QUEST

The party members avoided looking at their captors' grisly faces as much as possible while they were taunted and abused. This continued until a more imposing rat curbed the others' behavior. This particular rodent was different: its strong arms were attached to broad shoulders and its body was structured more like a human's. It walked upright, whereas its peers were hunched, their narrow shoulders almost clamped together.

The carts traversed a bumpy, narrow path deeper into the forest. Their progress was hindered by rocks, thick branches, and bushes. The vegetation became so dense that the captives felt leaves brushing their faces.

"I'm sorry," Marbel said, not really expecting an answer as he raised his eyes to a shining star.

"Your commander lost it. He cannot bear the burden of this mission anymore," Caleem whispered, his breath hot in Marbel's ear.

The prince's brown eyes reflected the faint starlight as the old man replied, "I can't say I understand Kamanar's actions. Nevertheless, he did bring us this far."

"This far? Look at us! We're probably being dragged to our doom. Where did he bring us? Straight into the Dalusian ambush!

Then to be trapped by the Guzuds, from whom we escaped only thanks to the boy and you. He was quick to leave me behind, knowing that I would get in the way of his scheme. He lost the sword in the thicket, and now, this rat nonsense … We could have overpowered them, you know.

"And that's not all. Do you know how I found you? I followed a diabolical-looking winged creature that was tracking you without your glorious commander even noticing. He was too busy carrying out his sleazy plot."

Marbel wanted to keep his thoughts to himself, but he felt Caleem's pressure for a response. After some uneasy pondering, he shook his numb limbs. "I have to agree with you. I never saw it that way."

"Then you won't doubt me next time?"

"If there is a next time."

"I'm going to lead the team from now on, with you at my side, like old times."

"I wonder where these filthy creatures are taking us." The older man peered at the rodents surrounding the cart.

"You're avoiding me."

"Caleem, please hear me out. For many years I've been alternating between the infantry and farming, trying to provide for my family. I'm just a simple soldier, you see. Kamanar is my commander, appointed by your father, the king. I only obey. I'm not allowed to choose or think. I must stay loyal at all costs."

"I know that, my friend. I simply need you by my side. Someone I can trust when things get rough. That's why I wanted you to join."

"I know you chose me for this mission, not Kamanar or your father. If we survive this, I only request that this be my last one. I'm too old for this sort of thing."

"What? Are you joking? Marbel, the veteran, is not up to the challenge?"

"I've changed. Since becoming a family man, my priorities have changed. It's not all or nothing anymore. I stopped taking chances. I learned to settle for less. But still, there's a reason why I *gladly* joined."

"What was it?"

"I have a son in the Black Company. I miss him very much."

"You are likely enormously proud."

"And … Nothing."

"Marbel, this faulty quest, it's all Kamanar's doing. Once I get us out of this predicament, I will take command, and then it will be steady all the way."

The older warrior's lips twisted in a sardonic smile. "Some aches can be shared only with those who have suffered the same kind," he whispered to himself and sighed. "This winged creature you saw, of what manner was it?"

The conversation was interrupted by a sharp jolt and panic-stricken rats shrieking. The cart began to accelerate downhill.

"What's going on?" yelled Marbel. He lifted his head and looked around, but all he could make out was the tumbling silhouette of a giant spider-rat.

"It broke loose from the harness!" said the prince, his voice shaking with the vibration of the speeding vehicle.

The cart continued to accelerate, and Marbel ground his teeth as he closed his eyes and waited for the inevitable crash.

The rats' screams faded out. The cart rolled, jouncing, about to come apart. The two men felt as though they were being hammered by an army of blacksmiths.

"This … our chance … Marbel … be … charge … after—" Caleem's speech ended with a final jolt.

***

"Wake up already," urged a pleasant voice. "Come on, get up. I already milked Jasmine so that you could have your rest, but that's enough."

Marbel lifted his heavy body and sat up. He surveyed the room until his gaze rested on his wife, Malika, and his face softened into a grin.

"Why are you looking at me like that?"

Marbel smiled, jumped out of his bed, and ran to his startled wife, whose first reaction was to warn him with the empty frying pan she was holding. Undeterred, he hugged her hard then lifted her up into the air and spun her around the cabin.

"Put me down, you madman!" Malika yelled, smiling.

Marbel lowered the petite woman to the bed and stroked her hair. He looked into her huge, bright eyes as his hand slid down her velvety cheek, widening the joyful smile on her tiny face.

"What's come over you?" she asked.

"Nothing. All is well. Even great ... Just perfect."

"Good. Last night, you didn't stop tossing and turning. You were sweating, too."

"I had a dream, a nightmare. I was out on a stupid mission with some crazy men. Absolutely everything went wrong. I don't remember too much."

"It's time to come back to the real world. Take the broom and sweep the front of the house. The cow left a mess over there. Then move the bales to the barn."

"What's that smell?" Marbel sniffed around the cabin.

"First get to work. Think about that belly of yours later," Malika said and lightly punched her husband in the stomach.

Marbel sprung up and planted a quick kiss on Malika's lips. He stretched and washed his face in a blue-and-white porcelain bowl. While he stood by the fireplace, he reveled in the enticing aroma of fried cheese bubbling in a pan over hot coals.

"It's great to be home." He snatched up a broom and skipped toward the door.

His wife, still puzzled, put her hands on her hips and laughed at her husband's unusual behavior. Marbel went outside, but not before blowing a kiss to his giggling wife.

Whistling the tune of a popular folk song, Marbel swept the cow dung away. When he was done dancing with the broom, he proceeded to move the bales one by one from the far end of the field into the barn. Once his chores had been completed, he hurried back to the cabin. Hani and Nola, his daughters, had set a table brimming with a variety of foods including his favorite fried cheese on a platter at the center. However, Marbel's attention was not focused on the food but on the two little girls, who sat next to each other and gazed at their father.

"Daddy, Daddy," they called.

Marbel ruffled their adorable curls. He seated them on his lap as they hugged and kissed him back. He wanted to caress their cute little heads, but his movements became sluggish, as if heavy stones had been attached to his limbs.

His legs wouldn't budge as if they were anchored to the ground. He tried to fight whatever it was that was happening to him. His wife and children's images faded away. Marbel screamed, reaching for them.

CHAPTER 32
THEY'VE GRILLED THEM!

The chubby man opened his eyes and gaped at the ceiling, which was not the wooden roof of his house but a dark, stony surface.

"Calm down," a familiar, echoing voice said.

Marbel saw the prince's stern face close to his.

"Caleem, what are you doing here?"

"You lost consciousness after we crashed into a tree. How are you now?"

"I can't move."

"We are bound together."

"I'm all right. My whole body hurts, but other than that I'm fine. Where are we? I hear dripping. Are we in a cave?"

"While you were passed out, you were smiling. You drooled all over my face. I suppose you were dreaming of food."

"Something like that. How did we get here? The rats?"

"Yes, them."

"What about the others?"

"I don't know. Somewhere in this cave. It's bigger than you might think."

"Somebody's cooking—smells good."

"It does … smells like roasting."

"I wouldn't mind a piece. I'm so hungry and so tired … and thirsty."

"Listen, Marbel. There's a puddle close to our feet. Let's try it."

Pushing and pulling, shuffling and huffing, they began to turn despite the painful bindings.

"Now I know how it is to be a worm," said Marbel.

"Let's work in coordination."

Using all the energy they had left, the two friends persevered until they could dip their sweaty faces in the puddle.

Caleem slurped, taking in a few labored gulps. "A bit muddy, but one can drink it," he said, then drank some more, spitting mud over Marbel's shoulder.

Marbel vacillated for an instant before deciding that if the prince could stomach it, then he could, too. Grimacing at the taste, he filled his mouth with the vile, muddy water.

Caleem saw the expression on Marbel's face and burst out laughing, spraying water all over his friend. Marbel, with his eyes shut, wrinkled his face in disgust, which delighted Caleem even more.

"Very funny," said Marbel before joining in with the hysterical laughter. They both laughed like lunatics, forgetting all about the rats and their precarious condition. Peals of laughter echoed inside the cave, and only when the men ran out of breath did the convulsions finally subside.

"That was liberating," said Marbel, grinning.

They heard clawed feet tapping on stone coming towards them. Seconds later, dark, squeaking figures besieged them. One of the creatures began to sever the bindings with a sharpened bone, while others began tugging and pushing them.

"Ugly mice, what are you doing?" asked Caleem.

Before they knew what was happening, they had been separated, yet each was still bound. Only their legs remained free.

Marbel gagged in revulsion at the paws shoving and tugging his body. "Don't touch me, you …"

The rodents' squeaks became louder as they kicked the defenseless men. "I think they want us to get up," said Marbel. The two stood up.

Caleem kicked the rodent nearest to him in the back, hurling the rats against the rock wall. "Kick 'em, Marbel! Kick 'em!"

Marbel did as he was told, kicking in the darkness. The men ended up kicking each other and the walls, unable to hit any of their aggressors, who dodged their swinging legs with ease.

"I can't see a thing. Damn you, ugly abominations. Where are you?" shouted Caleem. He continued to kick at the impenetrable darkness until he hit a bulging rock, lost his footing, and fell to the ground with a thud. In an instant, the rats lunged at him, pummeled him with their fists and claws, and tied his legs up. A bone hit Marbel's knees and knocked him down. The rats continued to beat him, leaving him prostrate, his legs tightly bound.

The rodents hitched them to a rope and pulled them across the rocky surface of the cave floor.

"Maybe that wasn't such a good idea … I think they just wanted us to walk with them." Marbel let out a moan as his head hit a stone. The soldiers' bodies jittered as they slid along the rocky floor, crossing the occasional puddle. The cave got brighter, showing stalactites hanging from the high ceiling. Caleem tried to look ahead, but it wasn't easy. Two torches burned, one on each side, making the hideous rats more visible. Hordes of rats gathered around the men, squeaking to each other and kicking their prisoners from time to time for no particular reason.

"I'll rip your tail off and then hang you with it!" Caleem raged.

The towing continued and they reached a large, well-lit cavern with several tunnels diverging from it. As they entered, the smell of grilled meat became stronger, overpowering the rotten stench.

"Caleem!" Marbel shouted, while dodging the bumps on the ground. "This smell … I overheard Gudjewkan telling Kamanar how these wicked creatures roast their prey alive! This smell could be our friends' roasted flesh!"

"What? Maybe he was joking."

"Gudjewkan does not joke."

The rodents halted and began a squeaky conversation.

Caleem and Marbel sat up and took in their surroundings, unconcerned with the bruises and gashes covering their battered bodies. They found themselves at the entrance of an enormous hall that looked like an enclosed coliseum. Numerous ladders made of wood and bones were set between the hall's various levels, each of which hosted holes and tunnels that led deep into the mountain.

Hordes of rats swarmed everywhere, in constant motion, crawling in and out of the tunnels, climbing up and down the many ladders. Beams of sunlight breaking through the ceiling illuminated columns of rising smoke. At the far end of the hall dangled a few cages. Closer to them was a round platform on which several small fires were burning. Involuntary, the smoky smell of meat made the hungry men's mouths water.

They exchanged glances of disbelief.

"I really hope this isn't our buddies we're smelling," said Marbel.

The two peered down. In between the columns of smoke, they noticed two huge bodies. "I think those are the two Guzuds I met a couple of days ago. There are smaller bodies lying there, too," said Caleem.

"Please, don't let it be!" Marbel said. "Oh, no, no, no. It's our friends. Look at their charred bodies. They've grilled them!"

Unable to identify the lumps of flesh, Caleem stared at his friend.

"Marbel, it's just the two of us now. We have to get out of here!"

"How?"

"I don't know yet, but we have to come up with something quickly, otherwise we'll end up like our guys down there."

"The tall one must be Kamanar. And that small one is probably one of the boys," said Marbel, tears welling in his eyes.

The strong smell now filled their nostrils.

What had awakened their appetites just minutes ago now made them retch. Marbel's head began to spin as his stomach churned.

CHAPTER 33
A GOOD RAT

They heard a rope creaking and then noticed one of the cages above them swaying as it descended. The cage landed near the two men.

"Listen, if they put us in that thing, it's over. Run, Marbel, now!" said Caleem as he tried to get to his feet. He bent forward and jumped to a standing position. After hopping twice, he lost his balance and fell face down on the floor.

"Come on, Marbel!" Caleem shouted. He refused to give up; he got up a few times but always fell back.

Marbel didn't even try.

Eventually, groaning in pain, Caleem became limp and as motionless as a corpse. The rats dragged him into the cage through a side door. Marbel rose to his feet, hopped into the cage, and joined his friend. The rats shut the door behind them and secured it.

"Are you all right?" the chubby man asked.

The battered prince lay on his back, his face expressionless, his wide-open eyes staring at the ceiling. "I'm fine, damn it," said Caleem.

As soon as the cage began to rock, Marbel was thrown aside. It started its ascent. Each man threw his weight to his own side of the cage.

"There." Marbel pointed with his nose.

Peeking over Marbel's shoulder at one of the upper levels, Caleem saw a system of pulleys and wooden cogwheels fixed to the wall. A pair of rats turned one of the many wheels, hoisting them up until they reached quite a considerable height. The pungent smell of charred flesh rose higher, becoming even more intense than before.

Breathing fast, Marbel lay down.

"What's wrong?" asked Caleem.

"Nothing, it's nothing," said Marbel. "I don't like heights."

"Heights? We've been trapped by a tribe of nasty creatures, soon to be grilled and eaten, and you're worried about the height?"

Marbel didn't answer. He just tried to steady his breathing while forcing himself to peer down between the cage's wooden bars. He saw the rodents picking small carcasses out of the flames then tearing and devouring their meat. Dozens of rats took part in the feeding frenzy, ripping and chewing in the ghastliest banquet the men had ever seen.

"Despicable beings," Marbel said and shut his eyes.

Caleem's derisive laughter, echoing in Marbel's ears, was slow to die out. Fatigue overcame the chubby man, and he dozed off.

"Hani, Nola, I hear you girls!"

Marbel awoke with a start. It took him a moment to return to his dreadful reality. "My mind is playing tricks on me. I thought I'd heard my daughters' voices."

"I also heard something. It sounded like those two imbeciles," said the prince as he peeked through the bars.

"Zag, can you hear me?" called Caleem.

"Zig," said Marbel.

"Zig, can you hear me? What was the name of the other one?"

"Marbel! Caleem!" a voice called back.

"I can hear you, boys. You, too, Motehro. You're alive!" called Marbel.

Beyond the empty cage in front of them, another cage swayed. Caleem and Marbel distinguished several figures standing inside it.

"Sarik," called Caleem, struggling to get up as he pushed his forehead against the bars.

"I'm here," said Sarik as one of the figures waved his arm.

Marbel leaned back, sighing with relief.

"The traitor didn't hurt you? He better not," said Caleem. "If you hurt him, blood will flow from your eyes, traitor."

No reply came.

"Answer me, hypocrite," said the prince.

An awkward silence filled the putrid atmosphere.

"Do you want to know why I did what I did?" Kamanar's voice resounded.

"No excuse can save you," said Caleem.

"Right now, we're very close to the Wall Cliffs."

"That doesn't mean a thing to me, Master Commander."

"Gudjewkan said that the rats' cave was close to the Wall Cliffs."

Raising his eyebrows, Caleem looked at Marbel again. Marbel nodded, whispering, "Now I understand. We are close to the cliffs!"

"So what? That doesn't explain why the hell he threw us to the mercy of these rodents."

"Don't you see? The Spy Trail must also be close. This means we're no longer lost."

"Had I been leading, we wouldn't have been lost for a moment," Caleem yelled. "You wanted the rats to capture us, just to find out where we are? Thank you for that. And now, how the hell are you going to get us out of here?"

"I'll take care of that. And then I'll teach you a lesson in respect," said Kamanar.

"I can hardly wait," the prince said and bit the bar of the cage in anger.

"I'm not sure about him anymore," whispered Marbel.

"About time you noticed," said the prince.

"Like you said—look where we are now. And honestly, I never understood why he disliked Sarik so much. He acts like he knows something we don't. This whole business with your sister really got me thinking. I just couldn't bring myself to see a traitor in Sarik. What was that lousy story about a raven?"

"The raven … What a dumb invention."

"I mean no disrespect to your sister, Caleem, but … Good heavens, the things a woman can do to a man's head."

"Nothing justifies his actions. Besides, she doesn't even like him anymore."

"I guess you're right, my friend."

"I'm glad we can still call each other friend."

"If it weren't for the ropes, I would give you a hug. Tell me, what about the sword?"

"We must find it. First and foremost," said Caleem, almost to himself.

"Kamanar?"

"Rest assured, I'll take care of him after we find a way out of this bind. I wonder how they got loose." Caleem gazed at their comrades who were moving freely in their cage.

"How did you cut loose from the bindings?" shouted Marbel to the other cage.

"With a knife. Znits gave it to us. Our bow and quiver, too," said Zig.

"Who is he?" asked Caleem, rising up to his knees and making the cage swing.

After a whispered exchange in the more crowded cage, Zig's reply came: "We can't say his name out loud."

"He's a good rat. He's on our side," said Naji.

"Do you hear yourself? A good rat? I trust no rat, and nor should you! Throw the knife," said the prince.

"How will we catch it?" asked Marbel.

The two men's thoughts were cut short by the whistle of a flying knife.

"There!" Marbel yelled.

"Move," said Caleem. They bumped into each other while trying to catch the knife that flew in through the bars. It bounced on the cage floor and rolled. Both men lunged at once, but it slipped and fell through the bars into the void below. "Damn it!" said Caleem, watching the knife plummet. "Get off me," he said to his plump friend, who was now slumped on top of him.

"Sorry," said Marbel, rolling off.

"It's not your fault," said the prince. He turned to the other cage. "You clown! Haven't you heard of one, two, three?" He looked around. "I don't need a knife. There's a splinter here," he said and rubbed his side against the bars.

While he sat quietly, Marbel watched Caleem twist and squirm like a crazed caterpillar. After several minutes of muttering and cursing, the grinning prince held his arms up.

"How?"

"Mule-headed determination," said Caleem as he released his friend.

Both men stretched their limbs to examine their bruises and wounds. Caleem tried to wrench the bars open then gazed up above the cage to the dark ceiling and down to the rock walls. "No chance. Even if we break free, there's nowhere to go," he said.

They leaned against the sides of the cage, soon falling asleep to the creaking of ropes.

Marbel snored and Caleem let out an occasional muffled curse while he tossed and turned.

CHAPTER 34

OLD GRANDPA RAT

A commotion at ground level woke Marbel. The beams of light coming in through the cracks in the ceiling were gone, and the scattered torches gave a dim light.

Caleem was still asleep, so Marbel peered down. No trace remained of any fire; the big cavern was clear of smoke. The rats were in upheaval. Emitting ear-piercing squeals, they seemed to be fighting among themselves.

"What's happening? What's going on down there?" asked Caleem as he sat up, his voice still sleepy.

"Good morning. Sleep well?" asked Marbel.

"Is it morning? I slept like a corpse. Something's happening down there."

"It's hard to tell. Looks like some kind of dispute."

Through the spaces between the bars, the two spectators watched as hundreds of rodents crowded around one who was different. It seemed to be the same one who'd saved them from the beatings while they were being towed on the carts. It was taller, and, apart from its long tail, its body resembled a human being's. The rats screamed at it but kept their distance. The tall rat responded in turn with more screams, gesticulating in all directions, even kicking some of his kin.

The agitation ebbed, and the rodents cleared a corridor

leading to the tall one at the center. Two rats appeared carrying a cushioned armchair, which they placed it in front of the humanlike rat. He stood waiting, his tail wiggling.

Not a sound could be heard. The captives' eyes were fixed on the bizarre scene.

The light of a flickering torch advanced down the corridor, and a figure appeared. It was a small, white rat, hunched over and leaning on a thin bone. In slow, short steps it shuffled to the center. Another rat followed, holding up a torch to light the way.

"Old grandpa rat," said Marbel.

The old rat halted in front of the armchair. One rodent prostrated itself, and the elderly rat stepped on its back, climbed up, and sat on the armchair. The elder began a speech in a tired, muffled voice, addressing the tall, humanlike rat. When it finished, the latter replied calmly. A squeaky conversation ensued.

Following the exchange from their cages, the men knew that all this was about them.

The elderly rat emitted a hoarse squeak and pointed up to a wheel resembling that on a ship. A couple of rats turned two cogwheels on the pulley mechanism, and the men's cages began to slowly descend.

"What do we do now, Master Commander?" Caleem called to the other cage.

The rats below reacted to his voice with a chorus of irritated squeaks.

Glaring at Caleem, Kamanar leaned on the bars. "If we want to escape this place, we have to work together. You will have to trust me, at least for now," he said loudly enough to be heard over the riot below.

"It was a mistake to ever trust you in the first place."

The cages halted right above the rats' heads. Some that had spears or pointed bones stabbed between the bars, aiming for the prince. "Disgusting, ugly abominations!" he yelled, spitting at them as he dodged the thrusts.

"They don't seem too fond of you," said Kamanar.

"Ask I you, no speak without permission," said the humanlike rat standing at the center of the circle.

"It speaks," said Caleem.

"Ask I you, do I say for your good," said the rat, its voice almost human except for a wheezing sound at the end of some syllables.

The leader of the rats raised his bone cane. The rodents fell silent but still glared at the cages. The leader squeaked at the talking rat. The latter turned to Caleem. "To say short. I am Znits. Me help you. You help us, please do thing for us."

"What in the bloody damn world do you want?" shouted Caleem, provoking the ire of the rats, who screamed and attacked him once again.

The white rat raised his bone cane and silence was restored.

"Please," said Znits. "This is chance to free some you."

"What do you mean *some*?" asked Caleem.

"Meat be important, there be not much and cannot go free, but this time, different. Kamakar, I tell him something to do, for help our people. But I say not what, yet," said the rat, looking at Kamanar. "Many time ago, we be slaves of bad magic man in big forest. He make us work hard. Rocks and stones, dig much. We wanted kill him, but he be strong very. He break us.

"But when he be old and sick, we run from forest to mountain. We build nice home, we happy and free. But bad magic man, before he die, send something bad, very big bad. He send snake. Snake was little, then big, very big bad. He eat rats, all the time hungry. He have poison in tooth, very pain ... Zusis great leader, smart hero. Zusis close snake below. Many years stay there, but now get out again and eat us. Wait below, always hungry, bite with poison and we die, much pain. We try close him again, but cannot." Znits paused for a moment, looking at Caleem. "I see what fighter do, he strong. He and you kill snake. I ask Zusis to ask you help us. You help us?"

"Of course," said Kamanar. "But in return, it's freedom for us. *All* of us."

Znits sighed, scratching himself behind the ear. "Meat important. Cannot let all go. If I decide, I free all you. But I … not decide."

"I don't understand. Do you want our help or not?" Kamanar said.

"Yes. But Zusis not want free all."

Everyone was speechless upon hearing this.

"Kamakar, Skarik, and crazy man. All other stay to be tasty food."

The agitation began again, this time from within the cages as the captives shouted in protest.

The rat leader raised his cane again. The rats fell silent, but the men raged on, despite Kamanar's efforts to quieten them down.

"This your one chance," Znits said and squeaked.

"I am not sacrificing any of my men, understand?" asked Kamanar.

The elderly leader squeaked to the rodents on the pulley level. Both rats began spinning the cogwheels to hoist the cages upwards.

"Well done, Kamanar. Your plan is working great. Now we're going to be *tasty food*," said Caleem. "You half-witted mouse! You will not decide who lives and who dies. If I could only put my hands on your filthy neck. Why don't you come closer, just a bit?" He reached out of the cage.

The riot below continued. Znits climbed up the ladders until he reached the same height as the cages hung high up under the stone hall's ceiling.

"He said roast you today. Why you no agree?"

"No deal. What about the other option we discussed earlier? We need more weapons. One knife … one bow won't do," said Kamanar.

"I try," Znits wheezed and climbed down.

"A contingency plan?" asked Marbel.

"What's in it for him?" asked Caleem.

"I promised him a dead snake."

A flash lit up the gloomy cavern.

"Lightning," said Marbel, his word followed by thunder and the echo of dripping water in the cavern. "The light broke through the cracks. This means we're close to the surface."

"It's no good. There's no way to climb up to that ceiling," said Kamanar.

"We need to think of something else, fast. Look down," said Caleem.

The rodents had begun piling up wood and charcoal on the lower platform.

"Let's hope this Znits returns quickly," said Marbel.

The rats were now bringing torches to light the fires. Motehro panicked and started his frantic gibberish.

"Dinner will be served … soon," said Caleem.

"What are we going to do?" asked Zig. The terrified boy looked at Kamanar, who paced about the cage, causing it to shake. His eyes went from the ceiling to the ground below.

"We must remain calm," said Kamanar.

The rodents below continued to add wood to the fires, which blazed, growing stronger. The few drops of rain falling through the cracks had little effect.

"What's Znits waiting for? Where is he?" asked Naji.

"I suggest we all pray," said Marbel.

The cage housing Marbel and Caleem moved with a creaking sound, but this time shifted sideways.

The rats spun one of the many cogwheels. The cage advanced a little with each turn, until it was aligned above the burning pyres. The two captives could now feel the heat very well.

"What a way to go," said Marbel. "What a way to go."

"Shut up!" said Caleem. "Let me think."

The fires below grew taller.

"Znits!" Kamanar's cry echoed off the rocky walls.

"I come," answered a faint voice amid the racket as the singular rat climbed up the ladders. When he reached them, he was empty-handed.

"Where are the weapons?" asked Caleem.

"Weapons in good place close. Cannot bring, much danger now."

"That's what you get for trusting a rodent," said Caleem.

The upheaval below calmed down, replaced by the elder white rat's screeches.

"He say drop you in fire," Znits said and squeaked.

Marbel and Caleem began to pace inside the cage. Marbel stumbled, fell face down, and his forehead bounced on the bars. As he looked down, he caught a glimpse of the raging flames awaiting them.

Chapter 35

Don't Think, Just Pull!

One of the rats operating the pulleys went for the wheel that controlled Caleem and Marbel's cage. Kamanar, realizing what was about to happen, yanked the bow from Zig's back. Drawing, he aimed at the rat who was now pulling on the release latch. Kamanar shot without hesitation. The arrow flew past his friends' cage, which hung above the flames. The arrow bounced on the mechanism and dropped near the rodent's feet. The rat released the latch, setting the gears free to spin at full speed. The cage plummeted, along with its screaming captives.

The rest held their breath, their eyes on the falling cage.

He shot a second arrow. It whizzed past the rat's head. At first, they were all convinced that it was another miss, but then the arrow slid into the hole where the latch was, jamming it and bringing the gears to a dead halt. The sudden tension in the rope jolted the cage, throwing the captives to the floor as the cage spun.

The two men hung close to the flames, right above the rats' heads. Dazed by the fall and the scorching heat, they couldn't comprehend what had happened. In the other cage, the string of the bow still vibrated, but, to everyone's surprise, it was in Zig's hands.

"Swing away, hurry!" the boy called, taking another arrow from Naji's quiver.

Everyone stood speechless. Caleem and Marbel, still stunned, did as they were told. Using their combined weight, they moved in sync, getting the cage to swing with increasing frequency. It swayed from side to side above the fire. The rats below went into a frenzy, throwing spears and sharp bones at the cage.

As the swinging cage gathered momentum, Zig drew his bow again while his anxious peers looked on. With a fierce expression, the boy sighed as he released the string. The arrow severed the rope that held the swinging cage just as it cleared the flames. The cage crashed down on the angry rats' heads. It tumbled twice, crushing several rats under it before coming to a halt. The dead rodents had softened the fall, yet the impact was still strong enough for the cage to burst open.

A little dizzy, Caleem jumped out to meet a contingent of charging rodents. He recognized the elderly rat leader behind them who stood on his short legs in front of the throne. The warrior lunged straight at it, ignoring the rats rushing in his direction. The rat leader fled, tottering on his cane while squeaking in terror. With a thrust of his shoulder, Caleem smashed two rats to the ground. Dozens of claws swung at him, tearing his clothes and scratching his body. The prince shook them off, focusing on the leader hobbling before him. He pounced on the little white rat.

They fell to the ground and rolled. After getting back to his feet, Caleem grabbed the rat and held him up in a chokehold with one hand. With his other, he grabbed the pointed cane and wedged it against the rat's neck. The minuscule leader stopped squeaking, his short feet dangling in the air. All the rodents now focused their eyes on Caleem.

"Not hurt him!" shouted Znits from above.

After a short struggle to extricate himself from the cage, Marbel raced unhindered to his friend.

"Get to the wheels," Caleem shouted. The chubby man

zigzagged between the rats, drawing as little attention as possible. The rodents' concern was only for their leader.

Marbel climbed ladder after ladder until he reached the pulley mechanism.

The rats surrounding the prince crept closer.

"I'll skewer him like a chicken!" he shouted, shaking the rat.

The rodents retreated.

Holding the furry, stinking creature tightly, Caleem felt a bit nauseated. "I'll crush his skull!" he said as he walked backward, making slow progress towards a ladder.

The leader squeaked at his subjects as they closed in on Caleem from all directions.

The warrior threatened again. This time the rats were undeterred, continuing their advance. Rows of rodents within arm's reach of the prince blocked the path to the ladder. Caleem lifted the white creature over his head and hurled him at the mass of fur. As he pivoted toward the ladder, he punched a couple of surprised rodents. The warrior jumped up and grabbed one of the rungs with both hands. Kicking his pursuers away, he climbed, managing to reach the level above. Once there, he kicked the ladder over, and it took a rat down with it.

Caleem flinched as another rat crashed at his feet. Realizing that Marbel had pushed it down from the higher level, the prince rushed to help his friend, who was struggling with yet another rodent. With all the turmoil, Caleem and Marbel couldn't even hear their comrades shouting from their cage. Before Caleem could reach the next level, another squeaking rat flew down past him, freeing Marbel to dash toward the gears. When Caleem reached the top, he toppled the ladder. Below him hundreds of rats pushed and nudged each other. More rats flooded in through the tunnels leading to the great cavern. Through the smoke, Caleem saw that his friends had already dismantled some of their cage's bars.

Marbel approached the many wooden wheels on the wall, but he had no idea which one operated the cage holding his friends.

Rats threw spears at them and were hastily erecting ladders.

"Quickly, Marbel! Don't think, just pull!" shouted Caleem. As clawed paws reached, he kicked them away, sending the rats plunging to crash on the crowd below.

Marbel pulled the first latch; a wheel spun loose, dropping an empty cage to the cavern floor and squashing several rodents.

"Yaaaa!" shouted Caleem. "Drop them all."

Marbel caught on, pulling out all the latches. The rats on the ground scrambled, but the cavern floor was too crowded, and they could only climb on each other. Caleem laughed as he watched the spectacle until his friends' cage was released, too, and his smile disappeared. Marbel ran left and right, looking for a way to break their fall, but the wheel was spinning too fast.

"Leave it," said Caleem.

Marbel froze and stared at the dropping cage. It crashed on the heads of the rats below, filling the air with the sudden, blood-curdling sound of cracking skulls and snapping bones.

"That's a fine rat cushion right there," said Caleem, laughing. He scanned the hall, which echoed with the screams of confused rats. Kamanar's group stumbled out of the cage, dazed but unharmed. The rats attacked Kamanar and Sarik, who were the first ones out.

The prince kicked a charging rat and snatched his bone-tipped spear, then dove into the pack of rodents heading towards the rest of his gang. Marbel released all empty cages, sending them crashing down. When he finished, the old man discovered a larger wheel. Out of nowhere, three rats charged at him, brandishing their spears. Marbel ran, the rats in hot pursuit. The level he stood on was not extensive. Although he could have jumped down to the other levels, he didn't want to leave the last, large wheel.

The rodents were in total disarray as they tried to escape the falling cages; one almost landed on Caleem's head. The prince, now at ground level, plowed on through a sea of rats. His advance was slow, the spear firm in his hands as he stabbed and kicked those standing in his way.

"Here, come," called someone from within the throng. Caleem looked in the direction of the voice.

"Here, here, come."

Getting a glimpse of Znits, the warrior had no choice but to trust him. "Marbel's still up there." Caleem pointed to the level above.

"I help him. Now come here," said Znits.

Marbel spun around and faced his pursuers.

"Come taste my fists!" he said, panting. The three rats, spears in hand, lunged at once.

The soldier dodged the offense and closed his grip around all three weapons. Pulling them backward with all his strength, he spun around, then let go, flinging the dumbfounded rats to the ground. Before he had time to consider his next move, more rats armed with sharp bones appeared on his right, and yet more rats climbed up on his left. Marbel tried to avoid the bulging, black eyes' chilling gaze. He turned his back on the aggressors and raced toward the large, wooden wheel. He yanked its latch out and it spun at an incredible speed. Two rats dropped their weapons and dashed toward the wheel, but it was turning so fast that they were thrown away from it. The other rats besieging Marbel were paralyzed as they looked up. A huge structure—some kind of wooden bridge or walkway—had come loose from the ceiling and was plummeting downwards. It crashed with a thundering sound.

"Oh, no," said the chubby man.

He closed his eyes as a gust of wind whooshed over his stunned face. The light in the hall became dim. When he opened his eyes again, a thick cloud of dust rose from the center of the hall. Only a few ghostlike auras of torchlight penetrated the gloom.

"Marbel," a voice called.

"I'm here! I'm here!" Marbel cried.

"Marbel, ladder here."

Marbel heard the ladder scraping the rocks on his right.

"Keep shaking the ladder," he shouted.

Groping along the edge with his shoe, he managed to get hold of the first rung and started a slow, cautious descent. When his feet touched the ground, he saw a figure in front of him.

"To follow."

"Znits …" he whispered.

"Yes, yes. Here come." Znits's clawed paw pulled on Marbel's arm. After a moment of hesitation, he went along.

As they raced ahead, they descended another level to the very bottom, making their way in the confusion. Marbel struggled to keep up with his guide because of all the dust in the air and the other creatures jamming the area.

"Hold," said Znits.

Marbel reached out and grabbed a warm, fleshy rope. Realizing it was Znits's tail jolting him forward made him a little sick. He fought off his revulsion and held on for dear life.

CHAPTER 36
ME FRIENDS CLOSE

"What about the others?"

"No worry," said Znits. "Duck now."

After crouching and running past the rats in turmoil, they entered a narrow passage that grew darker with every step. Marbel's head scraped the ceiling, and his belly rubbed against the walls. Not knowing where they were headed, nor what fate had befallen his comrades, the old man had no alternative but to trust the creature.

The heavy dust from the cavern lined Marbel's eyelids and mouth. Opening one eye first, he was relieved to discover it had suffered no damage. He opened his other eye; the dust had almost dissipated, and a faint light flickered at the end of the tunnel beyond Znits's bouncing shoulders.

As they entered a cave, Marbel needed only a moment to identify the tall Kamanar peeking out from behind a rock and holding a torch. The two boys were beside him. Everyone looked strained, but as soon as they saw the old man, a glint of joy shone in their eyes.

A great burden was lifted off Marbel, who could not contain his excitement. Behind the rock were Sarik and Caleem, safe and sound, absorbed in conversation. Next to them was Motehro, holding a second torch, its light dancing on his lustrous scalp.

Puffs of dust rose from Marbel's clothes as his friends patted his back. He wiped the soot off his face before turning to squeeze the boys in a warm embrace. Motehro, the only one left out, emerged from behind the chubby man, enveloping him and the boys in a big bear hug as he mumbled enthusiastically. Marbel hugged him back and patted him on his shoulders.

"Leave the kisses for later," said Kamanar. "We need to get out of here before Znits's friends give us their hugs."

"Here, come," the rodent said and ran into the darkness. Kamanar followed, holding the torch above his head. The rest, close behind, ran in single file.

As they descended, the passage became narrower. There was no sign of a ceiling above them. Znits squeezed through, but Kamanar struggled. The boys got through without any trouble. However, Marbel was stuck.

Kamanar went back and lit the way for Marbel.

"These tight passages like me so much they don't want to let me go," said Marbel.

"It's a good thing you've lost some weight."

"That's right. I think so, too. Unfortunately, these walls beg to differ," said Marbel. With a final thrust, he stumbled through. "Easy," he said, catching his breath. His shirt was torn around the waist.

Kamanar turned to Znits. "Are there more passageways like this one?"

"One more, fat man not pass …" he said while scratching his big ears.

"We'll cross that bridge when we get to it. Now, let's move," said Kamanar.

"How you to know there's bridge?" asked Znits.

"There's a bridge?" asked Kamanar. "'When we get to that bridge'—it's just a saying. Just go."

They hurried on, motivated by the sounds of the ugly creatures scouring the tunnels behind them. Their path intersected with several other tunnels. Znits seemed to know his way within the maze. "Me friends close," said the rat, throwing a few looks over his shoulder.

They came out into a wide area lit by a pink crystal protruding from the high ceiling. A ladder stood against one wall. Znits went up, and the rest followed. The rat pulled up the ladder with Sarik's help. On a flat rock outcrop a bunch of arrows lay on the ground.

"Shoot me friends!" Znits shrieked after moving to stand near the edge of the rock.

"Zig, ready your bow," said Kamanar.

"Come on, Zig. They're going to show up any second," said Naji.

The squcaking intensified. Zig looked down at the tunnel's narrow opening. Before he'd even set his first arrow on the bow's string, rats poured out. He stretched and released. The string vibrated, but the arrow fell near his feet.

The party members were stunned. Their eyes went back to the horde of rodents trying to climb up to the outcrop.

Sarik pulled the bow from Zig's hands and shot arrow after arrow.

The rats shrieked as they fell. His aim was amazing, and so was his speed. Marbel was barely keeping up with handing him the arrows. The rodents' bodies piled up. Before the arrows were depleted, the assailants were all motionless.

"That was incredible," said Marbel.

The pleased Sarik glanced at Kamanar, who gave an impressed nod in return.

"Let's go. More me friends coming!" Znits said then disappeared into a wide crevasse in the rock wall.

Kamanar patted the downcast Zig on his shoulder. "These things happen. Don't worry about it."

Sarik gave Zig back the bow.

"Yes, give it back. These things happen," said Naji, eyeing Sarik. "You were lucky—that's all."

"I guess I was," said Sarik with a smirk.

The commander prodded them into the crevasse.

They caught up to their rodent guide, again finding themselves running in a dark, narrow canyon.

Their general direction was still down, which everyone found strange, as if they were heading deeper and deeper into the mountain instead of out of it.

Caleem pushed through, overtaking the others, and caught up with Znits. "The long sword, where is it?"

"No worry, there is big sword," said the rat as he ran on.

The answer failed to satisfy the prince.

He let the others go past him and returned to the end of the column.

"Is there another way out?" Kamanar asked their rat guide

Znits looked back and slowed down. "Only straight or back. No more way. Back, me friends."

CHAPTER 37
GO ON WITHOUT ME

The commander's ears picked up the humming of roaring water. He assumed this meant the bridge Znits had mentioned was close. The rat slowed to a walk. Kamanar overtook him, lighting the way with his torch, eager to learn what awaited them.

The tunnel ahead widened and ended in a cliff. On the edge lay a thick log that extended into the darkness, and underneath water roared, spraying their faces.

"Bridge," said Znits.

Kamanar walked forward to take a closer look at the huge piece of timber. The light of his torch was not strong enough to show the other end. The foaming river below was fed by two waterfalls, one on either side of the log. One by one, the rest of the party arrived, gasping for air.

"What's that?" asked Marbel loudly over the noise of rushing water.

"Bridge," said Kamanar.

"It's just a log."

"Forward." Znits pointed and hopped onto the log. He did not seem concerned by the depth of the chasm or the intensity of the thundering current. He dashed ahead.

Kamanar lit the way with his torch. "Marbel, go after Znits."

The men stood, hesitant, daunted by the power of the waterfalls, the raging river, and the very narrow bridge. A slight slip meant a sure death. Their eyes shifted to Marbel. The reluctant old man avoided their gaze.

Screams approached from the dark path behind, getting closer by the second.

"Let's go," shouted Marbel. He leaped onto the log, ran forward, and disappeared into the darkness, catching everyone by surprise.

Kamanar followed suit, stepping on the smooth, wet log. With slow, cautious steps, he maintained his balance, the torch swinging from side to side. Naji followed, proceeding as slowly as possible. He crept forward with the help of Kamanar's swaying torch.

Zig and Sarik went next.

Despite the roar of the rushing waters, the screaming and squeaking became louder. Kamanar looked back and saw dozens of flickering eyes bouncing up and down, reflecting the torchlight. Caleem came last behind Motehro, muttering, "Come on, come on."

Kamanar heard a disturbance behind him and looked around, only to glimpse a dark figure charging the prince with a spear. Caleem swung and shoved the weapon aside. It fell into the foaming river along with its shrieking owner. Caleem lost his balance and stood on one foot, trying to steady himself on the slippery log, but he tipped towards the raging current only for Motehro to grab the prince's belt and haul him back up.

As the rest of them made it to the stone ledge on the opposite side, Kamanar watched Caleem backing slowly along the log, a rat pursuing him from the other end.

"Caleem, jump!" Sarik called. "There's firm ground here."

The prince pivoted and leaped blindly for the stone platform. He missed and stretched to grasp for an arm as he slammed against the rock wall under the platform's edge.

Kamanar had him. Gritting his teeth, he hauled the prince onto the ledge.

The prince stood for a moment, looking beyond the edge, trying to understand what had happened. Kamanar turned to assist Marbel, who was trying to push the log out of its niche. Lifting the heavy piece of lumber with the weight of the rodents was an impossible task until Caleem, Sarik, and Motehro joined in. Naji held Kamanar's torch.

The leading rat, his jaw open to reveal sharp teeth and a saliva-dripping tongue, charged and almost reached the ledge. Zig slung the bow across his back, picked up Caleem's torch, and threw it at the rodent's big, black, glaring eyes. With a chilling squeak, the rat stopped in its tracks and covered its burning face. The rats running behind slammed into it, and some fell into the void. At that very moment, the bridge was dislodged. The men pushed it aside, watching it hurtle down and disappear into the white foam along with the rest of the rodents. Some rats launched their spears as they fell, their weapons landing near their targets' feet.

"They good fighter," Znits said as he watched in awe.

Kamanar said nothing as he waited for his companions to catch their breaths. From the darkness on the other side of the chasm, loud squeaking and screeching could be heard even above the waterfalls' roar.

"How did you miss that? I don't understand," said Naji.

Zig lowered his head, avoiding his friend's eyes.

"When you jammed the falling cage, that was an impossible shot … and then the rope," said the commander to Zig.

The boy nodded, putting on a smile.

"It won't take them long to find a way around this obstacle. Come on—let's move," Kamanar said. He seized the torch from Naji and motioned for the others to follow.

As they left the rocky plateau, they entered a bigger cave where the thunderous roar of the waterfalls decreased to a murmur. After running for some time, Znits slowed to a walk before finally coming to a halt. He stooped down next to what looked like a an old door lying on the cave floor. They all knelt around the strange door made of thick wooden boards.

"This wasn't made by those rats," said Caleem as he caressed the ornate carvings.

"Help move," said Znits, shoving his claws under the heavy object. Sarik, Marbel, and Caleem helped the rat to move the trapdoor, revealing a hole. The sound of water rose from below.

"Go down," said Znits.

Kamanar peered into the narrow opening.

"Why don't we just continue ahead through the cave?" said Caleem.

"No," said Znits with a squeak. "Way is here."

All eyes looked at the chubby man.

"Come, Marbel, try to get in," said Kamanar.

The chubby man sighed. He dropped his feet down and tried to slide his body through, but his belly got in the way. "Give me a minute," he said, again attempting to squeeze his wide figure through. No matter what position he tried, his waist and belly were broader than the mouth of the hole.

"Not time. Me friends make new bridge. Me friends come here. Maybe better fat man stay, me friends have some meat, and us go—"

"Nobody asked for your opinion, rodent!" said the prince.

Marbel struggled to climb out of the pothole. "It's impossible … Go on without me."

"No!" everyone objected. "No way."

Marbel smiled. "So, what do we do, then?"

"There might be a way," said a gentle voice.

Everyone's attention turned to Sarik. Kneeling by the hole, he fingered its rocky edges. "These rocks are smooth."

Naji lit the opening with the torch as Kamanar listened without saying a word.

Caleem approached Sarik and peeked into the opening. "So?"

"Marbel, are you willing to try something?" asked Sarik.

"Of course. Anything."

"Start running."

"Running where?"

"Doesn't matter. Just run back and forth. Do it, please."

Frowning, the chubby man began jogging.

"Come on, faster," said Sarik.

"I don't understand. If this doesn't work, I will kick you in the butt," said Marbel.

"If it doesn't work, the rats will have our butts for super," said Naji.

"Come on, run!" Caleem shouted, chuckling. The rest soon joined, cheering Marbel on.

"Very funny," said Marbel, sweating and breathing heavily.

"Now, take your clothes off—all of them. You can leave your shoes on," said Sarik.

"Are you mad?"

"Please, do it."

The older man complained until he was done undressing except for his shoes.

Smiling, Sarik gathered up Marbel's clothes and dumped them into the hole before following them into the darkness. "Try to get in," he called from inside the hole.

Marbel approached the hole with a sour face and, dripping sweat, lowered his legs into the opening. He got stuck again. "It's impossible."

"Push him," came Sarik's muffled voice from below.

"What? What is he doing? He's pulling on my legs!"

Caleem and Kamanar pushed Marbel down, and his sweat spread on the smooth mouth of the pit. He finally slid through.

Kamanar looked down to see him stark naked, sitting in the dark. The shaft was not deep at all.

"Take these," Sarik handed the man his clothes.

The boys lowered their lean figures into the pit with ease.

"Be careful, there's another pit ahead," said Sarik.

The sound of flowing water was now louder.

Motehro slid through, even with his furs still on. Caleem

joined them. Znits descended, too. Kamanar was last, and he maneuvered his broad shoulders a few times until he managed to fit in. The cavern they were in now wasn't high enough for him to stand erect.

They slid the wooden trapdoor back into place. A few paces away was another hole. Kamanar placed his torch near the new opening and noticed that this one was wider, with water flowing below.

CHAPTER 38
OPEN CLOSE GATES

Znits made his way among the men, who were not yet accustomed to being in the company of a giant rodent. "Shadow," said Znits.

"What? Where?" asked the commander.

"Shadow, shadow."

Everyone peered down to where the rat was pointing.

"I don't see any shadows. It's too dark down there," said Marbel.

The rodent jumped down.

"Shadow, water shadow," said the rat, standing in a stream that was only knee-deep.

"Shallow … he meant *shallow*," said the chubby man. One by one, they all jumped in with a splash.

"The current is gentle," said Marbel, who was first.

Naji, cupping his hands and drinking, said, "The water tastes so good!"

Zig also took a few sips.

"Don't drink too much, or you'll swell up like a waterskin," Caleem warned as they all drank.

"Caleem's right. Don't drink too much," said Kamanar.

Everyone stopped, apart from Naji, who furtively sipped and sipped.

"Not far," said Znits.

"Not far to what, to where?" asked Caleem.

"To open close gates."

"'Open close gates?' Go figure," said Marbel.

"Is that the way out of this cave?" asked Caleem.

"Yes, there no danger. Me friends not come there," the rat said then squeaked and moved on.

"What about my sword?" asked Caleem.

"No worry. Big sword close," he wheezed and continued upstream.

Although it was gentle, the current still made their progress cumbersome. The stream was wide enough for them to walk side by side, apart from Naji, who lagged behind.

The boy held his bloated belly with his hand.

Kamanar's torch swayed from side to side, lighting the way. Their pace became sluggish, the distance between them and their guide widening.

"Fast," said Znits. "Is not far." His bulging eyes reflected the flame.

A faint light flickered from farther down the tunnel.

Halting, Caleem said, "Looks like a torch."

"No worry. I put," said Znits, pointing to the light with his claw.

"Any rats helping you?" Kamanar asked.

"No. Only I. No time questions." Znits sniffed the air. "Here come, quick! Me friends be close." He sprinted forward.

They raced after the rat as fast as they could. Soon, the sounds of rustling and thrashing water came from the darkness behind them.

The stream grew wider and wider, and became a large pool. Two torches lit the area, one close to where the water poured into the pool, the other inside a square opening in a massive wall built of blocks of stone.

"Open close gates," said Znits, hurrying forward.

The water was now waist-deep, and they did their best to keep up. Znits waited for them near the opening.

The high wall's big stone bricks were stacked together vertically rather than horizontally.

"That's an odd building technique," said Marbel, panting.

"This place was not built by rats," said Sarik.

The wall spanned the length of the pool and had additional square openings, similar to the one before them, except that they were dark. A stone staircase rose from the water inside the lit room beyond the opening.

Znits waited beside the opening. "Go under," he said.

The rat dove into the water, disappearing for a moment, and resurfaced inside the room near the staircase. Ascending a few steps, he shook his wet fur and gestured for everyone to follow.

"Here come, here come," he called.

The men looked at the mysterious gateway; they could not figure out why he had dived down when the staircase was right in front of him.

"It could be a trap," said Caleem.

"No … go under, no trap," said Znits.

Caleem advanced, testing the water ahead with his foot.

"Be careful, Caleem," said Marbel. The prince nodded, moving forward.

They all stared ahead, confused.

Kamanar waded forward. The rat flailed his paws, motioning for them to dive. "Down, water. Down water. Quick!"

Caleem and Kamanar slowed down.

"It's a trap," shouted Marbel.

The two men stopped and stared at the chubby man. "If you have something helpful to add, please do. Otherwise, shut up," said Kamanar.

Caleem moved ahead, and his forehead bumped against something. He recoiled slightly.

Everyone else took a step back.

"What is it?" asked Kamanar, waving his torch.

"I hit something," said Caleem. Placing both hands in front of him, he felt the air as if he were groping a wall.

As Kamanar approached, his torch was blocked by a mysterious, invisible obstacle.

"It's a transparent barrier of some kind." Caleem knocked on the unseen thing.

They all got closer to touch the bizarre obstacle.

"It's a wall, an invisible wall," said Zig.

"What kind of sorcery is this?" said Marbel.

"*Bajan! Majan!*" said Motehro, banging his head on what appeared to be thin air.

"Incredible," said Sarik.

"Quick, inside, danger behind!" yelled the rat.

Reaching for the submerged portion of the magical wall, Kamanar found a gap close to the bottom. He dove under the invisible wall, which turned out to be thicker than he had estimated, and surfaced on the opposite side. He was soaked and so was the torch. "Come on—dive," he said and wiped his face. He disposed of the wet torch and took the one that hung on the wall.

"Yes, yes, here come," said the creature, jumping up and down.

One by one, they dove through. They surfaced on the other side and ran up the staircase, out of the pool.

"Now I close, open close gate," said Znits. He inserted his paw inside a square niche in the wall, pulled on something, then removed his paw. Loud clanking came from the small opening. "Gate closing. No pass after."

The water around the invisible wall began to ripple as it shook. "Gate, never again open."

Zig spun around, looking for something. Turning pale, he ran down the stairs and got back into the water.

"What's wrong?" asked Kamanar.

Zig pressed his face against the invisible gate and looked at the edge of the dark pool.

"Watch your feet! The gate is still sliding down," said Marbel.

Zig turned to face the others. His voice trembling, he asked, "Where's Naji?"

CHAPTER 39
THIS IS ON YOUR HEAD!

Searching around, Kamanar confirmed that Naji was missing. He leaped to the niche. "Stop this thing!"

Caleem and Sarik jumped into the water. In the dim light, a figure jumped up and down on the other side of the pool.

"Naji!" called Zig.

"They're coming. They're after me!" cried Naji, his muffled voice breaking off. In water up to his chest, he flailed his arms, making little headway.

"No open after close," said Znits.

Kamanar grabbed the rat's furry neck and pinned him against the niche.

"It's not closed yet. Stop it, now!" he roared.

Znits inserted his paw into the slot and groped for something inside. Kamanar brought the light closer. There were several strange cogwheels turning in various directions. The cavity was deeper than he thought. The rat weaved its paw in between the wheels.

Marbel joined Caleem and Sarik in the water, but the three could only watch. Crying as he pushed forward, the boy was almost out of breath.

The squeaking intensified, and Naji's dark pursuers materialized at the edge of the underground lake, the glaring eyes multiplying as they poured in.

"Come on, boy," yelled Marbel.

Motehro dove into the pool, and then the tracker's bald head bobbed up on the other side of the invisible gate.

"What's he doing?" asked Caleem.

A loud yelp from behind startled everyone.

"What? Znits!" shouted Kamanar, seeing that the rat's arm was stuck inside the mechanism.

"I stop it. It still little open. Can't hold long time …"

Kamanar also entered the water and stood behind the others. Dozens of rodents were almost upon Naji. Motehro rushed toward him. Caleem and Kamanar watched the boy and the tracker.

"I can't hold more!" screamed Znits.

"Just a bit more," said Sarik, approaching the rat.

"Come on!" Zig shouted to his friend.

The tracker passed Naji, advanced toward the rats, and punched the nearest one. Beating on the water with his hands, he then began to scream at the top of his lungs.

"Keep going, Naji!" yelled Marbel.

Targeting the boy, the rodents tried to outflank Motehro. Motehro lunged to his left, wrapped his arm around a rat's neck, and sunk it under the water. A second one tried to go around from the right. The tracker leaped towards it and seized it with his other arm. While keeping the two flailing rats submerged, he yelled and growled, holding the rest of the pack at bay.

Naji was getting closer to the barrier.

"Dive! Go under!" they all screamed, pointing down.

Having no idea what his friends meant, the nervous boy smiled. He slammed into the structure. As he ran his hand over the barrier, his smile changed into a look of terror.

"Dive! Dive!" all his friends screamed.

Behind him, Motehro kept the two scratching and biting

rats under the water. A third rat lunged at Motehro's head. The tracker bit the creature's furry stomach and tore off a chunk of flesh along with some fur. Squealing, the creature recoiled in pain. Meanwhile, the other rodents overtook Motehro and closed in on the boy, who was stuck.

Caleem beat his fist against the invisible gate. "Everyone, shut up."

"Look into my eyes," he said to the boy.

Naji nodded and looked into the prince's eyes.

Aware of the approaching rats, Caleem locked eyes with the boy. "Dive."

Naji dived. The rats plunged after him. Kamanar knelt in the water, submerging his head and extending his long arm under the very tight gap.

"No more, hurt much. Can no more!" yelled Znits.

"Just a moment longer, please," said Sarik.

Kamanar felt Naji's fingers; he yanked him in from under the closing gate. Kamanar and Naji emerged from the water and fell back on the stairs. The boy was still kicking and screaming.

Znits yelled again, jerking his hand out of the slot. This time, the clanking was louder, ending in a final thud as waves swept the pool on both ends of the gate.

Marbel groped underneath. "It's closed. The gate is closed."

As the submerged rodents were crushed under the gate, their underwater squeaking stopped. One rat emerged on their side. Caleem intercepted the frantic rodent and, holding it by the neck, slammed it against the invisible gate. The rat squirmed to break free. Glaring into the creature's big, bulging, black eyes, the prince tightened his hold until it went limp, and then he let the lifeless figure drop into the water.

"Open it, Znits," shouted Caleem. Znits shrunk into a ball, shrieking in pain as a pair of broken cogs fell off his mangled paw.

The rats beyond the barrier piled on Motehro, his muffled cries barely making it through the barrier. The rats scratched against it with their claws, trying to find a way through. Some searched under water only to resurface and pound the barrier with their paws.

"No open again. Never," said Znits.

They all fixed their eyes on the gray mass overpowering Motehro.

"Open this damn thing now!" said Caleem.

"Is broken," said Znits. He pointed to the wrecked cogwheels lying on the floor then raised his mangled, bleeding paw. Sarik peered into the cavity in the wall

"What do we do now?" asked Marbel as they watched the retreating rodents and tried to spot Motehro in the furry pandemonium.

The captors left the pool and disappeared into the darkness, Motehro's screams fading away along with them. Many rodents remained on the other side of the pool, glaring at the men, yet impotent to do any more.

"I didn't expect Motehro to do something like that," said Sarik.

"The bald guy surprised," said Marbel, looking at Naji.

"You brought those boys. It should have been you out there," said Caleem, staring at Kamanar.

More rats entered the pool.

Kamanar got out of the water but said nothing.

His head drooping, Marbel ascended the staircase while shooting an occasional glance beyond the locked gate.

Zig helped Naji up the stairs. "What about Motehro? We can't just leave him," said Naji.

"He told you not to drink too much, didn't he? He told you," said Zig.

"Shut up," said Naji.

"This is on your head!" said Kamanar, pointing his finger at the boy.

Znits jumped back into the water and stood by the invisible gate. "No worry, me friends no come this side. I talk me father. Just little time."

"Father?" asked Kamanar.

Hundreds of rats filled the pool. After several stressful moments, the boys sat down on the steps in bitter resignation. Marbel soon joined them for a short respite.

As they waited, a small raft materialized at the edge of the pool. It carried the little white rat on a tiny wooden chair, with four rats tugging it from each corner.

"That's your father?" asked Caleem. Znits nodded.

"Something here isn't right," said Caleem. "Why do you want to speak to your father now? After helping us escape? After we sabotaged your stinking home, killing at least a hundred of you? No father would forgive such a deed. Unless you're leading us into a trap."

"No trap here. Father Zusis have many, many pups. A hundred hundred brothers. He not remember me. I not important. One not be important."

The raft floated closer to the invisible wall. The old rat, whose white fur glimmered in the light of Kamanar's torch, sat on its miniature throne and examined each one of the men. Its paws fondled the little bone cane. Caleem shot the creature a murderous glare, but the rat leader was clearly unmoved. He addressed Znits in quick, cutting squeaks.

The men relaxed a bit, feeling somewhat safe behind the strange, unseen barrier.

"I think I know what's going on," said Caleem.

"Really?" asked Kamanar.

"We're going from bad to very bad to unbelievably worse. You all saw—we managed to best the rats, it's possible. But now we're forced to deal with an even more powerful creature. That monstrous reptile and your friend Znits is leading us right to it."

"As soon as we get out of here, it's either you or me," said Kamanar.

Caleem brought his face very close to Kamanar's. "You mean *if* we get out of here. And if we do, at long last, you said something right. It's going to be you or me." After a long moment of frowning by both men, the prince looked away to keep an eye on Znits.

When Znits had finished speaking to his father, he nodded, making some gestures with his paws before approaching the men.

"Wait, Znits," said Kamanar, walking down the stairs toward the rat. "What about Motehro?"

"He be roast meat, of course," Znits said.

All were horrified by the chilling directness of the answer.

"One less in Kamanar's party," said Caleem.

CHAPTER 40

THIS MISSION IS MORE IMPORTANT THAN ANY OF US

"Ask him to give Motehro back. Our odds of defeating the snake will be greater," said Kamanar.

"Cannot do."

"Ask him!" said Kamanar.

Znits shrugged, turned to his father, and uttered a squeaky sentence.

The old leader coughed a few times, and Kamanar realized he was laughing. The white rat squeaked to the four rats around the raft, and they began to turn it around.

Kamanar scratched his stubbled chin. The raft returned to the far edge of the pool.

"Lots of meat … Lots and lots of meat, tell him," said Kamanar. "Tell him I will get him an amount so big that it will last a lifetime."

Znits squeaked to his father again. The old rat raised a hand, and the raft stopped. He made a circular motion with his tiny finger. The raft rotated back.

The rat squeaked. "Speak," Znits translated.

"Ask him if he knows what a cow is." Kamanar's eyes were fixed on the little rat.

Znits squeaked, and his father shook his head.

"Imagine an animal as big as ten hogs," began Kamanar while Znits translated. "Its meat is not as hard or coarse as a hog's, but soft and juicy, because a cow is lazy and doesn't like to move. It has but one thing in mind: grazing. It munches on green weeds all day, growing layer upon layer of delicious meat and fat. The cows compete among themselves to prove who is the most bovine. Very, very good for roasting. I promise you that I will bring you hundreds of these animals in exchange for Motehro. Alive and unharmed."

The mouths of the rats tugging the floating vessel began to water as Znits translated.

Turning to his friends, Kamanar smiled. "It's working."

The boys were drooling as well. They were quick to wipe their mouths.

Kamanar shook his head and looked back at the old rat, who was now talking to Znits.

"Why you take little meat and give lots of meat?" translated Znits.

"Why not?" said Kamanar. "He is skinny and all bones. Don't let his furs fool you. There's not so much tasty meat."

Znits and the old rat exchanged a few squeaks. "Only when bring lots of meat, Zusis release little meat."

"If you don't get your meat, you can keep Motehro. But it will take some time to make the arrangements."

Kamanar leaned forward and rested his hands on the invisible wall as he waited for the old rat's decision. The latter rubbed its furry white belly then picked its ear using the bone cane, scratching and enjoying himself. When the rat pulled the bone out of its ear, the sharp end was covered in a layer of greenish-brown mucus. The rat sniffed it, then licked it off the bone. The men's faces contorted in disgust.

The old rat squeaked at Znits as the latter nodded, turning to Kamanar. "Zusis agree. He want know when lots of meat come."

"Maybe a month or two."

Znits translated. The elderly rat motioned the rats to turn the raft away again, letting out a few squeaks in an indifferent manner.

"Much time. Father Zusis to think," translated Znits.

"What's there to think about?" Kamanar asked. "So much meat in exchange for little meat!"

Znits translated, but his words fell on filthy, deaf ears, and the raft disappeared into the dark cave.

"We have granted Motehro some time. That grandpa rat is not stupid, for a rodent. He won't hurt him. Now, let's get out of here," said Kamanar.

"That's it? We're leaving him?" asked Naji.

"The sooner we finish our mission, the sooner I'll return for him."

"Is this how the commander cares for his men?" asked Caleem.

"This mission is more important than any of us, and you know it."

"I know it. And I know that your personal gain is even more important."

Kamanar glanced at him but didn't reply.

Znits shook his wet fur once again and led them on. He went through a hatch in the wall at the rear of the room. Arriving at a dark canal, the rodent stopped for a moment, sniffed the air, and continued on. Kamanar lit the way with the torch as he walked beside the rat, the tired and slouching crew following behind.

After an hour of silent marching, Kamanar stopped. "I swear, once we finish this mission, I will come back to free Motehro. I give you my word. Even if it takes an army to do it."

"We'll come with you," said Naji.

"What if … what if he's already gone?" asked Zig.

"For those rodents' own sake, he'd better not be."

The commander's comforting words put smiles on their weary faces.

They soon found themselves in a corridor where Kamanar's torch illuminated sharp, angled patterns carved on the walls, unlike any they had seen before.

"This is intriguing," said Sarik, running his hand across the elaborate carvings. "Looks like there used to be some civilization here."

"These markings look ancient," said Caleem.

"Here big snake, here no life. Big snake, teeth, scary, poison, pain, death!" Znits whispered without looking back.

"'Poison, pain, death.' Why thank you, rat, for your comforting words," said Caleem.

"You welcome."

The men shuddered.

The narrow corridor merged with a larger one where Znits went to a corner.

"Things here, big sword, too," he announced, pointing to a pile on the floor. He threw aside a dusty blanket to reveal a pair of backpacks and a small pouch. Beneath one of the backpacks something glinted, reflecting in the prince's bright brown eyes.

"Could it be …?" Caleem mumbled, pushing the boys and Sarik out of his way. As he cast the bags aside, his face lit up with the widest grin anyone had seen him wear since the journey began. Taking hold of the hilt, he raised the sword high as they all stared in awe at the gleaming, bluish steel.

"Caleem … your sword," said Marbel.

"Yes, it is," The prince kissed the blade.

"Where are the other weapons I asked you to bring?" asked Kamanar.

"Here weapons," said Znits pointing at Caleem's sword. Kamanar puffed and said nothing.

"I smell something good," said Naji. The boys hurried to open the backpacks.

"Smells very good," said Zig.

Naji pulled out a handful of green roots. "What's this?" he asked, smelling the roots.

"Food," said Znits.

Naji bit into one. "Tastes like grass, but it's not bad." He put a few more in his mouth.

Marbel approached, drooling. "What do you have there, Zig? Looks like fruit."

"Wait a second. I know you're famished, and so am I, but let's sit down for a proper meal like almost civilized men," said Kamanar.

"Let's sit in a circle," said Marbel as he lodged the torch onto the wall between the vertical bricks. Marbel wiped the rocky surface clean with his hands, waiting for Kamanar to take out some more fruit and roots. "What's in the pouch?" he asked.

"Meat," said Znits.

Everyone stared at the rat.

"Problem?" he asked.

"What kind of meat?" asked Sarik.

"Tasty meat, snake meat." The rodent threw a few chunks of meat at each one of them. They all exchanged looks.

Znits bit into his share. "You not eat?" asked the rodent with its mouth full.

Naji examined his portion, sniffed the meat, and took a small bite. With everyone's gaze on him, he chewed, and his eyes grew wider. "So good," he said, little bits flying out of his mouth. Picking the precious morsels off the floor, he popped them back into his mouth. "Smoked snake."

"Snake eats rats, and rats eat snake," said Kamanar.

"This tastes really good," Marbel said. "When we're back home, you're all invited to my house for a banquet—main course, smoked snake."

No sooner had they finished their meal than they began to eye the backpacks and the pouch.

"No," said Kamanar. "I know everyone still has space in their stomachs, but we've had enough for now. We'll keep the rest for later. But we will take a break. Though it's not safe anywhere anyway, right, Znits?"

"Danger. There and here. Big snake."

Leaning back, Kamanar closed his eyes. "If we're to take that monster on, we'd better do it after a good nap."

"Who wants to stand watch first?" asked Marbel.

"Don't worry. Znits volunteers to stand watch while we rest. Right, Znits?" asked Kamanar.

"Yes … no … yes. You sleep not much," said the rodent.

"As much as possible," said Marbel. Before he had finished his sentence, the boys were already snoring.

"Sleep little," said Kamanar. He lay down on the ground and pointed at a tiny insect crawling by. "Until this bug reaches that exit."

The rat knelt closer to study the minuscule insect.

Caleem finished putting together a makeshift sheath for his sword made from one of the empty bags. This one only covered the blade halfway. He placed the sword next to him as he sat and motioned for Sarik to come closer.

Sarik lay down next to the prince.

"Don't become complacent. Keep your distance from Kamanar," whispered Caleem. Sarik nodded, falling asleep in an instant.

Everyone collapsed into a much-needed slumber.

Znits crouched beside the sluggish bug, waiting for it to reach the exit. All the while sniffing the air, the rat remained nervous and alert, peering into the darkness farther down the hall.

CHAPTER 41
I HAVE A BAD FEELING

"Bug, out. You sleep long time. Long time!" said Znits. "Bug too much, much slow," he whispered in a wheeze.

Sarik and Caleem woke up, as did Kamanar.

"Fat man, make much noise," said the rat.

Marbel opened his eyes, still bearing the marks of the rocks on his face. "I snored?"

"Yes, a lot," said Caleem. "I suspect there's no monster here. If there was, it would have found us. You shook the whole cave."

"Sorry," said Marbel as he rose to his feet and smoothed down his clothes.

"Wake the boys," said Kamanar, slinging on a backpack and picking up the torch. "This thing doesn't have much life left in it. Znits, I want you to lead us to the exit."

"Yes, me go there."

"Out. Not to the snake. Understand?"

"But you say you kill snake."

Kamanar stepped to the rat and towered over him. "I said that we'd do it if we were released! All of us. We escaped. We were not released. And this is not all of us. Deal? No! Now take us to the exit."

The rat grunted and squeaked. Whipping his tail about, he turned and continued on. He led them down a long corridor from which tunnels of different sizes branched out left and right.

They rushed along, glancing around without uttering a word.

"There's something up ahead," said Zig.

"Quiet," Kamanar said as he saw a faint flicker at the end of the tunnel.

"Is your light. No me friends. No snake," said the rodent.

Kamanar swung the torch from side to side, and the other light moved the same way.

"It's a reflection," said Marbel.

The closer they came to the object reflecting the light, the brighter it became, until they found themselves facing a large, jagged monolith. It blinked a few times, its flashing becoming more intense, until it outshone the torch.

"Incredible," said Marbel.

Stepping forward and touching the object, Sarik said, "I think the crystal has somehow absorbed the light from the torch."

Gaping in amazement, the boys began to grope the surface of the magical crystal.

"There's another one up ahead," said Caleem.

Moving toward the second monolith, which was identical to the first, they noted that Kamanar's light yielded the same exact result.

"Look there!" Marbel pointed to a third one, glimmering a few paces away.

More crystals, fixed at only a few paces apart, began to shine one after the other. The tunnel was becoming much brighter.

"Where can this tunnel lead … Out?" Marbel wondered.

"We'll know soon enough," said Kamanar, glancing at Znits.

"I can hear crickets," said Zig.

"I can hear them, too," said Marbel. "We must be close to the exit." The noise became louder as they approached two magnificent monoliths standing on either side of the tunnel. These were very tall, and their light shone bright green.

"Looks like a gate," said Kamanar. The moment he stepped in between the two monoliths, myriad crystals of various sizes affixed at different heights shone in shades of blue, green, and red.

"Dear lord," said Marbel.

"We're out," said Naji, skipping.

They marveled at the sight of the moon shining above the crystal-strewn valley.

"I swear I've never seen the moon and stars shine so brightly," said Sarik.

"Something's not right. That moon is too big … Unless we're at the top of the world," said Kamanar.

"It does look huge," Sarik said.

"The stars aren't where they should be. I can't find the Horn or the Arc Stars," said Kamanar.

"This isn't real," said Caleem.

A puff of smoke billowed from Kamanar's torch as it went out. Discarding it, Kamanar made his way to the crystals.

"What do you mean 'this isn't real'?" asked Naji.

"We are in an enchanted place, and this is all an illusion. I think we're still in the cave," said Sarik.

"The crickets and these bushes … Is it all an illusion?" Naji asked and kicked a nearby bush.

"That's not the night sky. There's a cave ceiling up there behind it … I'm sure," said Sarik, pointing up.

The vegetation was mainly bushes illuminated by the fake moon. There were also several dispersed piles of rocks among the colorful crystal ornaments. Gaping in wonderment at the display of lights, the men explored the terrain.

The sound of a sliding rock came from behind them and abruptly stopped.

"What was that?" asked Marbel.

"Something slammed shut," said Caleem.

In the direction of the entrance, the two bright monoliths remained firmly in place.

"Where's Znits?" asked Caleem.

Kamanar ran back toward the entrance, but something stopped him. "Damn it."

Caleem joined him, but he, too, was blocked by an invisible barrier.

"Another one of those gates," said Kamanar.

"Znits!" Caleem screamed, drawing his sword.

"Did he just lock us in here?" asked Marbel with a groan as he checked the invisible barrier for himself.

Running their hands over the surface, they all tried to find an opening or a way around it, but to no avail. Although they didn't see any walls around them, they all had the feeling that they were in an enclosed place.

"Znits!" Kamanar's cry was met by an eerie silence. "Znits, if you're up to something … I'm warning you."

"No surprise—looks like your rat friend has set his trap," said Caleem.

They all huddled together.

"I have a bad feeling," said Marbel.

"That snake monster is probably close," said Caleem.

After a few more stressful moments, they heard clawed feet tapping on the rock floor not far from them.

"Where are you, rat? We can hear you scampering around," said Caleem.

"Let's not sit here like easy prey. Let's look for a way out," said Kamanar.

Zig took an arrow out of Naji's quiver and drew his bow while he glanced at Kamanar for silent approval. Caleem tightened his grip on the hilt of the long sword. Quietly, they all crept forward.

Marbel, who carried no weapons, spoke for the rest: "All we can do is run."

"Maybe you won't have to," said Caleem, wielding his sword.

They heard the soft tapping of clawed feet again.

"What is that rodent up to?" asked Marbel.

"When I find you, I'm going to introduce your stinking fur

to this beautiful blade," Caleem promised, his voice echoing through the night.

The enchanted valley covered an extensive area. They advanced among a plethora of colorful monoliths and exotic greenery and soon found themselves marching up and down small hills.

"I hope the way out is close," said Naji.

"I th—" Zig began. The boy froze, his eyes fixed on a pile of rocks ahead. Everyone stopped to stare except Naji, who walked on, overtaking Caleem.

"Maybe we're not that far—" Naji stopped when someone squeezed his shoulder.

His finger hard on his mouth, Caleem frowned more than usual.

The boy stood still as a statue.

"Nobody move a muscle," whispered Kamanar.

Naji stared ahead at the pile of rocks glinting in the moonlight.

"Snake!" The whisper escaped Naji's lips.

Their eyes were glued on the enormous body, coiled in several layers, thick as the trunk of a giant tree. The skin was covered in hard, uneven scales made of stone and metal; weeds and mushrooms thrived on it. There were only a few patches where the skin was smooth and glinting. Scariest of all was the monster's humongous, triangular head. It's many long, blade-like teeth shot out in all directions, even piercing its own jaws.

Nothing could have prepared the men for the true magnitude of what they were facing.

"It's either dead or asleep. And we are *not* going to stay around to find out which," Kamanar said as he crept around the creature while motioning for the others to follow.

One by one, they walked as far away from the massive snake as they could. The creature still did not stir. Only Caleem remained in place, drawing his sword as he stepped closer to the snake.

"Caleem, what are you doing?" whispered Kamanar.

"It's sleeping. I'll drive my sword through its skull," said Caleem, closing the distance.

"No. Don't."

Kamanar watched in anguish. He signaled the others to move farther away from the beast.

Gripping the sword, the prince stood a few steps away from his target. His eyes locked onto it, and he raised his weapon above the gargantuan head.

Mucus dripped off the sword-like fangs into a slimy puddle right below the snake's mammoth jaws. Acid fumes rose to Caleem's nostrils as the corrosive saliva ate through the rock. Upon seeing one hideous, membrane-covered eye between the bulging teeth, Caleem heard Kamanar's words echo in his mind. Backing away, the prince returned the sword to its sheath, and Kamanar sighed with relief.

"We must find a way out of here," said Marbel.

"Indeed," said Caleem.

Pointing away from the beast and toward where the colorful crystals decorated the landscape, Kamanar said, "Come."

A few paces farther, Sarik stopped and glanced back at the monster.

"Znits!" he said. "What the hell is he doing?"

In the faint moonlight, everyone saw the rat standing very close to the snake's huge, triangular head.

"He's out of his mind," whispered Marbel.

The rat kicked the snake's head then picked up a large stone and hit it again.

The monster began to unravel its long body.

Znits turned to run, but after just one step, he disappeared between the snake's jaws. He only managed one last, feeble squeak.

Looking around, the snake inched forward. It halted, its eyes locked on the men.

"Scatter around. Run!" shouted Kamanar.

So they did.

Only Kamanar and Caleem stood their ground to face the beast.

As the monster slithered along the winding path of crystals, breaking them to bits, its mighty open jaws headed with great speed straight towards the two men.

CHAPTER 42
RUN!

Caleem stood alert with his sword drawn and Kamanar beside him. When the snake's massive head sprung forward, Kamanar dodged to the left while Caleem rolled to the right. The monster skimmed the ground in between them and slammed its head into a rock. Caleem raised his sword high over his head and brought it down as hard as he could onto the snake's slithering body, but the blade only grazed its hard skin, making Caleem gasp. The snake whipped its tail, hit Caleem behind his knees, and hurled him through the air. The sword flew out of his hands and disappeared into the darkness of the cave. Caleem cursed as he spun, then crashed face down on the rock floor between two blue crystal monoliths.

He lay motionless.

The menacing head slithered toward the prince. Kamanar leaped onto the snake and clutched its neck. He pulled as hard as he could, attempting to divert it, but it was like pulling on a tree trunk. He slipped under the creature and pulled on its lower jaw with both hands, trying to keep it from reaching the prostrate prince.

The snake continued to inch forward.

"Unworthy rodents. You will pay. You will feel my wrath on your flesh," boomed a voice inside the cave.

The snake's sword-like teeth almost touched the unconscious prince. In a desperate move, Kamanar swung his body to the side, twisting the serpent's giant head.

The enormous jaws slammed shut then opened and shut again, yet Kamanar held on. Drops of slimy acid oozed from the creature's mouth and splashed onto Kamanar's leg. The toxic liquid burned through his pants, reaching the skin. He withdrew his leg and moaned.

With perfect timing, Sarik appeared out of nowhere clasping a bunch of crystal shards. Facing the snake's fearsome jaws, he tossed the crystals deep into the creature's open mouth. The snake rattled its head. Every time it howled, Sarik threw in more shards. With a nasty grunt, the snake managed to spit out a few of the crystals then charged at Sarik. The young man dropped the remaining pieces and fled. The snake chased after him, abandoning Caleem as it crushed the colorful crystals strewn across the ground. Kamanar rode along, still holding on to the snake's neck.

"Marbel, Naji, where are you?" called Zig.

"Here!" the two replied in unison.

"We're here," Naji cried, but Zig still could not discern where his friend's voice was coming from.

"We're in a pit," shouted Marbel.

"Keep talking, so I can follow your voices," said Zig.

"We're here."

"Over here."

"That thing will hear us if we keep shouting," said Marbel.

The crystals made it easier to see, but the fake moon's dim light cast shadows everywhere, making some of the darker areas look like black pits. Zig stepped carefully, feeling the way with his feet. Kamanar's and Sarik's cries echoed in his ears.

A hand grabbed the boy's leg and pulled him down into a shallow pit.

"Are you all right?" asked the older man.

"I'm fine. I ran into a dark wall," said Zig, still agitated.

"Shhh …" said Naji. "I can hear only Kamanar and Sarik, but not Caleem."

"I hope he's safe," said Marbel.

"Ungrateful creatures! My relentless scorn is unleashed upon you," the booming voice echoed.

"There is it again. Who's saying that?" asked Zig.

"I have to help them." Marbel made to climb out of the pit, but Zig pulled him back in.

"Stay, Marbel," Zig pleaded.

"All right," Marbel said, clearly relieved.

A scuffle culminated in a scream.

"Kamanar." Zig grabbed onto the edge of the pit, and stuck his head out. Naji joined him.

"Stay put," said Marbel to the boys.

"What—?"

"I have to try," the chubby man said and jumped out to head toward the racket.

Marbel glimpsed a glint in the darkness. Slowing down to get a better view, he discovered Caleem's sword hanging from the top of the cave. The strange, fake, starry skies seemed high, yet the sword hung not very far from his head. He jumped as high as he could, but he failed to reach the hilt. Kamanar and Sarik's cries became more intense.

"I would give my cow for a ladder or something," said Marbel, searching for some useful object. "The boys …" he murmured while running back to the pit.

"Zig, Naji, where are you?"

"Where did you go? We're here," said Zig.

"Right where you left us," said Naji.

"Can you see me?" asked Marbel.

"Yes."

"Come on. I need your help." Soon enough, he saw their silhouettes crawling out of the hole. "Come quick."

The boys followed him.

"Up there. It's Caleem's sword," Zig whispered.

"Yes, yes," Marbel said. "We're going to get it. Come on, Naji, get on my shoulders." He spread his legs slightly while he arched his back and put his hands on his knees.

Naji looked at Zig, shrugged, and climbed up onto Marbel's back. The old man did his best to steady himself without complaining.

"On the shoulders," said Marbel, straining to keep stable.

Both of his legs trembling, Naji stood up on the fat man's shoulders. "I can't reach it."

"Damn it! It doesn't look that high," said the older man, shaking.

Zig climbed onto Marbel's back, then on to Naji's shoulders, making a tower of three.

"Zig … I can't hold you both!" moaned Marbel.

"Just a moment."

"I ca—"

The pitter-patter of feet approached. Marbel froze as Sarik raced past them, the enormous snake hot on his heels. Kamanar was still holding onto the beast's head. The creature crushed everything in its path while snapping its jaws nonstop.

Before Marbel could breathe a sigh of relief, the human tower collapsed. Moaning, Naji and Marbel stared at Zig, who jumped to his feet. He smiled as he picked up the hilt of the sword lying next to him.

"Well done. Give it here. Get back in the pit," said Marbel as he rubbed his aching back. He yanked the sword from the boy's hands and followed the trail of shattered crystals.

Sarik made his way among the colorful monoliths. After bumping into an invisible wall several times, he realized he was running around in an enclosed area. He still had no idea how to take on the fearsome creature. All he could do was lead the beast as far away from the unconscious Caleem as possible. The shattering of crystals grew closer behind him, and the smell of nauseating acid was strong in his nostrils; he glimpsed the open jaws right on his heels.

Kamanar still clung to the creature's neck, though he was clearly struggling.

The creature smashed its way through the cave. Kamanar tried to catch one of the crystal's flying shards.

The snake's body, twisting from side to side, advanced like a tumbling avalanche.

The mysterious voice reverberated again, coming from inside the snake. "Useless, ungrateful traitors …"

Sarik ducked behind a rock. The snake slowed down as it changed course. Not far ahead, Caleem still lay on the ground.

Unimpeded by Kamanar's grip, the large head hovered over the prince. Its powerful jaws opened, ready to devour the unconscious Caleem. Sarik was about to race in when Kamanar grabbed a crystal shard from the ground and, with all of his strength, jammed it into the snake's eye.

The creature let out a freakish cry and shook its head, trying to get rid of Kamanar. The warrior dropped the crystal and held on. The snake threw its head in all directions, slamming it against the floor and rocks, but the warrior retained his grip.

The snake went still for a moment, then its tail whipped around and slammed into Kamanar's back. The forceful blow flung him off and sent him rolling across the ground. Kamanar shook his head and bounced back to his feet only for the snake to start lowering its jaws toward Caleem again.

Kamanar sprung with his arms extended. The snake's jaws snapped shut, but this time not of its own volition. Kamanar had encircled the snake's upper and lower jaws, forcing them together. Each time the monster tried to open its mouth, Kamanar pressed it closed again, sending the beast into a mad rage. Kamanar was thrashed about. Glancing over at Sarik, he yelled, "Take Caleem away!"

The tail lashed at Kamanar, and he slipped himself below the jaws. The snake struck itself in the head. A muffled groan escaped its sharp-toothed mouth. The snake tossed its head, thrusting the commander into a large red crystal, shattering it. Kamanar moaned as his ribs cracked and sharp teeth pierced his abdomen. He let go and fell to the floor only to force himself back up.

Marbel blared behind the reptile, "Take this, you giant worm!"

The creature bent backward. Letting out another freakish cry, it turned away from the commander.

With Caleem's sword in his hand, the fat man came out from behind the squirming snake to run to his commander.

"I hit it! I hit it!" he cried. "But it's barely cut …"

Kamanar snatched the sword from Marbel's hands and patted the old man on the shoulder.

"Run!" he said.

While the snake was still twisting and turning, Kamanar noticed a tight crevice in the ground. He jammed the hilt of the sword deep into the crevice, leaving the blade pointing upward.

The snake crept toward Kamanar, who sprinted, leaving the planted sword behind. The snake passed the sword, chasing after the fleeing warrior among the glittering crystals.

Kamanar's lungs burned with each breath, and he had to slow down. The snake began to close the distance. Marbel and Sarik appeared at their commander's side, pushing him on, trying to outrun the monster.

"This way," said Kamanar, struggling for breath.

They could feel the snake's breath on their backs, hear its snapping jaws.

Sarik strayed a bit, and Kamanar pulled the young man toward him. "Stay close to me," he whispered as he raced on in a curving path.

As the commander began to falter, they pushed him on again.

"Go!" Kamanar ordered, pushing the two as they passed the vertical sword. He turned to face the beast.

The unrelenting snake slithered forward, its jaws wide open

and ready to devour Kamanar. He froze and closed his eyes, waiting for the jaws to slam shut upon him.

The snake rammed into the long blade. The beast's jaws split in half, splaying on either side of Kamanar. The blade bisected the entire head and some of its body. Blood mixed with other fluids splattered all over Kamanar. Silence ruled the cave.

Marbel ran to his commander and smiled in disbelief as he wiped blood and slime from his face. "Nice … to say the least. Are you all right?"

"I'm all right," said Kamanar, rubbing his eyes. "I think I broke a rib or two but nothing to worry about."

Marbel patted him on the shoulder then pulled his hand away. "It stings!" he said, wiping his hand. Using his sleeves, he wiped the remaining slime off his commander's shoulders and face.

"Thank you, Marbel."

"For what?"

"For being brave," said Kamanar, looking the man in the eye.

"You're the one who killed that damn thing," Marbel said, looking back at the hideous carcass.

"It was a team effort. I saw you three reaching for the sword."

"This thing stinks," said Naji, who popped out from behind a pile of crystals and kicked the motionless body.

Zig, who followed close behind, kicked the snake, too. The boys stared at Kamanar's torn clothes and lacerated hands.

"Are you all right?" asked Naji.

"What about Caleem?" asked Kamanar.

The boy pointed. "He's back there."

"Caleem, come. Your sword is here," Zig called.

His hand on his forehead, Caleem appeared with Sarik. "Where is it?"

"There." Zig pointed at the snake's split head. "Kamanar killed it."

"It was a team effort," said Kamanar.

The prince looked at the dead creature and the sword jutting out of its crevice, then at Kamanar and the gashes on his hands and torn clothes. Taking his hand away from his forehead, he revealed a massive bump throbbing between his eyebrows. The prince walked up to the sword, rattled it a little, then pulled it out.

His face twisted in disgust at the sight of the sliced head. Thick fumes and fluids were still oozing out of it. He wiped the blade with his sleeve then stepped carefully between the puddles of blood and acidic mucus.

CHAPTER 43
WHAT IS THIS WITCHCRAFT?

"We are not alone. You heard that voice: 'I will punish you, filthy rodents'," said Marbel.

"The voice came from the snake," said Kamanar. "I'm guessing it was the sorcerer's voice—Gudjewkan's father."

"But he died a long time ago," said Naji.

"True, but his curse apparently didn't," said Kamanar.

"Maybe he's … inside the snake." Naji shuddered, as did Zig.

The men looked at the boys with mocking expressions.

"Impressive," said Caleem, looking at the dead creature then at Kamanar. The latter's face broke into a smile then into laughter, his hand on his chest as the pain in his ribcage pierced him.

The commander struggled to calm down. "Sorry you missed it, Mr. … Unicorn!"

They all laughed while Caleem fingered the large bump on his forehead. "Fine. Very funny … Are you done? We need to get out of here fast."

"That Znits. We should have—" Marbel began.

"Kamanar's pal," said Caleem.

"I knew there was something rotten about him," said Naji.

"We're done with Znits and the snake. There's a black wall

surrounding this place. Let's split up and look for a way out. We need to get out of here fast, as the *unicorn* said." Kamanar chuckled, holding his chest. "Stay alert," he said and walked among the glinting crystals. Marbel followed.

Caleem motioned to Sarik. "Come. We'll go that way." The two of them disappeared behind a large rock.

The boys went the opposite way.

After the others disappeared from sight, Marbel approached his commander. "You know, Kamanar, when it was first offered, I wanted to refuse to join this mission, but there's a reason why I didn't."

"Really, what is that?"

"Criando … my firstborn. Ten years ago, he was drafted into the Black Company when he was nine. I know it's an honor and that I can't claim my boy back. But for me and my wife, this was devastating. We just can't get over it."

"What are you asking of me, Marbel?"

"I'm asking for my son back," said the older man in a quivering voice.

"You're asking for the impossible. Still, when we complete our task, I'll try my best. I'll personally request this of King Creeden."

Tears welled up in Marbel's eyes as he smiled.

The two reached the transparent barrier that had shut them in.

"There must be a way to open these things. Maybe it can be breached," said Marbel.

"The previous one had a mechanism that Znits was able to control," said Kamanar, touching the barrier

"But where is it?" Marbel wondered.

They heard the prince's voice nearby. "Let me try."

The two strode toward the voice. They found Sarik and Caleem tinkering with a little square box in the wall. At its center glowed two blue hexagonal crystals, one above the other.

"This might open the gate," said Marbel.

"Thank you for enlightening us," said Caleem.

The prince pulled on the lower of the two crystals with both hands until he ripped it off its base. The rock continued to glow while he held it.

Kamanar managed to pry the second crystal loose. "Give me the other one." Caleem handed the crystal to Kamanar. The commander faced the gate, raised the crystals over his head and pressed them together.

"Nothing's happening," said Marbel.

"Let me try," said Caleem.

"By all means, show us how it's done," said Kamanar.

Caleem approached the gate, pushed the crystals against it, then set them down at the base. "Maybe this way …" He took a few steps back. Nothing moved.

Marbel tried sticking his fingers into the box that had housed the crystals, but this didn't work, either.

The four men stood side by side pondering the mystery.

The dark sky brightened.

"What's happening? What is this witchcraft?" asked Marbel.

The stars disappeared, and the dark sky began to turn a bright azure. The faint moonlight shone stronger with a yellowish-white light, becoming almost blinding.

"The moon turned into—" said Marbel.

"Sun," Sarik said, finishing the sentence as he covered his eyes.

It took a short while to adjust to the intense brightness. In the fake sunlight, the tall, black walls surrounding the area became visible. They reached up and around the fake skies, revealing the domed shape of the cave.

"This place is getting stranger and stranger," said Marbel.

A few moments later, someone giggled and grunted profanities.

"It's the troublemakers," said Sarik.

They all walked to the two boys, who were still laughing.

Gray clouds gathered, covering the blue sky. The cave became darker. A streak of lightning flashed across the sky and reflected in thousands of crystal prisms, accompanied by loud rolls of thunder. An intense rain shower poured down.

Marbel and Caleem, followed by Kamanar, sought shelter near the curved wall. Still looking up, only Sarik remained where he was.

"It's another illusion."

Kamanar turned his gashed palm upwards. "I can't feel the drops."

"An illusion," repeated Sarik with a big smile on his face.

"It's all witchcraft and sorcery in this cave," said Marbel. "It's raining, but we're not getting wet." He looked up, blinking, although no real raindrops reached his eyes.

"You can even hear the noise of drops splashing on the ground," said the prince.

No puddles were forming on the floor, and no water flowed through the cracks. The ground was as dry as it had been before.

The boys' peals of laughter interrupted their discussion. The four warriors found the pair sitting on two small stools behind an arched rock table. They were banging on different sections of the table.

"Watch this," Naji boasted, pressing on something. The rain stopped and the clouds were gone as quickly as they had appeared. It grew dark again, with the moon shining as it had before.

"You did all this?" asked Sarik.

"Yes," said Zig. Noticing the others staring at them, he said, "It was Naji."

Kamanar popped up behind Sarik to examine the stone slab. Embedded in its surface were numerous crystals of different shapes and colors.

Caleem bent over the table, scanning its components. He slapped the back of Naji's head. "Bring back the sun."

"All right, all right." Naji pressed a round, yellow crystal. The sky cleared, the stars vanished, and the sun replaced the moon. Broad daylight shone across the cave.

"That's it. Now don't touch anything," said Caleem. "Get off—this is not a toy!" He pushed the boys off the stools.

"This thing controls the make-believe, but not the gate," said Kamanar. "At least now we can look for a way out." He scanned the black wall circling the cave's perimeter.

"I see something over there," said Sarik.

Following Sarik's glance, they all went to investigate.

"Two crystals again," said Marbel, gesturing to two transparent crystal cubes embedded in the wall.

"I think a different kind of people built this," Sarik said.

"What do you mean 'different kind'?" asked Kamanar.

"My grandmother, God rest her soul, once told me a story about magical creatures who lived in an underground world. They dwelled in a magical crystal kingdom. She said these creatures disappeared long ago. We thought it was just a fairy tale."

"The crystal people," said Marbel. "That's what they were called. The crystal people. I've heard that legend, too, also from my grandparents. It was even rumored that one could find great treasures in their caves."

"Enough with the bedtime stories," said Caleem. "With all due respect to your grandmothers, we need to get the hell out of here. Our mission is much more important than any treasure."

The prince approached the two small crystals. He pressed the top square and watched as it lit up bright yellow. A hidden door slid open with a rumble. "That's how it's done," said the prince.

Beyond the door was a smooth, round passage. Inside, small yellow crystal lights came on in sequence. Kamanar led the way, and they strode down the mysterious tunnel until they reached a junction.

"Left, right, forward … or backward?" Caleem asked with a snicker while staring at Kamanar.

Kamanar hurried ahead, his eyes fixed on some object farther along the tunnel. "I see a door," he said and walked up to a semi-transparent door tinted a light shade of blue. He was still considering his next step when it began to slide open, emitting a peculiar hissing sound that startled all of them.

"It could be a trap!" said Marbel.

"Stop with the traps," said Kamanar. "I'm going in." He stuck his head through the threshold and peeked inside the small, round room. Alert, he entered, and found three square crystals affixed to the wall. The top and bottom ones were yellow, and the one in the middle was red. After some hesitation, Kamanar pressed the bottom crystal. The semi-transparent bluish door hissed shut behind him, trapping him inside while his peers looked on, dumbfounded.

The entire room sank out of sight, along with Kamanar. His friends banged on the door, yet they were helpless to stop the fall.

"Kamanar!" Zig's yell was followed by silence.

"I knew it was a trap," said Marbel.

They all put their foreheads against the semi-transparent door and looked down to see the room rising back from the dark depths. The strange capsule whooshed right by the door, continuing up and vanishing once again. They managed to catch a fleeting glimpse of a stunned Kamanar standing at the center.

"What the hell?" asked Caleem.

A few moments later, the room descended back to its original location. The door hissed open, and Kamanar remained inside, smiling. His friends gaped at him.

"What happened?" asked Caleem.

"Come, get inside," Kamanar said, but none of them dared to move. "Don't worry, this is the way out."

"The way out?" asked Caleem. He entered and the others followed.

"Good," Kamanar said and pressed the top yellow crystal. The bluish door closed, and the floor began to rise.

"We're falling!" yelled Marbel in a panic, pressing himself against the rounded wall.

"Falling … but up," said Caleem.

"Amazing," said Zig, grinning.

Naji clung to the wall. "We're going to crash."

The commander crossed his arms over his chest and smiled.

After a few moments, the room stopped. The door slid to the side, and behind it an external stone door slid open. Naji and Marbel leaped out, panting, and the rest exited, looking around.

A large bush partially obscured the entryway, and golden rays of sunlight filtered in through the branches. They hurried past it to find a breathtaking sight.

"A bit chilly. But this is the most beautiful sunrise I've ever witnessed," said Marbel.

They took in the dawn's colors in wonderment as the cool mountain wind caressed their faces. The orange disk of the sun rose above the enchanted oak forest, which spread out like an ocean with its treetops jutting up like frozen green waves. High above, a blanket of gray clouds covered the sky.

"Finally," said Naji. "I'm so sick of caves and tunnels, and I'm hungry. Zig, come on—we'll look for some mushrooms behind those rocks."

"We must keep going. We don't even know where we are yet," said Caleem.

"We do need a little rest," said Kamanar weakly.

Caleem approached the tall man.

Kamanar's head hung low, and he said, "We're close to the Spy Trail. It's over there … I can see the trailhead. Down, near the Black Rock." He pointed to a ravine covered in abundant vegetation. "Let's rest for a while." He put his hand on his forehead and his legs trembled, then he swayed and dropped to his knees.

Marbel rushed to him. "Are you all right?"

Kamanar bounced back to his feet. "I'm fine. A little dizzy—nothing to worry about."

Caleem gazed at the ravine.

"Let's … let's rest for a bit," said Marbel, looking at Caleem.

"No. We've lost enough time already. It's not safe here," said the prince.

They all turned to Kamanar, but the tall man said nothing while staring at the sun while it disappeared behind the clouds.

"Maybe he's just hungry? Me and Zig will look for mushrooms," said Naji.

"This place could be teeming with Dalusians. And those are worse than the rats. We move now, and we'll rest once we're on the Spy Trail," said the prince.

CHAPTER 44
WHERE'S KAMANAR?

"Come on, Sarik, start walking," said Caleem.

Sarik, as confused as ever, took a few strides. Kamanar jumped to his feet, passed the young man, and took his position at the front of the line. "We'll continue, then," he said, setting off on a path between the rocks.

"Sarik, wait. I'll take the lead. You take the rear," said the prince, moving to the front of the team. "He's avoiding me," added the prince, skipping among the jagged gray rocks.

Matching Caleem's steps, Marbel whispered, "Listen, Caleem. This power struggle …"

The prince stopped and turned to face his friend. "There can only be one commander here, and it can't be him. How can you trust him? Just look at how he's behaving now."

The boys soon approached from behind, followed by Sarik.

"He saved your life down in the cave," said Naji while he helped Zig release his bow from a bush.

"That's right, those cuts on his arms came about when he pulled that monster's teeth away from you," said Marbel.

Caleem glared at Marbel. "It still doesn't justify what he's done. The fact that he did me a favor won't stop me from doing the right thing. I will resolve this issue," he said and ran forward to catch up with Kamanar, who entered the gorge.

They all descended, making their way among undergrowth and rocks. The slope was steep, with the occasional branch getting in their way. Nevertheless, sticking to animal trails allowed them to keep a good pace.

Caleem looked ahead from time to time, but Kamanar was nowhere to be seen.

"Mushrooms," said Zig.

"Silence! Didn't I make myself clear earlier? If you must talk, whisper," said the prince.

Zig dropped his gaze.

Naji strayed from the trail to pick a mushroom, thread it on one of the arrows from his quiver, then raise it up high for his friends to see. "Look at the size of this thing." The huge, spongy mushroom was deep red with white spots.

"Drop it right now!" Marbel commanded. "That's poisonous."

"But look at the size of this thing. It looks edible," Naji whispered back.

"Do as you're told," said Caleem.

Marbel said, "Let's catch up with Kamanar."

Naji tossed the mushroom then prompted Zig on. Caleem led the way up the narrow gorge. As the sky got darker, a light drizzle fell. No one spoke as the task of scaling the rocky slope demanded all their attention.

Looking ahead to where the gorge widened, his wet hands clenched into fists, Zig asked, "Where's Kamanar? Why doesn't he wait? Caleem is so annoying."

"It's really cold," said Naji, who hunched over with his arms crossed.

"You prefer the caves?" asked Sarik.

"Caleem is rubbing off on you," said the boy.

"No, you misunderstood. I was trying to cheer you up, to make you see the full half of the cup," said Sarik.

"That moving room did save us a lot of climbing," said Marbel. "Judging by the cold breeze, we're not far from the top."

Caleem said, "Could be—it's hard to tell, because the

mountain is too steep. I'm guessing it may take us another day or two of climbing to reach the ambush."

"A couple of days sounds too good to be true," said Marble.

"We'll make it eventually. Let's take a short break," said Caleem.

"Let's have something to eat," said Sarik.

"Half ration," said Caleem.

Zig asked, "What about Kamanar? We should keep some for him."

"Listen, all of you," said Caleem, "Kamanar is not fit to lead this mission anymore, and you all know it."

"That's not true," said Zig.

"He's more fit than you could ever be!" said Naji.

Caleem leaned his back against a rock. "Where's your glorious commander right now?"

"I—"

"You don't know. Neither do I. He just headed out on his own, abandoning you in enemy territory. What commander would do such a thing? He's unpredictable … and he's avoiding me, probably hoping that I cool down."

"Kamanar is no coward," said Naji

"That remains to be seen," said Caleem. "Besides, neither your opinion nor that of your friend count for anything. Once I catch up with your commander, I'll order him to go home. You two can join him."

"That will never happen. Kamanar would never back down," said Naji.

Caleem rose to his feet, pulled out his long sword, and ran his fingers over the blade. "I know," he said, looking at the blade with a menacing gaze. "We've rested long enough. If someone hasn't finished eating, he may do so while on the move," Caleem said and continued to climb.

The disgruntled boys got up and set out after Marbel, who remained quiet. Sarik, also offering no comment, was last. The ascent continued under persistent rainfall. The slope became steeper, forcing them to climb with their hands at times.

"After the rain comes the sun," whispered Marbel to the drooping boys, who walked with dipped heads. The two didn't bother even looking at the chubby man.

The march continued into the night, the pace slowing down. Every now and then, someone lost his footing, stumbling and falling among the slippery rocks. Much to Caleem's surprise, no one complained or asked to stop for rest. At around midnight, Caleem halted, noticing that the air was much colder than before. The group huddled around him. "Well done," Caleem whispered. "We've covered a lot of ground today. It wasn't easy. Dalusians can't see through the mist. We'll soon enter a foggy area where it'll be safe to get some rest. Stay close to each other. I don't want to lose anyone."

"It's impossible to get lost. There's only up or down," said Naji.

"That's right. But if you lag or somehow overtake us, we might mistake you for a Dalusian, and your friend Zig could shoot an arrow into your behind," said Caleem before he turned around and marched on.

"You wouldn't shoot me, right?" asked Naji.

"Of course not," said Zig. "Where's Kamanar? Why doesn't he wait a bit?"

Marbel pointed at a long footprint in a muddy patch. "He is somewhere ahead."

A thick fog began to envelop them, making the world even darker.

"Look for shelter among the rocks," said Caleem.

Without saying a word, they scattered among the rocks. Naji and Zig crouched down where they had stopped, clinging to each other for warmth. Sarik sat down next to the boys. Reclining against a cold rock, he tucked his hands in between his legs and rested his head on his shoulder.

"What's the matter? Come rest a bit," said Marbel.

"I'm not tired. I want to do some scouting. I'll be back soon," said Caleem.

"It's pitch-black."

"It is," the prince said and disappeared.

"Crazy ..." Marbel puffed and lay on his side on a small bush, using his arms for a pillow.

Caleem walked farther up the dark gorge where the vegetation was sparser. The drumming of the rain intensified. He heard squelching close by. His fingers stroked the hilt of his sword as he crept forward. Moving from rock to rock, he heard whispering. He inched forward, crouching, poised to attack.

He discerned a single silhouette standing among the rocks, its back turned to Caleem. The prince recognized the tall figure. It was none other than Kamanar, alone yet mumbling for some reason.

"Who are you talking to?" asked the prince.

Kamanar continued to ramble, his palms on the surface of two rocks blocking his way. He was trying to climb over, but each time he lifted a leg, he would slip back into a puddle.

"Turn around and answer—"

The tall man repeatedly strove to climb the obstacle in front of him and repeatedly fell.

Caleem backtracked, returning to where he had left the others. He stumbled over Marbel's belly. The old man whimpered in his sleep. Caleem lay down next to his friends and put his hand to his forehead, shielding his eyes from the spatter of the rain.

Birds tweeted in the treetops as the world became brighter and the heavy fog thinned somewhat. Caleem, who had not slept for a minute, got up, shook his cap and wet clothes, then proceeded to wake everyone else up.

"Oh, that hurts," said Marbel, placing his hand on his back.

"I thought you'd be used to sleeping on rocks by now," said the prince.

"Rocks and rain ... How about you? Sleep well?"

"Like a rock," said Caleem.

They all laughed at Caleem's joke.

"We're moving on," said Caleem, who stretched his limbs and began a new march up the foggy ravine.

Naji picked up his quiver and slung it over his back. "This pesky rain. I slept and woke a hundred times," he said.

"Remind me to lend you my duck-feather pillow," said Caleem.

"Very funny," said Naji.

Chapter 45

I Want to Feel the Rain on My Face

The prince stopped at two rocks blocking the path then looked around.

"What is it?" asked Zig.

"Nothing." Caleem jumped on the rocks and hoisted himself up.

One by one, they climbed over after him.

Out of the corner of his eye, Caleem caught a glimpse of Kamanar, who was lying face-down among the rocks on the side of the path. He carried on past him.

As they advanced, no one said a word, their only preoccupation being finding the next firm foothold to avoid slipping on the wet rocks.

"Who's there?" someone whispered.

Caleem turned around to see Sarik veering off the path.

"It's Kamanar!" Sarik called, kneeling beside him.

They stood around the tall man, with Caleem being the last to join.

"Kamanar, are you all right?" asked Zig.

The tall man let out a faint sigh. He raised his head and struggled to get up on one knee. With Naji's help, he managed to rise to his feet, his wet hair covering his face. "What's wrong?" asked Naji. "Kamanar!"

"His gashes …" Zig mumbled.

They all looked at Kamanar's mangled hands, which were covered in deep cuts, exposing raw flesh.

Marbel examined them up close. "What is this?"

Kamanar let go of Naji and placed one foot forward. He wobbled for a moment then took another tentative step and stopped.

"It's the venom," said Sarik.

The tall man took one more step forward.

"Come, Zig. Let's help him," said Naji.

Kamanar leaned on the boys' shoulders as they supported him.

Caleem took a deep breath then followed the boys, who struggled to prop the tall man up while they steered among the rocks.

"We can't go on like this," said the prince.

Naji said, "We're not leaving him here!"

"No chance!" said Zig.

Marbel and Sarik wanted to help the two boys, but Caleem, staring at Sarik, blocked their path. "You amaze me. Are you that naive? You want to aid the man who wanted you dead?"

Sarik lowered his eyes then glanced at Kamanar. "Look at him."

Kamanar was leaning on the boys, his head slumped to his chest, his feet dragging behind him. Caleem said nothing and marched behind, watching the panting boys maneuver around each rock. Naji slipped, pulling Kamanar down with him to the muddy ground.

Blood began pouring out of Kamanar's mouth.

"Marbel, come quickly!" Zig cried.

"Keep quiet," said Caleem.

"Don't tell him to *keep quiet*! Kamanar is dying because of you. You ungrateful bastard," said Naji.

"If you raise your voice one more time—"

"He's still bleeding," said Marbel. "Help me turn him over." Marbel palpated Kamanar's stomach then peeled back his shirt to reveal a horrible mass of festering wounds.

Kamanar moaned. His face, veiled by his dark, wet hair, contorted in a grimace. The commander whispered something while straining to get up. "Matar—"

"Lie down, Kamanar. You're not—" said Marbel.

Kamanar pushed Marbel away then struggled to his feet. He reached like a blind man then slouched. Zig rushed to hold him, followed by the others. Only Caleem stood by. Zig began sobbing while Marbel and Sarik picked up their wounded commander and helped him up the slope.

"Wait," said Caleem. "Let's find him shelter. We'll return for him after we complete our mission. It's the only way."

They all looked at Kamanar then at each other.

Naji asked,"Where will we find shelter?"

"First, we clear this part of the gorge. Follow me," said Caleem.

With great effort, they managed to lift the unconscious Kamanar out of the ditch. They plowed through the bushes and exited into a small green clearing.

"What a pretty place," said Caleem. "There—bring him over." He pointed to a dark gap between rocks and motioned them to follow. They stooped through the low entryway, finding themselves in a shallow cave. They laid their commander's body down, leaning him against the rocks with his head on his chest. Marbel knelt and lifted his head back up. Kamanar gurgled with every strained breath. His face was as pale as snow, the stubble on his chin soaked with the blood dripping from his mouth. His eyes, only half-open, were covered in a layer of some white substance.

"What do you think, Marbel?" asked Zig in a trembling voice.

"Not good," said the old man.

"What does that mean?" asked Naji.

"This venom is too strong for any man to endure," said the old man.

Naji asked, "What about that purple stuff we used before?"

"We don't have any. There's nothing we can do," Marbel said, his voice breaking.

"There has to be something …" said Zig.

"We'll come back for him as soon as possible," the prince said.

"We can take him back now. Maybe Gudjewkan can help—" Zig began.

"What would Kamanar say about that? This is not an option. Not when we're so close," said Caleem.

Naji stomped out of the cave, and Caleem followed the boy.

Sarik knelt and kissed Kamanar's forehead.

"Well done, Sarik," said Marbel.

Sarik got up and took a step back. He said nothing, and a tear rolled down his cheek. Zig began sobbing as he embraced Kamanar. Marbel put a comforting arm around the boy, who got up and left the cave along with Sarik.

Marbel remained alone with Kamanar, combing the commander's hair back with his fingers.

"Is it raining, Marbel?" asked Kamanar.

"What? Yes, it is."

"Sorry about your boy."

"Don't worry about that. I'm sure he's fine."

"Please, take me outside. I want to feel the rain on my face one last time."

Marbel nodded and carefully dragged his friend outside. He laid Kamanar on the grass under the foggy, grey sky.

"He loves the rain," said the old man, half turning to the men behind him as he wiped his moist eyes.

"Come on," said Caleem.

One by one, they made their way back into the gorge.

Marbel stayed behind, kneeling beside his motionless friend. Kamanar's eyes were still half-open despite the pouring rain.

Marbel placed a hand on the commander's chest but felt no heartbeat. "Much before your time. Farewell," he whispered, closing Kamanar's eyelids.

Marbel descended back into the ravine and joined the others. "Let's go," he said, his voice breaking.

CHAPTER 46
DON'T WORRY ABOUT IT

Caleem went last, watching his slouched comrades navigate the rocky terrain.

Zig tried to hide behind a boulder, but they all heard his sobs. Caleem approached the boy and put an arm around him. "Come here."

Zig shrugged, burying his face in the fold of his elbow.

"Please," said Caleem, pulling him closer as they walked to their friends.

"I know you all think I despise Kamanar," he said. There was no response. "It's true that we disagree on many things, but the fact remains that we have made it this far. I know that you're all—that we are all saddened by this. He does not deserve to die like this. Once we finish our duty, we'll take turns, and we'll carry him home. He can make it. You know him. Kamanar is a strong man."

Marbel wanted to correct the prince, but after seeing hope rekindled in everyone's eyes, especially the boys', he held his tongue.

"He can beat this," said Zig.

"Then what are we waiting for? Let's get moving," said Naji.

Zig nodded, beginning to move.

"Good. Let's get this over with, for Kamanar's sake," said Caleem as he set off. The fog thickened again, and the rain continued to pour down. Although they quickened their steps, it felt as if they were marching in place. All they could see ahead were roots clutching smooth, wet rocks. Sometime past noon, Caleem stopped to study the path ahead.

"The ravine is leading deeper into the mountain. It's not far away," said Caleem.

"How 'not far away' is that?" asked Naji.

"We'll be there by evening."

"Come on, come on," said Zig, prodding Naji to walk faster.

A stream of rainwater flowed down the already slippery gorge. There were no more trees, only thorny bushes that pricked and scratched their legs while the icy water permeated their worn footwear.

"You said we'd be there by evening," Zig whispered behind Caleem.

Caleem whispered back, "Soon."

"How soon?" asked Naji.

"We'll get there whenever we get there. Now shut up! It's not evening yet. It's just the mountain casting its shadow." The prince quickened his pace.

The constant cold stream hurt their feet, but still the march continued into the darkness.

"Caleem," Naji whispered then stumbled on a jutting stone. He fell face down on the wet rocks.

"What?" Caleem's voice came back.

"Damn these rocks. Damn this freezing water," said Naji, peering into the darkness. "Wait, we can't see you."

Caleem's disapproving sigh reached their ears. "Are you afraid of the dark now? You said it yourself, there's only up and down. You can't get lost."

The sounds of splashing indicated that Caleem was on the move again.

"Come on, Naji," Zig whispered. "Don't forget Kamanar."

Marbel, who was behind the boys, let out a mournful sigh. He knew that eventually he would have to tell them the truth about Kamanar. With another deep sigh, he continued on.

The march dragged on into the night, the rain not letting up for a second. The aching of their feet intensified, causing them to gasp with each painful step. Their soaking hands, noses, and ears stung with every gust of wind, but still no one uttered the slightest protests.

They pressed on in silence.

Caleem listened to their steady tread to make sure everyone was still with him. He could hear one boy's chattering teeth. For a moment, even he wanted to stop and take shelter somewhere.

As the night neared its end, it got even colder. They all shivered constantly. Zig and Naji's breath formed little white clouds, and Marbel had his hands tucked under his armpits.

"What the hell …?" asked the prince as he stumbled on a flat slab of stone and then noticed another one above it.

"Stairs," said Naji.

"Come closer." Caleem signaled the others. "All right. The Spy Trail ends here. We are now in enemy territory. We must stay absolutely quiet."

As they reached the top of the staircase, the sound of running water intensified. "A river?" asked Zig.

"Might be a waterfall," said Marbel. "Look ahead."

Zig got a glimpse of foam bubbling in the distance.

"Crouch down here, and stay quiet. I'm going to take a look ahead," said Caleem before crawling forward.

His subjects watched him disappear into the landscape, his shadow visible only against a backdrop of bright rocks, until they lost sight of him. The four waited while their surroundings became brighter. Looking around, they tried to familiarize themselves with the new environment.

After a while, the prince returned. The sword wasn't on his back.

"Your sword!" said Sarik.

"Don't worry about it."

"What do you mean?" asked Naji.

"I said don't worry about it. Dawn is breaking, and we're in enemy territory. We'll hide behind the waterfall until the sun is brighter. Follow me." They continued, hunched over and quiet. Caleem led them to a small waterfall, whose torrent cascaded onto a large, round slab and spilled over into two separate streams. Caleem gave the order to enter. One after the other, they squeezed into their new shelter. The water hit the rocks unrelentingly, spraying them. Marbel and the boys covered their faces.

"Not bad. The water isn't cold," said Caleem, his voice barely audible over the rushing water.

They didn't respond but squinted at him. The prince smiled, ignoring the spray.

"We made it … right? We made it," said Marbel.

"Our target's position is very close," said Caleem. "I saw a great spot on the bank of the elevated river to strike from." Caleem smiled, rubbing his wet hands together. "An ornate tower is clearly visible on the other side. It's the Dalusian general's house."

"Why don't we go now?" asked Marbel. "While it's still dawn."

"There's a Dalusian patrol. I barely evaded them. We'll wait until evening comes."

Resting in their new hideout wasn't easy. Although they tucked themselves as much as they could inside the niche, the spray kept them moist. Several hours went by. Marbel and the boys, leaning in various contorted, unnatural positions, somehow managed to doze on and off. Caleem and Sarik stayed alert. Toward the afternoon hours, the world beyond the waterfall became brighter.

"Look," whispered Caleem, his eyes fixed on something on the other side of the waterfall.

Following Caleem's gaze, Sarik discerned four shadowy figures standing motionless on the other side. Within a minute, more figures joined.

Marbel woke up and asked, "What's happening?"

"Quiet," Caleem whispered.

While slowly maneuvering to find a better position, Marbel's knee jutted out of the waterfall.

The figures on the other side stopped, and Caleem and Sarik held their breath.

"Pull it back!" snapped Caleem.

Marbel folded his knee back. He reverted to his original, awkward position, unable to see what was going on. He just watched his jittery friends.

The mysterious figures walked away and disappeared from sight. Only when the last was gone did Caleem relax. Sarik tossed his head back.

"You nearly exposed us," said Caleem.

"Are they gone?"

Caleem nodded.

"The blood has stopped flowing in my leg," Marbel said.

"Too bad it didn't stop flowing to your brain."

"Dalusians?"

Caleem nodded. "About ten of them."

The chubby man leaned his head back, shrinking into the constricted space. Only part of his face was now visible to Caleem. "So, we really are here."

"Did you doubt it?" asked the prince, who stared at the water, not bothering to cover his face.

"Motehro and Kamanar …" said Sarik.

Marbel glanced at the boys, making sure they were asleep. "I still have some hope for Motehro, but Kamanar is no longer. That's still hard for me to grasp."

"What?" asked the young man.

"He died just a moment after you all went down to the ravine. I just couldn't bring myself to say anything."

Caleem gestured to the dozing boys. "That was the right thing to do. It would have only hindered our progress if those two learned of his death."

Sarik turned his head, pretending to look elsewhere.

"Sarik, if I were you, I would never have forgiven him. But you did … somehow," said Caleem, patting the young archer on the shoulder. "When we head back home, I'll make certain that Kamanar is remembered as a hero and nothing else."

Sarik nodded. "Let's try to get some rest before evening comes," he said, leaning his head back against the rocks.

Caleem and Marbel followed suit. Although all three had their eyes closed, none got even a moment's sleep.

CHAPTER 47
HE'S GONE

"Wake up, you two," Marbel said as he poked Zig in the back. "Wake Naji."

"When it's a bit dimmer, we leave. Get ready," said Caleem. "Look at me," he said, making sure he had their attention. "Tonight, we will be running home like madmen!"

"With Kamanar," said Zig.

"With Kamanar," said Caleem.

Naji wrapped his arm around his friend's shoulders. "We did it."

"Not yet. Just a little farther to go. While the two of you were sleeping, the Dalusian patrol made its rounds. So be vigilant."

"If we run into two or three Dalusians, we'll take them on. But if we encounter the full patrol … then God help us."

"That sword would have been a big help, instead of waiting for God's help," said Naji.

Caleem said, "That sword is none of your concern."

"Wha—?"

"Shut up. I don't want to hear another word about the sword."

Sarik skipped ahead of Caleem and reached for Zig's back. "Give me the bow, please."

Relieved, Zig handed the bow over.

"No," said Caleem.

Sarik almost slipped.

"I can make this shot," he said after regaining his footing.

Caleem remained indifferent as he glared at Zig. "We have one bow. He'll do it."

Naji shook Zig with delight and said, "You can do it."

"I can do it," said Zig, facing Caleem.

"Well, we're ready. Follow me," said the prince. After peeking through the veil of the waterfall, the new commander jumped out and disappeared to the other side. Sarik and the boys followed. Last to step under the powerful blade of water was Marbel. The strong current pummeled the old man's shoulders, and he fell. He thrashed his arms about as he struggled against the current. Soon he found himself kneeling in a shallow stream, with Sarik and Caleem standing over him, smirking.

"A child couldn't drown here," said Caleem.

"I was just warming up, getting ready for the action," said the chubby man.

Caleem led them to dry land on the opposite bank. The rain had stopped, but the evening sky remained gray and cloudy. They reached an open green field framed by rows of trees. Next to that was a little pond fed by a small stream.

"This way," Caleem said and led them between the trees.

The sun had already set behind the mountains, and the sky was becoming dimmer by the minute. Staying under the cover of the trees, they were quick on their feet. A raven flapping its dark wings above them gave a gurgling croak, and they lowered their heads, treading more cautiously. Something tumbled in the bushes then came to an abrupt stop that ended in a familiar groan. Caleem stared at Marbel, who had fallen into a ditch.

"I did that on purpose," said the older man, "Come—take a look. I've found a concealed path."

Caleem gestured for the others to follow. The new path ran parallel to the one above it.

They pressed on, and Sarik lagged at the rear, glancing back all the while.

They made their way through a ditch, its banks high enough to provide them with cover.

"We're better hidden here. We don't want any Dalusians spotting us," said Marbel. "Right, Sarik?" He glanced back after he received no answer and saw the young man standing completely still. "Sarik ...?"

Sarik dove into the bushes and pulled something with both arms. He fell back, crashing into a muddy puddle, a dark figure on top of him. The two wrestled, and the dark thing managed to get to its feet, Sarik still clinging onto it.

Marbel tackled the creature from behind, and the tangled men fell. Marbel gripped the creature's neck as it stood with booth men clinging on. It sank its claws into Sarik's back, pulled away from his hold, and then punched the young man in the gut and hurled him away.

"You won't get away this time," yelled Caleem, recognizing the brown-winged creature. The prince sped forward only to be met by a strong kick to the chest, which threw him back.

Marbel still hung on to the creature's neck in an attempt to choke the winged demon. Naji threw Zig an arrow, urging him to shoot. Zig fumbled with the bow and dropped the arrow. Naji grabbed a rock and raced toward the thing. The strange creature spread its bat-like wings. As they whipped, one of the wings knocked him down with a powerful slap to the face.

Sarik lay squirming on the ground. Caleem, recovering from the blow, stood up with the support of a nearby bush. Flapping its wings, the demon attempted to escape, but Marbel weighed it down. It planted its legs then jumped backward to crush Marbel against a rock wall. Marbel's back made a horrible cracking sound. He released his grip and collapsed onto the muddy ground.

The creature flapped its wings and rose into the air. Caleem jumped and clasped one of its legs with one hand as it took off. He hung on, but before he could tighten his hold with his other hand, he slipped and plunged to the ground. His gaze remained fixed on the flying monster as it flapped its wings and rose out of reach. The creature swept over the treetops, leaving a whirlwind of leaves drifting over their heads.

"Damn it," said the prince as he stood and wiped the mud off his clothes.

As soon as the flapping of wings died out, everyone could hear Marbel's heavy breathing.

"Are you hurt?" asked the prince.

The man sighed, his eyes shut and lips quivering. He murmured something.

"No need to answer," said Caleem. "Just breathe."

They all huddled around the older man. Pressing a hand to his gut, Sarik was last to join. "I'm fine. Don't worry about me," he said.

Marbel's breathing became rapid, then he let out a harrowing moan.

"Marbel," Zig whispered.

The old man's breathing grew fainter and his expression grew serene.

"He's gone!" said Naji, whose face was bright red where the creature had slapped him.

"He's not gone. He's unconscious," said Caleem.

CHAPTER 48
END THAT EVIL BASTARD

After several long hours, Marbel opened his eyes. He stared at the bright half-moon that shone among the treetops and seemed to drift in and out of the fleeting clouds. He looked around without moving his head, comforted for a moment by the faces of his four friends leaning over him.

"Feeling any better? Is it your chest or your back?" asked the prince.

"My back …" he said hoarsely.

Sarik and Caleem lifted Marbel and helped him sit up against a boulder. He groaned once again, biting his lip. Sarik lifted the old man's shirt and studied his back.

"Oh, the pain. My spine … I think it's broken. I can't feel my legs."

Naji touched Marbel's leg. "Can you feel this?"

The old man shook his head.

"I can't get them to move. Let me try again." Marbel moved a bit to the side and moaned. "I'm sorry. I think this injury can't be fixed."

"No," said Caleem, "don't say that. You're not a healer. You don't know that."

"I've seen this kind of injury before. I'll only be hindering the mission. I suggest you leave me in some bush and continue on your way."

"No," said Zig.

"No way," said Naji.

"There's no other choice," said Marbel. "You don't have much farther to go. Go now!"

All eyes rested on Caleem.

"Come on, get out of here," said Marbel.

"What do we do, Caleem?" asked Naji.

The prince stroked his hat while looking at the boys then at Marbel. "I don't know—"

"I'll carry him," said Sarik. "I can do it. I've carried heavier things."

Marbel chuckled in his misery. "I'm not sure about that. And even if you could, I would just be in the way."

"You're not going to be in anyone's way. And look at yourself. You're lighter," said the archer.

"I guess I have lost some weight." Marbel forced a smile.

"Well," said Caleem, rising to his feet, "the two boys and I can keep moving. You and Sarik can start heading back."

"Caleem! You can't do this to us. A moment before the end you're sending us back," said Sarik.

"Sarik, leave me here," said Marbel.

The young man did not reply. He gazed at the prince.

Caleem took a deep breath. "You will compromise everyone's safety, and it's definitely the wrong thing to do … but you're coming anyway."

Sarik grinned. He turned and extended a hand to Marbel. With the boys' help, the injured man heaved himself up while suppressing a moan.

Sarik stood on wobbling legs with the old man slumped on his back. "Comfortable?" asked Sarik, steadying himself.

"No," said Marbel.

"Neither am I," Sarik said with a smile.

"Come on. Dawn is about to break. We can't afford to miss it," said Caleem.

Slouching forward, Sarik staggered yet managed to keep up.

At a bend in the ditch, Caleem climbed out. "This way," he said, stooping down to help Zig clamber up.

The boy knelt next to him while they waited for Sarik. The latter, still bent over under the old man's weight, looked up.

"Sarik, I think you should take it slow here," said Marbel.

Sarik charged up the bank. The old man shut his eyes and ground his teeth. The steep slope slowed Sarik's momentum. He stopped at the edge of the ditch, tilting backward and about to fall. Naji ran from behind and pushed the two. Still tipping backward, Sarik reached his hand to Caleem while Zig pulled Marbel's hand. Sarik stooped forward, and all four of them collapsed into a heap. Marbel was unable to suppress a whimper.

"On any other day, this would've been funny," said Sarik, panting.

"Indeed," said Caleem, jumping back to his feet.

The sky brightened. Once again, they heard the rush of a river. Caleem turned toward the tree line. Zig and Naji helped Marbel get back up on Sarik's back then followed the prince.

The water's gushing intensified so much that the rocks at their feet began to tremble.

Caleem came to a halt. "We're right on time. The sun's about to rise," he whispered, gesturing to Zig to come closer. "Are you ready?"

"I am," said Zig, stiff with apprehension.

Hunched down, Caleem moved forward and crossed between the rocks to a small clearing surrounded by thick bushes. Just ahead, on the edge of the clearing, was a narrow gap between bushes.

"Perfect," said Caleem.

One by one, they all arrived at the clearing.

"Zig and I will position ourselves right by that bush over there. I hope the bastard is home at this hour. Stay alert. And be ready to flee!" The prince ended his words with a smile. He crawled until he got a good view of the river then patted the ground beside him. The boy understood the gesture and crawled forward, taking his place beside the prince.

Zig peered over the edge at the wide river flowing below. The rumbling water pounded the stone banks, its velvet mist rising to refresh his face. Thinking of Kamanar, the boy whispered to himself, "You promised to be here with me …" He let out a long exhale and looked ahead.

Caleem whispered into the boy's ear so that Zig could hear him above the roar. "There. Can you see?"

Following Caleem's gaze, Zig saw a massive, lightly colored tower. It stood on the edge of a cliff, and its spire rose above the tight treetops. Around the narrow tip, a small balcony spanned its circumference.

"They won't be able to catch us, no matter what. The river won't let them or, at least, it will delay them. The question is, can you make this shot?" asked Caleem.

A figure emerged from a door to the balcony and became visible against the spire's bright wall. It stood motionless, as if looking straight at them.

"Come on Zig … It's now!" said Caleem.

Zig took the bow off his back, pulled an arrow from his pocket, and drew the bow. He aimed at the silhouette on the balcony. As the moments went by, his hands began to tremble.

"What's happening, Zig?" came a familiar voice from behind him, and a hand touched his shoulder. "Don't think about it," Naji whispered. "Just shoot. If you miss, I've got plenty more, right here." He placed the quiver on the ground before him.

Nodding, Zig faked a smile and fixed his attention on the tip of his arrow and his target.

"End that evil bastard," said the prince.

Zig focused, exhaling, ready as ever….

"Put the bow down," someone ordered in a clear, loud voice.

Zig relaxed his grip.

Sarik appeared behind them and walked tall on the edge of the bank until he blocked Zig's aim.

"Sarik. What are you doing? Get down!" said Caleem.

"Caleem, please remain calm and everything will end quickly," said Sarik authoritatively, a stiff expression on his face. His bright eyes shone in the sun.

"I said get down. You're giving our position away!" said Caleem, rising on his knee. "Zig, shoot."

Zig drew his bow, trying to take aim, but Sarik blocked his view.

"What the hell is wrong with you?" Marbel shouted.

There was a commotion in the bushes surrounding them. Hooded figures clad in dark cloaks and armed with bows emerged into the small clearing.

"What?" shouted Caleem, jumping to his feet.

"Surrender, and we will not use force," said Sarik.

Shocked, Caleem looked at Sarik. The young man seemed quite the opposite of the gentle Sarik he knew.

Naji began to crawl away only to be confronted by the bow-wielding figures. At least two bows were aimed at each of them.

Caleem placed both hands on his head. He glared at Sarik and recoiled. "A Khandalus," he said in a quavering voice.

Sarik did not offer anything.

Caleem scrutinized the hooded figures surrounding them as he peeled the hat, which had never come off during the entire journey, and dropped it to the ground. Bright gray, tangled strands dropped to his shoulders: the famous gray hair, the unmistakable mark of the Dummah dynasty. Caleem fought back tears of frustration as Zig circled around Sarik to take aim at the Dalusian general across the river.

An arrow whooshed through the air and hit the boy in the back of the neck. Zig's arrow sprung loose and fell into the raging river. He buckled to the ground.

"No!" Naji shouted. In a rush of unrestrained fury, he dashed toward the hooded figure, holding an arrow over his head like a spear.

Another arrow hit the boy square in the chest, silencing his scream. He fell at the Dalusians' feet. Caleem's eyes shot sparks at Sarik, and he lunged at the traitor. A flurry of arrows whirred from all directions and struck the prince.

He lost his balance and fell to his knees. The murderous fire in Caleem's eyes turned to sorrow. "Kamanar …" he said as his body crumpled at Sarik's feet.

"Bastard! How could you?" Marbel screamed, tears in his eyes. "We trusted you! You were like a son to me." Marbel hurled a stone at the traitor.

One last arrow was fired and struck the old man in the back. His head dropped to the ground. For one long moment, only the rumbling of the river could be heard.

"Round them up," ordered a voice in the Dalusian language. "Great work, Seonder. Well done."

Sarik turned to the river. He took a long breath as he gazed at the endless flow.

Darkness Behind the Mountain

Book II
The Legend of Broken Fingers

CHAPTER 49
SCUM

The tweeting of birds persisted in Marbel's ears. His body felt heavy and numb. Sleep was sweet, and he didn't want to wake up. He lay on his belly as questions ran through his brain. *Where am I?*

He opened his eyes and felt the smile disappear from his face as he pushed himself off the floor, making his head ache. He mumbled something to Naji, who was sitting against the wall close by, but the boy looked frustrated and didn't answer. The chubby man sat up then scanned the small, dark cell with the large, barred door. There were no windows.

His legs still motionless, Marbel dragged himself to the door and pressed his head against the bars. The only thing he could see was a wall lit by a flickering light. He clenched one of the bars and pulled.

"Forget it," said Naji. "It's stronger than steel."

Clutching his aching head, Marbel turned around.

"Damn sedative arrows again. It will pass soon … Sarik! Can you believe it?" asked Naji.

"Oh, Sarik. We were such idiots." Marbel laughed.

"Where are we?" asked Zig, who had just awoken. He sat up, shaking his head. "Where's Caleem?"

Marbel did not answer. Naji shrugged.

"What do you think they'll do to us, the Dalusians?" asked Zig.

"Interrogate us by torture … Kill and dispose of us in some despicable manner," said Marbel.

Zig's face turned grave, and he pressed his head between his knees. "We failed … After all we've been through."

Marbel laughed, but his laughter ebbed and ended in a desperate moan. "Kamanar was right all along …"

"He will save us," Naji shouted. "I'm sure."

"Kamanar is dead," said Marbel.

"What?"

"He's dead. Kamanar's gone. I couldn't work up the courage to tell you before."

Naji said nothing, just shut his eyes and threw his head back. Zig dropped his head onto his knees again.

"I don't know if anything matters anymore … Forgive me, I just couldn't do it," said Marbel.

Approaching footsteps echoed through the corridor. Three dark figures appeared at the door arguing in a strange language, then two turned and headed back the way they came. The third approached the bars and slid a tray beneath the door and into the cell.

The boys approached the tray. To their surprise, it held what looked like food.

The mysterious figure leaned forward on bars, revealing his face in the flickering light. "It's the traitor," said Marbel.

"What do you want?" asked Zig.

Naji took a step forward and spat at Sarik, who did not flinch.

"Well played. You managed to fool Caleem and the rest of us," said Marbel.

Naji said, "I bet this food is poisoned," and kicked the tray. Bits of food flew everywhere, some landing outside the cell by Sarik's feet. He remained impassive.

"Scum!" Zig shouted. "Where is Caleem? What did you do to him?"

"Caleem is alive and well," said Sarik.

"And what makes you think we believe a villain like you?" Naji asked and spat again, this time hitting Sarik's cheek.

Sarik stood up and disappeared into the darkness.

"Traitor!" shouted Naji.

"Scum," said Zig.

The sound of Sarik's footsteps faded away. The boys sat back down.

"He even looks different," said Naji.

Marbel pushed his back against the wall. "I heard that a Khandalus can be devious, but this one seems to be the Dalusians' best-ever creation. Sarik, that's probably not even his real name." With nothing more to say, the older man dropped his head, closing his eyes.

Zig studied the bits of food still scattered inside the cell. "Do you really think this is poisoned?" he asked as he picked up a piece of some unusual fruit. "Purple fruit."

"It could be poisoned, but it looks fresh," said Naji, taking the fruit from his friend's hand to squeeze and smell it. "Taste it, if you're man enough."

"You taste it," said Zig.

Naji took a small bite and spat it out.

"What? What?" asked Zig, staring at his friend.

"It tastes like—" Naji took a second bite and chewed. "I'm going to eat it. It tastes so good."

Zig bit into the colorful fruit. He and Naji finished off the rest of the food, down to the last crumb.

"We didn't leave anything for Marbel," said Zig

"I don't have an appetite anyway," he said, opening his eyes, looking first at the boys then at his limp legs. "It's so strange. Now the pain is gone. I try to get up, but they won't respond, as if they're not mine … as if they're dead." He folded his right knee to his chest with his arms. When he let go, his leg fell back down.

Naji said, "It can be healed—" but was interrupted by a terrible cry.

Zig hurried to the bars. "Caleem!"

They heard another scream.

"It's coming from below," said Naji, lying down and pushing his ear against the floor. Zig did the same. They listened to Caleem's distant yelling and nonstop cursing.

"What the hell are they doing to him?" asked Naji.

"Poor man. Are we next?" asked Zig, his face turning pale.

The screams went on for several hours. Apart from some profanities, they could not make out any words. Eventually, the screaming ceased, and the cell became quiet again. Each man reflected on his own morbid thoughts. A clatter of steps woke them from their lethargy, and Sarik appeared.

"What have you done to him, villain?" asked Naji.

"Caleem … he is—" Sarik began, his eyes lowered.

"Don't pretend you're sorry," said Marbel. "Kamanar should have gouged out your eyes when he had the chance. Sarik … did you pick that name by yourself, or did your Dalusian master pick it for you? Sarik."

"Marbel, you don't understand."

"Khandalus, that should be your name," said Naji.

"My name is Seonder."

"*Khandalus* suits you perfectly. Nothing else. Where are your masters? Why did they send their puppy to do their work?" asked Marbel.

"Do you think that I'm not sorry for what happened to you? To Kamanar?"

"Don't you say his name with that filthy mouth," said Naji.

Sarik took a deep breath, approached, and pressed himself against the bars. "If it makes you feel better, here I am."

Naji ran forward and thrust his fist between the bars to hit Sarik in the gut. Still grasping the bars, Sarik bent over. Naji hit him in the chest and abdomen again and again as hard as he could. Zig joined in, pulling Sarik by the hair, screaming and insulting him.

"Let him have it," said Marbel. He lifted himself up, trying to get closer. "I want a piece, too."

Sarik did not resist. He gritted his teeth while holding the bars.

The two cloaked figures reappeared on either side of Sarik. Each held a long staff with three small spikes at its end. They poked Zig in the chest and Naji in the shoulder. Reeling, both boys fell back, Zig almost crushing Marbel.

"It hurts," said Zig, holding his chest and squirming on the floor.

"It burns! It burns!" Naji said. He spat on his hand and rubbed his wound.

Sarik yelled at the two cloaked figures.

Marbel pulled Zig closer. "Let me take a look." The skin around the three small punctures had turned red, and the whole area had started swelling.

While Marbel was checking on the boys, Sarik had a loud argument with the two guards, gesticulating and pushing them back until they walked away, followed by Sarik himself.

CHAPTER 50
DALUSIAN WICKEDNESS

A minute later, Sarik returned. "I'm sorry. You're not in danger, but those wounds will hurt for a short while."

Still holding his shoulder, Naji yelled, "Shut up!"

"Go away!" said Zig.

"I'm not leaving until you listen," he said, dropping to his knees next to the bars.

Naji jumped and punched Sarik in the face again.

"Stop," said Marbel, but the boy swung once more. "I said stop."

"Why?"

"Just do it, please."

Naji returned to the back of the cell, glancing at their former friend all the while.

Blood began trickling down Sarik's chin.

"First, answer this: What have you done to Caleem? We want nothing but the truth," said Marbel.

"As I said, he's unharmed. He's just upset."

"Go on," said Marbel.

"What if I told you that you were deceived from the very beginning? I know it sounds strange. But please, hear me out."

Marbel chuckled bitterly while he pulled himself up to lessen his discomfort.

"Why would we listen to your lies, Khandalus?" asked Naji.

Marbel motioned the boy to calm down. "Come, sit next to me. Let him entertain us for a while. We have nowhere to go anyhow."

The boys sat on either side of Marbel, and the older man gestured to Sarik to continue.

"I'm sorry about your legs …"

"Stop. Your fake pity is irrelevant right now," said Marbel.

Sarik nodded and sat down while wiping the blood off his lips. "I will start from the beginning. The animosity between men and Dalusians is an ancient one. The origins of the conflict are unclear."

Marbel snickered. "I'm sorry. Go on."

"It's not important how it began. The origin of the conflict has been lost to time and, in any case, it's no longer relevant. The cycle of killing must end."

"Your masters, the hideous Dalusians, want to conquer the world, as they did with our stolen land, Anathoria," Marbel said. "They wish to spread their evil ways, enslaving everyone. Only thanks to the will and courage of our heroes have we managed to survive and frustrate their devious plans. For many generations, justice and valor have been our sword and shield in the battle against Dalusians' wickedness. But what really drives me mad is the men who accept them as their masters—men like you. I always thought the Dalusians cast spells on their servants, turning them into Khandaluses against their will. Seeing you now before me, I know this is not the truth. You serve them with your own free will!"

Sarik shot Marbel a piercing stare. The blood dripping from his lips formed a red stain on his shirt. "The Dalusians are not hideous," he said. "On the contrary, they are beautiful, peace-loving people who live in harmony with nature. In your minds, they are hideous and evil because that's what your king and your masters want you to believe. They would never harm other people or creatures of any kind, unless in self-defense."

Marbel and the boys sneered again.

"Please, don't mock me."

"Self-defense?" asked Marbel. "So, we are the villains who want to enslave the world? And we are the ones who drew first blood?"

Sarik lowered his head with a sigh.

"This game is pointless. Better just execute us as soon as possible and get it over with," said Marbel.

The boys swallowed nervously after hearing these words.

"Only he can do it," said Sarik. He stood up and left.

"What did he mean? Who is 'he'?" asked Naji.

"The executioner!" said Zig.

"No, no," said Marbel. "Maybe his master … I have no clue. It's all nonsense. I don't know what this Khandalus is up to."

They sat, contemplating things for a while.

"Did you know this is the third time we've been captives?" asked Zig.

"The Guzud pits, the rat cages, and now the Dalusians," said Naji.

Marbel asked, "Do you remember when we met Gudjewkan? Seems so long ago …"

As the long hours went by, the three friends reminisced about their unusual journey.

Zig opened his eyes to find himself lying between Marbel and Naji. They were both fast asleep and snoring. Dalusians whispered outside the cell. Then the door opened.

"Wake up. Wake up," whispered Zig as he shook his friends.

Three hooded figures, accompanied by Sarik, entered the cell carrying long, spiked staves.

Fists clenched, Zig and Naji jumped to their feet.

"I'm taking you to meet someone," said Sarik.

"We're not going anywhere," said Marbel.

"No way," said Naji.

"This is not a request," said Sarik.

The three cloaked Dalusians spurred the boys out of the cell with their staves.

"Marbel," said Zig.

Sarik approached the disabled man and said, "I'll carry him."

Naji blocked his path. "You are not touching him."

"So be it," said Sarik.

The boys lifted the man from either side, their eyes still fixed on the weapons trained on them. Marbel clung to the lads' shoulders as his feet dragged on the floor.

"Follow me," Sarik said and stepped out into the dark corridor.

The boys staggered out of the cell and climbed up a winding stairway. Behind them, the three cloaked Dalusians whispered among themselves in their strange language.

A bright light spilled through a doorway ahead of them. "A door … The first chance you get, you drop me and run," whispered Marbel to the staggering boys.

Sarik, having somehow overheard Marbel, mocked him. "There's nowhere to run to. You are in the heart of Dalusian territory. The heart of all evil." He slid the bolt and swung the door open.

Chapter 51
What Is This Place?

It took a moment for their blinking eyes to get accustomed to the bright surroundings. The birds were louder than ever, and the fresh air brushed against their skin. Far below, beyond the narrow wooden balcony on which they stood, stretched a vast forest bordered by massive cliffs. The gray rock walls merged with a great mountain range, now so familiar to them. Fluffy white clouds sailed past its jagged, snow-covered peaks.

"Dear lord! Look how high we are," Marbel said, not daring to look down again. "How did we even get here?"

"We don't have all day. Let's go," said Sarik.

The boys marched ahead, following Sarik, who was wearing a green cloak strapped at the waist with a wide, brown belt.

Looking ahead, Naji whispered, "A bridge."

They soon came to a long rope bridge with thick wooden planks. As they took their first steps, the planks swayed and the ropes creaked. The white tower that had been their prison rose above the trees behind them.

"What is this place?" asked Marbel.

The bridge was suspended over a huge lake, the forest bordering it on all sides. The crystal-clear water was as still as glass. A tree-blanketed island sat at the center of the lake. White towers shot out over the green canopy, mushrooming across the entire island and interconnected with one another by an impressive web of bridges like the one they were crossing.

"What's that line crossing the sky?" Zig asked.

High above stretched a different kind of bridge. Lighter in color, with no ropes or columns of support, it spanned an incredible distance to connect the two opposite ridges.

Interrupting their bewilderment, one of the Dalusians escorting them nudged them along with a swing of his staff.

"All right, all right! We're carrying a man," said Naji. A shudder passed through the boy's body as he stared for a moment at his faceless captor. He and Zig quickened their steps, but it was impossible to maintain the pace for long, and they soon slowed down again.

Another Dalusian appeared before them holding a spiked staff in one hand and dragging a wooden cart with the other.

"Put him in," said Sarik.

The panting boys placed him in the tiny three-wheeled cart.

"This is nice," said Marbel. "Comfortable."

"Can you please tell us where we're going?" asked Zig

Sarik pointed to a rope attached to the front of the cart. "Pull him."

Naji grabbed the rope and looped it around his waist.

"Good. Let's go," said Sarik, leading the way across the bridge while he chatted with the Dalusians.

The cart rolled over the well-crafted wooden boards, making their task easier. Naji pulled while Zig pushed from behind. They could see the blue waters of the lake far beneath them as they drew closer to the mysterious island.

"Do you think you can swim?" whispered Naji to Marbel.

Marbel's eyes were shut tight. Turning sideways in the cart, he opened one eye then closed it and cowered back into his seat. "No, no! No … if you want, you jump. Not me."

"Why? It's a great idea," said Zig.

"No."

"What are you up to back there?" asked Sarik.

The three of them fell silent and moved on with bowed heads.

"I would jump just for the fun of it," said Zig.

"Crazy, crazy." Marbel curled up in his cart, shrinking even more.

After a short walk, they reached a tower and circled around it, only to continue onto another rope bridge stretching before them towards the island.

"This Dalusian place isn't how I imagined it," said Zig as they got closer to the island.

"True … but this is our last chance to jump," whispered Naji. "Let's do it."

"Yes, yes. You can do it," whispered Zig, his lips pressed close to the back of Marbel's neck.

His eyes still shut, Marbel shook his head. "You boys jump. I prefer to die some other way."

"We will not get anywhere at this pace," said Sarik when the gap between him and Marbel's cart widened. "Even if you survived the fall, our boats would pick you up as soon as you hit the water."

The boys went back to a steady pace, and Sarik resumed his conversation with the Dalusians.

As it neared the island, the bridge widened. A large gate set between two white stone pillars, a sentry stood atop each one, appeared among the treetops. Sarik waved. A moment later, the portal opened. Sarik and the Dalusians entered. The three friends peeked through the gate, but all they could see was a mass of trees stretching to the horizon and more white towers.

Naji and Zig stopped and stood on both sides of Marbel's cart.

Sarik turned around, waiting for them as the three captives exchanged glances.

"Once we go through that gate, escape will be harder, maybe impossible," Marbel whispered. The boys looked at each other, shrugged, and went through.

Once again, the sounds of birds chirping and rushing water intensified. They reached a wide, stone porch, neatly lined with polished white cobblestones. The Dalusian standing next to Sarik took off his cloak. His face was gentle, his complexion light, almost pale. His brown hair had been pulled back to reveal oversized, pointed ears. He fixed his bright, yellowish-green eyes on the three captives while conversing with Sarik.

"Surprised?" Sarik asked.

The other three Dalusians also took off their hoods.

"You see? Not so horrible. Nothing demonic—no horns, no tail. And please, I don't want to hear a word about your shape-shifting nonsense," said Sarik. Two of the Dalusians had light hair and brown eyes; the third had dark skin, shimmering black hair, and sky-blue eyes.

"Humanlike. Except for the ears," said the old man while staring at the Dalusians.

Sarik leaned on one of the stone posts. "Come and see what the whole thing is about."

The boys advanced with the cart until they stood at the edge of the porch. Marbel nudged Naji aside to unblock his view. A sprawling tree-lined valley outlined by green hills and mountains stretched beneath them. More white towers emerged above the trees, both in the valley and on the hilly slopes. They also caught sight of white, globular structures of various sizes peeking out from the thick vegetation. A flock of colorful birds took off from the treetops, whirred by in their ascent over the green valley, and disappeared into the horizon under the magnificent white bridge. The captives took in the monumental structure, which was so high it looked like a string crossing the sky. Far away in the expanse of greenery, and somewhat blurred by an intervening haze, stood yet another strange structure like a great white sphere.

"Where are we?" asked Naji.

"Anathoria. Heaven on earth. Once a part of our Mellethya," said Marbel.

"Now home to the Dalusians. The heart of all evil," said Sarik.

Pointing at the three men, Zig said, "These people aren't Dalusians." Realizing the shift of attention, they stopped talking to each other and stared at their captives.

"Something isn't right here," said Marbel.

"What if …?" asked Naji. "What if a spell was cast on us, and all this beautiful scenery is actually ugly and terrifying? Maybe they do have sharp fangs and all the rest …"

Sarik burst into laughter. He turned to the Dalusians, gesticulating as he spoke. The Dalusians joined in with his laughter.

"That's foolish," said Marbel.

His voice taking on a serious tone again, Sarik said, "Let's keep moving."

Naji pulled the cart while a confused Zig pushed. Marbel shot one last glance at the enchanting valley. As they began their descent, the thick forest blocked most of the light. The ground was covered in dry leaves, whipping up into playful whirlwinds. They soon found themselves treading on the boards of a small bridge above flowing water. Naji slowed down, looking around then at the stream below, and his eyes stopped to focus on Marbel.

"If you're still looking for an escape route," said Sarik, turning around, "you're going to miss a hot meal that's waiting for us. Take that into consideration." Sarik crossed over to the opposite bank.

Naji and Zig looked at each other then thrust the cart forward. Marbel was thrown back into his seat.

"*Hot meal*," said Naji. "That's the only spell you need to make us fly."

CHAPTER 52
WHO ARE WE SUPPOSED TO MEET?

The canopy opened into a wide, sun-bathed street paved with square cobblestones.

As they walked, they were met by a multitude of figures clad in cloaks in various shades of earthy colors, some with leaf-shaped prints. Most of them sported wide, light, canvas belts. None of these Dalusians had their hoods up.

The three friends were intrigued by the Dalusians' soft facial features.

The street grew even wider as it stretched between rows of white, globular structures, each about the size of a small cottage. In the center of the street stood a circular stone planter that held a rich variety of flowers spilling over the sides.

"Pretty," said Zig.

"I recognize the white and blue windflowers. But what are those large blue and gray ones with the triangular petals? And the green, bell-like ones? They're so beautiful," said Marbel.

Naji stopped for a moment, stared at his friends, then looked back at the flowers. "What? They're just flowers. You two are worse than girls," he said and continued to haul the cart.

Dalusian pedestrians filled the streets: women, men, and

children all going about their daily activities, most of them showing little interest in the strangers.

"Red hair, yellow hair, black hair, green hair … there." Marbel stared at a young woman filling up a jug of water from a clear pool. Her cloak was embellished with a string of colorful flowers carved from wood. She looked their way; her long, green hair flowed down her back and shoulders, and her exotic eyes lit up with a glint of amusement.

"Beautiful … very," said Naji.

"Don't be rude," said Marbel.

"She doesn't speak our language," said Naji, still staring at the young woman as he walked. "Amazing, except for the ears."

Placing the jug on her shoulder, she smiled and hurried away.

Naji toiled with the cart, unable to take his eyes off the woman. He stumbled and fell, and the cart rolled over him, making him yelp. He pushed the vehicle off and bounced back to his feet. "Damn cobbles and damn cart."

His friends, Sarik, and the Dalusian escorts all burst into laughter.

"Look up. There it is again. Amazing … How's it hanging like that?" asked Marbel.

Beyond the rope bridges and the treetops, the long, white strip of stone stretched across the cloudy sky, dividing it in half.

"The water bridge," Sarik explained. "It's an ancient bridge connecting the two ridges surrounding Anathoria. It's an aqueduct, built by *Dalusian* ancestors to carry water over the land. Definitely not the work of humans. We'll be arriving soon."

The afternoon sunlight permeated the thick canopy above the path, which led them to a wide, circular plaza. The area was paved with rectangular, white cobblestones, but weeds sprung from the cracks and spaces in between. Several round planters displaying flowers of all imaginable colors were scattered about. Large, graceful marble statues adorned the perimeter of the plaza. The one nearest to the men was a masterful sculpture of a Dalusian girl clasping an arrow in one hand and bearing a leaf-shaped shield on her forearm. The three friends were captivated by the mythical Anathorian's breathtaking beauty.

Sarik led them to the center of the plaza from which a colossal stone building rose. A giant, spherical structure topped the low, wide, and ancient tower; it was dotted with innumerable windows above narrow balconies spanning its circumference, and a deep-green layer of moss and ivy covered its surface. Two humongous trees flanked the strange tower, their trunks thick and twisted, their branches and roots almost strangling the building. Sturdy roots had broken the surface and displaced some of the cobblestones at the base.

Sarik and his companions approached the entryway. Looking high up, the captives saw the water bridge passing precisely over the top.

The structure's double wooden doors were adorned with skillful engravings depicting forest scenes. A pair of sentries stood guard, each with a longbow across his back. Sarik exchanged some words with them then bent down to pick up a small branch with a few leaves on it. He folded some of the leaves and whispered something to the trees. Soon, a black raven glided down and landed on Sarik's shoulder. The bird snatched the branch with its beak and took off toward the top of the tower.

"The one we came to see is currently in a meeting concerning the war."

"War?" Marbel's face turned grave.

"I'd better leave the clarifications to—" began Sarik.

"Who are we supposed to meet? Who is *he*?" asked Marbel.

"Patience. I've sent him a message."

"That raven …" whispered Marbel to Sarik, making sure the boys didn't hear him. He didn't want to bring up Kamanar at that moment.

Zig sat down and leaned against Marbel's cart, soon joined by Naji.

"See that bridge over there?" Sarik pointed at a rope bridge that descended from the treetops to the plaza. "That's the short way here. We took the long way because I wanted you to see our land, our people, the 'evil' Dalusians, as you call them. I wanted you to perceive the truth with your own eyes."

"Your land? But you're as human as I am … aren't you?" asked Marbel.

"I was born to a human father and a Dalusian mother. I didn't get the pointy ears like the rest of my people."

"That's why they chose you to be a spy."

"Among other reasons. So, do you still think we're evil creatures?"

Looking at the four Dalusians who had accompanied them and at the sentries, Marbel shook his head. "There's no evil in this place. It's different from what I imagined. That doesn't mean we are not enemies anymore. Even if Anathoria is your land, what about all the wars and carnage that you initiated? What about wanting to conquer the world?"

"You have been deceived about our true nature. And with a false narrative you have been herded into the battlefield. You were all born into a lie."

The wooden door swung open. The sentries made way for someone holding a long staff who stepped into the light. The three friends were shocked. Before them stood a man with a scarred face, clad in a green cloak. His long, disheveled hair was bright gray, and he didn't have pointed ears. Despite the horrid scars on his face, he very much resembled Prince Caleem. His left eye was all white, and a long scar crossed his other eye and ran down his cheek. Tapping his ornate staff on the ground, he came closer.

"Is that you? Marbel of Rolia?" asked the man.

Marbel stared at his scarred face. "It can't be … Ansseur? Impossible. Is it really you?"

The gray-haired man's face lit up. "Yes."

"How? What …?" The chubby man bowed inside his cart.

"Raise your head. Bowing is frowned upon here," said Ansseur.

"Caleem's brother. He's blind," Naji whispered to Zig.

"Don't be rude," said Marbel.

"He's not blind. How did he see Marbel bowing?" asked Zig.

"You have been injured," said Ansseur.

"A little. It's nothing. But you, what have they done to you?"

"Don't be alarmed. This isn't the work of the Dalusians, as you call them. It's Dolegg's—you know him, my father's pet. He did it at my father's command, of course. But that's an old story. Right now, the first thing you should know is that you are all safe. You must be exhausted and starving after such a wearying journey. We'll talk more, all of us, over a good meal."

"An excellent idea," said Naji.

Still staring at Ansseur's mutilated face, Marbel said, "Indeed, I think we have a lot of learning to do."

Ansseur said, "Please, follow me."

"Leaving without me?" A tall woman wearing a green cloak with a flowery, white print crossed the doorway and wrapped her arm around Ansseur's. The pointy-eared woman was stunning, with long, raven hair and a tanned face. But her most striking feature were her sparkling, bright golden eyes.

"This is my wife, Narraneen," said Ansseur.

Sarik interrupted. "What about Caleem?"

"Seonder, as I already told you, my brother is tough and stubborn. He will need time," said Ansseur.

"You're his brother. Only you can talk to him, no one else. If only you'd come—"

"Not now. He needs at least another day. Your conscience is weighing on you. What you did is cumbersome on the soul, I understand … Don't think this is any easier for me. You may spend the night outside his cell. But still, I command you not to free him before I arrive!"

Seonder took his leave and rushed to the rope bridge.

"Apparently, he doesn't know my brother's hard head. I doubt he's changed over the years."

"About that meal, then …" said Naji.

"You're being rude … again," said Marbel.

Ansseur smiled as he began to walk while leaning on his cane and on Narraneen's arm. "You should all know that the term 'Dalusians' was invented by men. They prefer to be called elves," Ansseur said.

"Elves? I thought elves were naughty little creatures," said Zig.

"Those are of a different land. Here in Anathoria, the elves are tall and not so naughty," said Narraneen.

They all laughed as they took one of the paths leading away from the ancient plaza.

Chapter 53
I Believe You

Seonder crossed bridge after bridge, passing many elves. Some greeted him, inquiring about his journey, but he only waved without engaging with any of them.

"Caleem, Ansseur will come to see you tomorrow … Caleem, you're in good hands," Seonder mumbled. "Caleem, listen to me—I beg you … You have been deceived. Your father is an evil man of an evil dynasty …"

He found himself descending the spiral stairwell that led to the detention cells. Running past the first empty cell, where Marbel and the boys had been kept, encouraged him a little. He reached the bottommost floor and stopped in front of an oil lamp hanging on the wall that cast a dim light into the adjacent cell. Except for Seonder's panting, it was quiet.

Inside the cell, Caleem sat against the wall. His arms were folded around his legs, his face hidden between his knees. The silvery hair that he had gone through such pains to conceal was loose.

"Caleem," Seonder said. The prince remained motionless. "I don't know where to start."

The last time he had tried to speak to Caleem, the prince had gone wild, thrashing and screaming like a madman. Seonder tried to suppress the memory of their meeting the day before, when

Caleem had lunged at him with all the strength he could muster and tried to bend the bars, infinite hatred in his eyes.

"Ansseur will be here tomorrow," said Seonder. The prince raised his head. "He is alive and well. He even serves our great society as an advisor. He will come to see you. I'm sure it won't be easy for you to hear the truth. To realize that the Dalusians are a peaceful nation. And that your way was wrong. An entire dynasty of Mellethyan kings has perpetuated one big lie …

"'The Dalusians—those cruel, bloodthirsty demons, a danger to mankind, we must wage a holy war and fight them mercilessly. They took away our land …' What rubbish! How can an entire state be won over with just words? Despite all our attempts to stop the wars, to reveal the truth. Some of you unquestionably heard our words but didn't listen, didn't want to. They, like you, just stampeded on like a crazed herd, without question, without wanting to know. We tried again and again. Every emissary we sent has either disappeared or been murdered. 'We have defeated an agent of evil'—that's how you would describe it—'a glorious victory'." Slamming his fist against the bars, Seonder concluded with a bitter laugh.

Caleem was still curled up against the wall.

"When you do see your brother, don't be shocked like Marbel was. His face is scarred, mutilated."

Caleem stirred.

"And don't think for a moment that anyone here harmed him. When he was taken prisoner after the war, thirteen years ago, he saw Anathoria and its people. Within a day, he had the ability to observe, listen, and learn all about this beautiful place, soon realizing that evil was not evil. He volunteered and, against our leaders' will, insisted on going back to your father for answers. But your father … He had him thrown into the dungeon, along with the other soldiers who returned with him.

"A rumor was spread that he was ill, bewitched. Your father tried to *cure* him, but Ansseur, being who he is, would not stand for it. The king subjected Ansseur to torture—the heir to his throne, his own son. As ridiculous as it may sound, you'll hear this from your own brother. I am only trying to cushion the blow. If it hadn't been for the goodness of one soul, your brother would have died in that palace dungeon, far beneath where you and your sister slept soundly, away from the horrific screaming. Sadly, the other soldiers weren't as lucky … Ansseur escaped, making it back here barely alive. Since then, he's been more than just one of us. Your father declared him dead, but he's very much alive. I've no idea who lies in his make-believe grave." As Seonder finished, a sudden fatigue weighed on him. He rested his body against the bars, chaotic thoughts racing in his mind.

"I believe you," the prince said from inside the cell. Caleem stood up and approached the bars, catching Seonder off guard.

The half-elf retreated, but then he stepped forward, noticing that the hate had disappeared from the prince's eyes. "Yes?"

"Where are Marbel and the boys? I imagine they're safe."

"Of course. Right now, they're probably in bed after dining with Ansseur and his wife."

A smile appeared on Caleem's weary face only to vanish immediately. "I want to hear more about the Dalusians. I want to know the truth."

A wave of excitement flooded Seonder as he approached the bars. "You have no idea what this means to me. You can't imagine how I felt all this time, ever since we embarked on that mission … To have gone through so many adventures with all of you, discovering good, noble people. So many times, I wanted to scream the truth … but I couldn't."

"I wish I'd known all this earlier. And to think of how wrong we were, how stupid and shallow," said the prince, shaking his head.

The emotional exchange between Caleem and Seonder continued for some time. The prince even got his appetite back and ate some of the food brought to him by his friend. "Seonder. It's so odd to call you by this name," said Caleem, dropping his eyes. "I'm sorry. You have no idea how deeply—"

"Don't be. You couldn't have known, no one could. You have no idea how relieved I am," said Seonder, leaning on the bars.

Caleem moaned. "I feel so bad … Seonder, there's something urgent I must do." He stared into the half-elf's eyes.

"Whatever it is, I'll help you as best I can."

"You said my father is setting up a camp with the intention of attacking Anathoria. Is it far?"

"No."

"I can stop this war, Seonder. And you can help me," said Caleem, the light of the oil lamp shining in his eyes.

"Stop the war … How?"

"You'll have to trust me."

"Ansseur commanded me not to release you. Tomorrow morning, at the break of dawn, he will be here."

"Tomorrow morning will be too late! Every moment is precious. You have to get me out of here. You have to. Seonder, trust me, please."

The half-elf moved away from the bars and paced back and forth, his head down but occasionally glancing at the captive.

Caleem leaned against the bars, studying Seonder's every movement. "We can stop this war, together, you and I. Think of all the lives we can save, both men and Dalusian."

Seonder stopped to look into Caleem's eyes. He nodded, causing a wide grin to spread across the prince's face. "Let's do it." He unbolted the cell door and planted himself in front of Caleem.

Caleem opened his arms and embraced Seonder. "I'm sorry," said the prince.

"It is I who should be sorry."

Caleem took a step back. "We both made mistakes."

"I know, and it weighs heavy on me. But it's too late. Kamanar …"

"We have the responsibility to make things right. Can you smuggle me out of here? I have to reach my father as soon as possible. We can't risk any delays." Caleem placed his hand on Seonder's shoulder.

"I will help you," assured Seonder.

"Will you come with me, to aid me in presenting my case before my father? We owe it to Kamanar."

"Of course," said Seonder after a short pause. "Come on, follow me." They rushed up the spiral staircase.

Seonder opened the tower door and walked out onto the dark balcony. A cold breeze swept in. Two sentries leaned on the edge of the rope bridge, immersed in conversation. As Caleem stepped out they both became vigilant.

"No one said anything about letting him go," said one of the sentries in the Dalusian tongue.

The prince, his clothes little more than tattered rags, looked the pair over. Although their hoods were thrown back, their features were in shadow and their pointed ears silhouetted against the night sky. "I made sure that he was ready," Seonder said. "Ansseur allowed me to release him if he was ready."

The guards examined Caleem.

"He's under my full responsibility," said Seonder, placing a hand on his chest.

"Good," said one of the guards.

"One more thing … Your horses. We'll be needing them for an important errand, the details of which I don't have time to explain. I promise you—we are in great haste."

"We understand."

Seonder nodded, motioning for Caleem to follow him. "Come on."

He rushed past his peers and headed out across the rope bridge. Caleem ran after him, the bridge swaying with their hasty steps.

When they reached the next tower, Seonder made sure the two elves were out of earshot.

"Too bad you can't see the beauty of our land with your human eyes. When we come back, I'll take you all around Anathoria."

Chapter 54
Maybe It Was Fate

"I don't understand. They let us go, just like that?" asked Caleem, bouncing on the wooden boards as he held on to the rope railing.

"Not *just like that*. Trust," said the half-elf as he crossed to the second tower's balcony.

"Trust, you say. You said Ansseur had ordered you not to release me."

"You got me. Well, that must be down to my human side," he chuckled as they circled the tower. He then opened a hatch in the floor.

"What do you mean by your 'human side'?"

"I'm not a Khandalus. I'm half-man, half-elf."

Seonder lowered himself down through the opening and grabbed a rope ladder to begin his descent. He watched Caleem give the ladder a tug, presumably making sure it was strong enough before he followed. Seonder reached the bottom, and at a bush near the tower he broke off a dry branch. He folded some of its leaves. After a moment his black raven materialized to land on his shoulder. "You know where to take this. Do it with haste, my good friend," he whispered to the bird.

The raven squawked then took Seonder's branch in its beak. With a few flaps of its wings, it vanished above the dark treetops.

Seonder approached the two horses that stood quietly at the foot of the tower. One was black, the other grey. "There is an important task to be done," whispered Seonder. The black horse raised its head then, neighing, came closer to him.

Caleem jumped off the bottom of the ladder and to the ground, scanning his surroundings, alert.

"Calm down, you're safe."

"Men and Dalusians are bitter enemies."

"Oh, Caleem … Come on, follow me," Seonder said and mounted the black horse.

"There's no saddle."

"You'll manage."

Caleem gripped the horse's gray neck and mane and hoisted himself up on his mount.

Seonder whispered something to the horses, sending them bolting into a gallop. Caleem was almost thrown off. They rode through darkness. Every so often, a branch slapped the prince across the face.

"Where are we headed …? When … do we arrive?" asked Caleem as he was jolted on the horse's back. His host rode on and said nothing.

After about an hour, the horses began to slow down. Seonder jumped off. Caleem was slow to dismount, complaining that his groin and arms were sore. The half-elf whispered something to the horses and sent the animals trotting away into the night.

"What now?" asked the prince.

"Come," Seonder said, advancing in total darkness. As the clatter of hooves faded away, they could hear the soft splashing of water.

"A lake?" Caleem asked.

A few small boats were visible rocking on the surface. The half-elf waded into the shallow water and untied a cable then climbed into one of the boats. The prince entered the cold, black water and climbed aboard.

Seonder, already sitting at the stern, handed Caleem an oar.

"Now you can ask me whatever you want," he said as he dipped his oar into the water and propelled the little vessel. Caleem sat on the middle bench, immediately taking part in the effort as they floated away from the bank and into the expanse of the misty lake.

"Where are we heading?" Caleem asked.

"To the Yellow Plain. Where your father has made camp."

"Then we'll need to cross the Mobinar again. That could take a week."

"Don't worry, there's a shortcut underneath the mountain. We'll be there around dawn."

Caleem continued rowing. "What is my father doing there? He can't cross the Mobinar with an army."

"You're right. That is baffling our leaders," Seonder said. "The bulk of your father's army is marching toward the Mobinar passage from the south, as they have done in previous wars. But as to this small force on the Yellow Plain … We have no idea what your father is up to."

They were enveloped by the mist. "This is like sailing through a cloud in the middle of the night. I can't see a thing," the prince said.

"We'll get there."

"Tell me, what is a half-elf?"

"A half-elf is a half-man, half … 'Dalusian', for you. The Dalusians call themselves elves."

"So your father was human, and your mother was Dalusian—pardon me, an elf?"

"You've guessed right."

"Well, that explains your fitness and sharp eyesight. I had noticed them, but never figured … You look absolutely human. I assume that's why they appointed you to be a spy."

"Marbel made the same assumption. But to tell the truth, I volunteered. Growing up as part of both worlds wasn't easy. From a very young age, I was looked down upon. Actually, I think we were blessed. Me and the few others like me. We have been endowed with the best features of both races. I turned out looking like a normal man, which is quite rare. I decided to take advantage of that and volunteer. No one appointed me."

"Was it sheer luck that my father selected you for this mission?"

"Maybe it was fate … After all, I was the best archer in the infantry." Seonder stopped rowing. "An elf, a man, an angel with broken fingers … Does that mean anything to you?"

"No. Nothing."

"It's a riddle that many are trying to solve. According to the prophecy, one with broken fingers will tilt the outcome of the upcoming war."

"I don't believe in such prophecies and fortune-telling." They rowed in silence for a while. "How long have they been camping there, the force at the Yellow Plain?"

"Since yesterday evening. Both of them."

"Both?"

"Yes. A camp for Mellethyans, the other for Guzuds. It seems your father has made an alliance."

"I didn't know anything about this."

"They also brought some strange wagons, big and covered."

There was no response from Caleem, who continued to row.

"There's a chance that we can stop all that, you and I, right?" asked the half-elf.

"Right, right, we must stop it all. I'm just so mad at my father."

"You should be. We'll dock there." He pointed into the darkness.

"How is it to see in the dark?"

"It's a question all men are eager to ask. I can see the ridge rising high into the sky, then fading in the mist. I can see its jagged cliffs … the trees growing at its feet, and I can see the four boats moored at the jetty."

"That's a wonderful gift. Especially for a warrior," Caleem said. "Can you see through the mist?"

"No. Whatever I can see now is because the haze is getting

thinner. And before you ask me, no, I don't see everything as I do in the day. It's all less colorful and kind of blurry. I can see animals, thanks to the aura produced by the warmth of their bodies."

Caleem leaned back and went quiet; so did the half-elf.

"We have arrived." Seonder jumped into the shallow water and towed the boat before tying it to tree trunk on the bank. "Stay close to me so you won't get lost in the dark," said Seonder, laughing.

The prince leaped into the water and caught up with the half-elf. Seonder said something in the Dalusian tongue, and a reply came from the darkness. Soon they were surrounded by several cloaked figures.

"Give me your hand," said the half-elf.

"What do they want? What are they saying?" asked Caleem.

"They're wishing us good luck. Give me your hand. I'm taking you to the ladder."

"Ladder?"

"It's very long and goes deep down into the Mobinar. Kneel. Can you feel it?"

"Yes."

The prince started his descent, followed by Seonder.

Chapter 55
I Owe It to You

As they descended into the pitch-black pit, a strong current of air flowed up from below. Along with the creaking of the rope ladder, the gentle trickle of water echoed off the walls. Cool drops landed on the prince's head and shoulders. The two continued their way down for a few hours, Caleem's arms starting to shake from the relentless effort, though he didn't complain.

"My respect for the blind is growing significantly," said Caleem.

"We don't have much farther to go."

The splashing grew louder until Caleem found himself standing right in the middle of a puddle. He shook and stretched his aching arms. Seonder dropped beside him with a splash.

"This way," Seonder said, wading ahead.

"If you're pointing in some direction, it doesn't help. I can't see anything."

"Soon you will."

Caleem followed the sound of Seonder's splashing.

"I'm so sick of tunnels," he grumbled, feeling his way forward, careful not to stumble on any rocks or depressions.

"Can you see me now?"

The prince looked ahead and was surprised to see Seonder's silhouette before him. "I can … and that shimmer." Caleem pointed at the dancing dots of light on the surface of the water they stood in.

"And now?" Seonder stood grinning in front of the prince.

"I can see you." He noticed specks of light above the half-elf's head. "Stars. We're out."

The prince examined the peculiar way in which the stars were reflected in the water. "Green stars. What is this, Seonder? An illusion?"

"Glowing worms."

"Worms?"

"They glow to attract bugs that fly toward the light and become entangled in the worm's sticky web and, ultimately, get devoured."

"Lethal attraction."

"Do you think the bug knows that it's being lured into a trap?" asked Seonder, looking the prince straight in the eye.

Caleem evaded Seonder's stare. "Maybe. I don't know."

"I think it knows."

Seonder continued down the tunnel. The prince lagged behind, enchanted by the tiny, green, glowing lights. He picked up the pace, sprinting forward, and Seonder began to run as well. The two raced through the tunnel. Their splashing footsteps quietened as the puddles disappeared. They were hit by a gust of cold air, and they knew that they were no longer in the tunnel.

Breathing heavily and slowing to a walk, Caleem said, "We've crossed the mountain." Although there were no stars in the dark sky, it was bright enough for Caleem to see his immediate surroundings.

Seonder stopped next to a small creek that flowed out from the tunnel to merge into a larger one that wound among the rocks. "Yes, we have. The stars are veiled by the clouds," he said.

Wiping the sweat off his brow but still gasping for air, Caleem stood near the half-elf. He let his gray-white hair down to cool off before tucking it back up into his hat. "What happened? Why did we stop?"

"I think you should continue on your own. This creek will take you to the river. Follow it until you reach your father's camp."

Coming closer to the half-elf, Caleem gave him a wide-eyed stare. "No, no, no. You're coming with me."

"I'm not sure—"

"What? You released me, brought me all the way here, just to say, 'I don't trust you?' Why did you let me go in the first place if you don't trust me?"

"You're right … Come what may, I'm coming. I owe it to you!"

"We will go to my father, you and I, and we'll demand answers," Caleem said, staring straight into Seonder's eyes. "The two of us, we'll stop this war. I promise, no harm will come to you."

Seonder nodded.

"Good," Caleem said, and began walking.

The half-elf caught up. Caleem smiled, patting Seonder on the shoulder. After a short walk, the skies became brighter behind the veil of the dark clouds as the cold of the coming dawn grew bitter.

"There are three sentries ahead," said Seonder.

Caleem made out two silhouettes standing, the third sitting on a rock. He could hear them talking in low voices.

Seonder took a deep breath.

"Guards," called Caleem. Marching straight toward them, he took off his hat.

The seated one jumped to his feet, and they all drew their swords.

"Stop! Who goes there?" one of them shouted.

"Calm down. It's me, Caleem," said the prince, undeterred by their weapons, the half-elf at his heels.

The three guards waited in silence until the two were close enough for their features to be distinguished. "It is the prince!" said one of them and knelt before Caleem; the other guards did the same.

"On your feet. Stay vigilant," said Caleem, continuing on with Seonder at his side.

"Yes, Your Highness," said one of the men as the three of them got back up.

When they reached the outskirts of the camp, they were faced with numerous large tents pitched in neat rows. In front of the tents, several dozen soldiers were lined up in strict formation. While they stood as still as statues, Caleem walked right past them. They were clad in black armor and held hexagonal shields. All of them had black sheaths strapped to their hips, housing swords with blackened hilts. Some had long spears protruding over their shoulders, their angular blades reflecting the flickering of the torches.

"Look at this equipment." The armor they wore was different and of higher quality than any Caleem had seen before. The prince approached one of the warriors. The soldier's black helmet covered his face and head completely. The helmet had a pair of triangular holes for the eyes and a narrow slit that went from the tip of the nose down to the chin.

"My father's precious Black Company. Very much refined," Caleem said and continued toward the tents.

Simple infantry soldiers wearing basic helmets and armed with short swords appeared from behind the tents. As they recognized the prince, they fell to their knees and whispered to each other. "Welcome, my prince," said one of the men.

Officers and yet more soldiers began to pour out of the tents, forming a circle around him, their expressions brimming with flattery as they greeted the heir to the throne.

Caleem stood firm, returning their greetings.

"Who is our prince's honorable guest?" one of the soldiers asked.

Waiting to be introduced, Seonder looked at Caleem.

"I have brought with me a Khandalus, a traitor of the highest degree!" he said with a mocking glare then spat at Seonder.

For a moment, Seonder could not comprehend what was happening. He thought the prince was joking, and so did the rest. After a moment of confusion, the soldiers and officers lunged at him.

"Keep him alive for interrogation," said Caleem, still glaring at Seonder. The latter did not resist his assailants. "Take him away."

Wide-eyed, his lips quivering, the half-elf stared at him but said nothing. The soldiers dragged him into the camp.

"I want him tied. I want no less than six men guarding him at all times," said Caleem.

Seonder's terrified look was the last thing he saw before vanishing from sight. Wearing a cunning grin, Caleem walked deeper into the camp.

CHAPTER 56
A FALSE FABLE

"I will accompany you to your father, Your Highness," said Damian, the officer escorting him. Caleem nodded. All the soldiers bowed to him though he responded with a slight nod.

The sun had begun to rise, and its bright rays flooded the immense camp. Caleem headed toward the large, imposing tent at the camp's center.

At the camp's edges stood a few peculiar, massive wagons, all covered in black cloth. Near the wagons were even more tents, much larger in size, that seemed to belong to a different camp. When he noticed several gigantic figures walking among them, he stopped in his tracks.

"The Guzuds' camp," said Damian. "The great king has made a pact with them, as Your Highness surely knows."

"Of course," Caleem said as he quickened his steps toward his father's tent. Two guards wearing the Black Company's sophisticated armor stood at attention on either side of the entrance. Both were armed with sharp spears. The taller guard's arms were exposed; his right bore a dragon tattoo. The monster seemed to envelop the entire limb, creating the illusion that its claws were sinking into his flesh.

Damian remained outside. Caleem pulled aside the cloth that shielded the entrance and barged in. A torch hanging from a pole lit up the large tent's interior. To one side was a large wooden bed covered in bright silk sheets. On the other side, a lackey dressed in a traditional blue uniform held a golden towel. He bowed before the prince.Next to the lackey, his back to the prince, stood a man dressed in an elegant sleeping garment and fine boots. His gray hair reached to his shoulders, and he was washing his face in a bowl.

"Father," said Caleem as he knelt on the gold carpet.

King Creeden rinsed his face one more time before turning around. The lackey handed him the golden towel then took a step back as his sovereign wiped his face.

"Caleem." He spoke his son's name with reserved surprise. After throwing the towel aside, he smoothed his white eyebrows and beard with his fingers. He placed a hand on Caleem's shoulder, jolting him a little. "Did it reach its destination?" he asked in his thick voice.

Caleem looked into his father's eyes, which were framed by a web of wrinkles. He nodded, but the king rattled him again.

"Yes or no? Did it?"

"Yes, yes. I threw it into that river."

A smile appeared on King Creeden's face. He walked over to the bed, and Caleem heard him whisper, "He will come for it …"

"What did you say?"

"Oh, nothing," said the king, shedding his garments. The servant helped the sovereign put on his red cloak, fastening it with a wide, golden belt. The monarch stood upright in his ornate attire. The servant, standing behind him, placed a silver crown on his head. "I knew I could rely on you," said King Creeden.

"What do you mean? We failed. That Dalusian general is still breathing."

The king laughed.

"You're laughing? Had you appointed me commander, we would have succeeded."

The old man continued to laugh, infuriating the prince, who turned to leave.

"Nonsense." The king's grave voice resounded.

Caleem stopped near the entrance.

"There is no Dalusian general," said the king.

Utterly puzzled, the prince turned around. "What?"

"The whole tale of this 'Dalusian general' and his assassination was a deception. A false fable in case one of you got captured or turned out to have a treacherous tongue. The crucial part was that you delivered that sword."

"I don't understand."

"There's nothing to understand. The sword was the mission. It will bring the destruction of our enemies."

"Why did I not know anything about this? And your arrangement with the Guzuds? Do you know I killed two of them with that sword? Or did you think I had a treacherous tongue?"

"I'll allow your insolence. You've earned it. Go eat and get some rest. We have much to discuss."

"Request permission to enter, my king," said a voice from outside the tent.

"Enter," the king answered. "This better be important."

An officer was followed by three soldiers who dragged Seonder in, his hands tied behind his back. Two more soldiers followed them.

"Sarik!" said the king.

Caleem corrected him. "Seonder. That's the Dalusian name of our loyal friend. Speaking of treacherous tongues …"

"Well done, my son. Dolegg will take care of him. We'll see how useful he proves to be." The king motioned to one of the soldiers. "Go get Dolegg."

The soldier bowed and hurried out of the tent.

"Caleem, if you just—" Seonder began, but the prince had gripped his throat before he could finish a sentence.

"If you mention my name, or my brother's name, or Kamanar's … I will gouge out your eyes with my hands. You hear me?" His grip on Seonder's neck became even tighter.

Seonder stared into the flames of hate raging in the prince's eyes. When Caleem let go, Seonder coughed but didn't raise his eyes again.

"Permission to enter, my king," requested a voice from outside once again.

"Enter."

A short, plump man with a round face and flat nose entered. His short beard was as well-groomed as what was left of his black hair. He bowed, his almost bald head shining in the torchlight.

"My brave son has returned from his journey, bringing with him a Khandalus."

"Welcome back, Your Highness." Dolegg bowed to the prince while looking Seonder over with his tiny eyes. "I know his face."

"You would not believe it—he was one of our best archers. Take him in for a thorough interrogation."

"Of course, my king. It's a shame I don't have my tools with me. But I'll manage with whatever is available."

"I trust you will," said the king.

A wide grin spread over Dolegg's round face. He bowed again. "Bring him," he barked at the soldiers and followed them out of the tent.

The king motioned to the lackey, who ran to fetch something. "What of the others?"

"They're all dead," Caleem said.

King Creeden nodded. The lackey returned, carrying a large, ornate chair that he strained to place behind the king, who gathered the folds of his cloak as he sat down. "Kamanar?"

"Your true favorite son? He died first."

"My son? Don't be ridiculous." The king stroked his short white beard. "And how did you learn of Sarik's treachery?"

"I earned his trust. Bit by bit, he revealed various things about the Dalusians. He told me that he was half-man, half-Dalusian."

"Fascinating."

"He said that they are a peaceful race. And that my brother Ansseur is alive."

The king leaned back in his chair. "And do you believe him?"

"Of course not. I'm not that gullible."

"Naiya will be disappointed."

"The first thing I'm going to do when I return is slap her. How could she choose that vile Dalusian over Kamanar …? How could she not know?"

"I have a meeting with the Guzuds' commander. We will talk later. Leave."

Caleem exited to find Damian waiting at a distance from the king's two guards. "We have cleared that tent for you, Your Highness."

Caleem followed Damian.

"Fresh breakfast is ready for you, Your Highness."

Caleem bent down to enter the tent when loud peals of laughter from the higher ground above the camp caught his attention. There was Seonder, on his knees with his arms spread out and tied to tent poles planted in the ground on either side of him. A bunch of soldiers stood around him, laughing and kicking him. The captive's head drooped; his light-brown hair concealed his face.

Dolegg, with a sledgehammer on his shoulder, shouted non-stop, probing Seonder. The half-elf stared at the ground before him and did not utter a word. Then the plump officer swung the sledgehammer with all his might into Seonder's chest.

Although at a distance, Caleem heard the hammer crush Seonder's chest. He was sure no person could survive that blow. The captive coughed and moaned. Caleem strained his eyes but didn't step any closer. A trickle of blood ran from Seonder's mouth onto his chest.

Dolegg cursed once again, and then a second blow threw Seonder back, leaving him in a twisted position. The prince noticed a slight movement of his head. The soldiers' laughter rang in his ears. One of them took the sledgehammer from the officer, positioned himself behind the captive, and, to the others' further amusement, dealt him a third blow. Seonder hung limply, like a rag doll, only held up by the ropes binding his wrists to the poles. He tried to rise on his knees, but to no avail. His blood dripped to the ground. Despite the beating, Seonder made no sound.

Caleem turned and entered his tent.

CHAPTER 57
THIS IS MAZAHRATEE

The birds of Anathoria sang, and Zig rested his elbows on the white balustrade. The sight of the bridge crossing the sky high above was still astonishing. Lowering his gaze, he watched the tall trees' leaves riding on the breeze as they floated down to the wet cobblestones. On the street below, multitudes of elves swarmed, all rushing in the same direction.

Tears began to run down Zig's cheeks, and he buried his face in the fold of his arm.

"I'm hoping breakfast was to your liking?" Narraneen said as she approached then placed a hand on his shoulder. "What saddens you?"

The boy shrugged. The elf woman leaned on the railing next to him.

"It is hard … losing someone. One feels as though the grief will never go away."

Zig wiped his tears away with his sleeve and looked at Narraneen's golden eyes. "Few people were kind to me. He was so …"

"What was he like?"

"Brave, tall, strong. He cared … I know I shouldn't, but I feel mad at him. He made promises …"

"Life is beautiful, but also fickle. Death is stronger than all of us. It is the only thing that is certain. It's all right to feel sad and mad. Eventually these feelings will wither, and the pleasant memories of him will remain."

"What was that green thing?" asked Naji from behind them. He rubbed his belly with one hand while scratching his groin with the other.

"Talmara—it's made of bush leaves."

"Tasted like cheese to me," said Naji.

Zig was quick to wipe away his remaining tears.

"Where are all the elf people going?" asked Naji.

"An assembly is to be held this morning, to discuss urgent matters. You are welcome to join," she said.

"We'll stay here," Naji said, and then his eyes widened as they fixed on a figure marching below. "No, no, we're coming. Let's go."

"Wait just a minute. I have something for you two." Narraneen walked into the house then quickly reappeared carrying two brownish-green cloaks. "Wear these." She also offered them two pairs of canvas shoes.

"I'm staying with my blue ones," said Naji, pointing at his pair, which he had taken from the Allmother. Zig, on the other hand, was glad to get rid of his torn shoes in favor of a new pair.

"Two model elves," Narraneen said and chuckled.

Naji rushed down the stairs and out of the globular house. Zig and Narraneen followed.

"What's on his mind?" she asked after Naji ran off into the crowd.

"It's that green-haired girl," Zig said as he his stared at the white cobblestones.

She giggled. "I see."

"You live for a thousand years and we, a hundred at best … I don't think it's right."

"True. But on the other hand, here we are … Ansseur and I."

Zig blushed for a moment.

A large, formidable tree stood in the middle of the street, its thick roots displacing some of the cobbles. Elves brushed past the tree on both sides, as did Zig and Narraneen. After a short walk, the canopy opened up. They crossed the big square all the way to the massive tower, clutched by two giant trees, at its center. Zig studied the marble statue of the elf girl at the wide tower's entrance. Above them rested the enormous, spherical structure. Hundreds of elves of all ages sat around the square while more poured in. Zig was astonished by the sight of hundreds of colorful heads and the many planters in the square.

"Marbel," Zig called, recognizing the man leaning on the thick roots of a tree.

"Hey, boy, come sit next to me," Marbel said.

"Good morning," said the elf woman.

"A bit chilly, but still a good morning indeed," said Marbel, taking another look at the cloudy skies.

"Found her?" Zig asked Naji, who sat on a thick root as he glanced around at the crowd.

"She's over there. Akiena or Akeena …" He pointed then jumped down to sit down next to Marbel. "And she speaks our language."

"You talked to her?" asked Zig.

"Of course. After the assembly, there's some kind of briefing by a woman she really likes. After that, we can chat … She and I, that is."

"How are you feeling?" Narraneen asked Marbel.

The older man looked at the cart that leaned against a tree close by. "Better at times, worse at others. Definitely better right now." The paralyzed man smiled as he embraced Zig. "He's a good kid, isn't he?"

"He's special. Sensitive," said Narraneen.

"You mean a crybaby," said Naji.

Zig picked up a pebble and threw it at his friend. Laughing, Naji dodged.

"Ansseur is late. I hope everything went well with his brother," Narraneen said.

"He's so stiff," said Naji.

"After he meets your people, he'll understand," said Marbel.

The large doors at the base of the tower swung open. Four elf boys walked out and placed four chairs at the foot of the tower.

"The assembly is about to begin, and Ansseur is still not here," said Narraneen.

"I'm sure he'll be here any minute. With Seonder and Caleem," said Marbel.

Two elf women, one of them quite old, emerged from the tower followed by two male elves. All of them wore glossy white cloaks. The silence that reigned in the square was complete; only the sound of branches and leaves swaying in the wind could be heard.

"Who are they?" asked Zig.

Narraneen brought two fingers to her mouth and replied, "Now we must only whisper."

The four white-cloaked elves took their places on the tall wooden chairs facing the crowd.

"These four are the prime members of the Order of the Spider. They are Anathoria's mentors," whispered the elf woman.

"Order of the Spider?" asked Naji.

"The Order has eight members. Four couples, male and female. Each couple represents a different generation. Only the two eldest pairs head the assemblies in times of crisis. Decisions are made easier this way."

A fifth, gaunt elf came out to stand behind the chairs. He was dressed in a brown cloak and a wide black belt from which hung a large pouch.

"This is Mazahratee. The head counselor," said Narraneen in a voice so low that the three friends had to huddle closer to hear her. "He is the most unusual elf you will meet in Anathoria, and some say the wisest. He isn't too fond of men, especially Mellethyans."

The three friends were too far away to make out the features on the elf's dark face, which contrasted with the light-gray hair he had pulled back into a tight ponytail. The elf extended his left hand to the sky and began reciting a poem in a strange rhyme.

"Why doesn't he speak the common language?" asked Naji.

The elves around him stared at the boy, got up, and walked away.

"Please, speak with a lower voice," said Narraneen.

When he finished his chant, Mazahratee lowered his arms to address the crowd.

"What was that about?" asked Marbel.

"A preface to his speech," said Narraneen. "I'll try to translate the essence of what he says." All three listened in silence, waiting for the elf to begin. For several long moments, he stood as still as a statue. When he spoke, his voice thundered across the packed square.

The elf woman translated in a whisper: "We have known good times and bad ones. But the next few fateful days will be most dire, like we have never known. The Mellethyan king, Creeden Dummah, has made it his sacred mission to wipe the elves off the face of the earth. This is not new. In the past, we effortlessly halted his aggression, his and that of the wretched dynasty before him. But this time is different. This time, the Mellethyans are more determined, motivated, and better equipped than ever before.

"Our scouts have failed to bring us details of all the schemes and surprises Creeden Dummah has in store for us. Yet one thing is certain: his attention is mostly on the bridge of Anathoria! It is no secret that the blow he was dealt thirteen springs ago was humiliating, not only in the military and political sense but also on the personal. Now he is coming back for vengeance, his determination fed by anger, coupled with the humans' notorious lust for revenge." He extended a clenched fist then fell silent and turned his back to the crowd.

"I had the impression you Dalusians were invincible. I mean elves," whispered Marbel.

Narraneen seemed distressed.

"Is there a chance war can be avoided?" asked Zig, trying to keep his nervous voice as low as possible.

"Unfortunately, your king does not negotiate with us."

"We're human—the Mellethyan soldiers wouldn't harm us," said Naji.

"Out here, every human is a Khandalus," said Marbel.

The counselor began to speak again, and the elf woman continued to translate: "In my humble opinion, we have just a few days before war breaks. Therefore, I recommend that we begin—" Narraneen stopped. The citizens of Anathoria stirred, disturbed by the adviser's last word. They began to argue with one another in whispers.

"Begin what?" asked Marbel.

"Begin evacuation," she said, her golden eyes reflecting her dismay. "This option has never been considered before. I had no idea things were this dire."

Studying the audience, Mazahratee stood with his hands behind his back.

A short, clear call brought the uproar to a stop as a tall, redheaded elf woman appeared in front of the counselor.

"There seems to be a disagreement. This is Arizen. She's a former counselor," said Narraneen.

Arizen began a speech of her own to address the head counselor and the four members of the Order.

Narraneen translated the elf's words: "We will not abandon our Anathoria. For thousands of years, generation after generation, we have successfully defended it. What happened in the past shall reflect upon the future. It is not the first time we're being challenged on two fronts, the Mobinar passage in the south and the Wall Cliffs to the east. Many of you remember how, five hundred years ago, the humans tried to scale the Wall Cliffs while attacking through the Polikolion Valley at the same time. Thirty archers decided the fate of the battle at the cliffs, stopping the Mellethyans without a single casualty … and I was one of them."

Arizen, waiting for the counselor's reply, folded her arms into her green robe.

Narraneen translated Mazahratee's reply: "Why take the risk? It's a short way from the top of the cliffs to the water bridge. If the king's men reach it … As magnificent as this bridge may be, it is far from being indestructible. If it is brought down, Anathoria will flood in a matter of days. Our end will be swift."

Chapter 58
An Angel With Broken Fingers

The crowd became unsettled again upon hearing the counselor's words.

Mazahratee paced about, occasionally stopping to look at the female elf to size her up.

Narraneen continued her translation as the redheaded elf spoke: "Your words spread self-doubt and fear in our hearts, honorable head counselor. Now is not the time for such words. I believe in the skill, courage, and determination of our fighters. As before, we are ready for any challenge … We shall be victorious again. Furthermore, the Mellethyan king covets Anathoria, and therefore he will not dare to destroy the bridge. Your suggestion is preposterous!"

The counselor responded to her in an aggressive tone, accompanying his fatalistic warnings with vigorous gesticulations.

"He seems mad," said Zig. "What's he saying?"

"His cravings for our destruction are much stronger than his love for this land. And you say we are ready? Ready for the giant Guzuds, who have made a pact with the Mellethyans? Ready for the Black Company, a group of men bred from childhood for battle, who believe Creeden is God? Ready for the cursed sword the king's son threw into the elevated river, which is somehow destined to wreak destruction on us? Ready for Creeden's winged spy, out of reach, freely roaming the skies? And for the last thirteen years, King Creeden Dummah has been studying the arts of dark sorcery, which are forbidden for humans. Adding to all these, this morning, the Order and I have learned of a new peril …"

He paused and crossed the square after observing the worried expressions on the faces of his people. He drew close to the three friends siting with Narraneen. As he approached, his hands folded behind his back, his gaze scanned the crowd until his tiny, strange eyes rested on Zig. Years of fatigue had left their mark on the old elf's face, and a nasty scar stretched from his chin down to his neck.

"What peril are you talking about?" a voice from somewhere in the crowd asked.

The elf raised his thick, gray eyebrows.

"He's missing an arm," said Zig.

The elf's left hand clasped an empty right sleeve.

"Lower your voice. This explains why he doesn't like humans," whispered Marbel.

"A group of priests, by the order of King Creeden, has begun to mine through the Thousand-Year Rock. With bizarre rituals, they are reviving a dormant evil … the Dark Rider. A knight made from pure demonic steel," Narraneen translated as the counselor continued. "A blanket of secrecy was cast over the entire endeavor, which allegedly began at least a year ago. Our scouts were unable to find out any additional information on the matter. This evil knight's task is to lay destruction upon us. Great dangers await us should we decide to stand our ground. You have been warned!" The counselor finished and returned to the seated members of the Order of the Spider.

The eldest of the two females rose to her feet and spoke in a soothing voice. Narraneen translated: "The Order has heard the arguments. We will discuss the matter and come to a decision as soon as possible. Meanwhile, the preparations for war must continue."

Once again, they heard the head counselor's voice, this time addressing the crowd.

"What now?" asked Marbel.

Narraneen eyes were focused on Mazahratee, who spoke calmly this time.

"Look at this guy," said Marbel, pointing with his nose at Naji, who lay with his mouth open and eyes shut. "How can he sleep after hearing these things?"

"He can," said Zig. "The winged creature, the one that hurt you, it serves the king. How could Caleem not know about this?"

"I believe he was kept in the dark intentionally. As were we all."

Mazahratee went on, both his good arm and his amputated one moving about. Eventually, the elf ceased his inquiry and stood as though waiting for an answer. Yet none came. The old elf strode back to the tower. One of the members of the Order dismissed the assembly with an authoritative tone. The elves began leaving, and the congregation dispersed, the attendants disappearing under the trees surrounding the square.

"Could you please translate the last part for us?" asked Marbel.

"He was asked about the Alltree."

"Alltree?" said Zig.

"The Alltree is a sacred tree. Its location is unknown to most of us. Some say it is a magnificent tree, others that it is dead, with barely a leaf, and some say it's not a tree at all. Only a few have laid eyes on it. The counselor is among those few. It is said that through the rustle of the Alltree's leaves, one can hear whispers that are not meant for everyone's ears. These enigmatic whispers can alter fate."

"Have you been to this tree?" asked Zig.

Slapping the boy on the back of his neck Marbel said, "Don't answer this brat's rude question. It's sacred stuff. It's not polite to ask about these things."

"Why not?" asked Zig.

"Because I said so," said Marbel.

The number of elves around them dwindled; the square was almost empty.

"The counselor visited the tree multiple times. He heard the same prediction over and over: 'A broken-fingered angel will be our savior'," said Narraneen.

"An angel with broken fingers?" asked Zig.

"Mazahratee and the other counselors are trying to decipher what it means. They concluded that this 'angel' is a person—could be anyone, maybe one of us. However, a different explanation can always be provided. It's a riddle that many are trying to solve. Obviously, we don't occupy ourselves only with solving riddles. For many weeks, we have been preparing for the oncoming war. Many fighters have already been posted to defensive outposts at the Mobinar passage."

Taking in the serious news, the three friends remained silent. A big group of young elves congregated around one of the planters.

"Marbel, where will we be during the war?" asked Zig.

"Somewhere safe … I hope."

Naji woke up. "Where, what …?"

"Naji, war will break out soon. The king's army is attacking from the south, Guzuds and the Black Company from somewhere else, and a scary metal rider from who knows where. Yes, and a tree that knows everything says that someone with broken fingers will save everyone, but nobody knows who he is," Zig said.

"Give me a minute, will you?" asked Naji, looking around. "Where's Akiena?"

"Caleem's sword is also related somehow. Mazahratee says the Mellethyans will win this time," Zig continued.

"It's not our war," Naji said as he got up.

"Where are you going?" asked Zig.

Naji headed toward a group of elf girls seated near the planter. Without looking back, he said, "Go back to Narraneen's, or stay with Marbel."

Naji approached the young elves. Smiling, Akiena waved at him. He grinned then cleared a path between the other elves.

"Where is the woman you talked about?" asked the boy as he sat down behind Akiena, squeezing in between two elf girls who didn't disguise their annoyance.

"Her name is Nalahes, she is second to Ivest. She is brave leader," said Akiena. "Naji teach me speak?"

"I'll be happy to," he said, transfixed by the girl's beauty.

The elves stopped chattering when a tall female elf, her light-brown hair gathered in a bun, emerged from the tower and approached them. Her purple eyes were prominent in her noble face. She began her speech in the elven tongue.

Naji whispered, "She's tall," and poked Akiena in the back. She gave him a stare, raising a finger to her lips.

The tall elf walked about as she spoke, clenching her right hand into a fist every now and then.

"That girl's ears are the longest," he whispered.

Akiena threw Naji another furious glance.

"All right, fine," he said before getting up and making his way back to his friends.

"That was quick," said Marbel.

"Did you make her mad—?" Zig began, only to be interrupted by three riders galloping into the square. Assuming it was Seonder, Ansseur, and Caleem, they raced to meet the riders.

Ansseur dismounted next to his wife. He shook the dust off his cloak then handed the reins to one of the other two elf riders escorting him.

"Caleem and Seonder are gone," said Ansseur, panting.

"What?" asked Zig.

"Gone where?" asked Naji.

"Seonder released Caleem. They left for the enemy's camp last night."

Zig asked, "Why would they go there?"

"The mistake is mine," said Ansseur. "I sensed Seonder's great desire to free my brother, yet I gave him the benefit of the doubt."

"Why would he go with Caleem?" inquired Marbel.

Ansseur shook his head with a sigh. Narraneen clung to her husband, her arm wrapped around his. Naji, Zig, and Marbel looked at each other, not sure what to say.

"I hope the mistake he made won't cost him his life," said Ansseur gravely.

CHAPTER 59
NAIYA

Caleem entered his tent. Many servants wearing muddy blue uniforms were setting up inside. The racket and noisy conversations stopped, and the servants all bowed to the prince, their eyes to the ground.

"Continue," said the prince.

They fumbled around without uttering a word until they finished their task. A slight nod from Caleem sufficed for them to exit the tent in a rush. He touched the soft, white sheets of the well-made bed with his fingertips, then went to the table on the other side of the tent. On it were several large, silver serving dishes. Under the shiny lids, Caleem discovered plenty of warm, peeled boiled eggs, meat stew, and fresh vegetables. The enticing aroma filled the air. He took a moment to savor the scents then grabbed an egg and devoured it in one bite.

One of the servants returned bearing a loaf of bread wrapped in white cloth, a pitcher, and yet another serving dish, this one full of fresh fruits. He bowed and placed the items on the table. Caleem sat on a stool and reached for the warm bread. He dipped piece after piece into the gravy of the stew, savoring each bite. The servant poured wine into a silver goblet, then made to serve the prince only to stumble, sending some apples rolling on the floor. Caleem put the bread down.

The servant dropped to his knees.

"Please forgive me, Your Highness. Forgive me, please …"

Caleem remained where he was, observing the terrified servant. He took a sip of wine then grabbed a piece of bread and an apple from the floor before strolling out past the servant, who was still covering his face.

The sun had already risen above the clouds. The prince made his way past the camp's boundary. All the while, Dolegg's roaring laughter echoed in his ears.

Caleem noticed that Damian was following him. "I want no escort." Caleem turned, startling the officer.

"His Majesty ordered me to accompany you at all times."

"Is that so?"

"Yes, Your Highness."

"I'm going on alone."

The dumbfounded officer stayed behind as the prince continued on his way. As he reflected on the servant's behavior, a strange feeling of guilt swept over him. The few weeks he spent on the mission reminded him of when he had joined the infantry and first met Marbel. The soldiers had been simple, genuine people with a sense of belonging and a care for the collective. He has been respected and treated as an equal, even though he was the prince. Fellow soldiers had talked to him and looked him straight into the eye.

Are they dead, or are they captives being turned?

The morning chill had mellowed, and a light rain fell.

The thought of his friends being turned disgusted him. "They're better off dead," he said aloud.

After climbing up a small hill, he saw the river flowing before him. He took his clothes off and jumped in without a second thought. Upon contact with the icy waters, he gasped, then submerged his whole body, giving in to the gentle current. Below the surface, gray rocks and swaying plants clung to the river's depths. He stared into the blurred underwater world until a suffocating burn in his lungs forced him to surface. The drizzle had turned into a downpour, so he swam toward the bank to a large boulder around which flowed a warm current. The blissful crystal liquid washed over his weary body. Overcome with fatigue, he leaned on the boulder, hugging it, the music of raindrops plopping on the surface of the river playing in his ears.

In the foaming water he saw Marbel, Motehro, and the boys arguing and laughing; Kamanar's tall figure appeared behind them. Caleem choked as he tried to talk to Kamanar, but all he could utter was nonsense.

The long sword he had discarded in the elevated river was back in his hands. The bluish statuesque warrior lunged at him out of nowhere.

"Stay back!" he shouted to his friends.

The warrior swung at him as the rain thundered down and the wind howled. The dreadful scene went on and on as his friends watched. Caleem jolted and cursed, punching the boulder in this bizarre state of slumber. Despite the cold and the rain, his nightmares gave him no respite.

"Naiya!" he shouted, waking himself up with his own scream.

For a moment, he panicked, pushing himself off the boulder. His teeth clenched and his body shivering, he pulled himself out of the river to scan his surroundings. The rain had stopped, and the world began to darken.

Naked and barefoot, Caleem trembled. Bent over, with his arms around his body, he bounced from rock to rock on the muddy shore, searching for his clothes. He mumbled in his delirium, stumbling on the uneven ground, until he found them. As he was donning his wet clothes and shoes, he felt disturbed but didn't know why.

"Naiya," he said as he gazed to the other side of the river. While his eyes roamed over the clusters of trees, a vision appeared before him of his sister in a flowing, white dress, riding a horse as black as night. The vision faded into the darkness.

"Was it a dream?"

He made his way back to the camp. Running helped to relieve

his aches and elevate his temperature. As he wove between the tents, he heard the loud shriek of a familiar female voice. His heart sank.

It can't be. What the hell is she doing here?

He ran as fast as he could to the center of the camp, almost crashing into a soldier who was leading a horse by the reins. He recognized the magnificent stallion. "Autumn Wind."

He heard a second, blood-curdling scream, much closer this time, followed by sobbing. "Naiya!" he shouted and dashed forward.

He found her sitting on the muddy ground, her once-white dress now a brown mass of folds spread around her. Her hair had come undone; a few wet locks fell on Sarik's head. He lay on his belly in the princess's embrace, his right hand still tied to the wooden pole.

The princess wept as she held Sarik, her hand caressing his mud-smeared hair. "My love, what have they done to you … What have they done?" she murmured again and again.

The princess's cries tore at Caleem's heart.

"I have no idea how she got here, my prince. Do something, please," said Dolegg as he stood leaning on his sledgehammer.

"Naiya," Caleem called.

She raised her head, her brown eyes shining like two flames. Tears ran down her flushed cheeks and glittered in the torchlight. "What did I ask of you?" she said, her voice choking.

Caleem reached out his hand. "I'd like—"

"Don't touch me!"

Caleem recoiled.

"What was the one thing I asked of you?" she asked again.

"There are some things you need to—"

"I asked for one thing only … that you watch over him," she said, lowering her head again, never ceasing to caress Sarik's hair.

"You think you know him, but you're so wrong. He's a traitor!"

Watching the scene unfold, the soldiers surrounding them stood like statues.

"Did you hear me?" Caleem shouted, pointing an accusing finger.

"It is you who does not know this man. You are the traitor. You've betrayed me! I asked of you this one and only thing. What have they done to you, my beautiful Seonder?"

"How do you know his real name?" he asked, his eyes on the half-elf. A slight movement of Seonder's hand showed he was still alive.

"How do I know? How can you not know? I more than hinted countless times. You were always too stubborn to acknowledge anything."

Caleem raised his eyebrows in bewilderment.

"Don't pretend to be surprised! Or maybe you are, and you can't help being stupid."

While Caleem searched his memory, the soldiers in the circle began to retreat to give way to the king, who strode up to the trio. His two bodyguards, clad in their black armor, were by his sides. The larger one with the bare, muscular arms shoved the soldiers out of the way to remain close to the king at all times.

Dolegg bowed. "Your Majesty."

The king's voice thundered. "Those of you who value their eyesight better disappear at once."

All the spectators vanished except for Dolegg and the king's bodyguards.

The king looked at his daughter, whose only response was nothing but a frightened look.

"Get up," he said.

"I'm not going anywhere," she said, her hoarse voice trembling.

The king walked closer to her, and the princess recoiled, pulling Seonder with her.

"I said, get up."

"No!" she screamed.

The king yanked her up by the neck. Naiya dropped Seonder as she wrestled to break free from her father's strangling grip. She pummeled him with her fists and legs, but to no avail. Caleem lunged. Dolegg blocked his way with his big hammer. Both bodyguards drew their weapons.

"Lower your swords! Get out of my way!" said Caleem.

His sister's face was turning blue. Before he could attempt another move, the king let go of Naiya's throat. The princess collapsed on the wet ground, clutching her throat with her hands, coughing hard. The king turned to leave. The bodyguards sheathed their weapons, and Dolegg cleared the way for Caleem to rush to his sister's aid.

"Bring the prisoner to my tent," said the king as he left with his guards.

"Yes, Your Majesty," said Dolegg.

Caleem knelt beside her, but she pushed him away.

Two soldiers arrived. "Take him," said Dolegg.

They pulled Seonder by his bleeding arms and dragged him away. Naiya was still bent over, and she coughed until she threw up. Caleem wished to help her, but he restrained himself. A few servants approached, giving their mandatory bows before helping Naiya back to her feet.

"Seonder!" she shouted in between coughs.

"The king ordered you to the healer's tent," one of them said.

"No," said Naiya, gasping for breath. She picked up her dress and tried to free herself.

The servants grabbed her by the arms. "His Majesty said to take you, even against your will."

"No!" she screamed again, scratching the face of one of the servants holding her. Yet the men dragged her away as her brother watched: a silent, immobile witness.

Caleem could still hear her screams and curses as he walked toward the royal tent in a daze. With slumped shoulders, he entered his father's tent. The king sat on his chair scratching his short beard. Two servants knelt at his feet, brushing the caked mud off the hem of the royal red robes. His two bodyguards stood behind him, their arms crossed over their chests.

Caleem was but a few steps away from the king when a dark figure materialized from a corner of the tent. Startled, he leaped aside and faced the creature, his fists raised. The bodyguards drew their swords. To Caleem's consternation, their blades were pointing at him. Disregarding them, he focused on the shadowy creature spreading its bat-like wings, which touched each side of the tent. The prince was about to pounce.

"Caleem, stop where you are. Guards, sheath your swords," said the king.

"No! That thing is dangerous," screamed Caleem, his eyes glued to the winged monster.

"It is dangerous, but not to us," said the king.

"What?" Caleem glared dumbfoundedly at his father.

"This creature serves me. I possess something it needs."

Baffled, Caleem lowered his fists. "If it serves you, why didn't you give it the damn sword? It could've flown over and thrown it from the sky."

"Do you think I wouldn't have done that, had it been possible?" the king asked. "For some reason, it will not touch the sword. Its dark magic somehow disturbs my special servant. There is much mystery to that weapon."

"Who is coming for it? What other things don't I know about? Tell me now!"

Folding its bat-like wings, the strange creature curled back into its corner, its yellow eyes glowing.

"You know what you need to know."

"Father ... did the Dalusians ever try to negotiate with us?"

The king's face soured. He rose, sending the two servants at his feet crawling away. "What are these questions?"

Caleem approached his father. The bodyguards blocked his way. "These are questions that I should have asked long ago. I demand answers," he said, undeterred.

"Stubborn, a famous family trait," said the king as he returned to his seat. "Let us say they did try to negotiate. What difference would it make?"

"It could change everything for me!" said Caleem, and he glanced at the creature curled up in the corner, unsettled by its presence.

"If a party of Dalusians were to walk in here today claiming they wanted peace, do you think there would be any validity to such a claim? Every nation in the world wants peace … but at what cost? At what sacrifice? Don't be naive."

"I am not naive. We should hear what they have to say. What rightful claims do we have to Anathoria? How is it our land? Is it because it is written in some old book?"

"Hear what they have to say? Their tongues may be of flesh, but tongues can shatter bones. Words build kingdoms and worlds, and they can also bring them down in the same breath. Words are hot air—they reflect only the shallow reality. There are always hidden agendas. Understand this: It's not about Anathoria, and it never was. I'm going to drown it anyway. It's about Mellethya's pride. It's about the thousands of men who died fighting these devils. If you think I'd allow their sacrifices to be in vain, you are very wrong. And as far as I'm concerned, they are also to blame for your mother's death. So, no, they're not as hideous or devious as we've led the people to believe. We do that to preserve the hate and disdain. We're taking advantage of the commoners' need to see the world in black and white, beautiful and ugly, good and evil. For them, it's very simple. *We* are good and just, whereas *they* are cunning and evil. They need this as their truth. Otherwise, they will be baffled and, eventually, will turn on me! On *us*. There has to be something or someone to blame for their misfortune. They need to hate, and if it's not the enemy it will be their sovereign. Remember this!"

The king took a step forward. "You and I know that good and evil are a matter of perspective, but so many don't care to see it that way. For them, life would be senseless. For our purposes, that's a good thing. After all, why do you think God made Satan?"

He stood in front of his son, laid a hand on his shoulder, then looked into his face. "I hope you'll forgive me for keeping you in the dark. I did this for the greater good. It is my duty as king, and I am certain that when you become king, you will also place the good of the kingdom above everything else. I trust you, my son."

"The picture is clearer now. Forgive me, Father, for having doubts. What about Naiya?"

"That foolish girl. As if we had nothing else to worry about besides her silly affairs." The monarch scoffed, sinking back into his chair. "Don't let her bother you. I will take care of her." After a brief pause, the king continued, "It is going to be a monumental victory. After a millennium, I, Creeden Dummah, shall be the one to crush the Dalusians. Our forefathers will be avenged, with you by my side, the crown prince."

"I'm not familiar with the battle plan. What will my role be?" asked the prince, peering once again at the crouching creature.

"You will lead the Black Company up the cliffs," said the king.

Before Caleem could ask his next question, a voice from outside interrupted.

"Requesting permission to enter, Your Majesty."

CHAPTER 60
END HIS USELESS LIFE

"Enter," said King Creeden.

Dolegg entered and bowed. Two soldiers followed, dragging Seonder, his arms and legs bound. They dropped the captive at the officer's feet.

He lay on his back, covered in blood and mud all the way from his bruised head to his lacerated toes.

Caleem approached his father's chair and stood to his right.

"It took you long enough," said the king.

"I couldn't let this scum be brought into the royal tent without tying him up myself. We know what his kind are capable of, even if they're injured," said Dolegg, bowing again.

"And?" asked the king, looking at the captive, who did not move a muscle except for his chest, which heaved up and down as he breathed.

"Your Majesty knows these creatures. The trash didn't utter a word. His ears may not be pointed, but this creature is a Dalusian through and through. No man could endure such damage … Scum!" Dolegg finished with a kick to Seonder's head.

"Is he conscious?" asked the king.

"Yes."

"Do you want to say something?" the king asked Caleem while still looking at Seonder.

A puddle of blood began to spread beneath him.

The prince shook his head.

"Well … if you wish to be saved, you have only to request it," said the king.

Seonder turned his head and glared at Caleem yet didn't say a word. Caleem gasped when he saw Seonder's battered face. His right eye was so swollen it was sealed shut. There was some swelling on his right cheek, his nose was broken at an odd angle, and blood oozed out of both nostrils. His upper lip was torn, his front teeth broken. A gooey mixture of blood and saliva trickled from his mouth. When Caleem's eyes met Seonder's good eye, the prince froze. That one bright eye was the only thing left intact in his entire body. Seonder gazed at Caleem with an indifferent serenity.

"Dolegg, end his useless life. He had wasted enough of my time," said the king.

"As you command."

Dolegg drew a long knife from his belt.

With a kick, the officer turned Seonder on his side. He placed his boot on the captive's head and pinned it hard to the ground, then pulled on Seonder's hair to expose his neck.

From the moment his father gave the order, Caleem's heart accelerated. The closer the knife came to Seonder's neck, the faster his heart beat, until it became so intense that Caleem was convinced his father could hear it. The knife almost touched Seonder's throat, yet he still did not resist or make the slightest move. He only stared at Caleem.

The prince tried to look away from Seonder's accusing eye, but it was impossible. He tried to slow his breathing, concentrating on creating a semblance of detachment.

The blade of the knife pressed against Seonder's throat.

This is it. I couldn't stop it even if I wanted to.

Caleem's heart was about to explode. With great effort, the

prince managed to shut his eyes, blocking out the horrific scene that was unfolding before him.

"Stop," ordered the king.

Startled, Caleem opened his eyes.

"Do it outside. I don't want blood on my carpet," he said.

Dolegg pulled the knife, leaving a shallow red gash on the half-elf's neck. The officer exited and his two soldiers followed, dragging Seonder by the feet. Caleem exhaled, making sure his father didn't notice, then trailed after the soldiers.

"It is vital that you see," the king called after him.

Caleem stopped at the entrance. "Yes," he said, choking.

The prince followed in the dark of the early night. The strange group, led by Dolegg, took a path between the tents, heading beyond the boundaries of the camp toward a lone old tree. Caleem was careful not to even glance at Seonder. Dolegg began to whistle as they approached the tree, juggling his big knife, tossing it from one hand to the other.

"Enjoying all this? What a joyful task," said the prince.

"What did you say, my prince?" asked Dolegg as he spun around.

"I'm asking, is this joyful to you?"

"I will not whistle if it is not to the prince's desire," said Dolegg, continuing on his way. "Put him here," he ordered the soldiers, pointing near a thick tree root. The two soldiers obeyed then stepped back.

The officer put his foot on the captive's head once more, then bent down and held the knife to Seonder's throat.

"Wait! I want to ask you something, Dolegg," said the prince, approaching the officer.

The latter straightened up.

"You wouldn't be so brave if he wasn't tied up and wounded, would you?" asked Caleem.

"Sounds like this matter is not to your liking."

"Answer my question!" said Caleem, taking another step toward the officer.

"You said he was a traitor, not I. What's wrong with you?"

"You speak to me with such insolence and still won't answer."

The officer smiled, exhaling with a note of exasperation. "Your father holds me in the highest regard, more than anyone else, including you. If we have a problem, he'll stand by my side. And yes, I could overpower this traitor, even if he were fit and armed."

"Then take a try on me. Attack me!" said Caleem, putting himself on guard.

Dolegg was baffled. "The prince has lost his mind," he said and chuckled at the soldiers standing to the side.

"I'm standing here before you, not wounded but unarmed. I'm ordering you to attack me. Attack to kill!" Caleem shouted.

"The prince has indeed lost his mind."

Caleem leaped forward and slapped the officer hard in the face with his right palm and then again with his left.

The soldiers, befuddled, looked on without moving a muscle. Seething with rage, Dolegg raised his hands to his reddened cheeks.

"Attack me, you fat, ugly swine. You couldn't even beat a crippled grandmother. You coward."

"Insolent boy!" Dolegg shouted then charged, aiming the tip of his knife straight at the prince's heart.

Caleem deflected the knife then struck a hard blow to the officer's stomach. The latter folded over, moaning in pain. Caleem grabbed Dolegg's hand, which held the knife, turned it upward, and then inserted the blade beneath Dolegg's chin and drove it up into his skull. Dolegg's eyes almost jumped out of their sockets as he hummed. Blood splattered down Caleem's hands. The prince kicked the officer's limp body, sending it rolling until it hit the base of the tree and came to a sudden stop.

Glaring at the paralyzed soldiers, Caleem said, "Stay here, and don't move!" before running back to the camp. He kept his head down as he walked among the tents, avoiding the eyes of the soldiers who strolled about. As he wiped his bloodstained hand on a tent, he heard Naiya's muffled screams. Caleem followed her voice until he identified the healer's tent, which was guarded by two sentries on either side.

"Prepare Autumn Wind and another strong horse. I want to take the princess for a ride outside the camp to calm her down."

"Right away, Your Highness," one of the guards said and took off.

The prince barged into the tent. His sister was alone, her hands and feet tied to a bare wooden bed. Her mouth was blocked with a loose piece of cloth tied around her head. Her red eyes were wet, and tears rolled down her cheeks.

"Release me at once!" she shouted in a muffled voice.

Caleem covered her mouth with his hand. For a moment, she tried to scream again.

"I'm trying to help Seonder," he whispered in her ear.

Naiya listened, her eyes locked on her brother's.

"I need you to be quiet. I've just killed Dolegg. Seonder is lying outside the camp, Maybe we can still help him."

The princess nodded. Caleem removed his hand from her mouth, and untied her hands and feet. Once free, Naiya threw away the piece of cloth and leaped to her feet.

"Are you all right?" asked Caleem.

Wiping the tears off her face, Naiya nodded, saying nothing.

At the sound of approaching hooves, Caleem led his sister outside by the hand.

"Autumn Wind and White Dream are ready for you, sire," said the guard as he handed over the reins.

"Come, get on Autumn. He probably missed you already," said the prince.

With the guard's help, Naiya mounted the black horse.

Caleem mounted White Dream, whose appearance was the exact opposite of Autumn Wind: a horse white as snow, except for a black, arrow-shaped mark between its eyes.

"We'll do a few laps around the camp," said Caleem, pulling on White Dream's reins. He rode northward, down the path between the tents, with Naiya and Autumn Wind close behind.

Caleem spurred the horse to a gallop with his knees, directing it toward the lone tree. "Good boys," Caleem complimented the two soldiers as he dismounted. He knelt by Seonder, who lay as motionless as Dolegg's corpse. The prince turned him over, examining his wounds.

Naiya jumped off Autumn Wind and landed on the muddy ground. Stepping on the hem of her cumbersome dress, she stumbled and fell before getting back up, her eyes fixed on Seonder, who lay next to her brother. "Seonder," she cried. Sobbing and shaking, she knelt and hugged his still body.

"We need to hurry—enough of that! We have to get him out of here," said Caleem.

"Where to?" she asked, containing her tears.

"Ride after me," Caleem said before turning to the soldiers. "You two. Let's put him on the horse."

"He will ride on Autumn with me," said the princess as she began to take off her layered dress.

Caleem puffed but said nothing.

The princess was now in her breeks and tight, white woolen shirt. She mounted Autumn Wind. "Bring him here … Be cautious," she said.

The soldiers lifted Seonder's battered body onto the back of the horse and leaned him against the princess, who embraced him with both arms, holding the reins with her fingertips.

"Escort us," said Caleem to the soldiers as he jumped on his horse and prodded it forward.

Naiya and Seonder followed on Autumn Wind, and the two soldiers ran behind them.

The princess kept up the brisk pace, her attention drifting between the road before her and the unconscious half-elf on her lap.

The two soldiers, panting behind, could barely keep up.

Caleem heard the river flowing close by. Straining his eyes in the weak moonlight, he perceived the rushing white water. He rode faster along the river until it met the creek at the spot where he and Seonder had crossed the night before.

"Where to, Caleem?" asked Naiya, riding closer to her brother.

"Don't worry, just ride."

"Don't worry? Seonder might die at any moment," she yelled then began to cry again.

Caleem pulled White Dream around and rode toward the two soldiers.

"Your Highness," said one of them, trying to catch his breath.

"Thank you for the escort. You are free to go back."

The soldiers looked at each other then began to stagger back.

"We're going to the Dalusians," said Caleem.

"They're called elves," retorted Naiya.

"Doesn't matter. Follow me."

They rode up the rocks along the creek. After ascending the rocky slope, Caleem looked back to find his sister struggling with maneuvering the horse while holding on to Seonder.

"We'll have to continue on foot," said Caleem. He dismounted then reached for Seonder.

"Careful," said the princess as she lowered the half-elf into her brother's arms.

"Back to the camp," she said to the horses while clapping her hands. The animals descended the slope then galloped toward the dim lights of the camp. The prince placed the wounded half-elf over his shoulder and began to climb the rocks, choosing his footing carefully in the darkness, his sister following ably behind, her teeth chattering.

"Are you cold?" he asked without turning around.

"Cold? Why don't you ask me a different question? Like how and why I got here?"

"Why?" he stopped.

"Seonder sent me a message."

"A message?"

"Yes, delivered to me by his raven. It said—" The princess paused, gazing at her brother's back. "He was going to Father's camp, with you! And that he knew the risks. Look at me!" Her voice quivered.

Caleem turned around, struggling under Seonder's weight with every step. He stared straight into her gloomy eyes.

"He said that despite everything, he had faith in you. For the chance that you might listen, small as it may be … For the chance to earn your trust again, he was prepared to risk everything."

Caleem lowered his eyes, turned, and continued in silence.

"Had he known you and your true nature, he wouldn't have bothered," she shouted. Caleem gave no comment.

"But I was right … after all," a faint voice whispered in Caleem's ear. It took him a moment to realize it was Seonder.

Naiya rushed forward to help Caleem lay Seonder down on a flat rock. Seonder's eye opened. The princess kissed and kissed his bleeding face, and Caleem had to pull her off him.

"You're hurting him," he said.

Seonder struggled to smile as he eyed Caleem. "Here you are, with us."

Caleem nodded in return as Seonder's eye closed once again. Weeping, the princess wiped the blood off his face. Caleem pulled her off the young man again and continued, carrying Seonder.

"Why did you let them do this to him?" she asked, sobbing.

"Naiya, you're the most important person in the world to me."

"Tell me the truth, Caleem. How much were you involved with what happened?"

"I wish I could lie and tell you it was not my fault, or that I couldn't stop it …"

Making a huge effort to hold back her tears, Naiya stared at her brother.

"It's all my fault. I tricked him into coming with me. Then I accused him of treason and stood by while Dolegg tortured him."

Naiya stumbled up the rocks to him. "Put him down! Take your filthy hands off him!" she shouted.

"Stop it! I can't bear this anymore. I'm so sorry." Caleem refused to put Seonder down. Naiya tried to pull Seonder from her brother's hold. After she failed, she gave a terrible cry and struck Caleem's face with her fist. Caleem fell to the ground, Seonder's body still on top of him. It wasn't his sister's blow but the hatred in her eyes that wore him down.

Naiya pulled Seonder from his arms. "My love, I'll carry you myself," she whispered then stood up on shaky legs.

Caleem wanted to help but didn't dare suggest it.

The sound of stretching bowstrings reached their ears. Two dark figures stood above them.

"Help, please! Seonder is wounded," she said, walking toward them while she brushed her brother aside.

A third hooded figure appeared from the darkness, took Seonder from Naiya, and carried him up the mountain. Naiya followed then threw one last glance at her brother. "I will never forgive you!" she cried and spat in his direction.

Caleem froze as her words pierced his heart.

Ignoring the archers, his head down, he climbed up after his sister, whirlwinds of thoughts clashing in his mind.

CHAPTER 61
FALSE HOPES

"It's getting dark and cold. Come on, you two, pull me to Narraneen's. I'm tired of waiting," said Marbel.

The tower doors swung open. Scores of elves emerged, Narraneen among them, looking disconcerted.

"Narraneen, what's happening?" asked Marbel.

The elf woman looked back up at the sphere. Three long, red banners dropped from the balconies above. "The war has begun," she said.

"Already!" said Marbel.

"The battle at the southern front has commenced. The Mellethyan infantry is crossing the Polikolion Valley, aiming for the Mobinar passage. We'll stay here and help in whatever way we can. Our fighters are very capable. Let's hope for minimal casualties."

"Where is Ansseur? I have a request," said Marbel.

Noticing how nervous Zig was, the elf woman placed her hand on the boy's shoulder. "He'll be right out. The meeting has ended, and the resolution was not to his liking."

"What do you mean?" asked Marbel.

"It was decided that the last Ivest company, the best of our elven army, will reinforce the defenses at the passage. Ansseur and Mazahratee demanded that they be sent to the cliffs."

She pointed to a group of elf warriors, armed with swords and bows, hurrying out of the tower. They covered their heads with their hoods, crossed the square, climbed up a rope bridge, and disappeared between the treetops.

Ansseur walked out, feeling his way with his long staff while he argued with Mazahratee. "If you hadn't been so fixated on your 'broken fingers' fable, perhaps we could have convinced them." Ansseur's voice echoed through the square.

The head counselor mumbled as he rummaged through the pouch suspended from his side. "They would never have sent the company to the cliffs. Especially when neither the Guzuds nor Creeden's force has moved a pace, yet battle has already begun in the south.

"You heard what they said—they think it's a distraction to divide our forces. The order is relying too much on those cliffs. They think those rocks are unclimbable. I do think it's a distraction. But it's the other way around. We should be focusing on the Wall Cliffs, not on the southern front. This frustrates me more than it does you. And you should learn to respect the Alltree. The riddle is the key to winning this war."

"It's not only me. No one from the Order uttered a word about your Alltree prophecy," Ansseur said. "They want to win the battle at the cliffs with only thirty archers. They're really underestimating my father's eagerness."

"The Order is insisting on repeating the victory of the thirty archers from five hundred years ago. And you are still thinking poorly of the Alltree," Mazahratee said.

"I would rather focus on challenges that I comprehend."

"Apart from the enigmatic person with the 'broken fingers', there is the Dark Rider and your brother's sword, which remain a mystery. Too many unanswered questions. Come, let's go through the books, maybe find some clues."

"I must bring my wife, Narraneen, with me—she is my eyes. And she is smarter than both of us."

With a smile, Narraneen said, "I never imagined I would see

you two chatting like, dare I say, friends. Greetings, Mazahratee, honorable counselor."

"I wouldn't go that far … We are merely collaborating, momentarily. Greetings to you, beautiful and wise Narraneen," Mazahratee said.

"These are the newly arrived Mellethyans: Marbel, Naji, and Zig," she said.

"I doubt they can be of any help," he said.

Ansseur said to the three friends. "You may return to our home."

"I believe Marbel had a request," said Narraneen.

Marbel said, "Yes, yes … I know that the war has started, so this is not the ideal time to ask, but I will anyway. Is there any chance you could arrange to bring Kamanar's body here?"

"I'm sorry, my friend, but time is—" Ansseur began.

His eyes and mouth wide open, Mazahratee lunged toward Marbel. He put his hands on the cart and leaned in, face-to-face with the paralyzed man. "What did you say?".

Marbel shrunk back in his cart to get some distance from the elf's long nose. "I was wondering if our friend's body could be retrieved."

"No! You said something else."

"Counselor, what's wrong with you?" asked Ansseur.

He shook Marbel by his shoulder. "You said something else. You called someone something!"

"Who? Kamanar? I didn't call him anything," said Marbel, trying to push away the dark-skinned elf.

Mazahratee stepped back, almost treading on Ansseur's feet.

"Yes … no …" he said then mumbled in the elven tongue.

"Honorable counselor," Narraneen said in a stern tone.

He continued to mumble indecipherable phrases as he whirled in a dervish-like trance.

Ansseur placed a hand on the counselor's shoulder, jolting him. "Speak," he said.

"Kamanar. Kamanar! *Ka-ma-nar*. We must hurry. Kamanar. I

think we've solved the riddle. He might be the one. I don't know how yet. But it is Kamanar!"

The three friends looked at each other, then at the counselor, who seemed quite pleased with himself.

"Kamanar is dead," said Zig.

"That cannot be. If it were so, then the Alltree was wrong, and that can never be. He's alive, I have no doubt. He must be. He must be brought here as soon as possible. I need to see this Kamanar with my own eyes."

The counselor turned and ran.

"Could he be?" asked Zig.

"He died in my arms. Don't believe this lunatic. He's only giving you false hopes," said Marbel.

"Nalahes. Nalahes!" shouted the counselor as he walked toward the tall elf who had just exited the tower.

"Purple eyes … I remember her. She's a commander of something," said Naji.

"They are purple … What are you waiting for? Pull me closer," said Marbel.

"You said you didn't believe him," said Naji.

"Shut up and push!"

"Ansseur, you must understand. The word 'Kamanar' means 'broken fingers' in the ancient human tongue," said the counselor.

"It's probably a coincidence. It means nothing. The man is already dead." Ansseur scratched one of the scars on his face.

Mazahratee asked, "A coincidence? There are no such things as coincidences. Time and time again, you question the potency of the Alltree."

"You speak of this tree as if it is a god," said Ansseur.

"Careful, human! It is a holy entity you're talking about."

"Kamanar might be the one to save us? But he is a human being. You loathe humans."

"I don't loathe them. I just don't like them."

"Let us respect each other's beliefs. Maybe it's not a coincidence," said Narraneen.

"If Kamanar is alive, then the counselor is right. That's what I think," said Naji.

"Of course he's alive," said Mazahratee. "Nalahes, assemble a party to retrieve Kamanar."

Glancing at Marbel and the boys, the purple-eyed elf nodded. "Where did you leave him?" she asked.

"Where? Well … in a pleasant, green place down the creek from the ambush position. In a small cave, just above the gorge," said the chubby man.

The elf excused herself then dashed across the square.

"A female fighter," said Marbel.

"In Anathoria, both genders are equal in rights and, more importantly, in duties," said Narraneen.

"Until Kamanar 'broken fingers' is fetched, we will focus on the mystery sword and that Dark Rider. Are you coming?" the counselor asked Ansseur.

"Of course."

"There's no time to spare," said the counselor as he led the way.

Naji pulled the cart behind Mazahratee.

"You have helped enough. Thank you and farewell," said Mazahratee.

"Let's go have some food," said Naji, turning the cart around.

"Very well. I will tell you about the Dark Rider some other time. Let's go and eat some of that green cheese," said Marbel.

Muttering in the elven tongue, the counselor stopped in his tracks. "Wait! What do you know of the Dark Rider?"

"Take us along. We can help," said the chubby man.

Mazahratee frowned then turned and continued walking. "Come."

CHAPTER 62

SOMETIMES THE TEMPER OF MEN PROVES USEFUL

Leading the others, Mazahratee crossed the square and entered a narrow path lined with dense vegetation. The dark sky was concealed by a tunnel of thick branches. After a long walk, the vegetation grew thinner, but the canopy still masked the stars. The counselor halted and bent down to open a trapdoor in the ground.

"Through here," he said and lowered himself into the round opening.

Kneeling to feel where the opening was, Ansseur asked, "What is this place?"

"Can't you see? Oh, yes, you can't see. Wait." Mazahratee rummaged for something in the darkness.

Bright flashes came from the opening. Soon, a torch's flame illuminated the way. Ansseur found the ladder at the mouth of the pit and lowered himself down.

"Marbel—let me help you," said Narraneen.

"You go. I'll manage."

The elf woman followed her husband down the ladder. The boys turned to Marbel, but, before they had a chance to say a word, the man hoisted himself out of the cart and fell flat on his belly, flipping the cart in the process. He crawled to the opening and lowered his limp legs into the shaft. He awkwardly descended until his legs were sprawled on the tiles at the bottom and said, "See, no problem."

Naji and Zig followed into the small, round room lit by the torch. At the center of the room stood two tables, and on each lay a pile of books in complete disarray.

The counselor pored over the piles. "Speak. What do you know about the Dark Rider?" he asked, putting a book down and picking up another.

"What are all these books?" asked Naji.

"Don't touch," said the counselor. "I have arranged them in a particular order." He returned his attention to the one in his hand, flipping through the pages with his thumb.

"I can help you. I can read," said Naji. "Some 'particular order' you have here."

The counselor's odd eyes turned to the boy, but he said nothing and went back to the book.

Marbel dragged himself across the tiles. He sat up between the tables, picked up a book, and opened it. "When we were kids, the elderly used to taunt us with tales of a knight made of solid metal. Even his bowels and heart were solid metal. The Dark Rider, they called him. 'If you go there or there, the Dark Rider will come for you!'," he said, leafing through the book.

The counselor closed his book and knelt next to Marbel. "Go on."

"Some used to say this rider was possessed by a tormented soul seeking revenge. Others said that he was driven by a force of pure evil, an emissary from hell—"

"From hell? Nonsense … Go on," said Mazahratee.

"Maybe it was … but as soon as darkness came, you couldn't find even the homeless wandering outside. There was not a soul on the streets, for fear of the Dark Rider and his two vengeful swords. They say he used to emerge from the gaps in the great wall and massacre those who pushed their luck. After he was satiated, he would vanish …"

"Two swords?" asked the counselor before diving into the books once again. "I have read somewhere of a mythical rider armed with two swords."

"How do you know it's the same rider?" asked Ansseur.

"I don't. That's why you are here. To help me look through these books."

"This place used to be a shelter, right?" asked Narraneen.

"One of many. If Anathoria is flooded, these shelters will be useless, as they are under the ground," said the counselor.

"Do you really think King Creeden's army will reach Anathoria this time?" Marbel asked.

"Either they will, or … we will be flooded. Depends which front is breached first," said Mazahratee.

"Let's hope for a third possibility," Ansseur said then added a sentence in the elven tongue, directing his words at the counselor.

Mazahratee divided the books among them. "Each of you grab a book. Hurry up. There has to be some information here."

"Castle charts, poetry, letters, battle reports, chronicles. Most of these are stamped with the deer head! The Mellethyan royal emblem. Where did all these books come from?" Marbel asked after a while. "I noticed one of the tiles on the ground even has that emblem, too … There, near the ladder."

"That's none of your business and is insignificant right now," the counselor answered. "You said the rider appeared through gaps in your great wall. That means this happened after your war with the Wingaars."

Marbel said, "That was so long ago. Don't take it too seriously. It's all but a folktale."

"Maybe it is, maybe it isn't," said Mazahratee as he continued digging.

The entire party stood around piles of books, leafing through the pages. Ansseur exchanged whispers with his wife. Despite his impaired eyesight, he insisted on reading some bits on his own. Zig, who could not read, looked for the ones with illustrations or diagrams. As the hours passed, Ansseur and Marbel's eyes began to tire from reading in the dim light. The boys had long since fallen asleep sitting up against a stack of books. Naji's drooling head rested on his friend's shoulder.

Narraneen noticed the older man staring at the ladder's dancing shadow. "Is everything all right?" she asked.

"The battle at the Polikolion."

Narraneen closed her book and sat down next to the chubby man.

"Men and elves are dying right now. For what?" asked Marbel.

"They're fighting for the ambition of one arrogant man, from a long and corrupt dynasty," said Ansseur.

"If someone could only reveal the truth to those stupid soldiers," said Marbel.

Ansseur said, "The Dalusian image is deeply embedded in their minds. It appears to be an impossible task." He leaned over the pile, swapping his book for another one.

Marbel looked at the former prince's scar-covered face. "It's hard to believe that a father would do such a thing to his son."

"I accepted this a long time ago."

"I don't know how you accepted such a thing. Your father should answer for this evil deed," said Marbel, trying to get up but forgetting his injury.

"I'm merely another victim, one of many. I came to terms with my own tragedy. Sometimes I imagine myself confronting him, speaking my mind … Then hacking off his head."

"I would be glad to witness that," said Marbel.

The counselor, who had been quiet for hours, said, "Sometimes the temper of men proves useful," before returning to his book.

"Anger and the desire for vengeance can be blinding. You two should take a breath of fresh air," said Narraneen.

Ansseur chuckled. "We are nothing but a pair of cripples who can only wish. Don't worry, my dear, we can't harm even the feeblest of our enemies."

"I disagree," Narraneen said. "I believe you two are very capable. When you spoke of the king, I felt the vigor of your intentions."

"I thank you for the encouragement, my dear, gentle wife, but Marbel is a man of strong spirit. We both can face the truth of things. Isn't that right, Marbel?"

Marbel turned his gaze back to the ladder's shadow.

"We are not strong, sword-wielding warriors anymore," said Ansseur. "We will never again be able to defeat our enemies by force. We will never feel the fear and sense of sacrifice we once did on the battlefield. For better and worse, we are both changed men.

"I have accepted this, though it was not simple. You can keep feeling pity for yourself and be angry at the creature that did this to you, or hate your own legs for refusing to carry you. Believe me—I spent enough time feeling bitter and seeking to take my revenge on those who hurt me until I realized that revenge could bring about only passing satisfaction. What would happen to me in all that time until my sweet revenge came? If it ever came at all … Would I stay in limbo for years? For the rest of my life, maybe? No. I decided to continue. I decided to live. You and I can be of greater use right now. Perhaps we can't be a part of the actual fighting, but we can join the struggle using our minds, which can be more significant than wielding a sword."

Saying nothing in return, Marbel exhaled and went back to his book.

The torch's light began to fade. The round opening above turned from black to gray as dawn arrived.

"These swords look just like Caleem's," said Zig, who everyone thought was fast asleep.

The boy pushed Naji off his shoulder. The latter slumped over to his side, continuing to snore on the floor.

Mazahratee jumped, ripped the red book out of Zig's hands and studied it. His eyes scanned the lines written underneath the drawing. "Maybe this drawing is of the Dark Rider that Creeden Dummah is trying to revive. Are you certain that his son carried a sword like one of these?"

"Something is happening. There is a commotion at the tower," said Narraneen.

"I hear it," said Mazahratee, his eyes still fixed on the red book.

"I can't hear a thing," said Zig.

Narraneen put her book down. "I'm going to check what's going on. Don't worry, we are not being invaded. It's something else," she said with a smile after noticing Marbel and Zig's anxious looks.

"Maybe they brought Kamanar!" said Zig.

"We're coming with you," said Marbel.

CHAPTER 63
THE FIRST WOUNDED HAS ARRIVED

Leaving Mazahratee behind, they emerged from underneath the vegetation and into the square. The sky was overcast; the rising sun was not yet over the Mobinar peaks. A score of elves stood chatting before the spherical tower's doors.

Narraneen addressed them in the elven tongue, and after she received a reply, her expression became grave. "Come on, husband," she said, wrapping her arm around Ansseur.

"What happened?" asked Marbel.

"The first wounded has arrived," said Ansseur.

The two sentries opened the doors to the tower, letting the group through.

The small hall within was covered in shiny, light-brown, hexagonal tiles. At its center was a round planter upon which stood a masterful sculpture of an elf dressed in a cloak made with real fabric. He held a leaf-shaped golden shield in his right hand. A vine sprouting with wide, heart-shaped, bright-green leaves had climbed up to the elf statue's leg.

Narraneen walked past the statue with Ansseur, Marbel, and the boys in tow. Inside a large chamber, several beds were aligned along the curving wall, all empty except for one. A wounded elf lay on the bed as two nurses stood over him. One of them turned to the visitors and said something in the elven tongue as she smoothed her blood-stained apron. Ansseur stood motionless, oblivious to whatever she said.

"The healer is asking us to leave," said Narraneen. She noticed a slight tremor on her husband's lips.

Ansseur was not looking at the wounded elf but at the other figure leaning over him. Paying no attention to the visitors, the woman caressed the wounded man's head.

"I think that's my sister," said Ansseur.

Upon hearing him, Naiya raised her red eyes. She stared at him in utter shock then approached. "Ansseur," she said in a quivering voice.

"Naiya!"

The princess embraced her brother, caressing his scarred face with shaky hands. "Seonder told me."

"I've missed you so much," said Ansseur, embracing his sister as he kissed her cheeks. "Is that Seonder?"

"Look what they've done to him," she said, caressing his blood-soaked hair.

Ansseur scrutinized the unconscious man's pale, mutilated body and disfigured face. "Oh Seonder, why didn't you wait?" he asked.

"This is Seonder?" the healer asked in the human tongue, raising a hand to her mouth. Ansseur nodded.

"Please get out, all of you," said the healer, pushing Ansseur. "Undress him, carefully," she said to Naiya.

Ansseur stepped back, his slashed eyes shifting between Naiya and the patient.

Narraneen pulled him to the doorway, which was blocked by the boys and Marbel's cart, their expressions reflecting deep sorrow.

"This is all Caleem's fault!" shouted Naiya after them.

The healer slammed the door shut on them. Ansseur paused outside, staring at the closed door.

Breaking the silence, Marbel said, "Seonder doesn't look so good."

"But he's going to make it," said Naji, shifting his gaze back and forth between Narraneen and Ansseur. "His wounds will heal, and he'll be fine, right?"

"The healer said he's unlikely to make it to the evening. His wounds are grave," Narraneen said and led her husband to the exit.

"Poor bastard. But the way I see it, he's going to make it. Never met somebody with his kind of endurance," said Marbel. "I say, a couple of weeks from now, we'll all be sitting together with Seonder and maybe even with Kamanar! Around a big banquet, laughing about all this."

"I say it's next week," said Zig.

"Well done, lads. We must not fall into despair. Come, let's see if those fellows brought Kamanar."

They reached Narraneen and Ansseur, who were talking to a group of elves standing in the square.

"Any news about Kamanar?" asked Zig.

Narraneen glanced up and whispered something at the red banners draped from the top of the tower. Zig and Naji followed her gaze and perceived someone waving a reply from one of the balconies, but the voice was too far for them to hear.

"They have already passed the eastern gateway. They should be here soon," said the elf woman. She touched her husband's arm. "I'm going to fetch Mazahratee," she said and left.

"Soon we'll know if the Alltree is worth anything. Caleem came back with Seonder and Naiya," said Ansseur.

"What?" asked Marbel.

"The scouts say he walked back with them most of the way, but then he dove into the bushes and disappeared."

"It's impossible to understand that boy," said Marbel. "I can't figure whose side he's on. I hope he gets his head on straight before it's too late."

Nalahes, the Ivest lieutenant, galloped on a white horse along the rope bridge before pulling to a stop at the square. She alighted lithely; her short cape and pants were stained with mud. She addressed Ansseur, and her sentence began with Mazahratee's name.

While looking at the tall elf woman, Zig asked Marbel, "Where's Kamanar?" She was too far away to hear anything, yet she glanced at the boy without interrupting her conversation with Ansseur as though she had heard him.

Naji pointed at the swaying rope bridge. "There, look."

Another rider came down the bridge, this one dragging a wooden cart. A few elves ran alongside it, their cloaks and boots muddy. As he approached the tower, the rider slowed the horse to a trot. All the nearby elves approached the cart and peered inside.

"Make way! It's Kamanar, our friend," said Naji, pulling Marbel's small vehicle closer to the bigger one. Marbel grabbed the edge of the other cart, pulling himself even closer, as Naji leaned over it while it moved.

As the larger wagon stopped at the tower entrance, everyone saw Kamanar's tall body lying on a bed of dry, reddish-brown leaves. His long legs protruded out of the back of the cart. His torn sleeves revealed deep gashes in his arms, all covered with clotted blood and pus. His face was pale and his eyes slightly open.

A group of elves emerged from the building carrying a bed, which they placed next to Kamanar.

"Take it away. I told you he was dead," said Marbel, pushing himself away from where his commander lay.

Naji and Zig exchanged looks of disappointment.

Materializing out of the woods and accompanied by Narraneen, Mazahratee asked, "Where's the healer?" He continued to shout orders as he approached Kamanar's cart.

"It's all nonsense. The man is dead," said Marbel.

The counselor stopped as he bumped into the cart. He and Narraneen leaned over the body. "Dead, you say?" asked Mazahratee. He then shouted some more orders in his tongue. Multiple hands reached for Kamanar and lifted him up as though he were some precious artifact, then lowered him onto the bed.

The elves carried the bed into the tower, followed by Mazahratee. Before walking inside, he turned back, waved his arms and said, "No one comes inside. The healer mustn't be disturbed!" He slammed the doors behind him.

"I didn't see any breathing. I wouldn't keep my hopes up … I don't know," said Marbel.

"This healer is gifted, she masters the art of potions," said Narraneen.

"The fates of Seonder and Kamanar are out of our hands. We should let the healer work," said Ansseur.

"We agree—need to put some food in the belly," said Naji.

"Come on. Push," Naji asked of Zig.

"I want to stay here," said Zig.

"But there's food—"

Zig only exhaled.

"You can stay if you wish," said Narraneen.

Naji shrugged and pushed the old man's cart with the elf woman's help.

Zig left his friends and walked, head drooping, toward the tower's big double doors.

"He means that much to you?" asked an unfamiliar female voice.

The tall Ivest lieutenant walked toward him. "I suppose you know him well, then," she said. Zig could only stare at her purple eyes.

"My name is Nalahes," she said.

"Zig."

"I know. I'm going to check on Kamanar. Do you want to come along?"

"I just saw him."

"All right," she said as she grabbed the door handle. "I'll come with you."

CHAPTER 64
I NEED TO SEE SEONDER

The elf opened the door and entered, and Zig followed. Mazahratee sat on a stool next to the statue at the center of the tower's small hall. Several books lay scattered on the tiles before him. When Zig walked by, Mazahratee gave him a cold stare.

"He's with me," said Nalahes.

Mazahratee snorted and dove back into his books.

Zig followed the officer into the healer's hall. The healer was grinding herbs in a small clay bowl. She noticed the boy, but before she could say anything, Nalahes pulled him to her side. The healer sighed and continued crushing the herbs.

Zig approached Seonder's bed. He was naked, with only a thin strip of cloth covering his groin. An orange ointment had been applied to his countless cuts and bruises. Zig's eyes shifted up his body before he turned away; he couldn't look at his face again.

Naiya stood over him, spreading more of the ointment on his injured body, oblivious of anyone around her. Zig continued to Kamanar's bed; he had been undressed in the same manner. A pair of elves in gray aprons applied the ointment to his body. The boy stared at the wounds on Kamanar's abdomen plastered in blood and gooey pus. Careful not to disturb the nurses, he stopped next to Kamanar's head.

"I don't see anything special about him," she said. "I don't know why Mazahratee pinned his hopes on this Kamanar."

"He can do anything. He fought giant ants and rats … and he killed the monster snake inside the mountain."

"He killed the monster snake? Does he have any special power or magic?"

"Yes … No. He's strong. You'll see when he wakes up."

The healer gave the nurse a small, pipe-like object, which she placed in Kamanar's mouth.

"Ask her about Kamanar," said Zig.

The healer approached, holding a pot filled with a warm liquid.

"If he responds to this remedy, it will be a good sign," the healer said in the common language as she leaned over Kamanar's head.

"And if he does not respond?" asked Zig.

The healer poured the fluid into Kamanar's mouth. Shreds of herbs poured down the glass pipe, some of them spilling onto his face. The healer emptied all the contents of the pot into the pipe.

They all waited in silence. After several moments, the healer shook her head. She fumbled about with the pot. "I'm sorry, but—"

Her words were interrupted by a sharp cough.

Kamanar pulled the pipe out of his mouth and threw it away. His body shook while he coughed. The nurse turned him over to his side as he began to vomit.

"Excellent," said the healer. "You can leave now. There is nothing more for you to watch."

"Kamanar are you all right? What's happening? Is this good?" Zig asked as Kamanar continued to throw up, his eyes still shut.

"Very good."

"You heard her. Let's let her continue undisturbed," Nalahes said and walked over to the exit, motioning Zig to follow.

He hurried after the officer. The tower's outer hall had become gloomy, the small windows darker. Raindrops pounded on the glass. "I have to tell Naji and Marbel," said Zig, smiling. He dashed to the exit, rushing by Mazahratee.

"Watch the books," said the counselor, covering them with his only arm.

"He threw up. The healer said that's a good sign," said Nalahes.

"Of course," the counselor said and returned to his books.

Zig halted at the doorway. Outside four archers stood in the pouring rain, their bows drawn. They aimed at a man staggering toward the tower, but they kept their distance, allowing him to proceed.

"Caleem?" asked Nalahes. Zig nodded.

Behind them, the counselor leaped to his feet and stood beside them. "A third arrival … on the same morning. A coincidence, or is it fate?" he asked, his eyes wide. "The sword. He has it!"

Zig saw the dark hilt jutting out above Caleem's shoulder, the tip of the blade scraping the ground. The officer drew a knife from the folds of her cloak and headed straight toward the prince. Nalahes stood in the downpour, blocking his way. Caleem stopped.

"What are you doing here, Caleem Dummah?"

His torn clothes were soaked, and his bright-gray hair was scattered across his face, water dripping from the tangled strands. He raised his eyes to hers but said nothing. The prince placed his hand on the hilt of the sword.

Nalahes shouted an order and extended her knife. The elven archers drew their bows even tighter.

Caleem closed his grip around the hilt, and, in one smooth motion, he drew the sword and drove it into the floor, shattering the cobblestones. The sword rattled; its ringing sound reverberated across the square, even louder than the rain.

Caleem walked past the sword, advancing toward the officer. "I need to see Seonder," he said in a hoarse but clear tone.

"You need nothing. From this moment on, consider yourself a captive," said Nalahes.

Zig shuddered as she spoke. He ran out toward them into the rain. Caleem stood glaring at the elf, clenching his wet hands into fists.

"I need to see Seonder, now!"

The rain washed across Nalahes's bright face, and water dripped down her chin. She showed no signs of hesitation, her arm extended, her knife pointing at the intruder.

"Caleem," said a familiar voice.

The prince's gaze shifted toward the man before him dressed in green with long, gray hair. A woman was next to him, her arm wrapped around his.

"Can we say *welcome*?" asked Ansseur.

"Ansseur," uttered Caleem.

"How are you, my brother?"

"What happened to you? Who did this to you?"

"First, let's get some shelter from this rain."

"No! Tell me now. Who did this to you? Was it Father?" he asked, looking at his brother's scars.

"Father and his pet, Dolegg."

Caleem paused for a moment then continued, "Where is Seonder?"

Ansseur looked over his brother's shoulder and exchanged a few words with the Ivest lieutenant. She returned the knife into her cloak while commanding her men to lower their bows.

"How are you, Caleem?" asked Marbel from his cart.

Caleem looked at the paralyzed man, then glanced at Naji, who stood next to him, then back at Marbel and his cart.

"I'm …" he said, lowering his eyes.

"Let's go in." Ansseur and Narraneen led the way to the tower.

As they all entered, Mazahratee rushed out toward the sword, which was still jammed into the ground. The four archers were examining it, but the counselor waved them away. Taking the now-empty pouch from his belt, he wrapped it around the hilt and yanked the weapon free. Making sure it was as far as possible from his body, he rushed away and disappeared under the trees.

All soaked, the group entered the healer's hall, stopping near the two beds closest to the door. The pair of nurses were scattering aromatic flowers on and around the beds. Caleem walked on by himself and stood between the two beds. "Kamanar. He's alive!"

"Yes, he will be better. The healer said so," said Zig.

"I can't believe it!" said Marbel. "Push me closer."

The boys pushed the cart alongside the bed. The old man pulled himself up and climbed on his friend's bed. "The color is returning to his face. Amazing," said Marbel.

"I knew it. Kamanar is the strongest man in the world," said Naji.

Caleem turned to the other wounded patient, clearly wary of meeting his sister's eyes as she stood on the other side of Seonder's bed. Placing his hands on his own head, the prince stared at the unconscious half-elf. He took a deep breath followed by a long sigh. His demeanor changed. He dropped to his knees and, with shaking fingers, caressed his friend's shattered face. "Fair Seonder, what have I done to you?"

Caleem broke down into quiet sobs. His sister placed a gentle hand on his head. She couldn't contain her tears.

"I'm sure he forgives you. Such he is, my Seonder, his heart wider than the ocean."

Ansseur approached his sister to embrace her.

Caleem looked down, his wet hair falling on his face. Total silence reigned in the arched hall.

"I forgive you," said Naiya, tears cascading down her cheeks.

"I can't forgive myself," said Caleem in a clear tone. He stood up and stormed out of the hall.

CHAPTER 65
HE WOKE?

It was warm and pleasant inside Ansseur and Narraneen's house. Zig watched the downpour through the two small windows. Under the windows lay Kamanar, his wet cape draped over the thick mattress of leaves beneath him.

Holding a few towels, Narraneen walked in from the adjacent room. She handed one to Zig. Then, walking out to the terrace, she handed another to Marbel, who sat in a dry corner sheltered from the rain, his legs sprawled on the floor. "Comfortable?" she asked.

"Yes, thank you," he said quietly.

"Your injury?"

"Yes … No …"

"Criando?"

Marbel sighed.

Narraneen said, "If there is anything to be done, I know you will not hesitate—not for one moment, I'm sure. You already did your very best."

"I did nothing."

"You reached the end of the world—the Dalusian lair."

"I think a lot about the moment when I last saw him, when I let him go. It hurts me so much. I should have done something," Marbel said. "You know, the day before they came for him, we had an idea, Criando and I. I would break his arm, and he wouldn't be fit for the Black Company. Simple. If only we had gone through with it."

"I believe with all my heart that you will see your son again."

"You think so?"

"I do."

Marbel nodded and turned his gaze back to the rain.

Narraneen went back into the house where Zig was wiping Kamanar's face with the towel. "I have some matters to attend to. I'll be back in the evening," said the elf, putting the remaining towels at Kamanar's feet. She caressed the youth's wet hair and walked out.

Zig sat down on a small wooden stool next to Kamanar's bed. He leaned back on its backrest, his hands clasped before him.

Time flew by as the evening drew closer. The rain outside had almost stopped. Zig was stretching his arms when a voice, seemingly out of nowhere, said, "Thirsty."

He stared at Kamanar's face. Zig wasn't sure whether it was him who had said it.

"Can I have some water?" asked Kamanar hoarsely, his eyes still shut.

Zig hurried into the adjacent room and returned with a pitcher. "Here you go." Zig brought the pitcher up to Kamanar's mouth. As soon as the cold water touched his parched lips, they parted. The tall man, with noisy gulps, downed the whole pitcher. Kamanar sighed and opened his eyes.

"Thank you, Zig," he said and closed his eyes once again.

"I hope you're not talking to yourself," came Marbel's voice from the terrace.

"No!" said Zig. He saw Marbel's chubby face peeking in. Zig wiped the smile off his face when he noticed Marbel's teary eyes. He walked out to the terrace; the rain had stopped.

"Is everything all right?"

"It's just some old memories." He popped his head through the door again. "What about our big boy?"

"He woke up, sipped some water, and went back to sleep."

"And I thought he was gone. To hell with me."

The last traces of clouds floated to the east, unveiling the darkening blue skies. Through the branches came the twinkle of the first star. From behind the railing, Zig watched the street below. A group of young elves marched by, carrying swords on their backs and wooden, leaf-shaped shields on their arms. Coming from the opposite direction, Narraneen and Naji walked up the street, each holding a wicker basket. Zig hurried down the stairs to meet them and took the basket from his hostess.

"Kamanar woke up for a bit," he said.

"Wonderful, that's a good sign," said the elf woman.

"That's great … Do you think Akiena would come for dinner if I invited her?" Naji asked while rummaging through the baskets.

"She's a member of the youth company, Anathoria's last line of defense. They're busy right now," said Narraneen.

"But they're staying here. They're not going to fight anywhere, right?"

"I see you are fond of her. Don't worry, they're staying here."

"I'm not fond … I'm just asking about things. What about dinner?"

"Let's make it together," she said.

***

The almost full moon shed its light on the balcony. The lavish meal was set on delicate platters and dishes on a long, rectangular table. Marbel, ready and waiting, occupied one of the chairs at the table. Narraneen placed an oil lamp above Kamanar's bed and another atop the doorway to the terrace.

"Finally," said Naji when he recognized Caleem's light hair reflecting the moonlight. He was walking behind two whispering figures.

The two boys sat down beside Marbel at the table, ready to pounce on the delectable delicacies.

"There's no time. There is not enough time!" said Mazahratee, who was the first up the stairs, his arms behind his back. He approached Kamanar and examined him for a few seconds.

Ansseur and Caleem arrived a moment later.

"Please join the others on the balcony before the Mellethyans eat the plates empty," said Narraneen.

Ansseur strode to the table, Mazahratee behind him. Caleem lingered a little longer at Kamanar's side.

"Looks like this is my seat," said Ansseur after he stumbled on a chair.

"How's Seonder doing?" asked Marbel.

"Better, to everyone's surprise. But not to mine," said the counselor.

"Really? That's amazing news," said Zig.

"That lad is something—I knew it," said Marbel.

The counselor shifted to the right, then to the left, unable to choose a place to sit, muttering all the while.

"Is everything all right?" asked Marbel.

"No, everything is not all right. Nothing is." He gave Marbel a piercing look. "I have received ominous news. The evil Dark Rider was revived through some kind of occult ritual. He chopped up all those who had brought him back to life. He mounted his horse and is heading north, here!" He pointed at the floor under his feet.

"But he is only one rider," said Naji.

The counselor stared at the boy. "Only one?"

"Based on the little that we know of him, we have plenty of reasons to worry," said Ansseur.

The counselor shifted his mocking gaze from Naji to the others. "I found documents about this evil knight that concur with the legends about him. He obliterated thousands of lives. He tore through entire armies with his two cursed swords. He was unstoppable. This thing has been heading our way since this afternoon," Mazahratee said as he paced back and forth behind the chairs.

"The honorable counselor and I predict that he'll reach the passageway by morning or noon, the day after tomorrow," said Ansseur from the opposite side of the table.

"Can he be stopped somehow?" asked Marbel.

"That you should ask your friend, Kamanar. There's no time, no time …"

Mazahratee paused his ramblings as he caught a glimpse of Naji chewing on something. "You're so carefree. Everything is fine in Anathoria. This is the second day of combat at the passageway. Hundreds are dying as we speak!"

Naji stopped chewing.

"Go on, indulge, but when this rider arrives wielding his sword, food will be the last thing on your mind."

"Counselor, do not vent your frustration at the boy. It was my wish that we dismiss the war for this evening," said Narraneen as she placed another platter on the table.

Caleem stepped onto the balcony. He pulled out a chair and sat next to Ansseur. "Is there any news from the south?" he asked serenely, almost weakly, while staring at the rectangular plate in front of him.

The counselor sat between Caleem and Zig. "The wounded have begun to arrive. They said there have been losses, but we are holding up," said Mazahratee. "That will likely change when the metal rider knight thing makes his appearance."

"What about the cliffs?" asked the prince, his gaze still fixed on the empty plate.

"The camp was dismantled and packed. The Black Company and the Guzuds advanced up to a certain line. They are standing their ground, ready," said Mazahratee.

Caleem asked, "What about the oversize wagons?"

"Oversize wagons?" repeated the counselor. "What about them?"

"I don't know."

Yes, yes. I forgot about those," the counselor said. "This matter needs to be investigated." He stood up, toppling his chair with the back of his knees. “I have a meeting with the Order of the Spider tomorrow. They are expecting an update. I must go in haste—time is not my friend.” Upon reaching the doorway, he pointed inside the house. “I want to be informed the minute this man awakes.” He hurried in and disappeared down the staircase.

“He woke already,” Zig called after him.

The hurrying footsteps became louder, and the counselor reappeared on the balcony. “He woke? When?”

“A while ago. He asked for—” Before Zig could finish, the counselor rushed back inside.

The sound of a powerful slap came from the house.

Ansseur and Caleem rose. Narraneen entered, all eyes following her. They saw the counselor tumbling through the air across the room to the stairwell. Everyone crowded through the narrow doorway at once, pushing and shoving. Blocking the light of the oil lamp, Kamanar stood firm on his long legs, his fists clenched before him. Most of his face was hidden in the shadows.

Chapter 66
What Kind of a Name Is Kamanar?

"Kamanar," called Caleem, who stood in front of the imposing figure.

Narraneen held an oil lamp high to light up the room. The bright-red marks left by the counselor's fingers on Kamanar's cheek were evident. His fists tight, his expression was grave as he studied his surroundings. The counselor emerged at the top of the staircase, and Kamanar took a few strides toward him, his fists still clenched. The counselor backed up, almost stumbling down the stairs.

"Kamanar, calm down," said Caleem, taking another step toward the tall man. The latter reacted with a threatening gesture.

"It's me, Caleem," he said, placing a hand on his own chest.

"I dare you to come closer!" said Kamanar to everyone, his voice thick.

"Kamanar," said a soft voice.

Zig made his way forward without any trepidation. Kamanar's eyes were glued on the lad. "Zig, what are you doing here?"

"Kamanar, don't worry. There's no danger here," said the boy, placing his hand on his friend's fist. The latter let his hands drop as he surveyed the others.

"We are all your friends, sir," said Marbel, who had dragged himself inside.

"Marbel! Why are you crawling on the floor?"

"Don't worry about that. How are you feeling?"

A grin spread across the tall man's face. "I'm … hungry."

Everyone laughed except for Caleem, who embraced Kamanar. The tall man looked puzzled but hugged him back. After a long embrace, Caleem let go and went out onto the balcony.

"Caleem —" Kamanar began.

"You said you were hungry. You woke up just in time," interrupted Narraneen.

Kamanar gazed at the beautiful elf standing in front of him.

"I'm Narraneen. I'm Ansseur's wife."

Looking at the former prince, Kamanar said, "Ansseur!"

"Please don't ask me about the scars," said Ansseur, chuckling.

"You're alive. Who did this to you?"

"What about me? Remember me?" asked Naji.

"The troublemaker." Kamanar laughed and slapped the boy lightly on the cheek.

"There's food outside," said Naji, clapping his hands.

"Where am I?"

Ansseur said, "Don't worry. Each one of your queries will receive an answer after dinner." The host stepped aside, showing Kamanar the way out to the balcony with a sweep of his hand.

"And my name is Mazahratee. I do apologize for my rude action, but you were in dire need of it," the counselor said from a safe distance.

Kamanar studied the delicacies set out on the table, then stretched as he gazed at the moonlit treetops. "I feel as though I've been sleeping for years," he said, examining the gashes along his arms.

The counselor pulled out a chair and motioned with his empty sleeve for the tall man to sit. Kamanar eyed the counselor's ears, then those of Narraneen, who smiled at him.

"We are elves. You and your comrades stumbled into our land, and you are now safe, far from the evil Dalusians," said the counselor.

Kamanar noticed the two boys helping Marbel onto his chair before sitting down on theirs.

"Where is Motehro?" asked Kamanar. During the awkward silence, Kamanar searched all their faces for an answer. "What?"

Ansseur, who sat beside him, patted the tall man's shoulder. "Motehro returned home. I beg of you, please stop your queries for now," said Ansseur.

"Indeed, this evening is all yours, Kamanar. I promise you'll have all your questions answered by tomorrow … Before I leave, what kind of a name is 'Kamanar'?" the councilor asked as he put some fruit in his pocket, his eyes still fixed on the tall man.

"What kind of name is Mazahratee?"

"It means 'Happy-Beautiful'."

"It reflects on you nicely."

"What does Kamanar mean?"

"Kamanar was my grandfather's nickname; I was named after him."

"I gather he broke some fingers?"

Reaching out to grab a piece of fruit, Kamanar nodded. "His fingers were crushed by a log. He was a logger," he said and took a bite.

"So insignificant and yet very significant at the same time. I apologize, but I must leave. Please excuse me," Mazahratee said then left.

"Good appetite to everyone," said Narraneen.

They all pounced on the food, filling up their plates with fruits, cheeses, and cooked vegetables. Kamanar filled his plate with a mountainous pile of food that spilled over the sides. Splattering crumbs and sauce in all directions, he attacked his meal. Narraneen could not stop staring at the voracious diner.

"We have a saying, back in Mellethya: 'the only thing worse than seeing warriors fighting is seeing them eat'," said Ansseur.

"Have we met before?" Kamanar asked Narraneen with his mouth full.

"I don't think so."

"Are you sure? You look familiar."

"I'm sure," she said and looked away. Kamanar returned to his food.

Everyone ate to their heart's content, except for Caleem, who only moved his food around on his plate. As each had their fill, they leaned back on their chairs. Last was Kamanar, who raised his head from his plate and began to examine the rest of the diners until his gaze came to rest on Marbel.

"Was it a fall?" he asked as he wiped his mouth with a napkin.

"My legs?" asked Marbel.

Kamanar nodded. Marbel took a deep breath and looked around. "Ah—"

"This is not going to work," said Caleem. "This is foolishness. Tomorrow, Mazahratee is going to lay the weight of the world on his shoulders. He deserves the truth!" The prince stood up and tossed his napkin on the table.

"Caleem!" said Ansseur.

"Don't worry, Kamanar can bear it. It is imperative that he learns everything as soon as possible," said Caleem. He tapped Kamanar's shoulder. "Come, let's go for a walk under the moonlight."

Kamanar stood up and went after him.

"I will join you," said Ansseur.

"I would prefer if it was only the two of us," said Caleem as he and the tall man exited.

Caleem's whispers faded as the pair walked away from the house, their dark silhouettes vanishing down the street.

CHAPTER 67
I KNEW

Kamanar hung on to Caleem's every word while they strolled under the moonlight among the scattered, globular houses enveloped with thick vegetation. Caleem related the sequence of events, starting from when they had left the giant snake's corpse. As the tale progressed, Kamanar became disconnected from the reality around him, composing visions in his mind of all that had transpired. The moment Caleem reached the part about Sarik's betrayal, the tall man stopped in his tracks.

"I knew it … You wouldn't listen! I knew it," said Kamanar, clapping his hands and drawing glances from the elves who hurried past the two foreigners.

Caleem took a deep breath, and Kamanar returned his attention to the prince.

As he continued to relate recent events, they reached the banks of a small lake fed by a high waterfall on the opposite shore.

"The water in this lake is warm," Caleem said and sat down, staring at the water cascading over the tree-covered mountain above, which looked like a finger pointing at the moon.

Kamanar prompted him to continue. "You reached the camp with Sarik, and …?"

Caleem left out no detail. When he finished, he lay down on

the ground. Clasping his hands under his head, he gazed at the moon that was setting behind the mountain.

A long silence followed.

"The mission …" Kamanar said as if talking to himself.

"Everything is an absolute injustice—the mission, the wars … I'm sorry I've piled this news on you before you've fully recovered."

Kamanar chuckled then became serious again. "I've had my doubts, but I swept them into a corner in the back of my mind. I dismissed Naiya's words over and over."

Caleem winced at the mention of his sister's name.

Kamanar sighed. "All the acts of cruelty and rampant corruption that I witnessed under our king's patronage, and my part in them, haunt me. I avoided dwelling on things by keeping myself busy. I knew one day I would have to face up to my deeds …" The tall man lay down next to his friend.

"I wanted to earn the throne, not inherit it! I made the same mistakes," said the prince.

"What do you mean?"

"I wanted to be the one to lead this mission. I wanted it so much I didn't ask any questions. I didn't listen … to Naiya or the others. I was blinded by my own ambition. I always am."

"I think 'blind' is the right word for the both of us."

"What was it like when you were unconscious?"

"Red … I don't know why, but I remember redness all around me."

"Redness?"

"It probably doesn't mean anything."

"You know, I never thanked you for saving my life … twice," said Caleem.

"I think it was three times, no?"

Caleem smiled then raised two fingers. His smile faded, and he sighed before becoming grim again. "The day after tomorrow, the real war begins. What do you want to do?"

"How's that?"

"That's when the Dark Rider will reach the Mobinar passage. I presume Father will time his attack at the cliffs accordingly."

"These people, these elves, they think I'm some kind of savior?"

"Some of them."

"That's absurd."

Caleem sat up and gazed out over the darkening lake. "It won't be easy. If you choose to switch sides. To raise your sword against our own people."

"Facing your father won't be easy."

"I see him as the root of this horrible lie. Besides, he was a father to you more than he ever was to anyone," said Caleem.

"I was forced. Believe me, I didn't ask to be close to your father. I despised Dolegg for his sincere desire to please him. I'm glad you degraded that vile parasite before you disposed of him."

"Back home, do you think there are others who know the truth about the elves?"

"A few infantry officers—a minority. If it wasn't for your sister, I would have killed them all. They kept their mouths shut, and I reckoned they weren't capable of anything, so I let them be. Then, finally, Naiya stopped harassing me."

"You said you had *doubts*. It seems to me that you knew much more," said Caleem in a serious tone.

"I knew."

"Why didn't you do something about it?" The prince rose to his feet. "There's a difference between a stupid crime and a purposeful one."

Kamanar rose and faced the prince. "It's the same damage."

"No, it's not! I can't believe you knew."

"Lower your voice. It is what it is."

"How could you go along with it? I once looked up to you … Many did."

"There are things you don't know about me. Judge me as much as you want. I don't care."

"What things, Kamanar? I know you have secrets. How bad can it be? Tell me, and I can share the burde—"

"My demons are my own," Kamanar said and marched away. With moonlight illuminating the way, he retraced his steps back to the closest street, examining every object he set his eyes upon.

He arrived at a narrow wooden bridge crossing a gentle stream. A group of young elves approached from the opposite shore. He stood to one side, waiting for them to cross. They traversed one by one. Rays of moonlight lit up their faces. Kamanar nodded at them. The last individual to pass was a female elf, and the light revealed her pale complexion. She threw him a glance as if she recognized him and stopped. Kamanar looked around, thinking she might be looking at someone else. Her purple eyes glinted in the moonlight, the pale glow highlighting her delicate features.

A smile lit up Kamanar's face, and he let his eyes rest on hers for a few moments. "Hello," he said.

"I see you have awoken from your slumber, Kamanar," she said.

"You know me?" he asked.

She addressed the elves accompanying her, and they all continued on their way.

"My name is Nalahes, lieutenant of the Ivest, the elf forces."

"A woman warrior!"

"Surprised?" the elf woman asked and began to walk. As she moved out of the light, her features darkened, but her eyes were still shining.

"Every time," he said and joined her.

"So, you've met 'Dalusians' before."

"Not in as pleasant a manner."

"Here we have no predetermined allocation of tasks. We undertake whatever needs doing, regardless of gender."

"So, a male elf can give birth?"

"No," she said and smiled.

"You said tasks, like cooking and cleaning, but I didn't see Ansseur helping his wife at dinner. Is it because he's a Mellethyan?"

"It's because he's practically blind. I'd love to tell you more about our customs—maybe some other time. What have you learned so far?"

"I would say enough."

"Mazahratee and about half of Anathoria have pinned their hopes on you."

"And what about you?"

"I belong to the other half," she said without looking at him. "Your men seem to regard you highly, especially the boy."

"Zig, yes. He's a fine lad. Just needs to believe in himself."

"Come," she said, stepping from the path. She eased her way through the bushes as Kamanar stumbled behind her.

"We shouldn't get lost," he said, bending one of the branches blocking his way.

They made their way in the dark until they reached an enormous tree. The elf climbed up, as nimble and swift as a monkey. With an effort, Kamanar followed, his injuries still hurting. After a long climb, he caught up.

Chapter 68
I Couldn't Hide Them, Even if I Tried

"This way." Nalahes walked along the length of a thick branch and sat at the narrow end.

Kamanar shuffled, one foot at a time, then crawled out onto the rocking branch until he managed to sit down next to her. Glancing up, he saw a strip of brightening sky peeping between the broad leaves.

The elf woman gazed at the sprawling landscape. Kamanar was still stressed as he dangled between the earth and the sky. But as time passed, he became accustomed to the harmonic seesawing and creaking sounds of the tree's massive limb. The moon was setting in the west, and the sky became lighter. One last star twinkled beside a cloud.

From where he sat, Kamanar could appreciate how the Mobinar range surrounded the enchanted land on all sides. The water bridge, hanging high above and extending from the eastern to the western range—the same bridge Caleem had mentioned earlier—seemed to him an optical illusion. Beneath him lay

Anathoria like a smooth, velvety mass of green with scattered white towers. The island, floating in the center of the lake, had become visible.

"This is my home," said Nalahes. "Every time I come here, it's like seeing Anathoria for the very first time."

Dawn was breaking; the bright, golden-orange sun exposed itself from beyond the snow-covered peaks of the Mobinar, allowing living beings to lay their eyes on its beauty. The first rays of sunlight spilled down from the brows of the eastern ridge to the feet of the western one.

The rays inched forward until they conquered the island. Dawn light shone on the sloping hills, which cast long shadows behind them in the shape of upside-down bowls of differing sizes, covered in a carpet of lush vegetation. The towers sprouting among the hills shone in the pale light. Kamanar could discern several figures crossing the hanging bridges from the island to the shores.

"This is truly heaven on earth," Kamanar said. His gaze turned to the high, narrow waterfalls cascading from the western cliffs, glittering like magical silken sheets before spilling onto the surface of the lake, whose color was changing from dark gray to turquoise.

"Strange creatures, you men," the elf said. "Before you closed your eyes, you desired our destruction. Now that you've opened them, you want to save us … So, what will it be?"

Kamanar was still enthralled by the elf's purple eyes, whose rare hue could now be appreciated. "It's complicated. 'Save' is a big word. I would lower my expectations if I were you. And how do you know that I even want to save anyone?"

"Eyes don't lie. I wasn't observing you for nothing, back at the crossing."

"I thought you were just dazzled by how pretty I am. Were you reading my mind?"

"I haven't been endowed with that ability. I just grasped your intentions. Your eyes give you away despite those thick eyebrows."

"I thought I had my stiff expression on." He laughed then became serious again. "You are truly beautiful and intriguing creatures. I'd like to learn more about you. Maybe after the war is over … Is it possible for a foreigner like me to be accepted here, if I wished to stay in this wonderful land?"

Still wearing her smile, the elf turned her eyes to the landscape once again. "Perhaps. Probably."

"You know, when I was young, my mother always told me to be careful of Dalusians—especially Dalusian women, if I ever encountered one. 'They can bewitch you,' she said. 'Lure you to hell. Run for your life!'"

The elf woman laughed, and her eyes turned once again to Kamanar, who was staring at her. "Don't forget that I can tell your intentions. Your eyes are talking to me," she said.

"I couldn't hide them, even if I tried," he said in a serious tone, his eyes fixed on the two purple diamonds.

The elf's smile disappeared, and she got to her feet. "I see a crowd gathering at the tower. Looks like the assembly is starting earlier than planned." Nalahes pointed to the center of the island and walked back to the trunk. "They will be expecting you, too," she said, disappearing between the branches of the tree.

Kamanar remained seated on the swinging branch, still under the spell of the beautiful elf and the alluring land before him.

A heavy atmosphere hung over the morning; the closer Kamanar got to the tower the worse it became. He could hear the suppressed moaning from outside the healing room. Inside, many injured elves lay in numerous beds arranged along the curved tower wall. Kamanar surveyed the patients one by one. He could not help but admire the restraint shown by the wounded. Many had been hurt badly, and some had missing limbs.

The caregivers running around wore blood-splattered aprons.

"I'm glad to see you on your feet, but I must ask you to leave now," said the old healer.

"I assume I owe you thanks," the tall man said and bowed.

"Ignore me," he said before she could ask again.

The healer frowned and went back to her duties, all the while complaining in her language.

He recognized Naiya nearby leaning over Seonder's bed.

"Naiya," he called, bowing before the princess.

"Kamanar! How are you feeling?"

"Well. What about Seonder?"

"They thought he wouldn't make it, but here he is, doing better."

"He has a good reason to hold on to his life," he said, taking a deep breath. "I am sorry. I don't have the words."

Naiya remained quiet for a long moment. "I don't plan to throw anything at you. The past is the past … I am sorry, too."

"About what?"

"I warned Caleem about you. I assumed you were planning to hurt Seonder. I know my father urged you to do so."

"True, at some stage, I almost did, but not because of you or your father. I was convinced he was an enemy spy."

The princess closed her eyes and sighed. "Strange how things turned out in the end," she said as she continued to caress Seonder.

"You should know that Caleem did everything in his power to protect him during the journey. You can't blame him. He believed he was doing the right thing. If there is someone you should not forgive, it's your father."

"I did forgive Caleem …"

"I'm glad to hear that. I would—" He noticed Seonder looking at him. "Seonder!"

The princess jumped to her feet, ecstatic.

"Kamanar … I just want to say … sorry," said Seonder.

"You played your part with courage and true sincerity. Don't apologize for anything," said Kamanar.

"I feel better … just a little tired," the half-elf said and closed his eyes.

"Did you hear him? This is promising." Naiya smiled.

"He's going to be fine," said Kamanar, smiling back.

"Rest, my darling. I'll be here by your side," the princess whispered to her beloved.

"We'll have a lot to talk about—me, him, you, Caleem—when all this is done," Kamanar said to the princess then went toward the exit.

As he was leaving the tower, he bumped into Mazahratee.

"Where have you been?" asked the counselor, recoiling as he remembered his last encounter with the tall man.

"Around."

"Quickly, follow me," the elf said and entered the tower.

CHAPTER 69
WHAT IS MY TRUTH?

Kamanar followed Mazahratee up the stairs. He still felt a bit sluggish, so to wake his body up he skipped up the stairs with long strides—two, three steps at a time.

The staircase ended at an imposing ornate wooden door with a spider carved at its center. The crowded hall inside became quiet as soon as he and Mazahratee crossed the threshold.

Kamanar scanned the audience arranged in concentric circles rising to the domed ceiling lined with eight large windows. The morning rays poured in, lighting up long branches that protruded down from the windows.

Mazahratee hurried to the wide, circular deck at the center of the hall where the long sword stood, its tip penetrating a wooden block. He uttered something in their foreign language. Kamanar noticed four elderly figures dressed in white sitting apart from the crowd on large chairs; they were glancing in his direction. He soon realized that all the elves in the hall were staring at him. Most of the elves present were either elderly or youngsters. Among those present, Kamanar discerned an outstretched arm and a wide smile. "Zig," he called, smiling back.

Three more familiar figures sat beside the boy: Naji, Marbel, and Narraneen.

Mazahratee addressed the audience in their strange language, then translated, "This is Kamanar, Broken Fingers. The answer to the riddle and our savior."

Kamanar gaped then twisted his lips upon hearing the counselor's words. "Hello," he said.

The crowd broke into whispers.

"Say something more," said the counselor.

Kamanar shrugged.

Arizen, the redheaded elf woman, stood and addressed Mazahratee in the common language. "And why should this Mellethyan take the sword?"

"How can you be certain he is truly a friend and not a foe?" asked another elf. "We can't hand this weapon to him. It's too early. He could still turn back to his master!"

"It's our best and only choice," said the counselor.

"There is always another choice, if you care to look for one. We have misinterpreted the Alltree before," said the redheaded former counselor.

"I see my arguments were not convincing enough. Well, then, I invite you to take this sword. Go ahead, please." Mazahratee pointed to the weapon.

One of the elves from in the front row walked up to the sword and placed his hand on the hilt. But as he tried to yank it out of the wooden block, his expression became grave, then disconcerted. He relaxed his grip and retreated, making an emotive announcement to the audience.

"Indeed, great evil is hidden in this sword," said Mazahratee.

An elf wearing black gloves reached for the sword, but he quickly let go of it. The counselor shook his head and turned to the four members of the Order sitting behind him. "No elf, or even half-elf, can ever wield this cursed sword. When I first held it, I heard loud screaming. A strange sensation followed, and I felt something slithering inside my head, and the pain became intolerable. Somchow, I willed myself forward and reached the shelter. The sounds and headaches did subside eventually, but they still return in waves occasionally. Today, I wrapped it in blessed cloth. Yet even the sacred fabric could not block its malice. For some reason, humans are not affected by its evil. This morning, Ansseur carried it up here."

"If you have recognized its evil, why did you bring it here?" asked Arizen.

Emerging from a corner, Ansseur said, "Because this evil may be our salvation. Though pure souls like you cannot use it, we can." He placed his hand on the dark blue hilt.

"Out of respect to the men among us, we will hold this discussion in the common language," came the voice of an elderly female member of the Order of the Spider.

The youngest of the four stood up. "Counselor, you may continue your argument."

"Thank you. I will start from the beginning. About ten centuries ago, King Daneer Dummah, a deplorable monarch of the wretched Dummah dynasty, ruled over Mellethya at a time during which the enmity between our people was dawning. In his foolishness, he turned to the forbidden forces of the obscure. He invited heretic priests, witches, and sorcerers from all corners of the world. For weeks on end, they conjured spells until, ultimately, their vile rituals succeeded in bringing to life the Dark Rider, a rider wielding twin swords. The same rider who now rides here. At the end of the ritual, all of the participants lost their senses. A foolish servant accidentally entered their lair. His name …" Mazahratee paused, drew the red book out of his pouch, and thumbed through its pages. "Purmis, yes, he was called Purmis. This fool, in his innocence, stole one of the swords. The Dark Rider was somehow still inanimate at the time. Purmis took the sword back to his home in the south. It does not say where, exactly, this Purmis lived, just in the south."

Mazahratee crossed his arms behind his back, his single hand holding the sleeve of his other arm, and paced between the sword and Kamanar. "King Daneer was stupid enough to expect the rider to obey him. Little did he know that the knight was a servant of none. Lucky for him he wasn't at the end of the ritual. When this rider became animate, his first action was to slaughter his creators, be they sorcerers, priests, or even the guards … everyone! Then he sought his missing sword. He rode to pitiful Purmis's village, tracking his sword, leaving a long trail of death and destruction in his wake. He recovered the other sword, but not before killing Purmis, his family, his neighbors, his whole village. Kill, kill, kill—the monster continued unhindered in his massacre. Recovering his other sword made him different. He became much stronger!

"Once Daneer, the cretin, realized the gravity of his deed, he sent his army to stop the demon, but to no avail. No company or regiment was able to halt the ravaging pair of swords. Desperate, the king turned to his former deposed magician, who allegedly possessed great mystical powers. After a long, epic battle, this sorcerer defeated the knight and imprisoned him inside a rock."

"We must destroy this blade now!" interrupted an older elf from among the assembly.

"It's not possible—this metal is not metal. It's an indestructible substance. There is no way of destroying it. King Daneer tried that already. This is well documented," said the counselor.

The old elf said, "Then this evil should be driven as far away as possible before that thing reaches and defiles our land. He will clearly be seeking it."

"No!" said Mazahratee. "I've meticulously studied the books describing the creation of this knight. Although it seems he cannot tell the difference between men and elves, the reason he was given life was to exterminate our people. Understand this: when he first found his lost sword, he turned northward, to here! I recognized this by the sudden change of direction, which is written in another book. Back then, that fool Daneer didn't notice this, or he wouldn't have stopped him. So, wherever we hide it, he will eventually find it and will again want to accomplish what he was made to do in the first place. King Creeden is counting on this."

The older elf remained quiet as he returned to his seat.

"How did this magician subdue the Dark Rider, you wonder? With one of the creature's own swords. Unfortunately, the exact action is not described." He pointed at Kamanar. "No magician sufficiently powerful lives among us presently. Therefore, just as Creeden Dummah restored the Dark Rider, we have Kamanar here, who will replicate the feat of the magician … somehow!"

"This is absurd!" yelled Arizen.

Many more voices interjected.

"This man will take this indomitable weapon and confront the Dark Rider, who, I am certain, has the ability to tip the balance of forces at the passage against us," said the counselor. "The man standing next to me here, whose name the Alltree pronounced time and time again, is the only one capable of confronting that demon."

The counselor turned to the members of the order. Pointing upward, he spoke again, as if he had just remembered something. "In addition, Prince Caleem, King Creeden's second son, who, as we all know, defected to our side, will head to the cliffs and redeem himself by confronting his father … Anathoria shall prevail, as it always does."

The members of the Order had a short conversation.

The speaker turned to the tall man. "Are you, Kamanar of Mellethya, prepared to undertake the challenge that is being assigned to you, knowing that you will be confronting not only the Dark Rider but also your own people?"

"What if he fails?" came a question from the crowd.

Arizen said, "If the sword falls into the demon's hand, he will be much stronger, you said it yourself. I say we should not trust the two humans. Anathoria shall prevail without them!"

"On my way here," said Kamanar, "before I awoke, I wished death and destruction to befall your people. Before I lost consciousness, sensing my end was near, I was overcome with distress and a feeling of emptiness. This stemmed from the fact that I had not completed my mission. I failed my *great* king.

"After I awoke from my slumber, I was presented with this

wonderful new world. Despite the short time that has elapsed since then, my heart beats with the desire to redeem myself, to the best of my ability, for the pain and damage I and other men inflicted on you. Yes, I have fought against the elves in the past. I was so deluded that I pushed away all doubts. I did this again and again, until I couldn't tell right from wrong. And for me, as for others, this blindness was convenient—after all, what could I do? I'm merely another subject following orders without thought, without guilt. I had to stay loyal. Loyal to my king, my peers, my family, all those who had pinned their hopes on me. Loyal to Mellethya.

"Oh, loyalty … Loyalty is a good trait, right? Sometimes, maybe. But it can be evil—a tool for binding people, a very dangerous tool. I have learned this the hard way. It is crafted by master manipulators, like King Creeden and others, be they a community, a religion, an individual.

"The more loyal you are, the more blinded you get. The things I did in the name of loyalty, not only against *Dalusians*, but against my own people, my own friends … Still, I want to be loyal. Not to that monarch, no. And neither to any of you."

A whispering began among the crowd, but no one said anything out loud.

"I have decided that, from now on, my loyalty is to myself," said Kamanar. "To my truth, no matter the cost. I have learned that there are many truths that tell different stories of the same reality. So, what is *my* truth? Where do I find it? Do I choose it? Do I make it? To be honest, I don't know. But I do know that I like what I see here in your amazing world. People can speak their mind freely without fear. Where I come from, if someone talked in a manner not to the king's liking, they would be killed there and then. Worse, if the king was in a bad mood, he could order the killing of a servant who dropped a tray. But here, I feel that every person is important. Although, to me, it seems wrong that everyone can give his opinion, even stupid people or ill-motivated people, it still seems better than one opinion, one truth!

"I wish I could talk to my peers and convince them to explore this wonderful land with me. And to meet their kind, beautiful *enemy*! But the time for talking is over." Kamanar turned his eyes toward Ansseur and pointed at his scarred face. "The deep hatred ingrained in their hearts is too strong. There may be a solution for that, they may be persuaded … but not before cutting the snake's head off, which, of course, is my *dear* king!

"For all these reasons, I will not vacillate if I need to raise my sword against them. They will hate me, spit on me in the name of their senseless, distorted justice. I'm prepared to bear that … because now my truth is clear to me more than ever."

Kamanar closed his hand into a fist and brought it to his heart. "Once again, I have that same feeling of emptiness, but this time it's going to be different. I will only be fulfilled when your enemy—*our* enemy—is vanquished, even if it costs me my life." He approached the sword and drew it. "In my youth, I was taught 'If you feed, feed till satisfaction. And if you strike, strike till destruction'."

Ansseur and Mazahratee smiled at the tall man. Once again, there were whispers in the hall.

Brandishing the sword in the air, Kamanar moved aside.

"Mighty sword," he said.

"Quit playing with it," said Mazahratee, the smile disappearing from his face.

Chapter 70
You Will Swim Like Fish

"Where is the other Mellethyan, Caleem, son of Creeden?" asked the council's speaker.

"I'm here." Caleem's voice echoed under the dome.

Everyone's gaze was drawn to Caleem standing on a small balcony almost hidden by the vegetation lining the walls. Nalahes stood next to him, her arms crossed.

"Are you, Caleem Dummah, prince of Mellethya, willing to take on this challenge, as did your fellow Mellethyan?" the speaker asked.

"Words, arguments, explanations …" Caleem began. "You don't have the slightest idea of what is about to descend upon you. You bask in the glory of your past. You'd better bid farewell to your dear land because my father will ascend the cliffs and destroy your precious water bridge. All Anathoria will sink, and you will swim like fish."

The crowd went into an uproar.

"That means you agree, yes?" Mazahratee shouted to the prince above.

Caleem turned his back and disappeared.

Rushing toward a staircase, Kamanar said, "I'll talk to him."

"I apologize on behalf of my brother. He is being insolent. Please forgive him, for he has been through many trials and tribulations," Ansseur begged the audience. "My friend Mazahratee and I have not asked you to gather here only to provide explanations. We have a request."

Silence was restored in the hall. Mazahratee glanced at Ansseur, who scratched the scar on his chin. Before Ansseur uttered anything, the flapping of wings came from the upper part of the gallery. A raven flew in through one of the wide windows. With a muffled, gurgling croak, the bird landed on Mazahratee's shoulder. The counselor took the twig from the raven's beak and studied it.

"Commander of the Ivest, Azanus, has fallen," he said.

A great commotion broke out.

"But …" Mazahratee continued. His voice filled in the gallery, and everyone quieted down, one by one. "The fighters are standing firm, halting the Mellethyans at the passageway."

"The last company of fighters has already left to reinforce the soldiers at the passageway," said Ansseur. "The remaining company of guards, which counts about one hundred youths, is still here under the command of the second lieutenant of the Ivest." He approached the members of the Order. His one-eyed gaze shifted from one to the other. "We, the honorable counselor and I, would like to emphasize the urgency of sending the company of guards to the cliffs. The water bridge is a vulnerable …"

The rest of Ansseur's words were lost in the chaos of protests voiced by many of the elves. The four members deliberated for a moment.

"That is a company of youngsters who have no battle experience, and they are the last line of defense for Anathoria. Your request is denied!" said the speaker.

***

Kamanar found Nalahes standing on a balcony. Her back was

turned to him as she leaned forward on the railing and gazed up at the sky.

"Where is Caleem?" he asked.

The elf woman took a moment and wiped her eyes. "He went down the other staircase. That was quite an impressive speech," she said, trying to hide the tremor in her voice.

"I think that's the longest I've ever spoken in my whole life. What's wrong?"

"Look. Birds are tweeting, flying through the sky without a worry. There's no way out. This time it's going to be tough."

"What is?"

"Caleem spoke to me earlier, explaining everything. The Order is still insisting on grounding the guard company here. But I already instructed them to gather at the trailhead that leads up to the cliffs. We're going up to reinforce the archers. Caleem is joining us."

"Despite your Order's decision?"

The elf nodded.

Kamanar stood next to her, and they gazed at the horizon.

"Wise decision," he said.

"I never wanted to be a warrior," said the officer, her eyes still fixed on the view. "I've always wanted to do different things, like explore the world. Maybe become a builder or just make clay pottery, plant flowers, cook, raise a child …"

Kamanar listened. His eyes took in the distant waterfalls spilling from the various tributaries into the lake.

"I always excelled in archery and in handling swords," she said. "When I spoke, everyone listened. Gradually, and without intending to, I found myself rising up the ranks of the Ivest. My parents, my friends were proud, but I never craved it for myself. I just didn't want to disappoint."

"Good pleasers make good carpets," said Kamanar.

The elf exhaled and looked at the tall man's face. "I'm fed up with fighting these endless wars. I've seen so much death. I'm scared, Kamanar. Not for me, but for the youngsters."

"It's too late," he said. "There's no room for hesitation. You shouldn't be saying these things, even to yourself. Surely not now, before battle—"

"Don't worry, I'm a decent carpet. I'm well acquainted with the necessities of leadership … How lonely it can be."

"I'm sorry … You are confiding in me, and I'm treating you like one of my soldiers. When this ends, the first thing you should do is resign and start to make jugs. The second thing: find yourself a partner," he said with a playful smile.

A tear running down her cheek, Nalahes smiled. She clung to Kamanar, resting her head on his shoulder. Kamanar found himself drawing her closer as he rested his head on hers. They both stood silently in each other's arms.

"I have to go," said Kamanar.

"So do I," said the officer. "Did Mazahratee tell you that you're going to die fighting that metal thing?"

"He didn't emphasize that. Don't worry—prophecies are the silly words of overstressed people. Besides, I can't die yet. I have too many unfinished matters," he said and caressed her face before turning to disappear down the stairs.

CHAPTER 71
BID YOUR FAREWELLS

A myriad of elves hurried away from the tower. Kamanar slung the long sword over his shoulder as he exited to the square.

"There is little time to spare," said Mazahratee. "You should leave as soon as possible. The Dark Rider will reach the passageway tomorrow morning. I've ordered the best horse for you because it's a long ride. Come." He led Kamanar to Caleem and Ansseur, who stood near one of the trees adjacent to the tower. Marbel and the two boys joined them.

"Nalahes is taking the company to the—" whispered Kamanar. Both Caleem and Ansseur nodded.

Faking a smile, the counselor said, "Bid your farewells."

The first one to reach out was Caleem, who gave Kamanar a strong but brief hug then patted his shoulder. The rest took their turn hugging the tall man.

"Kamanar," called Marbel from his cart. "You, too, Caleem."

The two came closer. The older man looked at them with misty eyes. "You are going to battle. You might be confronted by the Black Company. Criando, my son, will be among them for sure. He's quite lean, a bit tall for his age …"

"When was the last time you saw him?" asked Kamanar.

His gaze alternating between Caleem and Kamanar, the old man said, "Ten years ago, when he was drafted. He was very young."

"Not a hair on his head will perish," said Caleem.

"I know how much he means to you," said Kamanar. Placing his hand on Marbel's shoulder, he continued, "I know that he is the real reason you came along on that harebrained mission. You are a great father. If Criando is somewhere out there, I promise to do everything in my power to keep him safe."

The older man tried to reply, but as he choked on his words, he just nodded with a smile instead.

"Here, we don't ask how friends met, but how they parted," said the counselor.

"Are you always this cheerful? Who said we're parting? It's just for a few days," said Kamanar.

"Before you go, can you come with me, Kamanar?" asked Caleem.

"Of course," he said, glad to end the awkward scene.

The two men waved to the others and walked away.

"Where to?" asked Kamanar.

"Not far. We won't be long." Caleem moved away from the paved square and made his way through the bushes. The long blade protruded above Kamanar's shoulders, slicing leaves and branches without him even noticing. After a short walk, they found themselves on the banks of the lake they had visited the night before.

Kamanar, seeing the black stallion tied to one of the trees, said, "That's Naiya's horse!"

"Autumn Wind. The elves found him roaming close by last night. It seems he doesn't like to be far from Naiya," said the prince.

Caleem took his shoes off and stood on the edge of the bank.

"You're jumping in? I don't know if there's time for this," said Kamanar.

"Only for a bit. Just to feel these warm waters. My soul has been craving this since last night. Besides, this may be the last chance for a decent bath." The prince grinned, looking at Kamanar. "I think this may be too high. Maybe we should try farther down," he said as he stooped down to examine the shoreline.

Kamanar burst out laughing and took the sword off his back, jammed it into the ground, then threw off his boots. "Caleem Dummah is afraid of a jump? I can't believe it!" He laughed.

"Just give me a moment. I'll go first."

"No, you won't," said Kamanar as he dived into the lake from the high bank. "Amazing! The water is great," Kamanar cried to the rocks above as he surfaced, brushing his hair away from his face. Caleem remained where he stood.

"Jump, Caleem," said Kamanar.

"I'm sorry."

"What? Caleem, no!" Kamanar yelled.

The prince drew the sword out of the ground. "I can't let you die again." He turned and disappeared from Kamanar's sight.

Kamanar hit the water with his fist "Caleem!" he raged.

He swam to the shore and climbed up to the bank. Above the rush of the waterfall, he heard sound of Autumn Wind's galloping fading away.

He put on his boots and ran after the prince, his mind racing. He slowed down after a minute and sighed. "To hell!" he said then turned back to the tower.

Beyond a group of elf children approaching the tower carrying baskets loaded with fruits and vegetables, Kamanar saw Mazahratee. Ansseur stood next to the counselor, his impaired eyes following the tall man's movements.

With his eyes wide, Mazahratee asked, "The sword! Where is the sword?"

Kamanar rushed to the pair, pushing passersby out of his way. "Caleem took it," he said, coming to a stop in front of them, his hair and clothes still dripping wet.

"That fool! Why would he do that?" Mazahratee raged. The counselor grabbed Kamanar by his arm. "Mount your horse and get the sword back from that insane man!"

"It's no use. No horse can catch up with Autumn Wind."

"No! No! The prophecy. The fate of our world depends on fulfilling the prophecy!"

"No," said Kamanar sharply. "I don't care about your prophecy. I care about the man! Mere foolishness, that's all. Believe me—I'm angry with him, just as you are. If that thing doesn't kill him, I will. He will face the knight, and I will go the other way, to the cliffs." Kamanar headed toward the brown horse.

The counselor followed him. "No, no, no," he said, his lips trembling. "Caleem is meddling with fate. This could bring calamity on the world … and surely on himself!"

Kamanar said nothing as he mounted the animal and headed east.

As he followed the straight road under the shedding canopy, he was no longer attentive to the beauty of the land. His mind was preoccupied with Caleem's act. Dismissing all doubtful thoughts about going back and fetching the sword, he focused his mind and soul on things to come.

He heard a familiar voice. "Stop, please!"

His horse halted, its hooves sliding, and the tall warrior almost lost his grip. "What the …? How did you get here? I'm not going after Caleem," said Kamanar when he recognized Narraneen standing on the side of the path among the green bushes.

"It's not about Caleem. I must show you something before you leave."

"I'm in a real rush right now."

"It's very important. Don't worry, Nalahes will not leave without you."

Kamanar hesitated for a moment but then he dismounted. "What do you—?"

"Come with me," she said and pulled him by the hand beneath the canopy.

"What's that dagger for?" he asked when he saw a small, adorned hilt sticking out of her dress.

"It's an ornament," she said without looking back.

After a short walk, they came to a secluded area. Narraneen gazed around, making sure they were alone. "Take off your shoes," she said.

"What?"

"Take them off."

Kamanar noticed that she was already barefoot. He took off his boots.

"Now, lie down."

"I'm not sure that Ansseur would like this," he said, chuckling. He lay down and then sat back up. "Narraneen, what is this? What are you doing?"

"We are going to a holy place—a place that has no location,"

"All right, that clarifies everything."

"You have the right to see it. It will be … very unfamiliar to you. You'll have to trust me."

Kamanar was intrigued and confused at the same time. He nodded then lay on his back and watched the swaying branches above.

"Open," she said, holding a small reddish seed near his mouth.

Kamanar sniffed the seed then opened his mouth. Narraneen put the seed on his tongue then lay down beside him.

"Go ahead," she said, staring at him.

He looked at her golden eyes, started chewing, then returned his gaze back to the branches.

Before he could discern the seed's taste, the world became dark.

Disruption I

The Realm of Souls

He jumped to his feet. His hand went for his sword's hilt, but then he remembered that he had none.

The trees and bushes had disappeared, and he was surrounded by a reddish darkness.

"I'm here. Don't be alarmed," the elf said.

She appeared out of nowhere, standing beside him. He took a step back.

"What's happening?"

"We have just left the physical world. Take a moment to compose yourself."

The warrior looked around, but all he could see was an endless red void. A familiar stench clung to his nostrils: the smell of decaying corpses. He realized he was standing in shallow water. When he looked down to his bare feet, the water was thick and red. "Is this blood?" he asked. "Don't answer."

"This way," she said, her feet splashing.

"Nalahes is waiting," he replied.

"Don't dwell on that. Here, in the realm of souls, time stands still."

"What?"

Narraneen turned and continued.

After a few steps, Kamanar felt some fleshy objects under his feet. He submerged his hand and pulled out a blood-drenched arm, cut off at the shoulder. He threw it and spat. "This is hell … We are in hell!"

"I was not sure about bringing you here. Yes, it is uncomfortable. I thought you could bear such things."

"I can," he said, relaxing his stance.

"Think of it as if we are in a dream. Nothing here is physical. Your body is safe, but not your mind. That's why I need you to control it."

Kamanar nodded and continued following the elf woman. "You mean a nightmare," he whispered to himself.

The warrior glanced all around, but there was only a never-ending span of red nothingness.

A pillar started to materialize in front of them. Its length stretched to an infinite height. As they drew closer to it, its form began to unveil. Kamanar was disturbed by the gruesome sight yet said nothing.

The giant pillar was made of innumerable decaying bodies and limbs, stacked layer upon layer. Some of the jutting limbs moved; muffled moans came from the structure, followed by sighs and hums.

Narraneen stopped and faced the mortal pillar. Kamanar went even closer to examine the inconceivable sight up close.

"You are the second son of men to ever step into this holy temple," said Narraneen.

"Who was the first?"

"An unworthy creature … He was of no importance, and he was led here by mistake. This is the Alltree. It is sacred to us Anathorians and all elves."

"This is it? Well, it does look like a tree … if you're really drunk."

"Please, respect this sanctum. Restrain your humor."

"Humor is the only thing that can keep me sane in this place."

The elf woman eyed Kamanar. He erased his goofy smile and nodded.

The gruesome spectacle of the decaying faces fascinated him. Some of them moved their jaws as if trying to speak.

"Are they dead?"

"They are not living, but the tree is very much alive."

Kamanar took a step back. Noticing their decomposing pointy ears, he asked, "Are they of your people?"

"Yes. This is the end and beginning for all elves. Once we die, our soul materializes here as an image of our former self, and then we bond with the Alltree."

"How is it a beginning?"

"After the soul bonds, it begins its journey up the ever-growing Alltree. First, it decays. Then it merges and becomes one with all the others. It will be a millennium until it ascends to the top, where it becomes a new being. Then it is reborn in the same image, but with none of its past."

"This is … hard to grasp."

As he began to circle the mortal structure, swirling blue lights shimmered around the pillar and took the shape of humanlike figures. The number of figures grew to many dozens. "What are these apparitions?"

"Look, and you will perceive."

Kamanar strolled between the bluish ghosts, studying them. They seemed to be preoccupied with their own matters, unaware of his presence. "I can hear them!" He glanced at Narraneen. "I know them … These are people I know, and some are already deceased. That is Naji, and over there is Zig … That's my mother!" He stood still and stared at the specter of his mother. He took a couple of slow steps toward her. She was picking up unseen objects from the ground. "Can she see me?" he asked but didn't wait for an answer. "Mother!"

"These figures are mere memories. Your mother's soul is not in this domain."

"She died a long time ago," he said, his voice breaking. He

shook himself and continued to roam among the ghosts. He took his time while Narraneen observed.

"Well, this is a nice surprise. Kamanar visiting me in my dreams," came a deep, familiar voice.

Startled, Kamanar found the ghost of King Creeden Dummah staring straight at him.

"Caleem said you had perished. I can see that is false," said the king's ghost as it approached the warrior.

Kamanar turned to Narraneen, who was as baffled as he was.

"This is not possible," she said, her troubled demeanor obvious. She vanished into thin air. Kamanar took a few steps back.

The red sky turned black, as did the water beneath him. The mortal pillar morphed into a monolith of bright-gray stone. The stacked bodies disappeared, as if they had never been.

"How are you faring? Where are you at the moment?" asked the king. He was now standing close to his soldier.

Kamanar looked around then faced the king. "I don't know what this trick is, but I'll play along. Tell me, king! Tell me about my 'finest hour', the 'mission of my life'!"

"A trick? No … Let's just say I have broadened my insights and my abilities by acquiring some artifacts," said the king.

Something flickered on his chest and shone for a moment from under his clothes. "You accomplished the real mission. I knew I could count on your relentlessness, you and that foolish son of mine, despite your mutual bitterness."

"You placed so much emphasis on trust … How can you demand it when you clearly don't apply it yourself?"

"Stop this nonsense! You are a man of war. If you don't understand the significance of secrecy, be off with you. Don't waste my time."

The king's ghostly figure began to solidify, transforming into flesh and blood wearing fine leather clothes and a red cape.

"You are right, it's a petty thing," said Kamanar. "Let's talk about more important things: about our lies, about Anathoria, about cruelty, you, and your evil dynasty."

"What is this insolence?"

Kamanar stood silent, his eyes fixed on the king.

"I sense this is not new," said the king. "How disappointing. Kamanar, the greatest soldier of Mellethya turned Khandalus."

"Anathoria was never a part of Mellethya."

"Of course it was, and soon it will be again. Don't pretend to be naive … You know what those Dalusians really are. You know everything—you are not a commoner. Don't let their gentle features deceive you. I thought you were better than this."

"I have finally opened my eyes. I am better … and I am coming for your head," said Kamanar, his finger pointing at King Creeden.

The king smiled. "You ungrateful fool. You will pay dearly for this act of treason. After all I have done for you? If it wasn't for me, you would still be a peasant, shoveling cow droppings. I treated you as my own son. I saved you! And regrettably, I believed in you. You gullible stooge, they got to you despite my many warnings."

"Stop trying to play my conscience. I won't have it. Especially from someone who has none. I saw what you did to Ansseur. How could you? Your own son!"

"You say I have no conscience, and then you proceed to address it."

The king's eyes shifted away from Kamanar for the first time, and he let out a short sigh. "He would not stop speaking against Mellethya. They poisoned his mind, especially that Dalusian witch. I could not have it. They brought this tragedy upon me! But eventually, this turned out to be an extraordinary incentive for the people to despise the Dalusians even more. Their king's firstborn, the prince and heir to the throne, murdered by those wretched beings."

King Creeden's gaze returned to Kamanar and he said, "How dare you lecture me about what I did to Ansseur, when you did worse? You hypocrite!"

"I had no choice!" Kamanar screamed.

"You had no choice, really? Amusing … You say that as if I weren't there."

"Shut your mouth!"

"I think this is the first time anyone has said that to me," said the king, giggling. "Yes … now I understand where this is coming from. You don't have any love for the Dalusians—this is all about redeeming yourself."

"No, it's not."

"Don't lie to yourself. I know what it is that haunts you—or rather, should I say who? I know you, Kamanar. I made you."

"You damned me!" screamed Kamanar at the top of his lungs.

"I understand you are forfeiting your reward. But I, being your merciful king, want to give you—"

"I want nothing from you."

"This is solely for your benefit. No one has ever received this kind of leniency, for it is demeaning to me. Can't you see how much you mean to your king?"

"I said I want n—"

"If you come back to your senses, I'm willing to take you back under my wing …"

Kamanar chuckled but didn't say anything.

"I'll make you my general. You will have everything," said the king. "With your exceptional talent and my guidance, we could conquer the world. Of course, you will again have to prove your loyalty to me. But have no fear. This time, it can be less agonizing. For my new invaluable artifact grants me the ability to enter minds and alter them as I please." The same light again flickered from under his clothes. "Hence your reward—let's not forget about that. I'm sure you didn't. You will have it. I can extract that dreadful incident from your past, as if it never happened. You will be free. I know how much this means to you."

Kamanar's heart sank upon hearing the king's last words. He avoided his king's stare. "I …"

"And if you refuse, you, your family, and everyone you know will be publicly shamed and executed. I think that goes without saying. But before all that celebration, I swear to you, Kamanar, I will make you relive your nightmare, that vile secret of yours, every single horrifying moment! I have the power to do so."

King Creeden's figure began to grow bigger and deformed as he continued to address the warrior as if nothing was happening. "I thank you for showing me this pathway. Now, it will be easier to enter your simple mind. When next we meet on the battlefield, which I'm sure we will, I will be waiting for your decision."

As the giant king's words reverberated, he stomped on Kamanar.

The warrior lifted his hands to guard his head. The giant king's form shattered into a million pieces and fell into the black waters.

After the king's laughter faded, the only thing Kamanar could hear was his own distressed breathing.

The skies and waters turned red again, and the endless gray pillar went back to its previous hideous form: the layered, decaying cadavers.

"Kamanar!" cried Narraneen, running to him. "I don't know how he did this … This is unsettling."

"Was this real, or was it in my head?"

"I'm afraid both answers are yes."

Kamanar stared beyond the elf. "Matar," he said.

Narraneen turned around. In the red void stood a tall young man staring back at them. Narraneen turned her eyes from the stranger to Kamanar a few times.

"Hello," said the young man.

The baffled elf nodded back.

"You can see him?" asked Kamanar.

Narraneen walked to the pale young stranger. She looked into his eyes and placed her trembling hand on his cheek as he looked back into her eyes. Tears began to trickle down the elf woman's face.

They both turned to Kamanar.

The bodies on the mortal pillar began stretching and pulling as they moaned.

"Murderer," a deep, reverberating voice came from the pillar. "Coward … Betrayer."

Kamanar covered his face, turned away, and ran. "Get me out of here!" he screamed. The moaning intensified so much that he couldn't hear his feet splashing in the red water. He stumbled and fell face down.

He plunged deep into the water. Kamanar threw out his arms and legs, reaching for the surface, but the more effort he made, the deeper he plummeted. Swallowing the liquid and feeling its taste in his throat and nostrils, he couldn't refute it anymore: he was drowning in a sea of blood.

He felt a pull on his shirt above his shoulder, reached, grabbed someone's arm, and clung to it as hard as he could to pull himself up. He surfaced, drenched in blood and gasping for air. When he stood, he struggled to keep his footing to avoid falling into another unseen chasm.

The warrior couldn't steady his breathing, and vertigo swirled in his head. "Get me out of here!" he screamed again, holding his head.

"Take this." Narraneen held a blue seed out to him.

The warrior pulled her hand to his mouth and almost bit her fingers when he took the seed with his teeth.

CHAPTER 72

DO WHAT YOU DO BEST

Kamanar blinked at the bright, blurry lights. As the brightness eased, he could discern the swaying branches above. He jumped to his feet and touched his face and hair; they were dry and clean. A strange feeling of displacement weighed on his chest.

He noticed the sounds of chirping birds and the light wind brushing the leaves above his head. The green scent of the bushes and plants filled his nostrils. His breathing slowed down, and the feeling of disorientation subsided. Narraneen was staring at him.

"Why would you do this to me on the eve of battle. Why?" he asked, leaping toward her, clenching his fists in a threatening manner. The elf woman was undeterred.

"This was very unexpected. I don't know how Creeden took control. It shouldn't be possible! That thing he was wearing on his neck—"

"It did happen. I can't even think!" He started pacing. "This is too much." His anxiety deepened. "So now you know?" he half stated, half asked.

Narraneen nodded and came closer.

"How do you expect me to fight after all this?" he asked, evading her eyes.

Narraneen pulled him close and held his jaw and cheeks in a firm grip, forcing him to look her in the eyes. Her gold eyes seemed different, and he couldn't look away, could feel himself falling into those two clear lakes. He shivered as an overwhelming feeling, a catharsis, rushed through his limbs. When he took a step back from the elf, everything became familiar again; he felt both serene and energetic.

"What did you do to me?" he asked.

"It will help a bit."

"This is a lot," he said and started laughing.

"Maybe … Put on your shoes."

"I will. Thank you. Thank you, very, very, very much," he said as he put on his shoes.

"Let's go," she said, both serious and amused at the same time.

She led him by the hand back to his horse and motioned for him to mount. "Take this," she said, offering a blue seed. "Take it immediately if that king of yours manages to snatch you to the other realm. This will force you out."

The warrior tucked the seed in an inside pocket.

"Go do what you do best. Good luck!"

Kamanar nodded and pressed forward, already starting to feel the effect of the elf woman's magic charm diminishing. The light, positive mood was being overtaken by harsh reality with each passing moment.

The farther east he advanced, the narrower the road became. The globular buildings were nowhere to be seen, but he could still distinguish a number of towers scattered through the landscape. The cobblestones gave way to a road covered in a carpet of autumn leaves, blown up into the air by his horse's hooves.

Narraneen's spell faded, and the unreal encounter at the Alltree felt like it had happened long before.

Riding bareback was challenging, but Kamanar was sure his destination was close. The gaps between the branches showed a mammoth wall of rocks rising to an awe-inspiring altitude. "The Mobinar," he uttered.

A bright round opening appeared at the edge of the path in front of him. The horse slowed down.

"Just a bit longer."

Beyond the opening were the still waters of the lake of Anathoria. As they exited the forest, Kamanar jumped off the animal and patted its long neck. By the lakeshore was a small boat tied to a wooden pole planted in the shallow water; like the boat, the pole was decorated in a motif of leaves in different shapes.

Leaving the horse behind, Kamanar waded into the cold water to the little boat that bobbed up and down in the waves caused by his stride. On the floor of the boat lay a small, leaf-shaped shield atop a sword. In the back of the vessel was a single paddle. He climbed into the boat and began to row.

He reflected one last time on the ordeal in that hellish place. Although he shouldn't have been, he found himself at peace with it, and he was sure this was Narraneen's doing.

Before him, the ridge extended high up until it disappeared into the clouds. At the foot of the mountain were several groves. On the shore stood dozens of elves waiting as the little boat approached.

"What are you doing here?" she asked.

Kamanar recognized Nalahes. All the other elves crowded around her, staring at him as he jumped out of the boat. "You're in luck—you get me instead of grumpy Caleem," he said, holding the sword and shield in one hand and tugging the boat behind him with the other. One of the elves entered the water, took the rope away from him, and pulled the little vessel to shore.

"When do we leave?" he asked, examining the strange weapon. The long hilt was about the same length as its narrow blade.

"Where's the sword?" asked Nalahes.

"Caleem took it."

The elf stood in silence, her subordinates whispering in the background.

"He insisted on changing roles with me," he said as he stepped out of the water, shaking his wet boots and glancing at the young elf fighters around him. "These are boys and girls. Are we going to war with children?"

"We are not children!" said a green-haired elf girl.

"It's not going to be easy, seeing them bleeding on the battlefield."

"They are very capable. What now?" asked Nalahes.

Kamanar puffed a few times. "To the cliffs!" he said, carrying the shield on his left arm, following the officer's example. He slung the sword on his back, with the handle above his right shoulder, but the blade slipped. Nalahes helped him insert the blade into a concealed sheath on the back of the green cape.

An argument broke out in the ranks of the young elven fighters. Nalahes pronounced one curt sentence, drawing their attention, but then the discussion went on.

"Enough!" cried Kamanar. "You should know that Caleem is a better warrior than I am. If there is one man who can stop that Dark Rider, it's Caleem … the prophecy notwithstanding. Besides, you all know that this front is more vulnerable, this front is more important. That's why you are all here despite your elders. So here I am, Kamanar, Broken Fingers, joining you, to battle at the cliffs … This whole argument is pointless. We are past the point of no return. There are no more decisions to be made and no more changes. We need to concentrate on our front and our front only."

The elves whispered among themselves once again. One elf girl stepped forward from among the ranks. "We're glad you have joined us, Kamanar," she said, smiling.

Nalahes said something in the elven tongue and moved ahead, followed by Kamanar and the rest of her troops in rows of twos and threes.

The path continued east, away from the lake, and ascended the range. The elves had no difficulty making their way up, whereas the tall man, despite his long strides, was already panting.

It was past noon, and a sweaty Kamanar had to push himself to near his limits. The purple-eyed elf skipped ahead, her light feet barely touching the ground. The elves' footsteps were so noiseless and their breathing so quiet that, once in a while, Kamanar glanced behind him to make sure they were all still following. In addition to the exertion, a piercing sensation burned in his abdomen and legs, but still he moved on.

The trail continued upward, winding north and south in sharp turns, like a snake slithering up the side of a mountain. Kamanar, huffing and puffing, slowed down. The tall man felt two hands on his back, pushing him. A smiling girl elf was prodding him forward. He smiled at her and at her peer, who was assisting from the other side.

With a second glance, Kamanar saw that the quiet elf boy supporting him was the spitting image of his friend Matar.

"How much longer do we have to push you?" asked Matar. "Why is it always the biggest man who's the slowest?" He chuckled.

Kamanar smiled but said nothing.

The elf force advanced under a blanket of gray clouds. The higher the trail led them, the thinner the vegetation became. To the west lay the island of Anathoria, a mass of green in a big blue lake, encircled by the high ridges decorated with waterfalls streaming down like white veils. Struggling to breathe, Kamanar had no energy left in him to appreciate the magnificent view. But he forced himself to study the monumental bridge extending across the sky all the way to the other side of the lake.

"We're almost at the top," yelled Nalahes for Kamanar's benefit.

Relieved, Kamanar smiled. Three bends later, they were at the end of the winding path. Nalahes stopped near a roaring river. The tall man halted near the officer, thanking the two elves who had helped him most of the way. He bent down, his hands on his knees, to try to slow his breathing. "Your energy … has no limits," he said, his voice breaking up in between gasps.

Nalahes waited until her entire force had reached the plateau and for Kamanar to catch his breath.

"Where the bridge meets the mountain, this is where the enemy will strive to strike," the officer said loudly while pointing at the edge of the bridge.

Kamanar looked at the high river spilling its waters into the strange, hanging bridge, which channeled the flow straight over the island across to the other side.

"The Bridge of Anathoria," said Nalahes.

In awe, Kamanar scrutinized the massive structure.

"This bridge, built by our ancestors, prevents the river from flooding the valley. If this bridge is destroyed, our land will be devastated within days," said Nalahes.

Kamanar advanced toward the bank of the turbulent river.

"Amazing," he said. "Indeed, this is where King Creeden will try to strike. Before we go on, I want to know the fighters' names. It doesn't feel right going into combat when I don't even know your names."

The first elf approached, offering his hand to the tall man. "Asahni," said the elf.

"I'm honored to meet you."

Stepping aside, the elf made way for the female elf behind him.

"Akiena, meet nice you," said the green-haired elf girl.

"Meeting nice you, too," he said, smiling.

One after the other, all one hundred elves introduced themselves to the warrior.

"We're moving on," said Nalahes. They continued their advance, with the river flanking them. The going was easier on the wide, paved, almost flat road. They reached a bend in the great river, which originated from the north between the snow-capped peaks. There, it meandered within the mountains of the Mobinar. After passing the curve, the officer increased her pace.

The elves' long shadows disappeared as the sun descended behind the gray clouds. The road became broader, ending in an open space. On the sides, tall rock walls stretched up to the clouds. Ahead, the stony platform ended abruptly. No one uttered a word; all were scrutinizing the edge of the cliff ahead and the immense gray space beyond it.

Nalahes led them to the edge of the wide cliff where the archers were positioned. All thirty elves lay on their bellies with only their heads protruding beyond the cliff's edge. Next to each was a long bow and a full quiver. Under each archer's legs was another quiver attached to a backpack.

Their eyes turned toward the approaching group, and one of them called to Nalahes, who stooped down and talked to him.

Kamanar inspected the wide ledge, which curved like a sickle and merged, on both sides, to the mountain. He then gazed down at the dense fog covering the world beneath like a frozen lake. The great shadow of the Mobinar extended across the sea of fog, almost becoming one with the cloudy blanket.

Hammering noises ascended from the void below. Kamanar approached Nalahes and the elf kneeling by her side. His pointy ears protruded out of his short, black hair, appearing even more oversized than the usual elven ears.

He interrupted their conversation and asked, "What's going on down there?"

The strange-looking elf shrugged.

"This is Lalandi, commander of the archers. He does not speak your language," said Nalahes. "They advanced closer by the cover of the fog, but they remain outside the range of arrow shot."

"What else did he say?" asked the tall man, glancing at Lalandi.

"The bulk of their force are armored giants, about four hundred, with another two hundred men, among whom King Creeden Dummah is counted. They brought along covered wagons, which, guessing by their size, don't hold supplies. The hammering began this morning."

"I don't like all this banging," said Kamanar as he approached the edge, scanning the misty space below. "They're building something ..."

Exhaling, Nalahes gazed into the void. They both scrutinized the invisible enemy lines. Kamanar placed his hand on her shoulder. She looked into his face, the heightened tension showing in her purple eyes.

"We'll give it all we've got, and whatever will be, will be," he said.

Chapter 73
I Want to Go With You

Night fell, and the cold air lashed Caleem's nose and ears while he rode Autumn Wind to the passageway. The deepening darkness forced him to slow down. Many thoughts raced through his mind as he galloped under the dark canopy.

"What would I do without you?" he asked, patting the horse's sweating neck. His words of praise did nothing to help the weary, royal animal, which, except for a few brief stops for water, had not had any rest. Slowing down from a canter to a wobbling, slow trot, it shook its head and neighed.

"You're right. You deserve a rest," said Caleem, dismounting, the pain in his stiff joints catching up with him. "Looks like I need it, too."

Autumn Wind grazed on grass by the roots of a nearby tree. From the pocket of the saddlebag, Caleem retrieved a piece of a long, red fruit and a pastry that had been squashed during the ride. After searching in the darkness for a place to rest, he slid into an alcove in a tree trunk. Taking the long sword off his shoulder, he savored the moist air filled with the scent of fresh leaves. He relaxed but kept the weapon close. He bit into the fruit and the pastry, all the while studying the smooth, shiny blade.

He heard galloping coming from far away. The clatter of hooves strengthened then faded as if carried by an errant wind. He stopped chewing and jumped to his feet, forcing the last bite down his throat.

The sound became stronger, breaking the silence of the night. Leaving his stallion, he dashed into the high bushes, then squatted with his hand gripping the sword's hilt. The mysterious rider slowed, coming to a halt a few steps from Caleem.

The prince's eyes were fixed on the dark figure as it dismounted and approached. He froze, ready to pounce.

"Are you going to strike me with that thing?" came a soft, familiar female voice. "I can see you," she said, getting even closer.

"Narraneen!" said Caleem, rising from the brush. "What are you doing here?"

"I wanted to know how you were doing."

After arranging the sword on his back once again, the prince came out of his hideout.

"You don't need to worry about me, or about the sword," he said, tapping the handle of the sword, which rose above his shoulder.

"I didn't come for the sword. Mazahratee doesn't know everything. I think you're capable of handling it," she said, walking up to Autumn Wind as he grazed.

"You don't know me … or what I'm capable of," said the prince. And then he addressed the horse: "Take it easy on the grass. We should stay light." He grabbed the reins and pulled Autumn Wind around to check the saddle. The animal continued to feed, almost unbothered.

Narraneen uttered a sentence in the elven tongue. The horse neighed, lifting its head from the dark vegetation. The moonlight filtered through the clouds, shining on the elf's face and light-colored cloak. Her golden eyes shone. "Come, sit with me," she said.

"I have to move on."

"You're closer to your destination than you think. Spare Autumn Wind a bit more time."

After reflecting for a moment, the prince returned to the tree, removed the sword from his back, and the elf joined him.

"It was brave, what you did," she said.

"I don't need any flattery … I'm questioning my every move."

"I believe you have a great role to play in these events."

"You said it—'a role.' That's what I have been doing my whole life: playing a role. I don't want to do that anymore."

"We all play roles. That's how things are. But very few can choose their role and change their destiny. I think that's what you are doing now. Maybe, if you ask yourself why or for whom you are doing this, the vagueness will dissipate."

The prince took a long breath. "You know, when I plunged into the river to fetch this sword, a part of me wanted to be swept away by the current, but another part couldn't accept this privilege. It's not only Seonder I've hurt. I've encountered Dalusians before, seen their faces. I was convinced that they were shapeshifters. I took pride in killing them. Now those faces are already coming back to haunt me," he finished almost in a whisper.

She leaned back and sat in silence by his side. The two remained quiet, listening to the wind blowing through the branches above.

"How come you don't have children?" asked Caleem.

"That's an odd question for someone who is about to engage in the battle of his life."

"Maybe I'm trying to clear my head from the mire of worries. Ansseur and you, you've been married for a few years now, right?"

"It takes time for an elf woman to conceive."

"Why is that?"

"You must understand, there is an equilibrium to life. The life span of our people is ten times longer than yours. This advantage brings with it some disadvantages. To have three children is a rare occurrence. Conception can sometimes take decades."

"So, there's a good chance I may not have any nieces or nephews."

"It is a possibility. But just so you know, mixed couples require a shorter period."

"Great," he said, and became serious again. "It seems remarkable that you look like you're thirty years of age, but you are actually much older than that. What will become of you and the children you bear? After Ansseur, you know … goes."

Narraneen stroked a leaf hanging beside her. "Time bears no meaning if there is no love. Ansseur asked me the same question before we married, and this is what I said to him: 'I love you. Do you want me to regret not being with you for the rest of my long life?' And there's always the possibility of marrying again!" she said with a laugh.

Caleem got up and placed the sword on his back. "I need to go now. Give my regards to everyone, and tell Seonder … that I am sorry," he said, lowering his eyes. Clenching his fists, he walked to Autumn Wind.

"You can tell him so yourself," said Narraneen.

Caleem mounted the stallion in silence and spurred his horse.

"I want to go with you," she said.

"Go back to your home and your husband."

***

Zig and Marbel sat by the lakeshore, each wrapped inside a warm cloak. After hours of staring at the dark body of water, the two dozed off to the soothing swish of the waves hitting the shore. The sound of trotting hooves woke them up. Ansseur appeared on a white horse.

"Have you seen Narraneen?" he asked before coming to a stop.

Zig shrugged.

"Did you, young man?" Ansseur asked.

"No, no, we haven't seen her."

"She spoke to me before she left," said Marbel.

Ansseur alighted from his horse. "Left? To go where?" he asked, coming closer.

"Don't worry," said Marbel, turning to face the lake. "She went to visit the five elders."

"The five elders dwell far to the north, up in the mountains … Very odd," Ansseur said and mounted his horse once again. "I thought she went to battle or after Caleem. You don't know her—she's capable of doing so." He whispered to the horse, which cantered back amongst the trees.

Zig returned to sit next to Marbel. Just like the older man, he continued to gaze at the surface of the water into the night. As they were starting to nod off again, Naji came running. "Did you—?" he yelled, still running, then stopping short. Almost out of breath, he bent down and rested his hands on his knees. He was back in his blue shirt. "Did you see Akiena?"

"No. And why are you wearing that?" asked Zig.

"I can't seem to find her anywhere."

"Are you stupid or something?" asked Marbel. "Your green-haired friend has gone up to the Wall Cliffs, together with the other young fighters."

"No, she was supposed to stay here, with her company. That's what Narraneen said."

"There has been a change of plans. Kamanar also went," said Marbel.

Staring at the lake, Naji shook his head. His breathing slowed down, and he kicked a pebble into the water.

"One king can do so much harm. He is just a man, not a god. Why does he choose to be evil?" asked Naji.

"Well, he is the closest thing to God. That is what many think, what I used to think," said Marbel. "Choose to be? I don't think it's as simple as that."

"This is not right." Naji turned to leave.

"Where are you going?" asked Zig, getting to his feet.

"To the cliffs … If she and Kamanar are going, then I'm going. I have to do something. I have to help," said Naji.

"You don't know how to wield a sword! This is war, not a brawl," said Marbel.

"Maybe I don't. But I have to try, I owe it to Kamanar. I've been nothing but trouble, and this is my chance," said Naji.

"I'm coming with you," said Zig, running after his friend, who stopped in his tracks.

"You're both nuts!" said Marbel.

"Don't even think—" said Naji.

"If you go, I go," said Zig.

"Listen, Zig, I have to tell you something. When I was looking for you, before all this, I ran into this fortune-teller. Do you want to know what she said? A knife in your chest, in a battlefield. That's your future. *A knife in the chest*—do you understand? You should be nowhere near any fighting."

Zig shrugged. "Maybe we won't have to fight. We're just going to support, somehow. Like maybe ask Gudjewkan for help—you know he hates those Guzuds … Caleem and Kamanar don't believe in fortune-tellers. It's all nonsense. Nobody really knows what will happen … Ask Marbel. What do you think, Marbel?"

"I think that you both should stay out of this."

"Gudjewkan is a long shot, but …" said Naji.

"If it were the other way around, you wouldn't let me go on my own. You already proved that," Zig said.

Naji tapped his thigh. "On one condition: whenever you smell danger, you run without looking back."

"Both of you," called Marbel, "come here to me."

The lads complied.. The chubby man hoisted himself up inside the cart and hugged the boys. "Take good care of yourselves, all right? You know I love you both like my own," he said with a tremble, holding them in his embrace for a long moment. When he let go, he wiped his eyes.

"That's enough mushy-mushy," said Naji, pulling Zig by the arm. "Let's go."

"You don't admit it, but you like it, too, mushy-mushy," said Marbel to Naji as the two boys ran on their way.

Chapter 74
I Have a Plan

The cold breeze brushed against Kamanar's face as he lay snuggled in a warm blanket. He opened his eyes and sat up.

The world was still enveloped in darkness, clouds concealing the stars and the moon. Behind him, the elves were scattered, busy with their final inspections. Some were fastening the straps of their high boots, others tuning their bows and checking their arrows.

The tall man rose, coming to stand close to the scouts who lay at the edge, their eyes scanning the depths of the fog. Kamanar settled at the end of the cliff with his feet dangling over the edge. The banging had ceased; only a disturbing silence came from the enemy camp below. He sat, watching the mist become lighter with the arrival of dawn.

"Eat," said Nalahes, sitting down next to him and offering him a handful of round, brown seeds.

The tall man took one and popped it into his mouth. "Bitter … and sweet. I like." He grabbed the rest of the seeds from her hand and devoured them a couple at a time. "How are the fighters?"

"Good," she said as she gazed to the east.

In front of them, far beyond the sea of fog, dawn began to break above the jagged peaks of the Tan-Mirus mountain range.

The sun rose quickly, lighting up the mist beneath them. The underside of the high, gray clouds was striped yellow from the sun's rays. The mask of fog began to dissipate, finally allowing the elves to see their enemies.

The members of the Black Company stood out on the field in strict formation. Kamanar and the elves focused on the lines closer to them where the giant Guzuds, some of whom sported armor similar to that of the Black Company's soldiers, stood in random groups. The rest had not yet put on their armor; it was piled up in large wagons parked nearby.

"Look at those two big ones." Nalahes pointed at two great wagons standing side by side, each much longer than the rest and with numerous huge wheels. Black fabric covered both vehicles.

"What do you think?" asked the elf.

"Maybe ladders of some sort. Maybe another surprise."

"Could be ladders. Surely, they intend to climb up here. Well, we're ready for them."

"Their numbers are greater than ours," said Kamanar.

"They seem strong, but also slow and heavy—look how they move. It's hard to believe they'll ever manage the climb."

"I worry about the smaller ones. I took part in their training."

"The Black Company?"

"They think King Creeden is their creator—as in the creator of all things. They are very capable."

"So are we."

"Are you trying to assuage my fears?"

"Yes. You worry too much!" She laughed then became serious again. "They'll be ready to attack soon. What do you think?"

Bewildered, Kamanar pointed north. "Do you see the smoke there?"

"Yes. Looks like it's coming from underground."

"The smoke *is* coming from underground!" Kamanar said with excitement as he placed both hands on her shoulders. "I've been there," he said, chuckling and shaking the elf woman.

"What's wrong with you?" she asked.

Kamanar fixed his gaze on the thin columns of smoke. He mumbled as he rubbed the stubble on his chin, his eyes moving between the enemy lines below and the twirling smoke.

"The distance between the smoke and the giants is less than a thousand paces," he said. "Listen," he shouted as he turned to the fighters lined up behind them. "All of you, listen up! We have a good chance of winning this battle. I know what I'm about to propose may sound crazy, but it's not." He walked among the young elves, looking each one of them in the eye. "We stun them by attacking first," he said and paused. Most of the soldiers looked disconcerted, shaking their heads. Many of them began whispered conversations.

Nalahes said, "You must be out of your mind … to give up our greatest advantage! To forego the high ground, in the daylight? No!"

"If we can lure those humongous fatsos to the columns of smoke, we will win the battle."

Shaking her head, Nalahes placed her hands on her hips. "Nothing you say can make us descend into a meaningless defeat," she said.

"Are we going to wait for them? Caleem said his father, King Creeden, has fixed an elaborate scheme. Are you all going to sit here waiting for his trap to spring? We'll get down there, wreak havoc, and run toward the smoking ground. And then … It will all be over, trust me. There is no time to go into detail. Look—they're not ready yet!" the tall man pointed at a big group of unarmed giants.

There was no reply, either from Nalahes or anyone else.

Lowering his arm, Kamanar glanced at the fighters. After reflecting for a moment, he turned to Nalahes. "Fetch me a rope, please. I'm going down by myself."

"Don't be foolish! Once you're down, there can be no climbing back. You'll be an easy—"

Kamanar waved his hand in dismissal. "You are their commander, not mine," he said. After receiving a coil of thin rope, he fastened its end around a jagged stone and threw the rest off the cliff. Armed with his shield and sword, he grabbed the rope. "I always knew men were braver than elves," he said, then lowered himself and disappeared from their sight.

Aside from the blowing wind, not a sound could be heard at the top of the cliff.

One of the elves stooped down to peer over the ledge, then looked back at Nalahes, who shook her head, triggering an argument among the fighters.

Using the cuffs of his sleeves to protect his hands as he slid down the rope, Kamanar dug his feet into the various niches and protrusions on the stony wall. At every opportunity, he threw a glance down behind to the enemy.

When a second rope was thrown to the left of him, Kamanar stopped. A third rope appeared to his right. One after the other, the fighters rappelled down, passing him on both sides.

Smiling, Kamanar recognized Nalahes gliding down. She stopped next to him.

"Your argument was far from compelling. Still, these youngsters believe in you … for some reason, Kamanar Broken Fingers," she said and winked. When she landed on the ground, her fighters huddled around her.

The first blaring horn echoed through the air, striking Kamanar's heart with anxiety. He accelerated his descent while the nimble, green-cloaked elves eased past him, until his feet finally touched the soft ground. He drew the sword, with its long handle and short blade, from the back of his cloak. A second horn joined the first, both resounding across the charged atmosphere.

"Well done, all of you. Don't worry—I have a plan!" said Kamanar. "What's the plan?" he whispered to Nalahes.

Nalahes issued orders in the elven language. The elves formed a long, green line, one next to the other at perfect, equal intervals.

"We'll storm the front lines, retreat to the range of our

archers, then run to the columns of smoke. Then it's on you!" said the officer nervously. She moved to stand at the front of the formation.

Kamanar joined her, looking ahead to the rows of giants preparing for the offense. Behind him, the young elves stood in a long line, their fists clenched, their faces grave, and their eyes locked on their adversaries.

Jumpy and tense, Kamanar asked, "What are we waiting for?"

CHAPTER 75
WE ARE AT WAR

The giants ran around in confusion. The officer reached for the hilt of the sword on her back and drew it out in a quick motion. The other elves did the same. Calling out a short command, she dashed forward, followed by her soldiers. Nalahes and the other elves were agile and very fast; Kamanar tried to keep up, but he was easily outrun.

The Guzuds began to raise their heavy hammers. Most of them had not yet donned their armor.

The elf officer broke through the line of baffled giants, her small fighters smashing into the orange-haired beasts, stabbing and slashing them.

The clash of metal filled the air, mixed with the groans of injured Guzuds.

A giant who'd given up on his armor charged straight at the elves, his huge hammer raised above his head. The hefty Guzud turned his gaze on Nalahes, rushed toward her, and struck with all his might. Nalahes leaped to the side, and the hammer came down on the ground, splashing mud in all directions. The elf jumped atop the half-buried hammer's head, and before the giant could pull it back up, the blade of her weapon had pierced through the skin under his fat chin, penetrating deep into his furry, orange neck.

Kamanar, the last one to arrive in the combat zone, watched the gigantic form collapse in front of Nalahes. The officer wove around the corpse and headed right for the mass of Guzuds.

The elves stabbed and slashed the panicking giants with unwavering determination. Kamanar witnessed a shield the size and shape of a door being swung at two distracted elves. They both fell back; one of them managed to roll away on the marshy soil. The shield swung aside to reveal a Guzud covered in armor from head to toe. He smashed the fallen elf with his hammer, spattering blood and mud everywhere. The sight made Kamanar shudder, and he moved to pounce on the giant. The other elf was terrified; still, he thrust his sword at the Guzud. The black armor was impenetrable, so he tried again and again, only to be repelled by the immense, rectangular shield. The Guzud lifted his hammer once more.

Finding a small slit between the plates of the armor, Kamanar drove his sword deep into the giant's tree-trunk-sized thigh. The beast roared, his blow barely missing the tall man, who bounced out of reach. Kamanar stabbed again, this time behind the knee. The giant let out a deafening scream as his legs buckled. Kamanar jumped on the Guzud's broad, armored back, clasped its thick neck right below the helmet, and slashed it without mercy. Dropping his shield and hammer, the Guzud fell, Kamanar still hanging on.

"Careful!" came a voice from behind.

Kamanar jumped back to his feet. He spun around, searching for the threat, expecting to see a hammer. Instead, it was another dead giant falling. A draft swept over the tall man from the crashing creature, blowing back his hair. Beyond the corpse, he saw a green-haired elf girl. She turned away, returning to battle.

In the pandemonium, the giant corpses piled up around him. But among them, he noticed a few small, mangled, elven bodies. The pointy-eared creatures lunged and stabbed without pause.

The giants had not yet managed to get organized, and their death count continued to rise. Nalahes issued orders to her green troops from atop one of the big corpses, and he rushed to her side.

"They never expected us to attack first," he shouted.

Nalahes jumped off the giant's back, about to reply to Kamanar, when she froze at the sight of something behind him.

"What?" Kamanar turned around.

Her eyes were fixed on two fallen elves.

Kamanar cupped her face in a firm but tender gesture. "We are at war. This has happened, and there is more to come … Don't let it get you down, not now. There will be time to for grieving later."

A Guzud's booming voice interrupted their brief exchange as the giant issued orders to his army. One by one, the Guzuds raised their rectangular, door-like shields and came together to form a tight, black wall.

Within moments, the elves found themselves shut out. Above the giants' shoulders loomed one Guzud astride a giant beast; only a section of its white back was visible behind the metal wall. This particular Guzud, smaller than his peers, was clad in armor only on his chest and back. A single horn jutted out from the left temple of his orange head. He held high a long, metal-spiked club and was spitting out orders to his soldiers, who continued to regroup and retreat. Before disappearing behind the bulk of his corps, he caught a glimpse of Nalahes and Kamanar.

"Fight, you fat cowards!" cried Kamanar, dashing toward the wall of rectangular shields. He tried to jam his sword in between them, but to no avail. The elves attacked without respite but could not break through the high metal barrier.

The Guzuds continued to move backward.

Nalahes yelled an order, and her soldiers were quick to form a line again.

"Prepare them for another offensive," said Kamanar, still trying to figure out a way to break the massive shield wall.

Small black figures emerged from within the iron wall and stormed ahead. The sharp edge of an approaching spear startled

Kamanar. It was by sheer luck that he managed to deflect it with his small, leaf-shaped shield. Kamanar was searching for the source of the spear when he was hit by a hexagonal shield, which sent him flying onto his back. Lying on the ground, he was confronted by a human-sized figure wearing black armor, his face hidden behind a black helmet. Through two tiny triangular slits, a pair of raging eyes flashed with hatred.

"Kamanar! You traitor!" cried the armored man, wielding his spear.

Kamanar diverted the spear with his elven sword. With his long legs he kicked his assailant in the knee, almost knocking him down. Kamanar rolled to his side and got back to his feet, staggering. He realized that an entire group of combatants like the one facing him were striking his young peers.

"Captain of the Royal Guard, and our former lieutenant … how could you?" the voice cried again.

Kamanar tried to identify the voice, all the while keeping a distance from his aggressor. For a moment, he considered explaining himself, but, seeing the spear thrown at him with force, he thought better of it. As the weapon flew toward him, Kamanar raised his shield; the lance shattered it.

The black warrior swung his sword at Kamanar, who was regaining his balance. The sharp, perforated blade whistled as it was thrust toward the tall man's face. He blocked it with the small elven sword, which he then aimed at his opponent's neck, the only vulnerable spot in the well-crafted armor.

The hexagonal shield repelled the short sword then swung with a vengeance to hit Kamanar's chest and forehead. The tall man bounced back; with a dizzy head he staggered backward, retreating to the elves.

"The Black Company," said Nalahes.

"Watch for them! They're very dangerous," he shouted, his eyes still fixed on the armored soldier lunging at him with the shield.

Kamanar kicked the shield, casting it far from the soldier,

who continued to advance, undeterred, his sword pointed ahead. "For Father!" he yelled.

Kamanar shoved the sword aside with his own. The two warriors collided, the black armor slamming into Kamanar's green cloak.

"For your evil father!" said Kamanar as he jammed the elven sword under his assailant's chin. Watching his opponent fall lifeless, Kamanar shook the blade free.

The Guzuds continued their retreat and regroup, but the Black Company still battled the elves with astonishing dexterity. Seeing that the fighting was becoming more difficult, Nalahes ordered her troops to fall back. Kamanar joined them while noting several green bodies strewn about among the few fallen black ones. The Black Company advanced, hacking at the small wooden shields with their spears and swords.

A cry came from above and Kamanar glanced up; the gray clouds overhead were striped with small, dark, flying lines. "Arrows!"

The elf archers shot hundreds of them at the Black Company. The arrows bounced off the armor and shields, only a few striking the weaker spots in between necks and shoulders. Despite the constant barrage, the armored warriors pushed forward. The shots were so precise that although they landed near the archers' comrades fighting below, they did not hit any.

Under the cover of the archers, the row of pointy-eared soldiers advanced ahead once again. In the meantime, out of range, the Guzuds, by their commander's orders, readied themselves for a new offensive, shields, hammers and all.

Kamanar and Nalahes, along with their subordinates, were engaged in fierce combat with the Black Company and didn't notice that the Guzuds were closing on them bit by bit.

CHAPTER 76
A MASK

A gentle wind blew at the Mobinar passage, carrying the fog between the two ridges to the south. The drifting clouds failed to squeeze through the narrow passageway, and they lingered over the battlefield, twirling in a sluggish whirlwind.

It was late morning on the fourth day of battle. The Mellethyan Breaching Company had pushed the elven defenses back into the confines of the passageway. The fog and the endless volleys of arrows originating from the high branches hindered the companies' advance.

Following the orders of Karagan, the commander in chief of the king's army, many trees had been felled to limit the Dalusian archers' concealed positions.

The soldiers advanced at a crawling pace, leaving behind a balding forest. The corpses of fallen combatants were removed to keep the morale of the troops intact. Karagan had learned this from the Dalusians, who never left their dead on the field.

The Dalusian arrows stopped, taking the soldiers by surprise. The baffled fighters at the front line peeked from behind the tree stumps.

"Stop," shouted one of the soldiers. The cry was directed at the archers of the Breaching Company, who hadn't ceased to assault the misty treetops.

"Stop!" cried the voice again, this time with more urgency. The archers lowered their bows.

The sound of a lone galloping horse came from the north, and the vague figure of a rider materialized in the haze. He was headed straight to the infantry's front line.

"It's Prince Caleem," said one of the soldiers.

"It is I, Caleem!" the prince shouted, riding among the soldiers. "For the moment, we are safe from the foul Dalusian volleys," he said to the fighters, who scattered behind the cover of the tree stumps and rocks, their shields still held high above their heads.

Behind the prince, another figure sat on Autumn Wind's back. The figure's hands were bound and its head hung low, covered by a hood.

"What the hell is going on here?" Karagan blared as he brought his horse to a halt in front of the prince. The commander in chief wore a chainmail. Under his shiny helmet, he had a trimmed, gray beard.

"Commander Karagan, one of my father's favorites. How are you?" asked the smiling prince.

"We are in the middle of a battle, as you can appreciate. Where the devil did you arrive from … and who is that?"

"I have just completed a mission of great importance, which has cost my men their lives. But not before seizing a prize from the enemy," said Caleem. He dismounted and yanked the figure down onto the ground. The cloak-clad form, whose head was still covered by the hood, let out a whimper, then knelt in front of the men.

"From now on, not one arrow will be shot this way because we hold this Dalusian hostage."

One after the other, soldiers and officers began to crowd around Caleem and his captive. Those in front were careful to maintain a prudent distance from the dangerous figure.

"Interesting. How exactly do you propose we use this prize?" asked Karagan, rubbing his short beard.

Caleem looked into the familiar faces of the infantrymen surrounding him. "This gains us some badly needed resting time. You have been fighting for four straight days," said Caleem, handing Autumn Wind's reins over to one of the men.

The kneeling figure, still staring at the ground, did not move.

"My troops need no rest, nor any prizes. We broke into the passageway, a feat never before achieved against these creatures. The soldiers can already smell victory in the air, right?" Karagan shouted out the last word.

"Yeah!" repeated the soldiers in unison, raising and rattling their weapons and shields.

"Long live the king!" cried one of the fighters, followed by a choir of his peers repeating his words. Their voices echoed off the walls of the tall rock formation. Their weapons rose once again in celebration.

The prince smiled. "High spirits, that's good. Maybe we should lift them up even farther," he said and kicked the Dalusian prisoner, who lifted up bound hands in protection. "Before we continue the battle, let's make use of this pleasurable moment, to enjoy decapitating this evil creature." The prince fixed his eyes on Karagan, who still sat atop his horse. Standing behind the captive, Caleem pulled off the hood, then yanked its head backward by the hair, revealing the Dalusian's countenance at last. The soldiers' murmurs stopped as they stared at the delicate, feminine features. The Dalusian woman attempted to avoid their gazes.

The prince surveyed the men around him. The suffering he was inflicting upon the woman became apparent to all. "What's the matter? Don't let this fragile look deceive you. We all know the Dalusians can transform themselves." He kicked Narraneen in the back. With a moan, she collapsed in front of the commander's horse.

The animal recoiled and the prostrate Narraneen began to cry. Her face was smeared in dirt, her hands were tied, and sobs shook her body.

The soldiers stood in silence; some climbed up on rocks or stumps to catch a glimpse of the creature. Those who were closer stood frozen.

"Get it over with," said Karagan.

"My pleasure," said Caleem, approaching Narraneen and grabbing her hair once again.

She dared to raise her head, her tearful eyes roaming over the bewildered soldiers.

The men were awed by the color of her bright, golden eyes, as well as by her features, still visible through the mud and tears.

Caleem pulled her hair away from her pointed ears. "Look at these ears," he said then chuckled as he pulled the long sword off his back. "Rot in hell, vile creature." He raised his sword high above his head.

Narraneen shut her eyes, taking short, spasmodic breaths.

One of the soldiers turned to look away from the delicate neck.

An archer watched with a disturbed expression, his leg shaking.

"Why do I detect compassion in your eyes?" asked Caleem, lowering his sword. He turned to the soldiers, addressing no one in particular. "Don't let her physical form fool you—it is just a mask. Beneath it, there is wickedness and cruelty."w

The prince approached the hesitant soldier, whose leg still trembled, and pulled him by his leather armor. "Lay down your bow," said Caleem, handing the long sword over to the soldier. Tossing away his bow, the man took the sword in his shaking hands.

Karagan spurred his horse forward. "I have no time for games!"

"Stay where you are!" blared Caleem, pointing at the commander.

The commander laughed. "You have always been impertinent. You may be the prince, but the highest authority on this battlefield is mine. The same authority bestowed on me by your father," said Karagan. "It is only out of respect to your father that I will ignore your last statement and tolerate your presence here for a few moments longer."

Caleem turned his back on the commander and faced the archer. "Your commander is in a hurry. Come on—relieve us of this demon," said Caleem, pointing at Narraneen, who still stared at the ground.

The horrified soldier raised the long sword, trembling with the effort.

"Be careful—don't get her green blood splattered all over you. I've heard it can scorch your skin," said Caleem. "Do it!"

Narraneen stared at the soldier with tearful eyes. As he lifted the sword over his head, the young soldier let out a heavy sigh, as though he were carrying a hefty rock.

Absolute silence reigned among the hundreds of soldiers crowding around them. They all seemed strained, except for Karagan, who exuded an air of boredom.

"Strike her!" the prince screamed into the soldier's ear, spraying saliva onto his face.

The young fighter shut his eyes. He released the sword.

"I can't …" he said, dropping to his knees with a whimper.

"Enough of this," said Karagan. Jumping off his horse, he unsheathed his sword and strode toward Narraneen. "I will show you how it is done." Raising the sword high above his head, he brought it down with full force. As it descended, the blade was intercepted by Caleem's weapon and shattered as if it were made of glass.

"What the hell?" asked Karagan, stumbling backward.

Pointing the tip of his sword at the officer, Caleem threatened, "Consider your next steps carefully!"

Karagan recoiled and then froze as if he had swallowed his tongue.

Caleem approached Narraneen, almost touching her. "Now, take another look at this creature. Is there anyone here capable of hacking off this gentle head?" He voiced his question for everyone to hear.

Narraneen raised her head once more and began to survey the warriors' faces. "Is there anyone here who believes this woman's shape is some kind of an illusion or spell? That this is a dreadful, wicked demon?" Confused, the fighters exchanged looks. Seeking a reply, Caleem looked around but was met only by silent stares. "All my life I had been told about the evil Dalusians and their devious ways, time and time again. I was told they drink blood and kill for pleasure, that they are instruments of the darkness. Yet now, as I look at this Dalusian, that does not seem right."

"What are you trying to do?" asked Karagan, casting away the stump that was left of his weapon. "The prince has been bewitched," said the commander.

"Do you want your head to roll before you?" asked the prince.

"Traitor. That's what you are, a traitor!" said the commander. "Apprehend him, now!" he said to the soldiers nearest him.

"Go ahead, Saffti … and Oulan, apprehend me," said the prince.

The two soldiers didn't even stir.

"Take him prisoner, I said!" Karagan kept his gaze fixed on the men. They avoided his eyes but still didn't budge.

"Unlike you, I was raised with these soldiers," Caleem said.

"You're both traitors. You'll be sent to the gallows," said Karagan, who then turned to other soldiers. "Take him!" he ordered, pointing at Caleem, who only smirked.

Again, the soldiers made no move.

"Traitors! You will all pay for this. Especially you, Caleem Dummah. After our unprecedented progress I don't know what you are trying to accomplish, but you will pay dearly," he said as he, mounted his horse and spurred it on. The soldiers opened the way for him as he rode by.

"He'll soon be back with other officers who are hiding somewhere in the back rows. But I'm not worried about them. Something much more dangerous is making its way here from the south. I ask you to listen to me. I will be brief," he said and cut Narraneen's bindings with the edge of his sword.

CHAPTER 77

SPIKES!

"Beyond the porcupine rock, walk three hundred paces to the east, then you'll reach the cliffs'," Naji read from the magic guidebook as he walked.

"Are you sure there are no rats around?" asked the navigation book.

"There are no rats anywhere," said Naji.

"After this, straight to the Allmother, right?" asked the book.

Naji noticed a strange boulder, hewn in vertical stripes.

"There's the porcupine rock," he said then shot a glance at Zig, who was limping behind him.

"I told you—I'm trying," said Zig. "It's so cold."

"If you'd hurry up, you wouldn't be so cold. Perfect time to sprain your ankle. There they are!" Naji pointed with the book.

Tucking the book back into his shirt, he dashed to the long row of crouching archers, who lined the curved edge of the cliff and shot nonstop. As he was trying to perceive what was going on below the ledge, loud, sharp cries filled the air, accompanied by the clanging of clashing metal. Naji knelt beside the archers, settling down to observe the battle below. The archers paid no attention to him.

A green group of elves were being squeezed against the

rock wall beneath him, besieged by a massive arc of gigantic black figures.

"Guzuds!" said Naji.

Zig crawled up from behind and peered down.

"And the Black Company … Kamanar is down there somewhere," said Zig as the black figures hacked and slashed at the elves.

"So is Akiena. So few against all of them. They have no chance," said Naji as he tried to identify his friend in the melee.

Zig pointed beyond the battlefield. "Over there!"

Naji followed Zig's finger to find two long wagons of extraordinary dimensions, each one fitted with large wheels. Dozens of ox-like beasts pulled the wagons to the rhythm of echoing horns.

"We need help," said Naji. "I have to hurry. I'll go alone. It's not that far—the book knows every shortcut," he said, gazing toward the tree line at the edge of the forest.

"What about me? Asking Gudjewkan for help was my idea."

Naji grabbed a bow and a bundle of arrows that lay in reserve.

"Now you're the thirty-first archer," said Naji and threw the bow and arrows at his friend's feet. Zig sighed and took the bow.

Naji took a dagger from a pile of available weapons, turned, and left.

Zig drew the string and took aim at the Guzuds. The arrow disappeared within the black mass, giving him no indication as to whether he had hit a target. He turned his eyes to the shrinking green cluster. A few of the minuscule figures moved forward, trying to push back the large metal shields, which stood as solid as a thick wall, not budging.

The boy shuddered at the thought of Kamanar being among the fighters. Drawing his bow, he took another shot.

Careful not to be seen, Naji shoved the long dagger into his belt and retrieved the navigation book from his pocket.

"I need to get to the Allmother. Give me the shortest way there," he said to the book.

"Hurray! Home!" The mouth drawn on the book curved itself into a smile. The book opened on its own, and the pages flipped, one after the other, until they stopped.

"'If you look to the north, beyond the cliffs, you will see a small gap in between the mounds of rubble. There lies a hidden passage to the forest'," Naji read.

He shot a final glance back at Zig, who was busy taking aim. He nodded then headed to the rocky edge where he climbed over the rubble until he found himself standing on a small, flat edge.

Two kneeling elves eyed the new arrival.

"Carry on shooting. I'm just passing through … on my way to the forest," he said, pointing to the Turundia Forest while hiding the navigation guide behind his thigh with his other hand.

"No, Zig, dangerous there. Big and dangerous thing there!" said one of the elves.

"I'm Naji," he said, patting his own chest.

"There giant," said the elf, pointing with an arrow at the tree line.

"Where?"

"Tree, look."

Naji caught sight of the top of a tree moving in an unusual manner. "Gudjewkan!"

He quickened his steps, the book open on his palm, and slid into a crack on the rocky ledge. "The hidden passage," he said and descended down the tight, dark passageway.

Resting his bow on the ground, Zig scanned the battlefield for his tall friend. "Where are you?"

Down below, the Guzud shield wall remained strong, as though it had been there forever. The Black Company warriors' long lances moved back and forth in front of the Guzud line in sharp, stabbing motions. Their dark armor blended with the black blur of their big allies.

Every so often, one of the small green figures from the elves' line attempted to break through the wall by lunging at the giants, only to be repelled by a huge shield or a long spear.

The archers poised next to Zig continued to fire without pause, but most of the arrows bounced off the armor while others were lost in the black mass. Zig noticed only a few casualties among the enemy.

The elf next to Zig called his attention to the two humongous wagons that began drawing closer to the battleground from the eastern side. Dark figures prodded the beasts forward with their whips. More Guzuds and other black-clad fighters moved around the strange vehicles. At their rear, a small group of cavalrymen followed, some carrying the deer-head flag on their spears.

Lalandi, the slender commander of the elf archers, got to his feet and issued an order to the elf force, indicating the wagons. Half of the archers trained their arrows on the towing beasts, releasing as soon as the animals came into range. The thick, protective layers of leather affixed to the animals' backs prevented most of the arrows from entering their flesh, yet two of the beasts hitched to the wagon closest to the cliff wall were hit. The elves went on shooting. From behind the wagons emerged four unarmored, orange-furred Guzuds that seemed even bigger than their already giant peers. The only garment they wore was a pair of gray pants. On their backs, they carried massive pieces of equipment made of metal and wood.

Zig's eyes shifted between the massive wagons, the riders advancing from behind the lines, and the four Guzuds who had begun to unload their burden onto the muddy soil, arranging the equipment in a straight line.

Soon, the four were standing beside four catapults. On one end of the beams, metal baskets were fixed. The giants struck the other end of the contraptions' beams with oversized hammers. It sprung up, and dozens of small, black, steel balls, each sporting long spikes. shot out of the iron baskets.

Zig's eyes were glued to the cloud of balls, which flew higher and higher. He couldn't guess whether they were aimed to strike the elves below or the archers beside him.

Lalandi shouted some orders to his men while the unnerved Zig shouted, "Spikes!"

The spiked balls whizzed above his head and he crawled backward in swift retreat. With his arms over his head and face buried in the ground, he braced himself. As the spikes scraped the surrounding rocks with a high screech, he waited with his eyes shut for what seemed like an endless moment.

The screeching stopped. Zig lifted his head to find nasty metal balls everywhere and long scratches on the stone around him. A few elves lay motionless and bleeding next to him. One with a spiky ball stuck in his thigh was able to drag himself upright. The elves ran to pull their wounded peers to safety. Two of them pulled Zig, who noticed a second volley of spiked balls flying toward them. Once again, the numerous balls struck the surrounding rocks, but this time, none of the elves were within their reach.

Following the youthful Lalandi's orders, the dead and wounded were evacuated to the rear. With perfect timing, consecutive salvos of the lethal spiked balls continued to hit the edge of the cliff wall, making it impossible for the archers to return to their position.

Below, the drivers spurred the beasts on, taking advantage of the respite. Lalandi did not wait but ran straight into the falling spiky balls, one of which slashed his right arm. Still, he continued to run. Stooping, he grabbed two backpacks and ran as fast as he could back toward his peers. A moment before he cleared the danger zone, a metal ball struck his back, throwing him face down to the ground. He clung to the bags he carried. Two elves dashed forward and pulled him to safety.

Zig came close, studying the elf with the cropped hair and the face of a child. One of his soldiers removed the metal ball from his back. Its nails were dripping blood. Blood trickled from Lalandi's mouth as he smiled at his friends. Then he closed his eyes. One of the elves shed a tear, got up, and began issuing orders.

The sight of the mounting dead and the endless volleys of spiked balls made it hard for Zig to breathe. He hobbled away while muttering to himself. "A coward. That's what you are!" He took a few more painful steps, placing his weight on his aching foot, on purpose, as a way of punishing himself.

Coming to a halt, he took a deep breath. He spun around and returned to the elves. The new golden-haired commander opened both backpacks and began to distribute wooden birds with long, fine, metal beaks. Zig received one as well.

The small, incredibly detailed mechanism was a work of art. He played with the wings, not knowing what the curious object was for.

The golden-haired elf gave an order. The remaining archers, about twenty in number, stood in line along with Zig.

The commander stood at the end of the formation. Upon her order, they all began to run, keeping a uniform distance from one another. As they reached the edge of the cliff, with an ear-splitting yell, she gave the command to release their devices. Their momentum was such that some elves almost fell off the edge. Last of all was Zig. The boy could not believe his eyes as he watched the mechanical wonders spread their wings to fly away. Moments later, they began to slow down, turning like vultures circling over their prey. They glided, spiraling down.

The volleys of black balls stopped.

The four Guzuds operating the catapults looked up while they scrambled about, trying to escape the spiraling, long-beaked birds. Two who crouched close to the wagons tried to crawl between the wheels. The other two ran in different directions, but the birds came at them from all sides. As the metal beaks stabbed into the orange fur, piercing the flesh, the four Guzuds roared in pain until their booming voices faded out.

Zig was still in awe. The archers returned to their positions and aimed their arrows at both wagons. But the giant carts had already been stationed close to the cliff walls, and the cloth covering them began to tear.

Two enormous figures materialized in front of Zig's eyes, filling him with terror: a pair of wooden statues, each carved in the image of a soldier. With the pulling of heavy chains, their arms extended upwards. Their enormous palms were now at the height of their chins, striking a threatening pose.

The towing beasts were released. Their places were occupied by Guzuds wearing their elaborate plate armor. The Guzuds pulled on more thick chains. Others, using long poles, pushed one of the gigantic statues from behind. To the echoing sounds of Guzuds roaring and the blowing of horns, the first statue started to rise.

Zig and the elves stood helplessly as they watched the giant statue rise to its feet. The stunned archers retreated.

The erect giant tipped and fell forward, and its enormous chest slammed into the high end of the cliff with a loud thud and a tremor that reverberated through the rocks. Its palms halted on the hard edge, creating the disturbing image of a giant clinging to the side of the mountain, its gargantuan head sticking well above the flat, stone edge of the cliffs.

Chapter 78
We Can't Stop Them

Kamanar snatched up a small wooden shield he found lying on the waterlogged soil. He sighed in frustration as he looked at the towering statue leaning against the cliff. "Damn."

He turned back to the large, metal shields deployed ahead. Despite the cracks and grooves on them, they still stood firm, and the black wall remained impenetrable. Before the barrier stood the Black Company warriors with their hexagonal shields and spears, stabbing and pushing the elves back. Each time the elves managed to strike an enemy, the black wall opened to pull the victim in. In a flash, a fresh, new warrior would jump out to replace him. Still trying to break through the siege, the young elves remained in a tight group.

The second wooden statue was erected until it also leaned on top of the cliff, shaking the mountain once more.

Nalahes looked at Kamanar and shook her head. The officer stepped out of the line of elf fighters, leaped forward, and grasped the end of one of the high, rectangular shields. The black soldier nearest her thrust his spear. Kamanar reached, grabbed the shaft, and pulled it. The soldier tried to jostle the weapon free from the tall warrior's grip. Kamanar drove the tip of his sword into the soldier's neck, but it was blocked by the soldier's gorget and slipped sideways. Kamanar yanked the spear again, causing his opponent to lose balance. Wrapping his arm around the soldier's black helmet, he cupped the man's chin and twisted until he heard bones snap.

The soldier's body fell limp.

Kamanar searched for Nalahes. She was almost atop the black barrier when she was thrown off by a sudden jolt of a shield. Several spears were aimed at both Kamanar and the officer. Kamanar intercepted the attack with his small shield, but the force of the blow sent him reeling back into the ranks of the green fighters. The spears threatening the elf woman were blocked by the shields of her comrades, flanking her on both sides. She recoiled and fell. Kamanar helped her up to her feet.

"We can't stop them. It's too late … They're going up!" she cried, pointing at the two giant statues.

"We must break through," said Kamanar, lunging forward.

One of the warriors shifted his hexagonal shield and swung his sword at Kamanar. The tall man dodged the perforated blade and kicked the shield, smashing his opponent against the unyielding black wall.

Kamanar tried to penetrate the barrier again and again until his small, elven sword was shattered into pieces. A shield's blow sent him flying toward his peers, an elf was swept back by his weight, and they both fell to the ground.

An armored Guzud dashed forward. He lifted his huge, rounded hoof above Kamanar then stomped down. A draft of air and splashing mud slapped the tall man, who had barely managed to roll out of the way. Kamanar jumped to his feet, placing the small shield in front of him. The Guzud, who was now in the elven frontline, lunged at Kamanar. Nalahes leaped and struck the giant's helmet with her sword. Faltering slightly from the blow, he regained his balance. He lifted his hammer and went for her.

A thunderous roar stunned all the fighters, and the Guzud

towering over Nalahes froze. Only the clanking of isolated swords continued. All the giants were paralyzed.

A second roar resounded, rattling the fighters' hearts once more. Looking to the north, the Guzuds began to growl to one another, some of them retreating, and the black shield wall finally broke.

Amid the confusion came the long, loud blast of a horn, and the Black Company soldiers disappeared behind the rows of Guzuds.

Along with her confused soldiers, Nalahes stopped fighting. "What now?"

"I think … It's too good to be true," said Kamanar as he, too, looked to the north.

The Guzuds on the northern flank were the first to be attacked. They fled in all directions.

"What is that thing?" asked Nalahes.

An enormous, silver-maned creature rose high above the Guzuds. The monster pushed on one of the massive wooden statues with his huge hands.

"Gudjewkan!" said Kamanar, as excited as a child. "We'd better not be standing here." He pointed at the statue, which was beginning to slide off the edge of the cliff, precipitating a small avalanche of rocks. The statue tipped to the side and crashed to the ground, crushing dozens of frantic Guzuds in its path. Chunks of mud flew everywhere as a cold draft blew over the battlefield.

After toppling the statue, Gudjewkan noticed a group of black archers readying their bows. Grabbing the trunk of a dead tree he had brought from the forest, he marched toward them, snarling with rage. Most of the archers could not even place their arrows on the bowstrings. Others fired, most of the arrows only hitting the trunk.

Ruthless in his advance, Gudjewkan swung the trunk, swatting the entire line of archers off the battlefield. He pulled out the two arrows that had penetrated his shoulder's thick skin and tossed them away. He turned toward the armor-clad Guzuds and slammed them with the trunk as he roared. The Guzuds seemed small next to the formidable beast that battered and broke the bones under their armor.

Chaos reigned among the giants, who only minutes earlier had seemed invincible. Their leader, the single-horned Guzud, rode back and forth on his white, furry beast, all the while emitting orders in guttural groans, even hitting his own soldiers' helmets with his spiky club.

"He's trying to bring them back together," said Kamanar but, when he turned to look, he realized Nalahes was no longer by his side.

She was kneeling over some of the wounded elves nearby. Getting back up, she began to issue orders, reorganizing her fighters. "We must take advantage of this," she shouted as she jammed her sword under the chin of a distracted Guzud who was staring at the formidable aggressor. The Guzud collapsed to the ground. Dozens of elves, joined by Kamanar, thrust and stabbed, renewing the offensive.

"That's my friend!" said Kamanar, pointing to the large monster wreaking havoc among the Guzuds, but the elves around him were too busy dealing with hundreds of giants who were, or were not, battling them.

Gazing north from his vantage point atop a dead Guzud, Kamanar could see dozens of Guzuds running for their lives. Far beyond them, where the field bordered the forest, about ten cavalrymen had huddled together, with the soldiers of the Black Company forming a circle around them. Despite the distance, he recognized the king's red cape. The monarch's retinue kept some distance from Gudjewkan, who was busy letting his wrath explode on the Guzuds, swinging the heavy trunk from side to side. The Guzud commander rode ahead toward Gudjewkan along with a few of his soldiers, who were dragging thick chains behind them.

Tightening the grip on his new sword—a sword with a black hilt and a perforated blade he had picked up from under a dead black warrior—Kamanar said, "They're up to something." He jumped off the dead Guzud and, crouching, made his way forward.

The Guzuds arranged the chains into a grid formation on the mud. Their leader rode his white beast back and forth, grunting to his soldiers. The Guzuds facing Gudjewkan began to retreat while the enraged giant continued his pursuit. The Guzuds who had not been bashed aside by the trunk turned to flee, stepping between the chains. One of them stumbled and fell flat on the wet surface. Gudjewkan tripped going after him.

"Gudjewkan!" cried Kamanar, but he was too far away for the giant to hear him.

Hammers in hand, two Guzuds pounced from the sidelines. The first one hit Gudjewkan over the head before he managed to rise to his feet. Stunned for a moment, the titan staggered, reaching for his forehead. The second Guzud did not delay and dealt him a second blow, which Gudjewkan blocked before snatching the hammer and casting it aside. The Guzud retreated in fear. The Guzud commander emerged, astride his white, woolen beast. A spiked club hung from his waist, and he held a pouch in his hand.

Gudjewkan, still dizzy, turned to face the impending danger. In an instant, the orange-haired leader flung the pouch at the beast's head. Before it could leave his grip, he pulled it back toward him. As the bag tore, spiked metal balls catapulted at Gudjewkan and struck his long face and eyes.

Growling, Gudjewkan covered his eyes and turned away from the assault. He ran toward the forest, tripping on rocks and mounds of earth in his path. The Guzuds hammered him again and again, until he managed to disappear among the trees. His moaning faded in Kamanar's ears.

Gudjewkan's intervention had inflicted great losses among the Guzuds, yet the bulk of their forces remained intact. They began to regroup to the orders of their commander, who seemed to be everywhere at once.

"We must strike him down!" said Kamanar, his eyes on the leader.

Nalahes followed his gaze to the Guzud commander, who looked at them and snarled before losing himself among his troops.

The young elves were forced to retreat. From time to time, the wall of shields opened and hammers were thrown at the elves, smashing and mangling them.

Nalahes and Kamanar found themselves retreating from the advancing wall of shields.

"Why don't we run to the smoke, like you wanted? What are we waiting for?" asked the officer.

"Not just yet ..." said Kamanar. "And right now, I don't think that's even possible. We're being surrounded again."

The advancing Guzuds became even more aggressive than before.

A horrendous roar sounded, and the Guzuds pivoted their shields and stormed the elves in perfect synchrony. Nalahes looked at Kamanar in despair as the limp bodies of her comrades flew through the air, but he was too busy dodging the hammers that slammed down without respite.

CHAPTER 79
HE IS HERE!

"Now that you have heard my words, I ask that you retrace your steps and reunite with your loved ones," said Caleem to the multitude of soldiers surrounding him as he scanned their faces.

Whispering, the soldiers remained in place.

Narraneen glanced with concern at Caleem. The prince took a step forward.

"Go on! Head back home!" he shouted, so that those farther back, who were almost invisible in the fog, could hear. "Go on, I said! The Dark Rider could materialize any moment."

"I must say to you, my prince, that nothing would make these men happier than to return home," came a thick voice.

The soldiers made way for an older warrior to walk through. The warrior tossed his helmet aside, exposing a solemn face with a short beard and disheveled, gray hair.

"Arod," said Caleem.

"My prince," he said with a slight bow. "Allow me to speak the mind of my fellow soldiers … During the last hour, you claimed that the truth is a lie, that black is white, that evil is good, and that our king has summoned a Dark Rider right out of hell to this battleground. This isn't something that can be fathomed with haste."

Knowing how much the men respected the veteran fighter, Caleem listened.

Arod moved to stand in front of Narraneen. "Are you a Dalusian?"

"I am a Dalusian, by Mellethyan naming. We call ourselves elves," she said.

"Allow me, please …"

After glancing at Caleem, she nodded with some hesitation.

Arod removed his leather glove and touched her cheek with his fingertip, all the while fixing his gaze on her eyes. He then looked at the prince before turning to the soldiers. "Who is the best fighter in the corps?"

"Arod!" chanted all the men around him.

"Do you know why I am the best? It isn't because of my father's legendary armor …" He lifted the fine panoply over his head and hurled it away. "And it's not because of this sword," he said while he drew his special weapon then jammed it into the moist ground. "It's not because of the many battles I have endured." He pointed at the long, deep scar across his neck. "I am the best because of my common sense!" He gestured to his head. "This woman has not taken any kind of shape, nor has she cast any kind of spell … And as for our prince, his head has never been more lucid. Every single word he said is the truth."

He drew his sword out of the mud. "I urge you, as your fellow Mellethyan, to heed his advice and go home. Remove all questions and worries from your hearts because today, at this moment, justice is being served as it has never been before."

The prince walked closer to Arod and placed a hand on his shoulder.

Whispers and arguments broke out among the troops. After a brief moment, the heads of hundreds of soldiers, whose silhouettes were amorphous in the fog, began to move south.

"How can you be so sure?" asked one of the fighters, emerging from the rear.

Arod sheathed his sword and approached the soldier. He

pulled the man up by his worn-out armor and brought his face close. "Do you think this is my first encounter with a Dalusian? Have I not fought Dalusians?"

He released the man and turned to the troops. "I had convinced myself that the delicate demeanors I saw wore enchanted masks and that behind those masks were horrible demons. But their faces came back to haunt me and many others. 'I'm just following orders,' I said to myself. Believe me—many veterans feel this way … These pointy-eared people are not so different from us. They dance, they sing, they cook, they laugh, they love. They are compassionate. Today we have a once-in-a-lifetime opportunity. With Prince Caleem on our side, we shall not fear the king's wrath! The winds of hope are blowing in a new direction."

Arod sighed as he watched the rest of the soldiers leaving.

"You are truly a great man. Thank you," said Caleem.

"I deserve no thanks. For I have done many wrongful deeds … I and many others were waiting for this catalyst, for someone as brave as you."

Narraneen covered her mouth with her hands, and a tear trickled down her cheek. "I saw this moment many times in my dreams," she said.

The prince embraced the elf woman. "We did well," he said.

"Don't fool yourselves into thinking that now it's all white and pink roses," said Arod. "It will be very difficult to reason with the people back home. Most men believe what they are told more than what they see with their own eyes. And the king's close circle of corrupted so-called noblemen—peace conflicts with their interests."

"I don't expect it to be easy, but it's a beginning," said Caleem.

"All beginnings are difficult, but I'm optimistic for this one … What about that rider?" asked Arod.

Patting Arod on the shoulder once more, Caleem said, "This evil does not care about friend or foe. Eradication of all is his only desire. You can't help—no one can."

Arod turned around and called the names of some of the soldiers.

The sudden shrieking of agonized men came from the south, and then the clash of metal reached their ears.

"He's here!" said Caleem to Narraneen. Tugging her arm, he led her to Autumn Wind, and she mounted quickly.

"Karagan is dead!" came the cry of one terrified man.

"Run for your lives!" came another.

To the sound of approaching hooves, Caleem unsheathed the sword. He gripped the long hilt and gazed into the fog ahead, attempting to discern the impending threat from among the sounds of screaming soldiers.

As the clatter of hooves became louder, their pace slowed. The horrified soldiers scrambled out of the way.

Straining his eyes, Caleem caught a vague glimpse of a dark figure: a silhouette of a knight of superhuman dimensions riding an oversized stallion. The rider slowed down, coming to a complete halt a short distance from the prince.

The haze surrounding the figure dissipated. The blood in the prince's veins froze; this was the same metal knight he had battled in his nightmares so many times. Seen close up, the rider was like a large statue of bluish metal sculpted with great precision down to the smallest detail: from the noble nose set between his eyes to the sculpted hair that cascaded to the nape of his neck. The metal had been chiseled along the lines of the muscles in his body and adorned with bizarre shapes and characters. On the left side of his chest was the engraving of a strange flower. The metal horse had been cast in a similar fashion down to the last element. It was bigger than any horse Caleem had ever seen. What caught Caleem's attention the most was the long sword the rider held in his metal fingers. The blood-dripping blade was identical to the one he was holding.

"Impressive armor, no doubt," said Arod, addressing the rider. "You've made it thus far … but you will go no farther." The veteran fighter signaled to the soldiers standing around him. They came forward, blocking the rider's way with their trembling swords.

"Dismount! Or we will force you down," said Arod.

The expression on the knight's face remained unchanged. His metallic eyes were fixed on the prince.

"Very well, you've had your chance," said the veteran, signaling to the soldiers again. More soldiers aligned themselves behind the first row of fighters.

Caleem stood his ground, planning his offensive while taking in the shape of the daunting figure. The world around him seemed to slow down, and the light dimmed. Sounds faded, and everything turned blurry except for the knight. The prince couldn't move his eyes from its painful stare. He tried to breathe, but his chest was as stiff as if restrained by undersized armor.

A grave voice resonated in his ears, echoing in his head. "Welcome to the beginning of your path."

The world returned to normality in an instant, and Caleem exhaled. Everyone around was indifferent to what had just occurred; he grasped that only he had heard the Dark Rider.

The knight's sword swung in a flash, striking the soldiers who stood in his way. With a single, broad motion, the formidable weapon hacked all the soldiers in its path, along with their swords. Their bodies, sliced in half, collapsed with a series of short, blood-curdling shrieks. Arod leaped back, barely dodging the blade. The iron horse galloped straight at Caleem, trampling the bleeding corpses lying in its way.

Watching the horrifying scene, Caleem froze in place.

"Get on, quick!" said Narraneen, and, somehow, he found himself on the back of Autumn Wind instead of confronting the threat.

"Hold tight," she said, spurring the stallion away.

Caleem held his sword with one hand while clinging on to the elf's waist with the other. He looked back; the metal knight held his sword up high as he galloped at full speed. His horse's iron hooves crushed the rocks beneath them.

"Don't worry. His end is near," said Narraneen, looking over the prince's shoulders.

Caleem tried to think, but his head couldn't keep up with what was happening. The image of flying, mutilated bodies would not leave his mind. He'd thought he was prepared for a confrontation with the knight, having pictured it so many times in his mind. But in this moment of truth, he was plagued by hesitation and fear.

"We are close," said the elf woman.

Caleem still didn't utter a word. They rode along a gorge that narrowed as they advanced, the knight still on their heels. Narraneen emitted a loud, sharp whistle that hurt Caleem's ears. Autumn Wind shot forward like he had never done before, increasing the distance between them and the demon galloping behind.

The earth began to shake. Huge boulders rolled down the sides of the gorge, leaving waves of dust in their wake.

Only when the knight and his mount had been completely buried in the rubble did Caleem breathe again. "Stop, stop," he said.

Narraneen brought the horse to a halt as clouds of dust covered them. The earthquake stopped, and just a few scattered rocks continued to roll. After the dust had settled, Caleem jumped off the horse, his sword ready. Narraneen followed suit.

"And I didn't want you to come," he said.

She smiled but very soon became serious again. Circling around Caleem, she studied the pile of rocks before them. "I think we stopped him," she said, still staring at the rubble.

"I lost my nerve! *You* stopped him," he said and put his hand on his head. "He said something to me … I could hear his words inside my head."

"What words?"

"I'm not sure."

"It doesn't matter. It's over now. We have to hurry to the cliffs," said the elf, walking toward Autumn Wind, who was still wheezing from the effort.

Dozens of elf fighters materialized from both sides of the gorge and climbed down to the bottom. They spoke with Narraneen while surveying the debris.

"Autumn Wind needs to rest. We'll go on foot, through a shortcut," said Narraneen.

"I don't think we should leave just yet," said Caleem.

The elves around him became alert and disappeared among the rocks.

Figures approached from the south.

He jumped on the rocks, waved both arms, and shouted, "No, please, these are friends!".

Narraneen delivered a loud announcement to the elves. One after the other, they reappeared, their heads covered in their green hoods, their bows ready. As Narraneen walked among them, she pulled back the hoods one by one, instructing the rest to do the same.

Gasping Mellethyan soldiers, led by Arod, appeared from within the fog.

"Where is the bastard?" Arod asked, catching his breath. His sword was drawn and ready. His eyes took in the grave expressions on the delicate faces of the elves surrounding him.

"He's under those boulders," said Narraneen.

The elves studied the soldiers, and the soldiers the elves.

Arod scanned the rubble, then looked up the slopes. "That avalanche was meant for us," he said.

"It was," said Narraneen. "Did you expect to cross the passageway unchallenged?"

"No. Of course not … He was lucky, that pile of tin, that he didn't face me. Here are the demons you've been fighting!" he turned to his troops. "Even their men are nice on the eyes," he said with a chuckle, coming closer to a tall elf. He extended a hand to the green fighter. The latter took his time, but eventually, he, too, stretched out his arm for a firm handshake. The two adversaries smiled at each other awkwardly. The fighters from both sides softened their expressions, coming closer to each other.

"Time for you to head back home," said Caleem.

"Leaving doesn't feel right, my prince. It is tempting, but we want to do more. Isn't that right, lads?" Arod yelled to the men beside him.

"Right!" they all called back.

The prince's feeling of relief faded as quickly as it had appeared.

One of the rocks rolled from the pile. A large metal arm rose from the rubble and began to grope around.

CHAPTER 80
WE MUST KILL THAT ORANGE CREATURE

As Zig lay at the edge of the cliff, his legs would not stop trembling, be it from the biting cold or from his fear. His hopes had disappeared along with the wounded Gudjewkan, who had vanished back into the forest; there was no sign of Naji, either.

He turned his attention toward the elf archers, who had crowded around the statue's frowning face. Some began to strike the thick fingers with their swords, while others tried to dig the rocks from under them. After this failed, they pushed, straining their trembling arms and legs to their absolute limits trying to topple it. But their light, elven boots only slipped on the wet surface, and the massive structure did not budge.

Zig observed the figure from its broad wooden shoulders down to its large feet planted in the marsh below. Several green fighters stood guarding the entrance to the huge feet, trying to block their enemies' way. The few were facing dozens of armored Black Company warriors, who were determined to ascend. Farther along stood a small group of cavalrymen, waiting, remaining outside the range of the few arrows being shot from the cliff top.

Zig gritted his teeth while watching hundreds of stomping Guzuds slamming their hammers at the dwindling elves.

"Kamanar," he cried, trying to find his friend among the pandemonium. He caught a glimpse of a tall fighter battling one of the Guzuds. Zig saw another Guzud coming up from behind, unnoticed by his friend. "Kamanar! Behind you!" he yelled.

The Guzud raised his hammer above the tall man. No matter how loud Zig yelled, his warnings could not reach Kamanar. The hammer landed on the warrior, crushing him to the ground. Zig could only watch the horrifying sight. The two giants turned to look for more victims, leaving the motionless figure on the ground.

A torrent of tears rolled down Zig's frozen cheeks. Ramming his head into the cold rock, he sobbed. Screams coming from below forced him to look down again. The Black Company soldiers had broken through the line of elves, gaining access to the wooden statue's feet. Only the soldiers' upper bodies were visible to the boy as they climbed up a channel cut into the back of the statue, from the feet all the way up to the head.

Zig crawled back. "Naji said to run away."

The elves standing near the statue's head were no longer trying to move it. They had rested their bows and stood poised with their swords drawn, ready to confront the armored aggressors. A pair of elves hurled two bags at the giant head. Crashing against the round wooden helmet, they burst, splashing a liquid that glided along the face and nape of the statue. One of the archers shot a flaming arrow into the wooden sculpture's eye. In a flash, the entire head went up in lashing flames.

The wooden giant's face was engulfed, and the blaze continued to spread to the neck. Another bag was thrown at the back of the sculpture, landing inside the channel. The hidden stairs caught fire, the burning liquid splashing down along them. The two black soldiers leading the march stopped just at the edge of the flames. Behind them were two long columns of soldiers lined down all the way to the feet. Placing the black shields in front of them, they dashed up the burning stairs.

"They're still coming," said Zig as he and the elves watched the undeterred soldiers.

The sculpture's mouth burst open. In an instant, from inside the blazing head, black soldiers began to jump out in pairs, lunging straight at the stupefied elves.

The new commander of the elves called on her soldiers to storm ahead as she led the way.

Zig turned to run away.

"A knife in the chest …" he said and slowed down. "No. I'm not running."

He spun around. His eyes locked on the fiery mouth, which continued to spit out black soldiers.

The black mass became wider, pushing back the elf fighters standing in its path. Zig forced himself forward. Taking the bow off his shoulders, he prepared to shoot, shivering while he looked for a target. As he reached the line of combat, he heard a furious cry. Zig turned and saw a shield coming his way at full force. The blow hurled him into the air. While looking at the gray sky above, he lost consciousness before he even struck the ground.

Kamanar jumped back and rolled on the ground. He crouched down in between two small rocks. Extending his sword and shield, he eyed the two Guzuds he had been fighting a moment earlier. They had lost him in the chaos; he was outside their field of vision, so they'd turned to the elves. Kamanar took a moment to catch his breath. From his hiding place, he watched as groups of Guzuds pursued the remaining elf fighters. Above, the fire at the top of the statue was abating. Among the two ascending lines of black soldiers, Kamanar recognized the king's red cape.

"All is lost," said Nalahes. Kamanar pulled her to him, forcing her to kneel between the rocks. "They're already on the cliffs. It's over!" she said.

"Pull yourself together! Your soldiers are still fighting. Believe me—the enemy will take no prisoners. We have to continue fighting," said Kamanar.

Astride his mount, waving his club, and issuing orders, the single-horned Guzud commander roared.

"He has no helmet on," Kamanar said. "We must kill that orange creature. We can do it."

"We have no bows. Even if we did, it's impossible to strike him, he's too careful. There's no way to get to him. They're defending him fiercely."

"Come," he said, pulling her by the arm. They dashed straight into the mayhem and dodged the walloping blows of hammers.

"Call him," Kamanar said to Nalahes, pointing to a blond elf who was battling three giants. Nalahes issued a command, and the elf jumped back.

"Come with me," said Kamanar.

"We'll outflank them, find a way to slip through and go for the kill," Nalahes explained to the elf. The three wove their way in between the moving shields. By sheer luck, they managed to evade the hammers as they sought to break through the lines. They went deeper and deeper inside the enemy ranks.

"There," said Nalahes, pointing with her eyes, careful not to reveal their intentions.

Breathing heavily, Kamanar saw him on his beast, whose fleecy legs were stained the dark color of the mud.

"Now!" He sprinted at the Guzud. On his left ran the blond elf, on his right Nalahes.

Two Guzuds appeared at their sides, their hammers raised.

"Go!" Kamanar shouted at the elf, prodding him toward the approaching Guzuds. Without flinching, the latter charged, his sword ready.

The two halted, aiming their hammers at the attacking elf. The officer circumvented, finding herself closer to the Guzud commander.

Two groups stormed the infiltrators from both sides. Nalahes pounced on a Guzud blocking her way. She jammed her sword into a small orifice in his helmet. The Guzud slumped and fell.

Kamanar rolled out from under the collapsing body and

bolted toward the Guzud commander, who panicked. Only a few paces away from the indifferent woolen beast, Kamanar tightened his grip on the hilt of his perforated sword. A wall of black shields closed in from the right. Another wall formed on his left. Kamanar was convinced he could squeeze himself in between the two rows before they came together. As he scrambled in the mud, for a moment his eyes met the tiny eyes in the orange head. The rows of shields slammed together. Instead of slowing down, Kamanar ran even faster. He lunged and hoisted himself up onto one of the massive shields and peeked over the top. He launched his sword with all his might, and the perforated weapon spun through the air, straight toward the commander's orange face.

For an endless moment, Kamanar hung on the shield, his eyes following the sword's path. He held his breath, oblivious to the threats around him.

The Guzud commander stared at his attacker. With no sense of urgency, he lifted his spiked club. The loud, metallic clang echoed in Kamanar's ears as the deflected sword flung away and landed in the mud far from its target.

The shield Kamanar was hanging onto tilted then slammed to the ground with him under it. Its owner stomped his huge, round hooves, but Kamanar managed to roll out from under the pummeling force in the nick of time.

Frustrated, he hurled a handful of mud at the giant shield wall, which swung open and made way for more rising hammers. The unarmed Kamanar had no choice but to break into a run and retreat.

CHAPTER 81
ONLY THROUGH PAIN

The metallic knight's body began to rise from under the rubble. His chiseled, statue-like face confronted a shocked Caleem.

Caleem charged.

Racing in between the rocks, he lifted the long sword with both arms above his head while his eyes fixed on the knight's hard face. Caleem brought the sword down with all his strength, striking the neck. The weapon bounced, as if it were made of wood. A painful tremor went through Caleem's arms from the vibrating metal. He struck again, but the sword ricocheted once more.

The knight freed the rest of his body from under the debris and loomed over the dwarfed man. In one swift movement, he swung at the prince, who jumped back using all his energy. Whistling as it split the air, the tip of the blade cut across Caleem's chest.

The prince staggered backward and folded over in pain. Touching his wound, he found the long, bleeding cut was superficial and had only scratched his ribs. He continued to retreat, all the while watching the stiff iron face fixed upon him.

"Go on! Cut this demon into a thousand pieces!" Arod shouted to his men, going for the rider.

"No!" said the prince.

The soldiers attacked, striking and stabbing the knight from all sides. The knight's shoulders and head rose high above the men, his face still fixed on Caleem.

With the sound of a metal blow, the entire front row of fighters was thrown back. Most of the men lay dead, their swords and shields shattered, and long, deep cuts bleeding across their torsos. Others twisted in the mud and shrieked.

The Dark Rider struck again, slashing through the rest of the soldiers as if they had no armor.

"Run away, you idiots. Run!" yelled Caleem. "Get out of here," he said to Narraneen, pushing her. Throwing an anxious glance at the prince, she turned and ran.

Some of the soldiers managed to retreat, but all those within reach of the long blade fell dead in an instant.

Caleem fled.

"What am I doing?" the prince muttered to himself.

Arod's voice resounded from behind. "Die, son of evil."

Caleem watched the veteran, who hung from the knight's back, stabbing his neck again and again. The metal fingers reached behind the dark-blue shoulder, grabbed Arod's armor, and sent him catapulting into the air until he landed on a pile of rocks.

Getting back on his feet, Arod prepared to charge.

"You have no chance … Let go!" said Caleem, pulling on the veteran's shoulder.

Arod shook off Caleem's hold. "Leave me be. I can do it!"

He wove around his men's dead bodies, looking for a chance. The knight thrust his sword straight through Arod's middle, impaling him. The long metal arm stretched upward and held the body on the blade like a piece of meat on a skewer. In a final effort, the wounded warrior stabbed the metal face with a dagger, sending sparks flying but inflicting no damage.

Arod turned his head to the prince. "A crack … in his back

…" he muttered, blood spouting from his mouth. Fighting to keep his eyelids open, he nodded at the prince before going limp.

The knight strode toward the prince, letting Arod's body slide off the bloody blade.

Enraged, Caleem clenched his jaws and charged. Leaping into the air, he aimed for the flower on the armored chest. The sword bounced off along with Caleem. The knight's weapon whirred down. Caleem jumped back, barely escaping, and scrambled away. The knight lunged again. Caleem rolled aside with his sword. The blood-dripping blade crushed the rocks on which the prince had lain an instant earlier. The prince jumped to his feet, hacking at the knight's foot; he felt like he was poking a rock with a stick. Caleem went for the waist, failing to make even a dent.

"Mazahratee was wrong … This sword does nothing to him!" he cried.

"Arod said something about a crack in his back," said Narraneen, who stood nearby.

The long sword came at him once more. He tried to intercept the blade with his own, but the blow was so strong his sword was ripped from his hands. It spun in the air and landed some distance away. Caleem noted that the knight's face had finally shifted away from him to his sword.

The knight stretched out his empty hand. To Caleem's astonishment, the sword's hilt, which was poking from between some rocks, lifted, and the sword began to move toward the armored fingers, its blade scraping the ground.

The prince dashed forward and snatched the rising hilt. Feeling the strong, jerky starts of the knight's supernatural pull, he had to tighten his grip on the weapon. "You want it? Come and take it," he said.

The knight lowered his arm and advanced in his direction. As Caleem prepared to flee, the Dark Rider widened his steps, quickening his stride.

"Where are you running to?" shouted Narraneen, joining him.

"I don't know!" Caleem shouted back.

The Dark Rider increased his speed, his feet smashing the rocks beneath them. Seeing the knight closing the distance, Caleem headed toward a small waterfall streaming from a cliff above. He waded into the water then jumped up in hopes of scaling the rocky wall. Glancing back, he saw the knight right behind him and ready to strike. In his haste, Caleem dropped the sword. He was pinned. He turned away, pushed his forehead against the rock wall and shut his eyes, waiting for the fatal blow. The sword cut through the air, then a loud bang shook the rocks, followed by silence. Dumbfounded, Caleem peered back. The Rider's blade was stuck in the rocks, inches from his ear. He reached down to the water for his own sword, but the big metal hand blocked him. He felt a pull on his shirt, then his whole body rose. He found himself face to face with the Dark Rider. The knight slammed him against the rocks, crushing his ribs. Acute pain pierced through his chest, and the gasping prince tried to resist, but the rigid fingers held him in a firm grip, slamming him once more against the wall. Caleem could taste the blood rising from his lungs.

"Must …" he mumbled.

The knight was ready to smash him again.

The prince's thumping heartbeat hammered in his head, along with that surreal feeling he had before.

"Ascension will arise only through pain," the knight's voice echoed again.

Seized by some kind of desperate madness and struggling for breath, Caleem squirmed, wriggling himself free. His body hit the icy waters, leaving the metal hand holding only his shirt. The freezing temperature made breathing even more difficult, yet he was able to wrench out his sword. Wading in the shallow stream, he gained a bit of distance from his assailant. His upper body was bare and wet, and he coughed blood into the current.

As he watched the Dark Rider pry the other sword free, Caleem caught a glimpse of a deep crack in his solid back. The rider turned, starting his pursuit once more.

Spitting blood and saliva, the prince retreated, barely able to make his way through the water. He faltered and felt a stabbing pain with every breath he took. The bleeding cut across his chest was deeper than he thought.

"Down!" said Narraneen from somewhere.

He glimpsed a long line of elf archers, ready with strung bows. Their aim seemed to be on him. He threw himself into the pool. Dozens of arrows whizzed by, followed by the clinking of metal. The knight's torso was engulfed in a fiery sphere of sparks.

"You're freezing," said Narraneen as she helped the prince get back to his feet. Leaning on the elf, Caleem hobbled, the long blade dipping in the water. The arrows continued to fly. Only once they passed the archers and were safe behind the line of fire did they look back. Despite the flashing sparks, the knight advanced, undeterred, his still eyes locked on Caleem.

The shooting stopped. They all scrutinized the target. Despite having obliterated some of the inscriptions on the metallic body, the arrows had not caused any damage.

Light drops fell from the gray skies, soon turning into heavy rain. Dropping their bows, the elves drew their swords.

"No. No!" Caleem yelled at the top of his lungs then coughed.

Narraneen shouted, but the elves seemed determined. In a synchronized move, they all lunged to attack.

The knight's long sword swung from side to side with its strange whirring sound, cutting through the elves and their weapons effortlessly.

Narraneen turned her gaze away.

"Fools," said Caleem. "It's impossible ... He can't be stopped!" His voice was drowned out as he stared at the horrific scene.

CHAPTER 82
TAKE ME TO CRIANDO

Marbel opened the squeaky door and walked out onto the porch carrying a clay lantern.

It was near dawn, and the world was still enveloped in darkness. Stretching his arms, the chubby old man yawned. He headed toward the crumbling wooden barn, shielding the flame from the gentle wind with his palm.

After placing the lantern on an old ladder near the doorway, he took two wooden buckets off the hook and grabbed his small stool. His cow mooed at him. "A good morning to you, too, Jasmine. How are you today?" Marbel placed the stool next to the stall and shoved the first bucket under the cow.

"How much juice do you have for me?" he asked, milking the animal.

A bucket and a half later, he hung the stool up once again. He opened the gate and prodded the cow out of the barn. The little cow strolled out into the field bordering the house and began to graze.

"Enjoy."

He blew out the candle and, leaving the lantern on the ladder, took the buckets and headed back home. Inside, he glanced at the bed. His wife lay covered from head to toe. His two daughters were curled up on either side of their mother. The flame of the candle above the headboard was making its last flickers before dying out.

Smiling, Marbel headed out to the field.

"Don't forget that spot over there," he said to Jasmine, pointing at a rock surrounded by dense grass.

The skies brightened. A wide orange stripe stretched over the horizon, signaling the arrival of dawn. Marbel began tilling the soil while humming a joyful tune. Row after row, he plowed the brown earth. The sun rose fast, and its warm rays started to punish his sweaty neck. His stomach began to rumble.

"Breakfast time," he said, tossing the hoe.

Wiping the sweat from his forehead, he walked toward the old fig tree at the far side of the field, climbed up the twisting trunk, and plucked a few fruits. He whistled a melody on his way back home.

"Daddy … Daddy," cried the two little girls as they saw their father approaching. The two curly-haired children ran to him.

"My two little big loves," he said, lifting them up and twirling them around.

"Late for breakfast? That's rare," said his wife as she set the small round table on the porch.

"Eating outside. I love it."

"The sun is pleasant—not too strong," she said and sat down.

"It is." He planted a long kiss on his wife's cheek.

"Come on, girls," she called to her daughters, who were huddling over an insect.

"Come on, I'm hungry. Do you want me to have you two for a side dish?" asked Marbel.

The table was set with a bowl of creamed cheese, pickled olives, and six boiled eggs—three for Malika and the girls and three for him. As was the custom every morning, wrapped in a white piece of cloth at the end of the table was a freshly baked loaf of bread. Its aroma drove Marbel crazy. "Raisin bread, my favorite."

He took the figs out of his pocket. "One got squashed—not a big deal," he said, setting them on the tabletop. "These are for dessert."

Marbel unwrapped the warm bread and tore it into chunks. He noticed his spouse's expression turning gloomy, her big eyes becoming moist. He became serious despite himself.

"What a wonderful thing … if Criando were here, with us, having breakfast …" she said, tears streaming down her cheeks.

The bread fell from his hands

"Criando …" he said. "Criando!"

Marbel was woken by his own voice. He found himself in his cart under a balcony. The rain pounded the roofs above and ran down the trees opposite the building. Exhaling, the older man gazed ahead as raindrops fell from leaf to leaf and then onto the thick foliage covering the trunks, ultimately splashing down on the cobblestones.

Lightning lit up the sky, followed by the rumble of thunder.

"Is everything all right?" asked Ansseur, appearing as if out of nowhere and wearing a hood over his head. He walked quite fast, using the white cane to feel his way. Ansseur tapped the base of the cart with his stick. "Marbel," he called again.

"Nothing is right," said the old man. "Kamanar, Caleem, and the lads are fighting, right now, alongside the elves and against my friends. And probably against my son."

"I would like to comfort you with some good news, but there is none. The ravens returning from the battlefields carry disturbing news. It's just a matter of time now … On the other hand, if they win, your son wins," said Ansseur, bending down to lean on the cart.

"It's a sad ending anyway. Fate has betrayed us—Mazahratee's prophecy was nonsense. It's all nonsense. Even if Criando were to stay alive, what kind of life would he have under the wing of that tyrant? There is no justice in this world. You know, Ansseur, I'm no elf, and yet, I can feel my friends' distress. Fear and despair have been gnawing at me from the moment the two boys left. Everything will be lost."

Both men sat in silence under the balcony.

"What will become of all who stayed?" asked the older man. "The elderly and the young elves?"

"And the invalids."

"No one is evacuating. We all want to face the end here, be it the flood or fighting that evil knight—whatever comes first. You don't have to stay. I can arrange shelter for you in the mountain. There is still time."

"This is the end of the road for me."

Behind Ansseur's cloak, Marbel saw Mazahratee hurrying past them. The counselor seemed anxious, almost terrified.

"Who is it?" asked Ansseur.

"Mazahratee."

"Counselor, wait," Ansseur called as he rose. But the counselor had already vanished along the path leading to the tower. "I'm going after him," said Ansseur.

"Take me with you," said Marbel, rising in his cart.

Ansseur tossed his staff into the vehicle and pushed it down the path in the pouring rain.

"A bit to the right," said Marbel. The path sloped downhill, and the nervous Marbel gripped the railing inside the cart. Branches smacked his face and arms.

"Stop!" said Marbel when he spied Mazahratee, wet to the bones, crouching behind a tree.

Ansseur steadied the cart, bringing it to a stop. "We're not at the tower yet," said Ansseur.

"If you weren't mostly blind, I'd be mad," said Mazahratee, waving with his hands. "Over here, behind me."

"The enemy?" asked Marbel as he wiped his wet face with his hand.

Ansseur pulled the cart to the counselor's nook. Mazahratee's gazed above the trees. The clouds showered the world with rain.

"Just one," said the counselor, his head shifting back and

forth from the top of the tower to the clouds. "I saw it a moment ago, flying above."

"The winged creature?" asked Marbel. "What does it matter? Nothing matters anymore."

The counselor brushed the gray hair from his forehead, exposing his grave, aging face, and stared at Marbel with his tiny eyes. Lightning flashed, lighting up Mazahratee's figure. "If I'm going, I'm going fighting. I'll be smiling when I cross to the other side," the counselor said and gripped the hilt of a sword hidden in the folds of his cloak.

"Words to my liking," said Ansseur.

"But I'm not planning on leaving any time soon. As long we're moving, we're winning," said Mazahratee.

"Moving isn't one of my stronger attributes anymore," said Marbel

"Too bad for you," said Mazahratee.

"Good luck on your going out in a blaze of glory," said Marbel.

"What's it up to?" asked Ansseur, blindly staring beyond the bushes to the square.

There was nobody to be seen among the puddles, nor was there anything in the sky.

"It was here earlier, flying in circles … There it is!" said the counselor, pointing up.

Between the clouds, the bat-winged creature appeared, carrying something.

"Is it flying above shooting range?" asked Ansseur, facing in that direction.

It vanished again behind the treetops.

"It's spying. Caleem said that was its purpose," said Marbel.

"Yes, but what—" Mazahratee began but stopped as dozens of black balls descended on the tower and the square. The spiked balls whistled as they fell and crashed on the stones, bouncing and scattering all over the tiled surface.

"They're not hitting anyone," said Marbel.

"Maybe it's trying to lure the elves out. Maybe it's trying to stir fear," said Ansseur.

The winged demon emerged once more, flying lower this time, holding a rock and releasing it over the spherical structure. The stone struck the top and shattered tiles. The winged creature disappeared only to return with another load. A group of hooded, old elves came running out of the tower. Mazahratee shouted at them, but they didn't answer and instead disappeared through the gateway to the western trail. There they met a group of young elves. The counselor yelled a warning to them, too, sending them scrambling away into hiding.

"I don't know which are more foolish, the elderly or the young," he said.

Marbel threw his weight to the side of the cart, overturning it. He pushed himself out and crawled as fast as he could toward the center of the square.

"What are you doing?" asked Mazahratee, fuming.

"Marbel!" cried Ansseur.

Marbel used his arms to pull his incapacitated body farther into the square under the pouring rain. Using his stick, Ansseur raced after Marbel then stooped over him.

"What's come over you? Get back!" he said.

Marbel continued, crossing a puddle. At the center of the square, he turned onto his back, sopping wet and covered in mud.

"Are you insane?" asked Ansseur, bending down to grab his friend's foot.

"Leave me alone!" screamed the old man.

Ansseur began to pull the invalid back. Marbel grabbed one of the spiked balls.

"If you don't let go of me now, I'll—" he said, blood dripping from his fingers.

Ansseur relaxed his grip.

"I know it seems hopeless. I feel the same," said Ansseur.

"Let me be. Please!" The chubby man looked at Ansseur's scarred face then to the sky. The creature was approaching, clutching another rock in its claws. "Be careful! Here it comes!" said Marbel, throwing the spiked ball away. Ansseur spun around to return to the counselor.

"Get him back here!" shouted Mazahratee.

Ansseur mumbled something, triggering an intense debate between the two men.

Marbel lay on his back. "I'm here, you oversized bat-chicken!" he shouted, flailing his arms, mimicking a chicken and laughing as hard as he could.

The creature spiraled down, releasing the rock.

Mabel rolled to the side. The rock crashed where he had been a moment before and bits of shattered tiles showered his body. The chubby man continued to laugh hysterically. "Missed me. Who would send a cross-eyed bat-chicken to do a … vulture's job?" he asked, laughing even louder under the rain and flashing skies.

The dark-skinned creature left and soon returned with another load and swooped down to drop the rock on Marbel. He rolled over on the tiles, and the creature missed again.

The whole square trembled to the echoing of thunder.

"You are even uglier than I remember," Marbel shouted. Hoisting himself up with great effort to sit on one of the rocks, he went on roaring with laughter. While the rain washed his face, his eyes were fixed on the creature.

The thing circled back toward the man. Folding its wings, it swooped down, accelerating as it dove head-on for the madman. Marbel could now distinguish the four tightly curved horns on the creature's head. He froze as he held his breath.

"Marbel!" cried Ansseur, rushing toward his friend.

Its wings hissed as the creature glided close to the ground with amazing speed. It rammed Marbel and went on.

Ansseur stopped in his tracks, unable to comprehend what had happened. Squinting against the sudden glare of lightning, he faintly saw the chubby man clinging to the creature and rocketing upward. Swinging in the air, the two of them hit the top of a lofty tree. Screams and screeches echoed across the square as tree branches shook. Mazahratee pulled Ansseur toward the tree, but the winged demon flew off again with Marbel hanging onto its back. In a moment they faded beyond the clouds.

Marbel pulled the belt looped around the creature's neck hard with his right hand while his left held onto the curving horns. He pushed his face into its rigid back. The creature batted its wings, thrashing the man, trying to free itself from the stranglehold.

"I'm not letting go … not letting go!" screamed Marbel, pulling the belt even tighter, undeterred by the sharp claws shredding his sleeves and skin.

The creature shrieked and squirmed as it tried to tear the belt loose. Marbel tightened the belt more, until the creature could not scream anymore and its wings slowed.

"I'm not letting go. Take me to the battlefield. Take me to Criando!" said Marbel, lifting his head and opening his eyes for the first time. Below, beyond the freakish head, he saw an amazing spectacle: a sea of gray clouds lay beneath them, and higher above were white clouds sprinkling snowflakes that began to cover his arms and shoulders and most of his face. On the horizon, between the blankets of clouds, enormous whirlwinds of snow twisted. Lightning like giant roots flared right before Marbel's eyes, followed by an explosion that hurt his ears.

Screaming, the chubby man buried his face into the back once again. "Criando!" he screamed.

The wings' flapping settled into a steady rhythm, and the creature maintained its course. Marbel loosened the belt a bit, his trembling hand ready to pull again if needed.

"I know you understand me. Take me to the cliffs now, or it will be the end of both of us … Take me there, you owe it to me!" Marbel screamed in the creature's ears, making sure he was heard above the powerful winds lashing at them.

"Criando!" he called again and smiled.

Before his eyes stretched the great peaks of the Mobinar impaling the gray mattress of clouds. The winged creature began its descent, diving below the clouds between two mountains. Marbel discerned movement on the landscape far below: black fighters were huddled behind a strange, cone-shaped, turbulent wind. The creature began to glide down in a wide spiral. Marbel tried to figure out what was going on beneath.

"Down!" said Marbel. "Criando!" he shouted, but his cry was lost in the wind.

With a sudden jolt, the winged creature rolled upside down, dropping the man.

Marbel fell.

CHAPTER 83
KILL ME!

Careful to avoid slipping in the mud, Kamanar stooped as he ran, again snatching a sword from the hand of a dead soldier.

It was past noon. The cold had become harsher, made even worse by the drizzle. The wet earth could not absorb any more water, and pools were forming in the Guzuds' deep, rounded footprints, which were scattered throughout the vast area.

The small group of surviving elves drifted to the south end of the field, forced together against the rock walls by the large shields and heavy hammers closing in on them. Kamanar threw himself down from behind the last row of Guzuds. Rolling, he emerged on the other side and joined the elves. Their soaking green cloaks had been tainted brown and red. Despite the dire situation, the young fighters continued to pound the high metal shields to stab the Guzuds hiding behind them.

Someone lunged at Kamanar from the side, bringing them both down to the ground. Before pushing the attacker away, he saw it was Nalahes.

"We should never have descended the cliffs. It's all your fault!" she said, her face stained with mud. Her wet hair was loose, and her purple eyes had a crazed look.

"Judge me later. Your soldiers are still standing firm. Get up and fight by their side," said Kamanar, shoving her aside and getting back on his feet.

Lying on the ground, she began to cry. Kamanar saw that the elves were still resisting the wall of Guzuds. Feeling confident for a moment, he approached Nalahes. Another elf came, and they both helped her up. The elf tried to talk to her calmly.

"It's all over … We failed. They will wreck the bridge. Anathoria will be no more. All because of me," she said.

Kamanar pulled on the elf's cloak.

"She isn't well. Take her behind the lines. Don't let the others see her like this," he said before hurrying back into combat.

"I never wanted to be a fighter, I never wanted to hurt anyone," said Nalahes, leaning on the elf.

Her hand relaxed its grip on the sword, which the defeated elf officer did not even bother to pick up. Their short march was disrupted by the deafening sound of an explosion coming from behind. The Guzuds had broken through the elves' line of defense, beating and squashing them with their hammers.

The elf whispered something in Nalahes's ear. After setting her down near a small rock, he drew his sword and raced to help his friends.

Nalahes surveyed the battle scene as she sat crying. The elf who had just left her charged at one of the Guzuds, who, before her very eyes, slammed his hammer into the elf's chest, sending him flying back. His body slid in the mud, leaving a smooth trail until it came to a stop near Nalahes's feet. When she looked into her dead friend's open eyes, she screamed and kicked her feet. Crawling away from the corpse, she stumbled upon the body of another elf victim, its face buried in the dirt.

The officer pushed herself back up to her knees only to see Kamanar besieged by warriors in black armor. Even after they lay dead, her subordinates were being battered by hammers. The blows never stopped. Nalahes pulled her hair, her crying only getting louder.

"Kill me," she shrieked with her eyes closed. "Finish me!"

She sat waiting for the final blow amid the screams of her young soldiers and the clashing of steel.

She heard a roar and growl that sounded like a bizarre chuckle. Filtering out all the other noises and focusing her eyes, she found herself staring at the one-horned leader beyond the rows of Guzuds. His cranium and shoulders rose above the Guzuds swarming around him. He was delighted, and his malevolent laughter pummeled Nalahes's head. She gritted her teeth, her breathing grew heavier, and her heart began pounding. Fixing her eyes on the orange head, despair and fear gave way to hatred and fury.

Although she remained motionless, her breathing and heartbeat accelerated as though she were sprinting. Out of the corner of her eye, she caught a glimpse of a broken spear. The spearhead was intact, still attached to a what remained of the shaft.

Nalahes drew it out of a puddle while her eyes remained locked on the leader's wide face. The Guzud commander, astride the white beast, continued to joyfully dole out orders.

Both Guzuds and elves became as insubstantial as shadows to the elf officer; their battle cries faded from her ears. Only one thing stood out in sharp contrast against the blur: the Guzud commander. Dashing forward, undeterred by any danger, she was dominated by one thought only.

Kill!

After only a few paces taken at astounding speed, she broke through the Guzud line. Nalahes jumped up onto a big, armored corpse. She held her breath as she launched herself over the black shields. She flew above the enormous helmets, over the first, second, and third rows. Her impetus was so great that none of the hammers could reach her.

The elf raised the spearhead above her head, poised to hit her target. Her eyes locked on their objective, not wavering even once. The only sounds she heard were the whistling wind and the pounding of her heartbeat.

Drawing his club in a panic, the Guzud commander lost his grip and dropped the weapon.

Nalahes's body curved backward like a sickle as her hands tightened on the spearhead. With unrelenting determination, she jammed the weapon right between the tiny eyes of the gape-mouthed giant.

She crashed into the Guzud, and they fell together and landed in the mud. The white furry beast, now without its rider, trudged aside. Nalahes found herself staring into the commander's vicious, still face. Blood gushed around the spear buried deep in his forehead.

Nalahes rested on the giant's chest for a moment. She thought she heard her name being called. Turning her head, she found Kamanar looking at her from behind dark figures. Nalahes gazed at him dreamily, a smile appearing on her face.

Kamanar's mouth opened in a shout, but she was detached.

"Nalahes, watch out!"

As soon as she understood his words, she turned. A hammer head was coming her way. She held up the wooden shield. It shattered on impact, and she was sent tumbling in the air until she landed, motionless, on the muddy ground.

Kamanar fell silent. Clenching his teeth, he kicked aside a Guzud's iron shield. The giant struck back with his hammer and Kamanar dodged, rolling away. In between dozens of thick Guzud hooves stamping about him, he went for Nalahes's prostrate body.

He dashed, bent low to the ground to make his way in between the mayhem of thumping hammers and armored legs. He managed to get lost in the black mass, his small, crouching figure going unnoticed. When he reached Nalahes, he turned her on her back. No sooner had he lifted his head up to assess the danger than he saw that all the Guzuds were looking in the opposite direction. Grunting and roaring, they were pointing at their fallen leader.

Kamanar dragged Nalahes by her hands across the wet

surface. He glanced at her pale, dirty face and his heart shriveled. "To hell!" he said. "I've only known you for a couple of days, and already my heart is aching for you."

He carried her in his arms. A few paces farther, they entered the green cloaks' zone. Sighing, he fell on his knees. He swept back Nalahes's hair and wiped the mud from her face. He placed his ear above her pink lips. Hearing one breath was enough to elicit a smile.

"You are alive," he said.

He got back to his feet and carried her over to the cliff wall where he hid her behind a boulder. He stayed on a moment longer, contemplating her serene face speckled with raindrops. He could not help but steal a kiss from her warm lips before covering her body with the big shield.

"I hope we … Sleep here until it's over."

Kamanar grabbed an abandoned, hexagonal, black shield, clasped his sword, and turned to the battlefield.

To his astonishment, the elves stood close to the giants' front line, but they were not engaged in combat. They stood with their weapons and shields ready, talking among themselves. As he got closer, he noticed the Guzuds were wary of the elves but were more focused on glancing behind at their leader's corpse. They grumbled and growled, pushing and shoving their peers in some sort of disorganized retreat.

"The orange head is dead. We must take advantage of the confusion," Kamanar shouted.

"Nalahes is hurt!" said one of the elves.

"Nalahes is all right, but she will no longer be your commander. Do you remember why we gave up the high ground?"

"Columns of smoke!" said a green-haired elf girl, whose face was caked in mud.

"Exactly. We must run to the smoke," he said. "Everyone, run to the smoke, and I promise you victory!"

The green-haired girl looked left and right, exchanging a few words with her peers. The Guzuds continued to retreat.

"Nothing left to lose," she said.

The young elves ran.

"I will be right behind you," Kamanar shouted.

As he followed, Kamanar noticed the big, four-legged beast strolling among the remaining Guzuds. He dodged through the confused giants and ran straight toward it. Grabbing the white fleece, he hoisted himself up and straddled the freakish creature's back. He found himself surrounded by hundreds of Guzuds, who soon recognized the tall figure sitting above the tumult. They growled and raised their hammers.

"Giddyup!" Kamanar tried to spur on his mount, but it didn't budge.

Bleating, the animal broke into a sudden wild run, trampling anything that stood in its way.

Clinging to the velvety wool, Kamanar kept trying to get the beast to move in one direction, but it darted, making random turns. The pain of stretching his legs enough to remain astride the wide back was offset by a surprisingly smooth ride. To his good fortune, the beast carried him past the Guzud crowd.

His enthusiasm was short-lived: the creature was heading away from the columns of smoke. Kamanar felt a sharp prick on his right hand. He frisked the soft, braided fleece with his fingers, soon finding the object. It was the dead commander's spiked club. He pulled, disentangling it from the fleece until he had a firm grip on the heavy weapon. He poked the enormous right flank with the thorny end, and the beast turned to the left. Now equipped with the means to control the animal, he prodded it away from the Wall Cliffs.

"Your stupid commander sends his regards from orange heaven," he shouted, raising the club over his head. "I'm keeping this, as a reminder of my brief friendship with one-horned orange head."

As per Kamanar's instructions, the green fighters still raced toward the smoldering columns in the distance. Nudging his mount, he found himself riding alongside them.

The entire army of raging Guzuds was now in pursuit.

Soon, the elves reached the smoking columns, but they stood there, seemingly engaged in an argument.

Kamanar yelled, "A line! Form a long line."

They complied, and Kamanar rode past the elves and the smoke, poking the white animal in the head to make it slow down. The ground under him shook from the stampeding Guzuds' heavy footsteps.

Bringing the beast to a halt, he commanded the elves, "Split up and flank me. Over here."

Racing past the smoke, the elves came to stand on either side of Kamanar, facing the fast-approaching Guzuds. He considered turning the animal around to face the giants, but he gave up on the idea and instead stood up on its almost flat back.

"Be prepared," he said, brandishing the club above his head. "Come on, you blobs of fat! We're ready for you," he shouted at the top of his lungs.

The elf who stood nearest the beast asked, "Be prepared for what?"

One of the fighters took a step backward.

"Stand your ground. Trust me this one last time," said Kamanar.

The elf returned to his spot and took a deep breath, his gaze turning once more to face the enemy.

"Hold the line, no matter what. Nobody charge," Kamanar said and turned his attention to the black mass of Guzuds racing their way.

The earth trembled. Kamanar and the elves stood frozen, while the white beast became restless. "Everything will be over in a moment … I hope," Kamanar said and jumped off the animal, which galloped away in terror of the impending stampede.

The Guzuds raised their hammers as they drew close. Those at the head of the line shoved their peers, trying to get to Kamanar.

"Come and get me!" Kamanar yelled.

The tall man's eyes swept over the ground beneath the black

mass, then shifted to the jittery elves, who stood firm, holding their small shields and swords.

Taking a deep breath, Kamanar returned his gaze to the first Guzuds, whose eyes were fixed on him as they accelerated.

"Too close … damn it!"

CHAPTER 84
BE BRAVE

Motehro sat up in the dark cage. His relentless efforts to free his hands had resulted in deep gashes. He tried pulling, biting, disentangling, and rubbing the thin ropes against splinters protruding from the wooden bars. He even spat on and cursed the ropes, but to no avail. The frustration pushed him to his wit's end, and he gave up.

It seemed so long ago that his friends had abandoned him to the mercy of the rodents. He could not even tell night from day. The only thing he could see from his gloomy confinement was a boulder that reflected a dim, flickering light. Occasionally, the light was obstructed by the silhouettes of pointy-eared, furry rodents. His blood froze each time his squeaking and screeching captors approached the cage, often lashing their claws at him. But as soon as they disappeared, his horrors vanished with them, allowing him to go back and hide in his thoughts.

Motehro's nostrils had become accustomed to the foul odors filling the moldy air. Although he hadn't had a bite to eat in days, he felt no hunger. The drops of water trickling down one of the bars were enough to moisten his tongue. Leaning over from his corner to lick the wet bar every few hours was his only activity.

"Damn you, Grandpa!" said Motehro after several days of complete silence. He stood up. "Damn you."

Furry figures leaped from beyond the rock, their squeaks and tapping claws getting closer.

"Don't worry—I'm still here. Where would I go?" he asked, glaring at the dozen nefarious rats congregating around the cage.

"It's all your fault, Grandpa," he said, pacing. "Be brave!" he said and giggled. As he strode back and forth, he began to recall that fateful moment when he sprung to Naji's rescue. "So stupid."

The rodents searched around the cage, trying to figure out who the captive was talking to.

One of the rats lashed out at Motehro.

"Leave me alone!"

One by one, the rodents receded, leaving him to continue with his soliloquy. His revolving thoughts and memories propelled him to replay the events of that day when he, his brother, and his grandfather went to Shark's Fin Beach.

The sun had long risen, its light flooding the world. Motehro and his older brother Rialto had been waiting for their grandfather.

"Let's join these guys, until Grandpa comes," Rialto had said. The two had approached a group of children playing with sticks and doing all sorts of acrobatics.

"Go on—ask them," said Rialto.

"You ask!" said Motehro.

"Can we play with you?" asked Rialto.

One of the older kids approached. "Sure, you can. Know how to play Ambush?" he asked.

"No," said Motehro.

The boy pointed to the closest palm tree. "Go stand by that tree." And so they did. The boy winked at his friends. The group huddled around, all of them quiet before the boy screamed, "Ambush!"

All the kids threw their sticks at the two brothers. "Ambush, ambush," they chanted.

Rialto threw back a few random sticks, but Motehro ran, tugging his brother along behind him.

"Dumb brats. I'll get them one day," said Rialto.

Motehro was shaken but didn't say a word.

"Never go where you are not invited," said their grandfather, who appeared out of nowhere.

"But they started it," said Motehro.

"Never mind. Now, come along."

The two brothers followed their grandfather past the square straw huts. Soon, the encounter with the bullying kids faded from their minds. It was still early, and the tribeswomen were setting out to work at the banana groves. A week before, all the men had left on their monthly hunting trip. It was the custom of the Taggs, Motehro's tribe, that grandparents stayed behind to look after the children's education and well-being. The Taggs were the inhabitants of an archipelago in the middle of the Great Blue Sea. They lived off fishing, hunting, and basic agriculture. All the men were bald, the result of rubbing a special ointment daily on the scalps of all male toddlers, starting from the moment they could walk, until eventually, several months later, all hair growth stopped. All tribe members had a dark complexion, and most of them were slim. Life on the islands was comfortable, so people almost never left. The few who did were usually rebellious or misfits.

Motehro, his brother, and his grandfather were walking past the largest hut in the village when about fifteen children came out of the door, one after the other. The last person to appear was an elderly man; he waved at them with a broad smile. Motehro's grandfather waved back briefly, faking a smile in return.

"Quickly!" he said to his two grandsons, prodding them.

The boys' grandfather was always annoyed by this neighbor, who never ceased to brag about his numerous grandchildren. Of all grandfathers in the village, he had the largest number, whereas Motehro's only had two. Having many offspring meant greater security and more working hands for the family. For the Taggs, this promised a higher social status.

Heading to the beach, the three left the straw huts behind.

The brown earth soon gave way to pearl-white sand, and the rich foliage of the fruit trees gave way to palm branches and coconuts waiting to be harvested. Past the reclining palm tree, the last one on their short path, Shark's Fin Beach stretched ahead in an arc. Gentle waves rose and receded, licking the hulls of some of the long canoes resting upside down on the shore.

"Let's go," said Grandpa, pointing at the boats.

The sand glistened, its grains like chips of shattered crystals in green, white, and orange stripes.

After they settled in their small family canoe, Grandpa threw each boy an oar. "Row," he said.

They both rowed, one on the left, one on the right, propelling the boat away from the shore. Once they were far out and their island seemed like a small mass of green, the old man looked down into the clear water.

"Here. Don't bother with any crab smaller than your heads. I want only big ones. Watch out for eels."

With a chuckle, Rialto dove headfirst into the water. Motehro arranged his wrinkled shorts, the only item covering his body, and peered in after him. Schools of colorful, glittering fish swam away from Rialto, who dove deeper and deeper. Taking a deep breath, the child jumped in, feet first. After the initial bubbles from the splash scattered away, he plunged, head down, into the deep. Using powerful strokes of his arms and legs, he descended. Despite his young age, like all his fellow Taggs his eyes were already immune to the sting of salt water.

Motehro swam toward a long reef lined with red coral. This dense population of polyps and tentacles resembled the branches of trees. Between the swaying, red limbs, he could discern his brother's legs, his head and torso buried among the coral. Before heading out to the reef, he looked around at the fish of all colors swimming about and the infinite blue beyond. The canoe's hull floated on the water's shimmering surface above. A bit farther, the sun was like a blinding circle broken into glossy strips, its rays penetrating the water to light up a rainbow of underwater creatures, reaching even the depths of the reef. Once he was sure there were no eels around, he made his way down the reef, past a rock devoid of corals. This was the home to a family of sea urchins resembling thorny, black flowerpots.

A huge orange crab with white-striped legs came crawling out; Motehro was elated. As the boy let out an involuntary gasp, the bubbles sent the creature scurrying away sideways to hide behind a stone, but three of his legs and a pincer were still in sight. The boy, wary of the sea urchins, reached for the crab.

A dark shadow fell over the stones and sea urchins. The boy tensed. Looking up, he saw a huge shark. He gasped, releasing more bubbles, and saltwater entered his mouth and nostrils.

Motehro shook his head, waking up from his musings. He was still in his cage within the rats' lair, yet he felt safe. The memory of that moment when he caught sight of the big shark still made him shudder.

He went back to reminiscing about the events of that day.

More bubbles had risen up toward the shark as Motehro had propelled himself with his arms. He never took his eyes off the predator searching for food among the corals.

The shark scanned the reef above his oblivious brother.

"Rialto!" he shouted, his voice trapped in the rising bubbles. Motehro swam up to the surface with all his strength. There was almost no air left in his lungs as he pulled and pushed, focusing only on the boat. Breaking through to the surface, he gasped. "Shark!" he yelled between coughs.

Motehro's grandfather pulled the boy to the safety of the boat then jumped into the water. The boy continued to cough, spitting water and phlegm over the side of the boat as he watched his grandfather fade into the depths.

"Grandpa! Rialto!" he cried. Trembling and sobbing, he shrunk into a bundle inside the boat.

Rialto surfaced with a large crab in hand, and he tossed his catch into the boat. The old man appeared on the other side.

They both climbed in.

"What's wrong, Grandpa?" asked Rialto.

Staring at Motehro, he replied. "Your brother decided to pull a prank."

"There was a shark … There *is* a shark," said Motehro.

"It's not shark season. If there was the slightest chance of danger, would I let you anywhere near the water?" asked Grandpa.

"I saw it. It was gray and huge!" said the boy, glancing into the water.

"This is not the first time. These pranks will cost you," said Grandpa to Motehro.

Pointing to the three tattoos on his own head, Rialto smiled at Motehro. As soon as a child's head became permanently bald, the Taggs wrote on every male's scalp the first guiding phrase: *Love the Sea.* This sacred tradition had been practiced for centuries. Before puberty, they were given a second tattoo: *Selfishness I Heed You.* These two were common to all, but the third was specific to each individual, usually depicting or rectifying a negative trait in that person. Motehro's brother bore *Don't Be Lazy*. This was due to his profound love of sleep and his tendency to shirk his chores. Grandpa's third tattoo said *Respect Fire.* Many years ago, during the dry season, Grandpa and his friends were playing with torches and set fire to the entire side of a mountain. Were it not for an unexpected downpour, the whole island could have caught fire. The memorable event granted all its participants, including the man with the fifteen grandchildren, the same phrase. The most loathed phrase was *Do Not Lie.* Some Tagg children crafted different kinds of mischief, lest the humiliating label be engraved on their heads forever.

"Row back … Prepare your head for your final guiding," said the grandfather.

"But—"

"Quiet." Grandpa settled down at the stern next to Rialto and lavished compliments on his oldest grandchild as they both examined his catch. Motehro sobbed while rowing back to shore.

"Take it like a man."

The feeling of despair and injustice would remain imprinted in Motehro's mind for the rest of his life. Before reaching the shore, his brother bent over toward him. "Do not lie," he said and laughed. Then his brother's face froze. Motehro followed his stare, and, sure enough, he saw a huge fin cutting through the water close to the canoe.

Grandpa got up, only to be thrown back down by the ripples that rocked the canoe: ripples made by the silent creature.

Relief and satisfaction overwhelmed Motehro's fear. "Shark!" he said, smiling. The shark disappeared back into the deep and did not harm anyone that day. The two brothers rowed to the beach, each pulling with all his might. Only when their feet were on dry sand did they relax. Motehro felt chills all over his body.

"I have never seen a shark out of season in all my years," said Grandpa. "I learned something today, and you should, too."

Motehro thought he had managed to dodge the tattoo. His grandfather, however, had other plans, and he inscribed *Be Brave* on the boy's head. "Upon seeing the danger, you escaped to the surface, failing to warn your brother."

Although a long time had elapsed since he had left his island, when he'd seen Naji struggling in the pool, the phrase *Be Brave* had jumped to his mind.

Lying on the cage's hard floor, he sighed and said, "*Do Not Lie* would have been a blessing." Eventually, he smiled before falling asleep.

Motehro's slumber was interrupted by a commotion, and he awoke to see a host of gruesome silhouettes. The cage began to swing amid squeaks coming from all around. Paws lashed out at him, and Motehro tried to retreat into the cage's corner. They grabbed his arms, shoulders, and head, trapping him.

"Stop. What do you want?" he shouted. His efforts to break loose failed; with every attempt came a squeak and another pair of paws tearing into his flesh.

Motehro's feet were tied up and he was dragged away. As the

rats pulled him, their course, sticky fur brushed against his skin. Their squeaks penetrated his ears, and their foul, moist breath was hot on his nape, but now he offered no resistance.

His pulse began to accelerate when he found himself back in the large, multi-leveled hall.

The gloomy space was teeming with rats. The light of a smoldering bonfire flickered on the round platform at the center of the hall. Dozens of rats crowded around him. They all pulled on him and screamed in his face for no apparent reason, the fire reflecting in their bulging, black eyes.

"Where are you taking me?" asked Motehro, his eyes glued to the small fire where the skulls and bones of various animals were scattered. "Help!" he shouted as the rats carried him to the platform where others were setting up a wooden pole. Motehro shouted and wailed but offered no resistance. Within seconds, the rodents had tied him to the pole.

"Be brave, be brave … Be brave!" he said and closed his eyes. He repeated the phrase over and over again until he was able to steady his breath. He imagined himself rowing a wooden canoe, not far from his island, in the calm sea. The sun rose above …

A stinging slap pulled him out of his daydreaming. Rats climbed up and down the ladders to the different levels of the hall, scrambling in and out of the many entrances to the cave. The two rats on the platform shoved bundles of dry roots on and under the captive's feet.

"No, no, no! You filthy mice!" he yelled, struggling against his bindings.

The rats shoveled red embers under the roots. They blew on Motehro's feet until the roots began to smoke.

"Stab me first or something? I promise I'll stay fresh!" he said. "I hope it ends fast."

The rodents surrounding the stage parted, giving way to the old white rat leaning on his small bone cane. Tilting his tiny head sideways, he squeaked at Motehro. Soon thereafter emerged a tall, broad-shouldered rat that walked upright.

"Znits … Znits!" called Motehro.

"I is Krits," said the rat in the common tongue.

"Znits, Krits, Blits … *Poldani, poldani*!" said Motehro.

The stooping, elderly rat squeaked at him. Krits began to translate. "You friend lie," he said.

"*Toldon aranga* … Not lie … Not lie. Wait more!" said Motehro, already feeling the heat around his feet intensifying. The two crouching rats were still arranging the twigs and blowing on the small flames.

Leaning on his bone cane, the old rat turned around and walked away.

"Wait, please …"

Krits issued a set of orders, all the while pointing at the tracker.

"What? What … what?" asked the anxious bald man.

"I ask right side, your behind, not much fire. I like not cooked much," said Krits, licking his snout with his long tongue.

Motehro closed his eyes and screamed.

As the flames started to gnaw at his feet, he slammed the back of his head against the wooden pole over and over again. "I'll knock myself out!" he said and continued to knock his head against the hard wood. The world around him blurred and began to spin.

He heard a commotion building up. Taking a break from the self-abuse, he looked around; the rats were panicking, climbing one on top of the other. He thought his battered head was playing tricks on him.

The whole cave vibrated. The squeaking rats scrambled in all directions. The tremor turned to an earthquake. A boulder dropped from the roof of the cave and landed next to Motehro, smashing the edge of the platform. Mud and water poured down from the ceiling.

Motehro was shaking. All he could do was close his eyes.

Chapter 85
Keep Yes Promise

The roaring Guzud army charged, their hammers ready to strike.
The mud under Kamanar's feet trembled. One of the giants leading the front line lunged, aiming the heavy black cube at Kamanar. The tall man's blood froze in his veins; he had no way of staving off the impending blow. Yet he stood as firm as a statue, not even blinking. The elves on his side were hesitant but still stood their ground.

The Guzud slipped, slamming his hammer right next to Kamanar's foot, and his huge body disappeared. Kamanar gasped, and the earth tore open like a piece of cloth right in front of him.

The ground succumbed to the weight of the hefty giants, sending them plummeting, armor and all. The crevice expanded, swallowing almost all the Guzuds. An enormous cloud of dust erupted from the immense pit, engulfing the elves and Kamanar. The rain soon washed it all away, revealing a reality incomprehensible even to Kamanar, who stood at the very edge of the pit.

Pointing down, the young elves paced back and forth. The few Guzuds who had not fallen in stood dumbfounded on the other side of the pit.

Kamanar shifted his gaze from the idle Guzuds to the terraces below, where rats had begun to pop up, sniffing around like anxious hounds. Among the rocks and giant corpses were many crushed rodents. The chaos and destruction were so great that Kamanar wasn't sure it was the same place in which he and his friends had been held captive only days earlier. Above the ground, the few surviving Guzuds cast aside their hammers; some had even discarded their helmets and armor as they all retreated.

"How do that?" asked the green-haired girl.

"You know hole in ground?" asked another elf.

Kamanar looked at them without replying.

"Kamanar!" screamed a familiar voice.

The shout came through loud and clear, beyond the squeaks of the rodents. In the center of the pit Kamanar saw a bald head.

"Kamanar!" Motehro yelled again at the top of his lungs, laughing and crying at the same time.

"Motehro!" the tall man cried back, recognizing the tracker's mud-splattered face. In between two dead Guzuds, Motehro was tied to a pole, mud covering his feet and the inanimate bodies lying next to him.

"Bring a rope or something," said Kamanar.

But the elves only stared at him in awe. Before he could say anything, the top of a ladder slammed onto the rim of the crater. He approached the edge to see Motehro climbing up.

Below, amid the chaos, the white figure of the old rat stood out, accompanied by another creature identical to Znits.

"Many meat! Keep yes promise," he shouted to Kamanar, who nodded as he helped Motehro out of the pit.

The tracker embraced Kamanar with all his strength and began to blabber in a mix of languages. The battered, bald man had lost a considerable amount of weight, but aside from the words "thank you" and "rats" Kamanar could make out nothing else.

"Relax, Motehro. Everything is all right now. Go to the forest. You'll be safe there," said Kamanar, pointing to the tree line.

On shaking legs, the tracker began plodding toward the forest, not looking back.

A shiver shook Kamanar's entire body, and he dropped the club. His heart raced, and his legs wobbled as he broke into a bizarre laughter. "It worked."

"We need to hurry," urged one of the elves. "Your king will reach the great bridge any minute."

Kamanar nodded. He took a deep breath then ran toward the gigantic statue standing at the cliff. Behind him followed the rest of the elves. He felt that from that moment onward, those young elves would follow him even all the way to hell.

The tall warrior and the elves climbed the smoldering staircase to the top of the cliff.

Leaning on a spruce tree, Naji stopped to catch his breath.

The sizable and widely spaced footprints left by Gudjewkan in his hasty retreat were swiftly filling with rain water. Spruces and pines stood tilted and shattered, indicating the giant's passage.

"This could take days," he said as he followed the footsteps. "Even if I find him, then what?" He turned and headed for the cliffs.

What was that noise? he wondered as he dodged slippery roots and fallen branches, trying to make sense of the loud, thundering crash. Gasping, he emerged from under the trees and continued to the edge of the battlefield, where there was not a soul to be found. "Where is everyone?"

Reaching a small elevation, he saw a great pit that had not been there before. Near the pit, a man walked toward him. "Motehro!" Naji shouted and ran.

The young man threw himself into the bald man's arms, almost knocking him over. "You're alive," Naji said and relaxed his hold on the tracker.

"*Bnoga Naji.*"

"Thank you … for saving my life."

"Kamanar, hole … *Dovta doro* Guzud!" said Motehro, holding

his head between his hands. "*Nalbe ulda nogogo.* Boom, bam, boom!" He pointed at the pit then continued hobbling toward the forest once again.

"Where is he? Where's Kamanar?" Naji asked.

The tracker turned and pointed up at the blackened, smoking statue.

"With the elves?"

Motehro muttered something as he tramped on.

Naji ran up and pulled on his torn shirt. "Where are you going? You said Kamanar and the others went up the cliffs." Naji looked Motehro in the eyes. Motehro only mumbled.

"Zig is also up there. We need to help them. You're a man—you can fight," said Naji, but Motehro continued on his way. "Coward …"

Motehro turned around and limped back to Naji. "I brave … I life you," said Motehro.

"You're not brave … You helped me because you wanted to belong. You were always a worthless outsider. No one understood you. You offered nothing … Me and Zig were much more valuable than you."

"Me brave!"

"No, you're not. If you were, you would come with me right now … to help our friends."

Motehro dismissed the boy's words with a crude gesture and turned to go.

"Stop!" said Naji.

The tracker stopped his mumbling when he saw Naji was pointing a dagger at him.

The two exchanged looks.

Motehro took a few steps back. "Crazy *baboola*!" he shouted then ran away, limping.

Naji exhaled and said nothing more. He tucked the dagger back in his pants and headed to the leaning statue. The closer he got, the more corpses there were, with the giants' large bodies the most prominent. The sight of elves sunken in the moist earth, bloody and mutilated, disturbed him. He fixed his eyes on the wooden statue's feet.

"Zig," he mumbled and jumped into a murky puddle at the base of the statue. As Naji scaled the big steps, his feet became numb from the ice-cold water flowing down the strange stairway. Still, he continued ascending without looking back.

After entering the scorched head, he jumped out of the mouth on the other side and tripped. Raising his head, he found himself looking into the lifeless eyes of a gaping elf girl staring back at him. Naji screamed and scrambled back to his feet.

He was surrounded by the bodies of elves lying in graceless postures. Blood from their mangled limbs flowed through the cracks in the rocks. Among them lay many Black Company soldiers.

"Zig!" he yelled as he scanned the dozens of corpses. A few moments into the macabre search, Naji caught a glimpse of Zig's curls peeking out from underneath a hexagonal shield.

"No!"

He ran to him and cast the shield aside. Zig lay on his back, his eyes wide open. Naji knelt beside his friend and began to sob.

"I told you to run!" he said, pummeling his buddy's chest with his fist.

Zig lifted his hand to his chest. "Ow, ow,"

"What … what …? You are not even injured?" said Naji. "Did you see Kamanar and Akiena?"

Zig got up, only to grimace in pain. He limped to a pile of rocks, found a small niche, and crawled into it.

"Motehro is alive," said Naji.

Zig curled up in his shelter, hugging his knees. He stared at his friend but didn't utter a word.

"You're all right," said Naji examining his friend once again. "Get down." He pointed to the statue's head. "Run to the forest. It's safe there. Maybe you'll run into Motehro or Gudjewkan."

"Gudjewkan is hurt," said Zig.

"I know."

"Kamanar is dead."

"He's not dead."

"I—"

Naji forced his friend out of the shelter and hauled him toward the statue. "Don't look at the bodies. Now go!" Naji pushed his friend and turned the other way.

"I can help, with the bow," said Zig.

"What? No."

"You can't stop me," said Zig, his expression graver than ever.

CHAPTER 86
HE'S ALWAYS FACING ME

Caleem struggled to keep his balance as he ran, the long sword dragging at his side. Narraneen clutched his arm.

Coughing, he asked, "Where to?"

"There," she said, tugging his arm.

Cold drops of rain fell on the prince's naked back while the freezing wind lashed at his exposed skin. The shadow of the metal warrior closing in on their heels was so disturbing to him that neither the cold nor his broken ribs troubled him even one bit.

The two ran on the slippery ground.

"Turn around, stand here," the elf said and stopped, turning to face the assailant.

Exhaling, Caleem spun around, unable to fathom what the elf woman had in mind. He perceived the figure of the metal rider trailing them. The bluish-white flash of lightning crossing the gray sky, followed by the roar of thunder, made Caleem shudder.

"Let him come to us," said Narraneen, standing close by his side.

Although Caleem was puzzled, he stood his ground and extended his arms, holding the sword in a firm grip.

With a slight inclination of her head, Narraneen drew his attention to the metal knight plodding across a large muddy pool they had both just circumvented. Although his feet were sinking in the wet dirt, the knight continued his advance without any signs of slowing down.

"That wasn't very smart of him," said Narraneen.

The farther he went, the deeper his body became submerged in the marshy pool. Caleem did not dare take his gaze off the thing until the figure's eyes disappeared under the dark bog. Only then did he relax his grip on his sword and smile.

"This will only delay him," said Narraneen.

Caleem's smile disappeared as he saw the tips of chiseled curls rising above the surface. Sure enough, the metal warrior continued his relentless advance.

"There's no stopping him," said Caleem. "This was a mistake. I shouldn't have taken this sword from Kamanar."

"You are not lesser than him."

The prince looked into the elf's golden eyes. Lightning lit the skies once more, followed by thunder. Several elves began to crowd around Narraneen, engaging in a nervous conversation before rushing to the small waterfall.

"What now?" asked the prince.

"Whatever happens, he must not take your sword," she said.

The ripples of mud moved closer.

"The crack on his back—try to stab him there," she said.

"He's too big, too fast. He's always facing me."

She looked at the waterfall falling from a small cliff. "Follow me," she said, dashing to the base of the cataract.

Eight elves scaled up the cliff wall and disappeared behind the protruding edge. After fixing the sword in his belt, Caleem followed suit. His numb fingers clung to the sharp, wet edges of the rocks as he climbed. With trembling arms, he hoisted himself up, acute pain stabbing his chest with each pull.

"Almost there … Come on," said Narraneen, climbing after him.

When he reached the top, he flung his body over the edge and found himself on a ledge dotted with small rocks. Against a background of foliage stood a large, isolated tree, naked of its leaves. There was no trace of the elves who had climbed up minutes earlier.

"There's not enough room here to maneuver," said Caleem to the elf woman.

She pulled back her long, wet hair and fastened it into a bun at her nape. "Correct," she said. "We lure him around."

"What do you mean?"

"Just keep him close to the edge."

Below them, the mud-covered knight began his climb. Narraneen went behind the tree. Caleem receded a few steps, taking deep breaths, his eyes fixed on the cliff's edge.

I'll give it my all.

Shifting his weight from one foot to another, he strengthened his grip on his sword.

The metallic arm slammed onto the edge. Caleem's breath stopped as the knight's entire metal body rose before him. His bluish blade had been washed clean of mud and blood by the rain. The prince backed up toward the tree, his foe closing in. The metal knight leaped, swinging the blade. Caleem ducked and stabbed, but his sword slipped off the impenetrable metal chest.

He took a few steps in retreat, then lunged forward to strike. Using all the strength he had left in him, he jumped as high as he could. The blade bounced right off the armor. Caleem crashed into the cold steel body and felt more cracking in his ribcage.

He fell to the ground then struggled back to his feet.

As the knight's sword whizzed by again, Caleem intercepted it with his own. When the blades clashed, lightning lit the world, and deafening thunder roared louder than ever, shaking the mountain. The prince felt as though his arms were about to be torn off his shoulders. He watched his sword swish through the air and fall into a stream. He collapsed, the bones in his arms still rattling.

The Dark Rider turned his gaze to the sword lying in the

shallow water. He extended his arm, and the weapon began to slither toward him. Caleem threw himself toward the levitating hilt but fumbled. He lay watching as it almost reached the knight's hand.

Narraneen kicked the handle away and sent the sword flying to the other side of the ledge. The rider turned, his arm extended toward the sword once more. Narraneen grabbed the hilt, her body shrank, and her eyes closed. Unbearable screams grew louder inside her head. His arm still outstretched, the knight inched closer to her. She fell to her knees but didn't loosen her hold on the hilt. The terrible screams pierced her ears and oppressed her heart, forcing her to keep her eyes shut.

The Dark Rider hovered within striking distance of her, poised to deal her a fatal blow.

Carrying a heavy tree trunk, eight elves leaped from their hiding place and ran toward the knight. An instant before the knight's sword hit Narraneen, they slammed the hefty trunk into its broad metal back. Losing his balance, the Dark Rider stumbled, almost crushing Narraneen, who lost her grip on the sword. He wobbled at the edge of the cliff. The elves and their load bounced off the knight and landed atop one other in a heap. The rider had not yet regained his footing when a scream from Caleem punctured the air. He charged ahead, ramming the metallic back with his shoulder and pushing the rider off the edge. The prince collapsed again and lay motionless, his eyes open in the pouring rain.

Narraneen, still dizzy, crawled to him on her hands and knees. She mumbled something.

Caleem turned over and dragged himself to the edge, blood and saliva dripping from his mouth. Far down, the steel figure lay face down in the shallow waters. In the center of his dark, blueish back, Caleem discerned the crack.

He pulled the sword close then rolled over the edge.

Narraneen screamed his name. The cold air whistled in

Caleem's ears as he plunged down. The knight began to stir far below. Caleem focused on the bulging back. He knew that he would not survive this fall. He pushed thoughts of death away. His only objective was to jam the weapon into the crack.

The tip of Caleem's blade zeroed in on the crack and penetrated the knight's back. Its limbs rendered useless, the clunky mass splayed face down in the stream. Caleem crashed on top of its hard metal body.

Fumes rose from the crack, forming a strange cloud that soon dissipated in the rain. The dark-blue steel turned into rusty scrap.

Caleem's broken body lay on top of the inert pile of metal. He smiled before he drew his last breath.

"Caleem Dummah … you are deserving," a grave voice echoed in the pitch-blackness.

CHAPTER 87
THE MONUMENTAL EVENT

The remaining young elves halted their march on the cold, stone path and huddled around Kamanar. The tall warrior dropped the hexagonal shield and fell flat on his face. Gasping, he pulled the spiked club to him, scraping the flat rocks.

"I will only delay you … Creeden and his vile company will reach the bridge. Continue on …" He tried to get up to a crouch, but his head remained on the ground.

"Prophecy tree everything true. Kamanar Broken Fingers, we not go without you," said one of the elves.

Kamanar held his belly. With each breath he felt the venom from the snake stirring again, stinging him from the inside. It felt as though one of those spiked balls were trapped in his stomach. He studied the elves encircling him, nodded, and stood back up, his breath becoming steadier. "All right, Let's go."

One of the elves took the heavy club; a green-haired one took his shield.

The wind moaned as the lightning flashed and the thunder resounded from the surrounding peaks.

Kamanar smiled, hung the black sword on his belt, and hurried on. Along with the remaining thirty elves, he continued the pursuit. Their breathing almost casual, the elves raced. Kamanar, on the other hand, ran with his head low, pressing his side with his hand, trying to relieve the throbbing pain. The tall warrior allowed his thoughts to distract him from the exertion. Despite the turmoil in his soul, he thought about what Nalahes had shared with him about wishing to be a housewife rather than a glorious warrior.

What does a warrior do? Kill or be killed.

He made a resolution then and there: as soon as the war was over, on the remote chance he survived, he would adopt a simple life. *Fisherman or farmer.*

He pictured himself returning after a day of hard labor to a cottage, to Nalahes. He saw her waiting for him on the front porch, surrounded by children.

He shuddered, his heart shrinking. He could not understand how his feelings for the purple-eyed elf could have grown so strong in such a short time.

The roar of the elevated river flowing down from the mountains yanked him back to reality. Ahead was the river bend where the flow continued adjacent to the flat road to the west. He raised his eyes, but he still could not see any signs of the Black Company.

Running along the river, the small force passed the bend. Fatigue slowed him down again. A pair of hands pushed him from behind; he was too exhausted to even turn and look. The world became a bit darker as the sun, hiding behind the gray rain clouds, began its decent.

The elves came to an abrupt stop.

Ahead were two rows of black warriors, one kneeling in front of the other. Their hexagonal shields formed a tight barrier. Behind them, at the edge of the mountain, water flowed from the river onto the elevated stone bridge.

The elves marched forward, alert and ready, their small shields held up and their swords drawn. Kamanar took back his hexagonal shield in one hand and the Guzud commander's club in the other. He stopped not far from the enemy. The elves formed a line on either side of him.

With exhausted eyes, Kamanar scanned the enemy lines as he gasped for air. Behind the shields, he counted at least twice as many black soldiers as there were elves. The rain had softened to a drizzle; he now could hear his anxious peers' griding teeth. He knew their eyes were locked on the small, triangular orifices in the black helmets as they awaited his orders.

Before the tall man could issue any command, the black shields at the center swung apart, opening the way for a tall, burly warrior to come forward. His muscular arms were bare of any armor, and one arm sported a dragon tattoo. Kamanar recognized this soldier as one he had trained when the man was still a boy. He was the best and most brutal even before he grew so big. The intimidating soldier stepped aside, his perforated sword drawn, and from behind him emerged the king himself. Like his men, he was clad in armor, but his face was exposed. On his shortened helmet rested a simple silver crown with a single clear stone in the center.

"At last … I was a bit worried you'd miss the monumental event when this bridge comes crashing down. But, as always, you never disappoint. It will be a spectacular scene," said the king thickly. "So … *Broken Fingers*, are you the savior of Mellethya or Anathoria? Men or Dalusians? Have you decided on which side you want to be? Good or evil? Can you even tell them apart?"

Lightning crossed the sky and, an instant later, the ground trembled with the powerful, ensuing thunder.

"I can. I learned how."

"Did you? Why don't you enlighten us with your wisdom."

"Through the lens of values: my values," Kamanar said. "Not with knowledge. Knowledge can be twisted and manipulated, molded to bricks inside the mind, especially when dispensed by someone like you. I should have taken this step long ago."

"Why didn't you? Maybe you weren't man enough? I think you couldn't build up the nerve to face the consequences, to face me. Am I wrong?"

Kamanar lowered his gaze. "I was a coward—that is true. For that, I've been paying the price my whole life."

"Brutally honest! Good for you … I have fathomed your aim. Still, I want to hear you say your final answer. Will you accept my offer?"

"No. I forfeit your heinous reward and any other of your distorted proposals."

Kamanar tossed the heavy club, and the spiked weapon scraped the flat rock floor until it came to a halt at the king's feet.

There was a moment of silence.

"That's a shame … Have no doubt, after we are done here, I am going to keep my promise. I will execute everyone who is dear to you. And when I write about this great day in my history, you will be portrayed as the cowardly traitor that you are, the worst Khandalus Mellethya has ever known."

"Before we commence, allow me to ask one question. Why destroy Anathoria?" asked Kamanar, pointing at one of the black soldiers, on whose back was strapped a large hammer, one of many that stood out in Kamanar's eyes.

"You are so simple. Perhaps it all began because of Anathoria, but it has evolved to a greater significance. The people need something tangible to believe in, so we chant 'Anathoria.' It is about the human spirit! The spirit that was broken by those who stand next to you, despicable murderers hiding behind angelic faces. It's about the honor of those who have died on the battlefields, like your two uncles. It's about Mellethya's pride."

A bolt of lightning lit up the wet, red cape hanging from the king's shoulders. Thunder roared.

"You mean it's about your pride and your personal revenge!"

"Mellethya is me, and I am Mellethya—we are the same."

"These holy wars, all those men, dying because of your vanity. You and your evil dynasty. There is no pride in that."

The monarch burst into laughter. "Tell me, righteous Kamanar, who do you think built this magnificent bridge? Thus, creating Anathoria?"

"Not us. We do not possess that kind of ability. Don't even try to suggest differently."

"That is true. But it was not them, either. They do not hold such knowledge."

"What fairy tale are you going to tell me now?"

"Spare yourself a few moments, and I will lay out the historical events that brought us here. Do you not have the desire to learn the truth? Just before the end."

"Let's finish this. We shouldn't play his games," said one of the elves. Kamanar raised his hand, gesturing the elf to silence.

"Thank you," said the king, faking a smile. "A millennium ago, this bridge was built as a gift to our nation from the cave-dwelling creatures, the crystal people. A shy but very capable civilization. It was a time of great desperation for Mellethyans: famine and plague struck the land. Then came these strange, truly altruistic beings, who hung this remarkable structure. The lake retreated and the island emerged: what we now call Anathoria—"

"Liar! You lie. Elf ancestor make bridge," the green-haired elf girl shouted. "He lies," she said, addressing Kamanar.

"Why should I lie? For all of you will soon be dead. I want you to know the truth, merely to make your descent into hell an even more bitter journey."

"And then came the elves who snatched it from us. And that's why?" asked Kamanar in a mocking tone.

"Some years after the crystal people's disappearance, the Dalusian menace emerged, conjuring their frightful schemes, swiftly driving all Mellethyan farmers out. They imposed a depraved sanctity on this new land, and it was not to be defiled by men. They viewed raising cattle and cutting trees as blasphemy. Bit by bit, they took Anathoria while King Zarmem stood idle. The plague and famine were ending, so that coward king forfeited the land. However, when his son Daneer rose to the throne, he had a different position. Appalled by his father's impotence, he took action against the aggressors, thus igniting the cycle of holy wars."

The king's statement shook Kamanar, who paced, holding

the shield in one hand and gripping the black hilt tucked into his belt in his other. "Even if what you claim is true, it's not worth this cycle of death—nothing is."

"The longer this argument continues, the less I think of you. You are unable to fathom the machinations of the principle of things. If you think acquiescing to an aggressor is right or noble, then you are the equivalent of a gullible adolescent. This will only be perceived by the enemy as fear and cowardice, ultimately compelling them to demand more. It would have been the same as handing them all Mellethya on a platter. Aggression should be met with greater aggression. Daneer understood this. That's why he summoned the Dark Rider in the first place."

"You said it yourself—they used scare schemes, not real raids or massacres. This says a great deal about this peaceful race."

"You fish for the wrong arguments, Kamanar," said King Creeden. "To drive farmers out of lush land at a time of famine is effectively dooming every Mellethyan man, woman, and child to starvation. A slow, agonizing death, worse than any massacre! This eventually came about. But fortunately, Mellethya's fate was one of salvation when rains poured on the thirsty land, halting the famine, no thanks to that coward king. Mellethya healed, but the wound made by these demons endured. Can't you see? Their agenda is worse than ours. We want to destroy them, but we are honest about it. On the other hand, they want to eradicate us by stopping our progress and expansion. All the while playing the angel and the devil at the same time. Both masks appeal to different demographics, spurring doubt and confusion across our beloved nation. A great scheme indeed."

"A very amusing story. You should author fables. Why am I, or any of your children, not familiar with it?"

"A millennium and dozens of wars waged can alter many facts. While the chronicles of victors are eternally cherished, the accounts of the defeated are buried in anonymous graves. As much as Daneer strived, in the end, he lost his battles to the Dalusians.

"As for my children … I take full responsibility for their

ignorance. I had better things to do than deal with spoiled brats. For the sake of Mellethya, I would sacrifice them all in an instant. These are my true children, the true sons of Mellethya!" The king patted a big soldier on the shoulder.

"My mind is set. I know my truth," said Kamanar.

"There is no truth, no reality, nor good or evil! If there is a truth, it is reserved for simple, beastly creatures and gods, nothing in between," said the king, taking a step forward. "This is too incomprehensible to you because you are only a soldier. A soldier does not think, he only obeys. Speaking of children, you know I cared for you, more than any of them. And this is how you repay me? Bearing this argument is blunt proof of my feelings for you. You don't have to love me anymore, only be on my side again, my right hand. I can fix your head, if you are willing. Consider my words. Instead of being the greatest soldier, you will be the greatest general." The king's eyes flared under his white eyebrows.

Kamanar sensed the jittery elves' eagerness to pounce as they waited for his command.

"Your elaborate argument is very compelling," he said. "But there is a truth, and there is good and evil. Tyranny, cruelty, manipulation, and blind loyalty are evil. Kindness, tolerance, and forgiveness are good. I won't be a part of your vile ambitions anymore."

"Having to carry the weight of a nation requires a great deal of sacrifice. You speak as if I relished ordering people to their death. This is a heavy burden for the sovereign to bear. What about you? Kind and virtuous Kamanar, how many died under your sword? What is your truth, your real motive? Be honest about it—it is *your truth* after all."

"My truth … is vengeance!" shouted Kamanar.

"Thank you … That is why nothing I can say will change your mind. So let us resume this day—for all my life, I have been waiting for it," said the king, pointing the tip of his sword at Kamanar.

CHAPTER 88
HOLD ON

Kamanar stared the king in the eye, screamed, and charged. The elves followed, their swords drawn. The black soldiers thrust their weapons at the green fighters. In the lead, Kamanar went straight for the king. The burly guard lunged at him, overtaking his comrades. The bodyguard's massive figure blocked his master from Kamanar's view. As an elf leaped to intercept the tattooed man, the big man pitched his sword and the weapon twirled through the air and impaled the elf's chest, the force throwing his body back.

The huge attacker continued his dash. Kamanar jammed his sword into the man's shield. Shifting his shield aside, the bodyguard swung his fist and punched Kamanar in the chin. Then he clasped Kamanar with his big arms and pressed his body against the cold, hard armor. The tall man tried to raise his arm to strike back, but he was unable to move it even one bit. He struggled for breath.

The elves collided with the hexagonal shields, their swords swinging up and down, stabbing and slashing. The black warriors struck back.

Fighters on both sides fell between the black metal and green fabric boots thrashing around in the mud.

An elf girl emerged; the tip of her sword went for Kamanar's aggressor's neck, but he dodged, and the sword almost hit Kamanar. The tattooed arm struck the confused elf in the head, and he then yanked her by the hair. She was pulled onto Kamanar's back. The giant bodyguard had a grip on both of them, trapping the tall man in the middle almost to the point of suffocation. Kamanar felt the elf's ribs cracking. The young female soldier gasped in pain.

"Back line!" said the king, his voice coming through loud and clear above the clatter of clashing metal. The black soldiers thrust their shields forward in a single, coordinated motion, forcing the elves back. Then, in a quick, ordered manner, they took their positions behind the king. The bodyguard released Kamanar and the elf and kicked them both away. Then he, too, returned to stand beside the king. Kamanar fell, coughing, and the motionless elf girl slammed to the stone ground beside him.

Kamanar didn't understand what was going on, and neither did the elves. Kneeling on the ground, Kamanar raised his head, catching a glimpse of what appeared to be a plain stone in the king's left palm. Spreading the fingers of his right hand, the king began to recite unintelligible phrases.

The tall man jumped to his feet. "Attack!" he shouted at the youths.

A powerful wind carrying mud and dust from the ground struck them with overwhelming force. Kamanar and the elven fighters were knocked off their feet. The green fighters tumbled away, their rolling bodies curled up. Kamanar stretched his limbs as his large frame slid over the stone ground. Groping with his hands, he managed to hold on to a crevice. His attempts to glance forward were futile; his eyes were blinded by sandy particles. He turned his head aside and caught sporadic glimpses of other figures holding on for dear life, just like him.

The blast of wind from King Creeden's fingertips blew everything and everyone away.

"Fly off, menacing creatures!" The king's shouts carried above the howling wind.

The black soldiers remained in the rear.

"Get to work," said the sovereign. "Archers, stay beside me." He focused once again on the wind wreaking havoc. His eyes were fixed on the silhouettes hanging onto the rocks, their legs flailing up and down.

Kamanar squinted to see the three archers and the tall bodyguard, who had found himself a new sword, next to the sovereign. The rest of his troops advanced to where the water bridge met the cliff's edge. After putting down their shields and tucking their swords back into their belts, they climbed up to the structure that crossed the skies of Anathoria. They pulled their hammers and began to pound on the bridge's base.

Kamanar's legs thrashed up and down, striking the ground. It was impossible to do more than to hold on as the powerful wind continued unabated. His fingers hurt and his arms were about to give way, and it was difficult to hear over the wind. Kamanar rolled to the side to try to reach the riverbank. But as he relaxed his grip, he was sent tumbling over the flat surface, knocking into the elves behind. He frantically clawed at the ground with his lacerated hands. His fingers slipped into a protrusion, and he held on again. He spat dust from his mouth and nostrils while his legs flailed above him in the unrelenting wind.

"Strike it hard. Let it fall," said the king, the stone still held in his raised hand.

The soldiers hacked at the corners of the bridge, breaking off bits of stone. A crack had begun to slither across the structure.

Frustration gnawed at Kamanar's heart; he felt helpless. Breathing was becoming difficult. His body bounced against the hard surface countless times.

"Let's see how far you can fly," the king said and mumbled another verse, repeating it several times.

The wind grew stronger, howling so loudly that the mountain seemed to tremble. The currents came in waves of ever-increasing intensity, tearing the elves away in a dizzying vortex. All the silhouettes vanished from the king's view, except for one.

Although the wind had reached a peak, the regent did not stop reciting the verses. Streams of fire began to flair in the air around Kamanar.

Despite the superhuman effort, he did not let go.

"Archers!" yelled Creeden. "Aim for his limbs. I don't want him dead yet."

All three archers drew the strings of their bows and released, their arrows flying with the wind to reach vast distances. One struck Kamanar's arm, penetrating all the way to the other side. His grip released. Rolling away, he flailed as he tried to find purchase on the ground and succeeded in grabbing onto a protruding rock. His injured arm felt heavy and lazy, and the effort was excruciating.

"Hold on, just a bit more," came Matar's voice out of nowhere.

The warrior glanced to his side. Matar was holding on, the same as he was.

"You don't have a damn arrow sticking in your arm!" said Kamanar.

"Stop complaining. It's just pain. You know how to take pain."

"Then what?"

"I have a feeling we'll be meeting soon, just hold on …" Matar said and faded away.

As the hammers continued to pound, the crack in the bridge grew longer and wider, and a stream of water began to trickle through it. The king's men channeled their efforts into the already weakened spot.

"Good work, lads. Glory is upon us."

Kamanar saw some of the soldiers look up, and he followed their gaze to see a chubby man falling from the sky. The screaming man, who had materialized out of nowhere, landed on top of their monarch.

The mighty wind stopped as though it had never been.

Dizzy, Kamanar lifted his head to find a commotion taking place among the enemy.

He and the elves did not linger. They charged at the enemy line, picking up whatever weapons they could find, even those the black soldiers had dropped.

"Kamanar!" came a familiar voice.

The tall man halted. Naji, weary and bruised, emerged from a niche in the rocks on the side of the road. Zig followed, carrying a bow.

"What in the name—Go back, now!" Kamanar said and continued ahead. He wobbled and fell flat. Naji and Zig ran to him.

"There is an arrow in your arm," said Zig.

"Have to stop him … before he calls the wind again," said Kamanar as he tried to get up.

The king appeared to be searching on the ground for something. The green elves were again engaged in combat with the black soldiers, some of whom had to abandon their work on the bridge. Kamanar took this all in before he blacked out.

***

Kamanar was still slumped over. Naji reached for Zig, pulling him by the arm. They approached the scene of the battle.

"What are we doing?" asked Zig.

"Look at me. You are going to shoot the king," said Naji, looking Zig straight in the eye.

The stupefied boy placed an arrow on the bowstring. "Where?"

Looking beyond the fighting soldiers, Naji caught sight of the crown atop the king's helmet. He tucked his head between his friend's legs and lifted him on his shoulders.

"I still can't see him," said Zig.

On wobbling legs, Naji climbed atop the corpses of two armored soldiers, stacked on top of one another.

"Now?"

"No … no!" said Zig, on the verge of tears.

Kamanar's yelled from behind. "He's there! The stone in his hand!"

Zig scanned the scene, his mood grave. He drew the string and Naji steadied his stance, not even breathing.

Kamanar caught up. He grabbed Zig's shoulder to get his attention. "You know you can."

The boy nodded. Their eyes shifted to the king, who once more held the stone high over his head. The king's lips moved. Kamanar stood in his place, not uttering a word. Zig steadied the arrow's shaky tip and focused his one open eye.

The arrow whooshed through the air and disappeared in the turmoil. Kamanar scanned the battle line, his teeth clenched.

The arrow struck the king's hand, flinging the stone away.

"I got his hand!" said Zig.

"Great shot!" said Kamanar.

"It's a miss," said Naji, dropping Zig.

Zig jumped off his friend's back. "No one asked you. It was a great shot," he shouted.

Naji's lips moved but he just couldn't respond. He stared at his friend.

"Go, both of you. If I see you again, I'll strike you. Go!" said Kamanar, tightening his hand on the hilt of the perforated sword and sprinting forward.

A black soldier charged at him and Kamanar struck, but the soldier deflected the blow with his sword. He rammed the soldier with his shoulder, throwing him to the ground. The soldier's armor shifted, exposing his abdomen. Kamanar jammed his sword into the bare skin. The aggressor screamed then lay motionless.

The elves around him were outnumbered, yet they fought on, their small blades slashing and stabbing. As the tall warrior pushed toward his former liege, he found himself face to face with the king's bodyguard, his sword drawn. Behind him stood the three archers, their bows drawn.

"I don't need the stone," said the sovereign, nursing his wounded hand. "Look at these outstanding men."

The black soldiers were pinning the elves to the walls on both sides of the road. The young fighters clung to their shields, which were no longer leaf-shaped after the relentless hacking.

Standing behind his bodyguard, the sovereign said, "Look! The end of Anathoria is drawing closer." He pointed at the fractured side of the bridge. "And so is yours. But before Cri here slices you to pieces, I will grant you your reward. You earned it. To me, it is equally important as seeing this bridge fall."

Kamanar lunged forward. The king signaled with his arm for the archers not to shoot. Something glittered on his chest under his armor.

Disruption II
The Realm of Dreams

The world became dark in an instant. Kamanar fell face down in the shallow water. He jumped to his feet. Everything was pitch black, and the awful sounds of the battlefield were replaced by a sudden, unsettling silence. For a moment, he thought he had been killed by a blow that he had failed to notice. His surroundings began to brighten. He saw the silhouette of an immense pillar. The arrow that impaled his arm was gone. He had no trace of any wounds on his body, and there was no longer any pain. The never-ending pillar was now visible; it was the same monolith of gray stone that he'd seen when he'd encountered the king in the realm of souls. He wanted to move, but his feet were chained to the ground beneath the shallow black waters, and now, so were his hands, shackled together by a heavy, rusty chain.

King Creeden's voice resounded. "An eventful day, isn't it?"

The monarch materialized wearing a bright silk robe and a simple crown. "Welcome to the realm of dreams, a domain so intriguing that it makes the tangible world feel bland … This is where minds and souls meander. I have only begun to unravel its mysteries—so much to unearth, so much to learn. Access to forbidden knowledge and power that can alter fate. Not even time abides in this realm. The possibilities here are limitless."

The pillar faded from sight, and shadows began to appear in the void, taking the shape of the young elves and the black soldiers fighting them. The whole battlefield unfolded in front of Kamanar's eyes. But the warriors were as still as statues, their expressions and piercing stares frozen. Rain drops hung suspended, as did splashes of mud and splattering blood.

"What sorcery is this?"

"You would think time ceased for the squabbling children. But in fact, we are the ones trapped in this moment. Think of it as a much-needed respite, just for the both of us, for some reminiscing." The king chuckled.

The warrior gazed across the battlefield, noticing himself and the tattooed bodyguard lunging at each other, about to clash, yet both frozen like the others.

Farther ahead, beneath the hammers, a frozen cascade of water gushed from the ruptured bridge.

"We could have explored this realm together, you and I."

"The real world is enough. It is bland only in the eyes of the dissatisfied and greedy. I am no longer your puppet."

"This wasn't a suggestion, for you have relinquished your power to choose. In the end, what is a king, if not a puppet master? Make no mistake about it: you have always been and still are a puppet. If not in my hand, then in that witch's."

"What does she have to do with anything? Stop babbling and speak to the point."

"Why do you think she took you to that hellish place? She wanted to learn your true intentions. Do you think our meeting there was coincidental? She tampered with your mind without you even knowing. Did she bring a dagger?"

Kamanar remembered the ornate dagger that Narraneen had tucked in her cloak.

"She did," said the king, smiling. "You know, I was her *guest* long before you were. She took me to that horrifying pillar. And when I failed her test, she tried to kill me with that dagger. But I was ready, for I have foreseen her scheme."

"She is a sublime creature."

"Eventually I escaped, but not without a cost. This is her doing, you know, this mark." He pulled down his robe, exposing a nasty scar on his chest.

"That's not true," said Kamanar, yanking his chains.

"She is far more dangerous than you can ever imagine. She has the blood of thousands on her hands. Why, of all people, do you think she married that gullible fool, Ansseur? Love?" asked Creeden and laughed. "Love is merely the daughter of selfishness. And it is, after all, the finest tool for manipulation. Her every move is masterfully calculated."

"Even if what you say is true, I would still gladly choose to be her puppet."

"Puppets cannot choose anything … Let us make use of this respite and proceed to your reckoning."

The void enveloped the battlefield, and it disappeared only for another scene to unfold.

It was the old great courtyard, with its dirty, gray cobblestones and high, surrounding walls. There was something different about it, but it was the same courtyard that Kamanar knew. It was almost empty; only a few soldiers strolled at its far corners.

"Look. To the north wall." The king pointed. "Can you see that aspiring young soldier?" Under the blue skies on the high wall stood two figures. One wore a red cape and a crown on his head, the second was tall and held a stretched bow in his hands. He was pointing his arrow at the top of one of the towers. "Recognize yourself?" asked the king.

The tall figure released the arrow, which struck a big bird standing on a ledge above. The bird fell like a stone outside the wall.

"The young you just shot that magnificent eagle, the one I proudly hung above my throne. It was so long ago, yet it feels like yesterday. I'm sure you remember this day. We'd just had—"

"Glazed deer …" said Kamanar weakly.

"Correct," the king said with a smile. "Let's get a better view, shall we?"

As Creeden finished his last word, Kamanar found himself standing on a thick, old beam protruding from a deteriorating stone balcony. The chains on his feet were screwed to its edge. To his side, the king sat on a chair, still in his silk robe.

"What a beautiful day it was. See, the sky is clear, the birds are singing," said the king.

The events of that awful day began to stir in Kamanar's mind. He yanked on the chains a few times but did not say anything.

"This balustrade offers a delightful view, don't you think? We can enjoy everything from a new perspective. Behold! Your reward is in the making … Look at our former selves, going down the stairs, so close together like father and son."

Kamanar looked at his younger self, immersed in conversation with the king; they both emerged into the courtyard and drew closer together. Trembling and reluctant, he turned to look to the other side of the courtyard where a small wooden stage had been set up. There he was: Matar, lying prostrate, chained to the stage. His body was bruised and bleeding, his face covered with his blood-soaked hair. Standing on the side of the stage was the executioner wearing his eerie, metal-skull mask, his big ax slanted across his shoulder.

Kamanar became grimmer by the second. He felt as if he were choking on every breath; his heart was thumping so hard that it hurt his chest. Becoming dizzy, he knelt and held the beam with both hands, his eyes still glued to the tragic event unfolding close beneath him.

"What is this?" shouted the young Kamanar, casting away the bow.

"Your final and most important trial," said the other King Creeden.

"What did he do? Whatever it was, I'm sure Your Highness will forgive him! For my sake."

"His crime was the same as yours, remember? A year ago?"

"I thought you banished him to some island."

"I kept him—solely for today's purpose," said the king. He gestured in a calming manner and continued. "I'll elucidate. When I learned that two dozen of my men barely managed to seize two boys, I had to see both of you with my own eyes. There you were: two furious beasts, rage and violence beaming from your eyes. Though bound, you made those cowardly soldiers tremble. Then and there, the design of the Black Company took shape in my head. Not the spoiled sons of avaricious nobles or slothful city-dwellers training to become superior soldiers. But the sons of farmers and miners, already harsh and hardened, trained to be extreme warriors, to be the protectors of Mellethya … I figured I should start with just one, for I hadn't any knowledge of taming wild beasts. I choose you."

"Why? Why me?"

King Creeden didn't answer. He came closer to Kamanar.

"What is it you want me to do? What is my trial?"

"Swear your loyalty to me, by the way of sacrifice … with your own hands."

"What? No! You know I would give my life to Your Majesty without flinching … I will prove my loyalty in any other way. I would march on Anathoria right now. Ask anything of me, but not this—there has to be another way!"

"There is no other way."

"What purpose does this serve?"

"It is beyond your grasp."

Moaning, Matar stirred and tried to sit up.

"Matar!" cried the young Kamanar. He hopped onto the stage, knelt, and helped his friend.

"Do what you have to, brother," said Matar weakly.

"No, what are you saying? This is wrong!" Kamanar rose to his feet. "I want to trade places with him." He jumped off the stage and knelt before his liege. "He is stronger than I am. Your Highness knows this. He could be a better soldier—please!"

The king remained quiet.

"Do you want the both of us to die?" asked Matar. "Don't you understand? This the only way."

"No!"

"Do it for the both of us. Do it for me."

Multitudes of soldiers began to gather behind the king.

Kamanar jumped back onto the stage, pushed the executioner out of his way, and knelt beside his friend. "We could try—" he whispered.

"Shut your mouth! Please, don't make this harder than it is … I had the best life, with the best friend. I'm ready."

Kamanar looked at his friend's bleeding face and began to sob. Matar raised his chained hands and tried to hold Kamanar. The young warrior embraced his shackled friend for a long moment. "I love you, Matar," he said, his voice breaking.

Matar put on a smile, something that seemed impossible to Kamanar. He then pushed his friend away, knelt, and set his chin on the scored wooden stump.

His eyes wet, Kamanar rose. He approached the executioner, stared at his skull-shaped mask, and yanked the ax from his hands.

"Don't do it. Please, don't do it!" screamed the current Kamanar from the elevated beam. "Kill that snake!" he screamed at the top of his lungs.

Down below, no one seemed to hear his cries. Kamanar broke down and started crying with all his heart.

"You were right after all. You didn't have a choice. As I said, puppets can't choose," the current king said and chuckled.

The figures down below froze; the sounds of the world muted, and the sky took on a reddish shade.

Creeden jumped from his chair and slammed his hand to his own chest.

A sudden strong gust of wind pushed Kamanar back and he faltered, almost falling from the beam.

A vertical, crimson ray of light appeared out of nowhere,

in midair, right in Kamanar's face. A woman's hands erupted through the crimson shaft, pulling and tearing, widening it.

"Kamanar!" Narraneen's voice resonated. "You don't have to endure this torment. The blue seed in your pocket—take it! It will cast you back to the material world."

"Witch! Go back to your hell," yelled the king, tightening his grip on the small object on his chest under his robe. It flickered with flashing white lights. The red crevice began to close.

"Take the seed!" Narraneen screamed, still trying to tear through.

Kamanar took the seed out of his cloak, drew it close to his mouth, then paused.

"Take it. He will break your spirit. Take it!" the elf woman screamed.

The crevice shrank back to a line; her fingertips were barely clinging on.

The wind bursting from the crimson rupture still whipped Kamanar's face. He looked away from the strange spectacle and lowered his gaze to the wooden stage. He opened his palm, letting the blue seed slip from his hand. It fell and disappeared among the gray cobblestones.

"No!" screamed Narraneen.

"Depart, demon!" shouted the king, throwing his hands forward. The flickering lights around the mysterious object on his chest intensified.

The crimson line shrunk until it vanished, and the skies became blue again.

"How I long for her demise. This will be my first concern after sinking Anathoria," said Creeden.

Kamanar said nothing. He continued looking down.

The figures in the courtyard became animated again, continuing from where they had stopped.

The young Kamanar walked—inched—toward Matar, who was bent down, gazing at the ground in front of the stage.

His heart racing, his breath loud, Kamanar lifted the ax over his head.

The yard felt silent. The soldiers stood like statues, holding their breath.

Kamanar's hands began to shake. He let out a scream and discarded the ax.

The executioner chuckled.

Kamanar broke down again. He held his friend with both arms as hard as he could. "I can't. This is wrong," he said while he sobbed.

"Come on, Kamanar. You can do it," whispered Matar. He kissed his friend on the forehead and went back to his previous posture.

The young soldier took the ax, raised it over his head, and slammed it onto the stump.

His eyes were glued shut—he didn't dare open them—but he still heard the horrible thud when his friend's head fell to the floor. The soldiers cheered.

The current Kamanar, staring down from on high, didn't even blink. Tears cascaded down his cheeks.

The young Kamanar turned away, fell to his knees, and began to cry and wail, pounding the ground with his fists like a child. The executioner, wanting his ax, came closer and grabbed its handle. Kamanar pushed him back and jumped to his feet. With a scream, he struck the executioner with the ax between the neck and the shoulder. Blood gushed, and, before the masked man could fall back, the crazed warrior hacked his head off.

Kamanar jumped off the stage and charged at the soldiers, striking them left and right.

"No one dare touch him," said the king.

The current king leaned forward in his chair. "Witness your birth. My finest creation, the birth of a monster … The best is yet to come."

After killing several soldiers, the fatigued young Kamanar dropped to the ground, still sobbing. King Creeden came closer to him and lifted the tormented soldier up to his feet.

"All pain shall pass, my son," the monarch said and embraced the tall warrior.

Up on the balcony, the current king was elated. "Here it is—look. Look how you rest your head on my shoulder while you are sobbing … I was deeply moved by that gesture."

The courtyard blurred and faded, the world became dark again, and the gray pillar reappeared.

"I delivered what I promised. You deserved every moment of it. You traitor!" Creeden finished his sentence with a roar.

His head still drooping, Kamanar stood on his feet and gazed into the black waters.

"We are finished here," said the king after a prolonged silence. "But we still have a glorious day to continue. Ready yourself. You're about to clash with Cri."

The warrior's shackles slipped from his wrists and fell to the water.

CHAPTER 89
STORM OF HATE

The cries of the battlefield erupted in Kamanar's ears, and blurry green and black figures scrambled around him in the gray world.

The bodyguard charged, and Kamanar tried to swing his sword, but before he could land his blow the big soldier struck him in the chest with his fist. Kamanar faltered back, placing his pierced arm on his chest, and retreated with a moan.

"Let the duel begin. Who shall be the victor? Cri, the champion of Mellethya, or Kamanar, the betrayer?" asked King Creeden. With his arms folded across his chest and a smirk on his face, he circled around the two combatants.

The two warriors hacked and stabbed, punched and kicked each other.

"A magnificent culmination. I'll have the pleasure of witnessing the bridge collapse and your demise at the same time."

Kamanar's arms were sore from dueling. He stole a few glances and saw the number of elves dwindling. Behind the king, the men still clobbering the bridge were joined by more soldiers keen on destroying it. The three archers remained poised, ready to shoot on command, their arrow tips trained on Kamanar.

The bodyguard swung at Kamanar's face. He dodged, but the blade slit the left side of his neck. Blood spurted from the deep cut onto his chest and flowed warm on his cold skin. Realizing what that meant, Kamanar pressed on the wound with his left hand, retreating a little from his enemy.

"Exceptional maneuver, Cri," said the monarch, relishing every moment. "Try not to finish him off too fast. I want this thankless traitor to suffer."

Kamanar wobbled. He couldn't feel his left hand anymore. The stabbing sensation inside his stomach intensified.

His entire body ached, and blood was still spurting out of his neck.

"What matters is that we tried," came a calm and familiar voice from somewhere. Kamanar glanced at the dead bodies. Under one of the armored corpses Marbel lay on his stomach. Ice flakes covered his shoulders and the thinning hair on his head.

For a moment, Kamanar thought this was another of Creeden's tricks.

"It's your friend," said the king. "How fortunate."

Cri, the burly bodyguard, swung his sword at Kamanar's neck, but he dodged. Cri swung again with all his might, hit Kamanar's blade, and it hurled to the ground. Kamanar crouched and slammed his shoulder into his opponent's stomach, but he did not budge.

Kamanar noticed a strip of exposed flesh in between the plates of black armor. He broke the arrowhead that impaled his arm and stabbed the guard in the waist.

Cri recoiled with a gasp. The king glowered. The tail of the broken arrow protruded from the black soldier's side. He attempted to pull it out but was in such agony that he failed.

Kamanar wrenched his sword from the mud and slashed the muscular, tattooed arm and then, with all his strength, gave a mighty blow to the black helmet. Dazed, the faltering soldier recoiled. Kamanar kicked the hilt out of his hand, hurling the weapon away.

"Show him what a true warrior is," shouted Marbel, still trapped under the weight of a heavy corpse.

Before Kamanar could continue, the king pulled the bodyguard to him.

"Wait, wait, wait," said Creeden while untying a string at the back of the soldier's helmet. He lifted it off Cri's head.

Kamanar was filled with an odd sensation as he gazed into Cri's youthful face. The lad's hair was cropped short, and his small, timid eyes looked more familiar than ever. Though he knew this young soldier, he was unable to discern what was different about him.

"Criando! Criando!" yelled Marbel, startling both Kamanar and the young soldier.

Marbel continued to shout his son's name. He pulled and thrashed with all his strength, trying to free himself from under the weight of the corpses.

"Kamanar! No, please! It's Criando. Listen, Your Majesty …" said Marbel.

"Fate delivered you one final surprise," said the king to the puzzled Kamanar. "This is going to be intriguing."

Marbel would not stop yelling as he struggled to extricate himself. Kamanar, his hand pressing on his bleeding neck, shifted his gaze between his squirming friend, the king, and the befuddled youth with the innocent eyes in front of him.

"Marbel, this …" said Kamanar.

Criando took a few steps to the side and grabbed a new sword, his eyes never leaving Kamanar.

"Criando, no … Stop. He's a friend, he's a good man, Criando!" shouted Marbel.

Cri showed no reaction to Marbel's words.

"Criando, it's me … your father," said the old man.

The young soldier dashed at Kamanar. The two began to fight once more.

The monarch, huddled in his warm red cape, stood atop the dead soldier that was atop Marbel. "What will you do, Kamanar? Submit? Or kill your dear friend's beloved son right in front of his eyes? Will you betray your friend? Again?"

Kamanar was immersed in battling Cri. Both were wounded and near exhaustion. They fell, one on top of the other, got back up, screamed, and wrestled on and on.

"He doesn't remember you," said Kamanar hoarsely to his sobbing and yelling friend.

"He'll remember me—I'm his father!" cried Marbel, pulling and squirming, trying to release his body from its trap, but to no avail.

The king tapped him on his head, laughing at his awkward attempts.

"I'm sorry, Marbel," said Kamanar.

Marbel screamed at the top of his lungs, "No! You promised to keep him safe!"

Kamanar tossed his sword at Criando's face then rolled on the ground toward his foe. Criando intercepted the weapon with his own sword and sent it flying away. He raised his sword above his head, ready to strike. Kamanar shoved the end of the protruding arrow deeper into the man's torso. Criando moaned and slumped on Kamanar. Their eyes met for an instant before the boy fell dead.

The king jumped off the corpse and backed away.

"You promised! You promised!" Marbel's horrified screams rose as he finally managed to squeeze out and crawl to his son. He hugged the cold armor, crying as he never had before while uttering unintelligible half phrases.

A sudden, acute pain made Kamanar fold. The piercing pangs came from his chest, from which jutted the sculpted hilt of a dagger. Its curved blade resembled a twisting snake. A stinging sensation swept his body before he went numb. He fell to his knees.

"Tell me, virtuous Kamanar," the king said and stepped back, leaving his dagger plunged in his former captain's chest. "Did you really think you could have your revenge? Even if you miraculously had your way, would that redeem you? That poor boy, Matar, was an orphan—no brothers, no family. You practically wiped him from the face of the earth. And now … your friend's son. How cruel."

The king paced about between his three archers, their strings still stretched, aiming at the injured warrior.

"I, Creeden Dummah, triumphed where all other kings in a long, impotent dynasty failed. I will return to Mellethya as an exalted hero, unequaled by any other. I will secure glory and immortality when my name is pronounced by all, young and old, for years to come. I will become a legend while you'll rot here. Look …"

Kamanar, unable to grasp half of what was said, turned his heavy, glassy eyes. In the distance, the tight group of soldiers, like a pile of giant ants, hammered the bridge. On its side, a large triangular stone broke free; as lightning flashed it shone and fell to the dark void. The cascading current turned into a waterfall.

The cold bit into Kamanar's bleeding, weak body. He pulled a perforated sword from the mud. While still on his knees, he tried to raise it, but the tip of the weapon didn't lift off the ground. His eyes rolled back to the king, who rambled on. He lowered his heavy head, blood pouring from his mouth, his limbs trembling. Raindrops splashed on the puddles around him, but he did not feel them on his flesh anymore.

"You want to know why I chose you as my prime soldier? Matar was just as capable, and so was Caleem. But they lacked a significant trait: obedience. That was what set you apart. You were as obedient as a sheepdog."

Kamanar's vision blurred, and the pain spread to every single part of his body. The world around him darkened. Marbel's sobs and the thumping hammers faded into whispers. He could no longer make out the king's words. The hilt teetered in Kamanar's hand, almost slipping through his fingers. He tried to gather his wits, but his heavy head and weary mind drifted into submission.

"The gate is open. I'm just a moment away," said a calm voice.

Matar was clear among the blurred figures. He knelt beside Kamanar and leaned his head against his friend's.

"It's you, Matar. You are the answer to everything … In that moment, when I saw you at the center of the scale, I learned to recognize evil."

Matar smiled. "You can do it. One last time … Today is that day: when the puppet cuts its own strings."

Kamanar raised his eyes to the king's silhouette. He tightened his fingers around the hilt. "Storm of hate," said Kamanar.

Lightning flashed as he jumped to his feet and took giant strides ahead.

The archers released their arrows.

He cried as loud as he ever had while he swung.

The terrified king raised his hands. Kamanar chopped off his hand and then his head. The sword continued and slammed the helmet of the archer who stood closest to the sovereign, knocking him unconscious. The sword slipped from Kamanar's grip.

"Vengeance for me … Justice for many," said Kamanar.

Stupefied, the two remaining archers stood motionless and faced the warrior who stood tall above the body of the fallen king. The king's rolling head stopped at their feet.

Lightning flashed again, though the thunder was more distant this time. Two arrows were lodged in Kamanar's torso, and the snake-shaped dagger was still deep in his chest. Yet he remained standing.

The two archers cast away their bows and broke into a run.

"Father is dead!" they shouted.

The banging on the bridge halted; the clashing of steel dwindled. One by one, the black soldiers approached the site where their king now lay. Shooting the king a silent glance, they left their task and fled, one after the other, back to the statue from whence they came.

Naji and Zig came out of their hideout and headed toward the scene of the battle.

Their cloaks stained and tattered under the bleak evening sky, the elf fighters regrouped, surrounding the tall warrior, who stood with his head down.

"Akiena!" Naji cried, recognizing the green hair of the elf girl. He walked over but remained speechless upon seeing her bloodstained face. Her eyes glistened as she looked ahead.

Naji followed her gaze to Kamanar, who stood among the elves. Zig overtook his friend, marching with trepidation until he stood next to the tall man. Zig began to sob.

Naji froze when he saw the strange dagger jutting out of his friend's chest.

The tall man's cloak turned crimson. Although he stood upright, his head hung over his chest, and his wet hair streamed down, hiding most of his face.

Naji burst out crying.

The sobbing boys came closer, and their friend's tall body tipped over into their arms.

Motehro came shouting out of nowhere. "Kamanar! Kamanar!" He discarded the sword from his hand and hugged Kamanar from behind.

They stood, cradling their dear friend for a long time.

The storm moved away, and the last roar of thunder was almost inaudible.

The rain stopped.

EPILOGUE

The battle ended and, with it, the war.

A week later, after Ansseur assigned him a permanent servant, Marbel journeyed back home to his wife and daughters. "Our son died fighting for what he believed in," was what he said to his wife.

Seonder recovered, but his many scars remained. Zig and Naji spent the long, cold winter in Anathoria. Naji became quieter and sought to be alone most of the time. Zig, on the other hand, integrated with the elven population, becoming an active member of their community.

Motehro dedicated his time to bettering his linguistic abilities, and when the weather permitted, he wandered around the surrounding mountains.

Caleem, whom everyone presumed was dead, woke up from his coma, somehow recovering from what had appeared to be fatal wounds. He hoped that confronting the Dark Rider would atone for some of the damage he'd done, but that did not happen. He hardly ate and didn't speak to anyone as he roamed throughout Anathoria like a ghost, keeping his distance from his friends. Many tried to console him, but he avoided everyone, especially Seonder. He continued to distance himself until, one day, he vanished, his fate unknown.

***

"Marbel …" called Zig, running to his friend. The latter embraced the young man.

"I've missed you," he said, tightening his arms around Zig in a long hug that rocked his cart.

"How are you, Marbel?" asked Naji.

Marbel let go of Zig and looked to Naji. "Aren't you going to give me a hug?"

Naji gave Marbel a light hug.

"Where is Motehro?"

"On the mountain searching for Kamanar's soul. Don't ask me about that," said Zig.

"I see that Motehro is still Motehro. Let's go—we don't want to be late," said the older man.

Naji pulled the cart, and Zig pushed from behind.

The three, wearing festive clothing, made their way on the winding trail around the lake, passing many Mellethyans and Anathorians strolling to the same event.

"What a beautiful day," said Marbel, gazing at the blue skies and flocks of white birds flying up high.

"How was the winter?" asked Marbel.

"Cold. A bit snowy. We helped fix the water bridge with wood and stones. That was hard work," said Zig.

"Judging by your plump cheeks, Anathorian cuisine is to your liking."

Zig laughed. "And your winter?"

"A bit rough. But it wasn't all sad. We have a new king, and he is stirring things up. Good things are happening in Mellethya."

The trio joined the crowd assembled in the field. They walked among the quiet elves until they reached the front.

At the edge of the field in front of a cluster of giant trees, Mazahratee stood perched on a big rock, his arms crossed behind his back. "Today is the first day of the flower festival," he said loudly. "We are all gathered here to attend to a painful wound. Beneath the green grass and flower buds you stand on a bed of heroes. Heroes who have given the greatest gift of all. Their sacrifice birthed hope for a life of peace for all of us. Therefore, it is our obligation to remember and to cherish this precious gift … You may distribute the seeds." Before descending, he threw his arm in the air. "Wait, I have something more to say."

The crowd went silent, and Mazahratee took a deep breath. "A few weeks ago, as I was preparing for bed, I imagined myself sitting beside my unborn child. To be clear I don't have an unborn child or any child. Not that I would mind, maybe, in the future. Anyway … I was sitting beside him and telling him the story of Kamanar Broken Fingers. He argued with me, telling me that the story could not be, that Kamanar's tale was only a legend. And I said yes, Kamanar is a legend, but a very real one. And that I had the honor and privilege of meeting him in person … Now you may plant the seeds."

From the crowd emerged young elves wearing festive cloaks in bold colors. They handed out seeds to the families.

Akiena, the green-haired elf, walked up to Marbel and gave him a brown seed. "We plant these special seeds on the graves of our beloved. The trees will rise to great heights and grow soft, evergreen leaves. These trees live forever. Plant it over your son's resting place," she said, closing Marbel's hand around the tiny seed.

The elf girl glanced at Naji, who stood in the background. He returned a look of indifference. The green-haired girl went back into the crowd, handing out seeds.

"You taught her well. She speaks very well," said Marbel.

Naji didn't reply.

There were no tombstones or markers on the graves, yet everyone knew where their loved ones had been buried.

Marbel gazed at the other end of the field and saw a large cluster of people. He could tell they were farmers and simple people, just like him. The older man indicated his son's burial ground to the two boys, and Naji and Zig pulled his cart there and helped him out. Marbel sat on the ground and felt the short grass with the palm of his hand. He dug a small hole with a flat stone, dropped the seed in, and covered it with dirt."Your mother didn't come. It's still hard. She sends you her love, and so do your sisters," said Marbel as he patted the dirt.

Seonder and Naiya stood across from him, close to Kamanar's resting place. His scarred face lit up with a smile, Seonder approached Marbel. "I am sure the two of them will be friends for all eternity," he said to Marbel, patting his shoulder.

"You know, Seonder … Kamanar kept his promise to Zig and Motehro. He kept his promise to your people, even to those hideous rodents. But he didn't keep his promise to me. I know, I know. It was impossible, but … funny how things ended. Maybe *funny* isn't the right word."

Seonder rubbed Marbel's shoulder but said nothing and just gazed ahead with his friend.

The soft sound of a crying woman reached their ears. Wearing a hooded green cloak with a pattern of tiny, royal-blue flowers, Nalahes approached. She knelt beside Kamanar's resting place and planted her seed. The tall elf became quiet, stood back up, and stared at the grave.

Under the warm sun, the grieving families lingered across the great field. When the evening drew close, they all made their way back to the tower, leaving the green field empty.

In the square, the sounds of cheerful melodies were heard as string music was played. When the friends entered, they saw the square and the spherical tower as they had never seen them before: the whole area was decorated with leaves and colorful flowers; from the balconies hung long banners in white, yellow, and blue; and across the square numerous tables covered in white tablecloths displayed an assortment of dishes. A multitude of elves wandered around, all wearing an assortment of brightly colored cloaks.

Three young elf women dressed in white sat on small stools at the base of the tower. Each plucked the strings of a round instrument, producing soft but cheerful melodies. One sang with a pleasant and gentle voice.

"Come," said Naiya, wrapping her arm around Seonder's. "There are some important announcements."

She walked ahead, arm in arm with her man. Naji and Zig followed, pulling Marbel's cart.

Both Narraneen and Ansseur, wearing light-colored garments, stood next to one of the planters filled with colorful flowers. The couple jumped on a bench as the public gathered around them.

"We have some good news for all those who wish to listen," said Ansseur. On his head rested a simple silver crown embellished with a single green stone at the center. Narraneen's crown was more delicate, decorated with a blue diamond.

"Ansseur, my dear king, has ordered that a palace of gardens be built at Polikolion Valley so it can become a place of pilgrimage for both elves and men," said Narraneen. Cheers and applause came from all directions. "One more thing," said the queen. "Seonder and Naiya's wedding is scheduled for tonight."

"Hurray," said Seonder, taking Naiya in his arms and kissing her to the delight of his fellow elves.

The voices of the elated crowd rose to the sky.

Mazahratee got up to stand next to Narraneen. He raised his good hand, gesturing the audience to calm down. "Now, I command you all to eat, drink, and be merry on this joyful day. But don't overdo it, because we have a long day—and evening—of dancing ahead of us."

Everyone cheered and scattered about the square to take a seat at one of the tables. The new king and queen of Mellethya strolled from table to table, inquiring about the well-being of their people. They lingered a little longer with the foreign guests, the parents of fallen Mellethyan soldiers who had been sacrificed so far from their homes.

Zig helped Marbel to his seat.

"I love this purple fruit, but it reminds me of that ointment," said Marbel, reaching for one in a wicker basket.

"Here, try it with this orange cheese," said Zig, offering a slice to the old man.

"Where's Naji?" asked Seonder from the opposite side of the table.

They all looked around. The boy was standing by himself, looking somber.

"Why don't you join us?" asked Marbel.

He stood still, staring at his peers with his light brown eyes. "I don't know how you can pretend to be so merry," he said.

"What's wrong?" asked Marbel

"I think the only person who has grasped the significance of what has happened is Caleem. How can you all look at Seonder's face and pretend everything is normal?" He fixed his eyes on the half-elf's disfigured face.

"I'm all right. I'm still—" Seonder began.

"Yes, you are fine, just like Marbel … What about your son?" Naji lowered his eyes to Marbel's plump face. "Gudjewkan is hurt, and none of you seem to care. Kamanar is no longer with us, and his dim-witted family hasn't even come to visit his grave. Doesn't this mean anything to you? The Mellethyan people are already divided, and some are speaking against the new *Dalusian* queen."

"This isn't appropriate," said Marbel.

"It's all right. He's speaking his mind," said Narraneen.

"The war is barely over, and already there is talk of another," said Naji. "This new alliance is not to the Wingaar king's liking. He is gathering his forces. Someone should bring order into this world. Tyrant kings and authoritarians should be eradicated without delay … all of them!" Naji finished, raising a clenched fist.

"That's a bit extreme," said Naiya.

"You shouldn't dwell on unfortunate events, especially if they are out of your hands," said King Ansseur.

"It's over. 'We should look ahead, not back.' That's what Kamanar would have said," said Zig.

Naji offered Zig the copper coin that he had held onto for so long.

"What's this? I don't want it."

"Did you do it on purpose, your *great shot*? If you hadn't missed, Kamanar would still be alive," Naji said and threw the coin away.

"Stop it," said Marbel.

The others stood up and protested simultaneously. Naji turned and stormed away.

"That is not like him. He'll calm down—I'm sure. He needs just a bit of time," said Marbel.

They all finished their meals then danced until dark. The wedding ceremony was conducted under the light of colorful lanterns hanging throughout the square. After the ceremony, the feasting and dancing continued, and even Marbel swayed in his cart to the rhythm of the music while the bride and Narraneen danced around him. The party went on and on …

***

Gloomy thoughts occupied Naji's mind while he strode through the night. Wearing his blue garments, he had covered a great distance on his way to the Allmother. Descending into dark caves and without any respite, he crossed the Mobinar.

At dawn he reached the first oaks of the Turundia Forest. A chilly wind shook the tops of the great trees. As he walked, engrossed in his contemplations, he heard growling. A couple of Guzuds wearing tattered clothes were down on their knees grazing with their thick lips on stems of green grass.

"What are you doing here on this sacred ground?" asked Naji, tucking the navigation book back into his shirt.

The startled Guzuds picked up their hammers and stood to face him. They charged, closing the distance between themselves and the young man. One lifted his hammer, about to strike.

Naji did not budge.

A bizarre thrill filled him. He shut his eyes and extended his palm. Two green rings glowed on Naji's eyelids. As he lifted his palm, the two beasts rose into the air. They grumbled and roared, squirming, trying to break free from the invisible force gripping them. Yet they could not extricate themselves from the uncanny stranglehold.

Naji closed his hand into a fist. The two giants squeezed together. They yelped as their bones cracked, then they became quiet, and their bodies went limp.

Naji swung his arm aside, and the motionless corpses were hurled into the distance.

Naji relaxed his hand, and the two green circles disappeared.

"Out of my hands?" he said, grinning. "This is not over. This is only the beginning: the beginning of the end for all kings."

He opened his eyes and strode into the call of the howling wind under the swaying branches.

***

In an uncharted forest of a far land, Caleem crawled on his knees.

"Kamanar! Where are you …?"

He crawled closer to the tree. Tears welled up in his eyes as he gazed at the long-cursed sword planted in the tangled roots.

"Kamanar, help … Something is wrong with me."

He let out a scream that reverberated across the forest.

Caleem stared at the mesmerizing blue blade. He extended his trembling fingers to the weapon. As a tear trickled down his cheek, the dark hilt shifted ever-so-slightly toward him …

The End

If you enjoyed my novel, please rate it on Amazon. This means a lot to me. And even better, share your thoughts on your social media.

Thank you,

Amir

ACKNOWLEDGEMENTS

Contributors

Editors

Tiffani Angus

Jonathan Oliver

Mary Hargreaves

Translator

Julia Ehrenfeld

Special thanks to Maha Abu Sada

Printed in Dunstable, United Kingdom

72083669R00316